The Ladies of Llanfairpwll

LK Wilde

Copyright © 2025 by LK WIlde

Cover Design by Jarmila Takač

ISBN 978-1-0685491-5-1

For Althea and Frank,
whose stories are just beginning...

Men may laugh at the 'little woman', but the time will come, when that Little Woman without tying herself to railings, or knocking off policemen's hats, will, simply by making her views known throughout the Institute, be able to demand and get healthful improvements in village life, up and down the land... Use that Power to its full.

Madge Watt

Chapter One

Angharad

Weekends are not my favourite part of the week and Sundays even less so as they mean encountering Bryn. I suppose deep down I must love him, but sometimes I struggle to remember why. When he looks at me, his mouth forms a half smirk, as though he's remembering what I did and enjoying my self-imposed exile from the world. But as much as I loathe that look, it's probably the least I deserve.

Despite it being a Sunday, my day starts right enough with a visit to my girls. It was Eddy's idea to get the hens, and at first I'd been reluctant. Bryn once told me my hands were too big to care for animals. He said I was too strong for my own good and would cause them an injury. The face Eddy pulled when I recounted Bryn's words was a picture.

I lean against the hen coop and close my eyes, reliving the moment, pretending I'm back in the bothy on that winter's night, sitting beside the fire with Eddy.

"Hands too big to look after animals? What rot. We're getting hens and I'll hear no more about it, *cariad*."

Thinking of Eddy sends a sharp pain across my chest, and I grip the coop so tight my knuckles turn white. Tears burn in my eyes and at the back of my throat. A black cloud drifts across the sun and the sudden darkness feels fitting. That thoughts of Eddy can still provoke such a reaction is quite something, but I should be used to it by now. It's part of my penance, a bit like a haunting, only worse.

After several deep breaths to calm my trembling limbs, I open my eyes and return to the present. Eddy always taught me to look for the good in the world, and that's what I try to do now. *Vegetables. Now they never fail to put a smile on my face.*

Beyond the hen coop, my precious veg patch is blooming. It turns out I'm rather green-fingered, a revelation which surprises me as much as anyone else. Bryn says my abundant allotment is attributed to soil, not skill, but I'm not so sure.

"Girls? Where are you?" One step ahead of the weather, the hens are hiding away. "Come on, ladies, I need my morning chat. It doesn't seem right taking your eggs without a quick hello first. Dafina? Delyth? Dwynwen? Gwyneth? Bethan?" I crouch down and give my best clucking impression, but despite the sound of scratching from inside the henhouse, none of them venture outside. "Suit yourselves."

With my basket full of eggs, I trudge back across the grass to my bothy, unreasonably sad from missing my usual encounter with my feathered friends. Each time they let me pet them, I feel I'm proving Bryn wrong and Eddy right. So long as I feed them regularly, the hens are happy to take me as I am, and there aren't many around these parts who'll do that.

"Stop it, you daft old thing. Hens aren't friends. Keep this up and you'll be dragged off to the madhouse."

The rickety wooden door to the bothy needs looking at, with its rotting wood and rusty hinges. I kick it open, promising myself I'll repair it tomorrow. It only takes two strides to get from one side of the bothy to the other. As I place water to boil above the fire, I continue muttering to myself, even though I know it's a habit I need to break.

"It's a blustery old day today, Eddy. But don't you worry, I've still been out to collect the eggs. They've managed six today, not so bad, although the girls seemed rather grumpy this morning and wouldn't come out to say hello."

I shiver as the windows rattle in their frames. It's barely six months since I last painted those blasted windows, and the black mould is already appearing through the white. The last time Bryn visited my bothy, he stuck a finger into the spongy wood and tutted. Another failure on my part, was the intimation.

As rain begins its pitter-patter against the window, I pull my shawl even tighter around myself. This is meant to be summer. Summer, my foot! Wales: land of wind, rain and the all-too-frequent storm. I've read about other faraway places in books, and always marvel at their climates. I've grown up among damp, blustery days and always lived in dank, draughty homes. It's a wonder I haven't turned mouldy myself.

But mouldy or not, the bothy is my sanctuary. Out on its own in the middle of one of Mr Stephens' fields, and no one disturbs me here. I'm out of sight and out of mind, just as Bryn likes it. Though I'll not admit it to him, I like it too. Out here there's no one I can hurt with my careless words, and I'm oblivious to the sharp-tongued words of others. Yes, I'm sometimes lonely, but loneliness is a price it's only right I pay.

Betty, with the sixth sense most dogs seem to possess, comes barrelling into the bothy, jumping up against my legs and licking my hand until it's sodden. "I'm sorry, *cariad*. Of course, I can't be lonely when I've got you for company."

Betty cocks her head and looks at me as if she can see deep into my soul.

"Best not look, Betty. You'll find nothing you like in there."

The pan of water bubbles on the stove, as steam fills the room and clusters in droplets against the cold windowpanes. I take a moment to dry the windows with an old rag, then I make myself a pot of tea and carry it to the small table that sits neatly in the alcove beside the fire. A newspaper lies spread across the table and I push it aside, not wanting to read of more tragedy and death from a senseless war. Mr Stephens gives me his old newspapers for the privy and for starting fires, at least that's my excuse should Bryn ever find them.

In the hearth the fire burns bright and Betty curls herself up in front of it, drying out fur damp from an early morning roam in the meadow. I should save my coal for winter, but the nip in the air is more reminiscent of early spring than summer, and besides, who's going to find out about my little luxury?

Breakfast is over all too soon, and there is no avoiding the inevitable. If I could, I'd live in men's breeches, a jumper and a sturdy pair of old boots, but God gave me the misfortune of being born a woman, so I have no choice but to change into my Sunday best.

My jacket is wearing through again on the elbows and will soon need a third set of new patches. My shirt has been adjusted from a man's garment, and I've cobbled my long skirt together from two that once belonged to my mother. Sewing has never been my strong suit, the needle fiddly between my long sausage-like fingers, but by making and mending I've avoided the dressmakers in the village for years.

Despite all my adjustments, my clothes still strain at the seams, making breathing tricky and adding to my ever-present sense of shame. There is no mirror anywhere in the bothy to check my appearance. I can't bear to see the woman I know will be reflected at me.

The clock on the mantel chimes nine times and I button up my jacket and set off on the long walk into the village, Betty by my side. As an intelligent dog, she knows our routine and where we're going, and delays the journey as best she can, darting into the occasional rabbit hole then rolling in a cow pat so I have to stop and wash her off in a stream. Today the mountains have disappeared beyond a sheet of thick cloud and rain, and the Menai Strait, dazzling on a fine day, is camouflaged among all the surrounding grey.

Despite Betty's best efforts, I arrive in Llanfairpwll just at the right time; not late, but not early enough to be caught up in any conversations. Through the thick walls of the chapel, comes the sound of an organ playing and the low hum of conversation. I tie Betty's lead to a railing and steel myself to step inside.

I slip into the back of the chapel and find my usual position on the pew. From here, no one in the congregation can see if I keep my eyes open during the prayers, or grind my teeth through yet another lengthy sermon. I can be as invisible as it is possible to be in a crowded chapel full of local people who would hound me out of the area if they knew what I'd done. If anyone glances my way, I know what they'll be thinking. *Look at that poor spinster. What an embarrassment she must be to her family.*

The pew creaks as I lean back against it. My eyes are damp and I swallow the lump in my throat. If it were up to me, I'd never set foot in the blasted chapel again. But there is no getting away from the fact I am a Williams, and the shame I would bring on the family if I publicly denounced my faith is a step too far, even for me.

Chapter Two

Angharad

C hapel is less of an ordeal than usual, thanks to a young lady sitting in the pew in front of me. I've never seen her before, but the way she nods to other members of the congregation tells me she is local. Her mousy blonde hair sits trapped on top of her head by a hat that has seen better days, but she has made some effort with her appearance and her jacket, although worn, is clean. When we reach the prayers, she clasps her hands tightly together, rocking back and forth in her ardour.

But it is none of this that causes me to notice her. What grabs my attention is her voice. On a usual Sunday, I mouth my way through the hymns, unable to say out loud the words I no longer believe in, haven't in fact believed in for quite some time.

But there is no pretending or mouthing words from the young lady in front of me. Her voice soars with each melody, her tone sweet yet determined in equal measure. She has the voice of an angel, and it steals my breath. Listening to the stranger sing, I feel a tiny stirring in my soul, an echo of the past, when I still prayed to a paternalistic God. But a paternalistic God would have watched over Eddy. And despite all my prayers, God has been missing in action, just when we needed him.

Above a sea of hats, Bryn is holding forth at the lectern. He is not naturally gifted as a speaker, frequently checking his notes, and pausing each time he loses his place. But his face is set in an expression of conviction, his beady eyes narrowed, and his tidy moustache glistening with a mixture of sweat and spittle.

Bryn turns and lifts his arm, emphasising a point, and the light from a nearby window catches the bald patch on the back of his head he tries so valiantly to hide. Behind the lectern, he appears even smaller than usual. Bryn inherited our mother's neat proportions, whereas I take after Father. It is an inheritance that has left us both dissatisfied, and I wonder whether Bryn's theatrical gestures while speaking are an attempt to make up for his lack of stature.

Attuned to the exact timings of Bryn's sermon, having heard it many times in rehearsal no doubt, my sister-in-law Anne slips from her seat and makes her way down the side of the chapel. Her waist has thickened several inches lately, and the pretty face she had when we first met is now pinched by piety and etched with lines of disapproval and judgment. I shake my head, remembering how foolish I was to once consider Anne a friend.

My attention returns to the woman in front of me. Even during my brother's monotonous dirge of a sermon, she nods her head, clapping her gloved hands lightly together at certain points. I try to tune in to what Bryn is saying, but it makes me too cross. How can I take any form of spiritual guidance from the hypocrite standing behind the lectern? Christian compassion is sadly lacking in the Williams household, despite what Bryn's congregation might think.

I slip out of the chapel during the last hymn, just as I do every Sunday. On my way out, I nod to Anne, who is taking up her position to send the congregation on their way with a kindly word or two. No kind word is offered to me, just a frown of disapproval and an almost inaudible tut.

As I untie Betty and walk away into the fresh spring air, the sound of 'Lead Kindly Light' follows me. From a distance, the young woman's voice is no longer distinguishable from the rest, the male baritones drowning out any sweetness or nuance. For a moment, I stop to wonder what it would be like to be the young woman's friend. Perhaps in another life I could have been. Is she as sweet as her voice suggests? I hope so, even though I know I'll never be granted the opportunity to find out.

The hymn's words haunt me as I walk, and even though I can't relate to their plea to a higher being, with so many young village men away fighting, the lyrics cause tears to spring to my eyes. I may be isolated from village life, but that doesn't mean I am unaware of or immune to the collective suffering inflicted upon the community by a senseless war.

Lead kindly Light, amid the encircling gloom,
Lead Thou me on!
The night is dark, and I am far from home—
Lead Thou me on!
Keep Thou my feet; I do not ask to see
The distant scene—one step enough for me.

I hurry on through the village and the lyrics take on an even greater poignancy as a door is flung open and a young woman bursts out onto the street, falling to her knees and letting out a howl of pain. In her hand is an envelope, which she clutches to her chest, her body heaving in violent sobs. An older woman rushes from the house, wraps an arm around her daughter or daughter-in-law, and ushers her back inside.

Another loss. Another young woman widowed. Another son of the village never to return from the fields of France.

All the way home, I try and fail to push the young woman out of my mind. Shame rather than exertion causes my face to redden as I realise I am jealous. The woman is in mourning, but at least she has someone to mourn and can do so as loved ones hold her in their arms. My grief is shameful, hidden, an unspoken secret that weighs me down and taints my thoughts.

I mentally shake myself. That poor woman doesn't deserve my jealousy. What she needs is compassion, just as I fear many others will before the war reaches its end. There's talk of it being over by Christmas, but with every passing day, this seems increasingly unlikely.

Mr Stephens is crossing the yard when I reach the farm, and gives me a brisk nod. There's never any conversation between the two of us given he's deaf as a post, and I suppose in some ways that makes things easier. So long as I stick to our routine, feed him regularly, and work hard, we rub along well enough.

Back at the bothy I change out of my Sunday best, cover my old shirt and long skirt with a pinafore apron, then make my way back to the farmhouse. Tomorrow I'll arrive early to prepare a cawl that will simmer above the fire all morning, but given I've been out at chapel, Mr Stephens knows to expect a simple dinner of bread, cheese and whatever cold meats we have lurking in the pantry.

He arrives at the farmhouse on the dot of one o'clock to find a table laid and dinner ready to be served. If there is important information to impart, he will attempt to lip read, or write a simple note, but our meals are mostly conducted in silence. Before the war I always ate separately from the family, but since his sons went away to fight, we have taken to eating together. I sometimes wonder if Geraint Stephens is even lonelier than I am.

Before he sits down, he produces a newspaper from his back pocket and throws it across the table at me with a grunt. I thank him with a smile, then we get down to the business of eating.

Mr Stephens cuts himself a hunk of bread and smothers it in butter, followed by a thick slice of ham and an even thicker slice of cheese. The bread disappears in two mouthfuls and he repeats the process. Since war broke out, and his sons went away, Mr Stephens has no time for chapel, he has no time for anything but work. He's a dour old fellow, but I can't blame him when he's trying to do the same amount of work as before but with half the labour.

As far as Bryn knows, I'm just a cook, housekeeper and occasional milkmaid. If he knew the amount of labouring I'd taken on since the younger Stephens men went away, he'd be horrified. But I enjoy putting my strong limbs to good use, and there's no doubt I'm a better worker than the old codgers who've been called upon in the younger men's absence.

With a swig from his glass of milk, Mr Stephens is up and ready to get back to work. He stomps out of the farmhouse, and I stand to clear away the dishes, but an official-looking letter on the mantelpiece catches my eye. With the plates discarded on the table, and a quick glance over my shoulder to check Mr Stephens has indeed left, I pick up the letter and read.

The sound of footsteps in the yard makes me jump and I replace the letter with haste and pick up the pile of dinner plates. From the kitchen window, I see Mr Stephens wielding a shovel ready to muck out the byre. My heart twists as I watch him. Is the news in the letter evident on his face? Are the lines around his eyes deeper? Has he lost weight?

The more I stare, the more I recognise the tell-tale signs. I can't believe I haven't noticed, given I'm an expert in concealment myself. His knuckles are white as he grips the shovel, his jaw clenched, the loose skin around his eyes pink. Mr Stephens is doing an excellent job of hiding it, but as I watch him, there is no doubt the news in the letter is true. His youngest son is missing, presumed dead, somewhere on the Western Front.

If Mr Stephens could hear me, would I tell him I understand? Would I share in his grief and provide a listening ear? I shake my head. Of course I wouldn't. But I know what I can do. Tomorrow his portion of cawl will be larger than usual, his bread as thick and fluffy as I can make it. I will work even harder on my daily tasks and take on any extra work I can find. If Eddy taught me anything, it's that sometimes the smallest actions mean the most.

Chapter Three

Ffion

June, 1915

The curse of daylight strikes again as I study my reflection in the entrance hall mirror. In the dull glow of a dinner party's candle and lamp light I can still pass for twenty-one, but in the harsh light of day I look every one of my thirty-five years.

"Is there anything I can get you before you leave, madam?"

"No, thank you, Susan. Help me with my riding jacket though, please. I always find these buttons rather fiddly."

"Of course, madam."

Susan helps me slip my arms into my jacket and I remember to smile. She is a sweet young thing, and less likely to go running to Hector than some of the other servants. I'm tempted to tell her where I'm going just to see the look on her face, but decide against it. "I shall be back in time for lunch, but I am going out this afternoon, so please tell Mrs Edwards to prepare something light."

"Of course, madam. What time shall I ask Mrs Edwards to have your lunch ready for?"

"Midday should do it and remember to tell her I want something light. I'll be eating alone, so there's no need for her to go to any fuss."

"Very well, madam."

I leave through the front door, then make my way around the house to the stables. As much as I complained when my husband first rented the property, I have since grown rather fond of the view across the Menai Strait. Mind you, the view hasn't come cheap, with Hector forking out four hundred pounds per annum for the privilege of living in a house far too big for the two of us and a handful of servants. It's slightly better when the children are home from boarding school, but even then, there are innumerable rooms left gathering dust.

Thoughts of my children provoke their usual response, and I dab my eyes on the corner of my jacket. Each time they return home from school, they seem more changed. The last time I saw them, the boys' voices had deepened, and the girls had grown at least an inch between Christmas and Whitsun. Not to worry, thanks to Colonel Stapleton-Cotton's invitation, I finally have something to take my mind off my missing children other than tea parties or choosing the fabric for a new gown.

The lawn behind the house slopes gently down to the water. Already I'm sure I can taste salt on my tongue. I check my wristwatch and realise I have time to spare. According to Mr Banbury, the woman I need will be busy milking for at least another hour, and given the imposition I'm about to place on her, the least I can do is allow her time to finish her work.

Instead of making my way to the stables, I cross the lawn, then walk through a small copse and skirt its edges, following the water line. It's low tide, and the smell of seaweed hangs in the air. Sometimes I walk along the shore towards the Britannia Bridge, but at low tide it can be especially slippery and even in my sturdiest boots I've had a couple of near misses.

The day is remarkably clear, and I settle myself on a large flat rock and gaze at the Snowdonia mountain range visible across the water. It's at times like this I wish I could paint, but I'd never capture such a beautiful scene on paper. Perhaps instead I should take up sailing and experience the beauty of my surroundings from the water? I'm sure if I asked, Hector would buy me a pretty little dinghy. Anything to keep me happy, and therefore out of his way.

With a sigh, I push away thoughts of my errant husband, currently living it up in London with his chums, and make my way back up the hill towards the stables. There I find my favourite mare, Bluebell, who shakes out her mane and nuzzles into me.

"She's all ready for you, madam," says George, who has had 'stable hand' added to his list of tasks since the younger chaps went off to war.

"Thank you, George."

"It's a fine day for a ride out."

"I know, and such a relief after the awful weather at the start of the week."

"You going anywhere nice?"

"Nowhere in particular."

"Right then, I'd best get back to the garden, have a pleasant ride, madam."

"I'm sure I will."

Bluebell and I walk at a stately pace along the driveway, then trot towards the village. We continue along a wide street and keep to the left as carriages on their way to Holyhead trundle past. Rows of stone terraced houses flank us, their front walls butting up against the road. My curiosity is piqued as I glance into the sitting rooms of women who live such different lives to me. The sound of children playing fills the air as we pass near the school, and I envy the huddle of women chatting and laughing outside the post office. As we pass the substantial white building housing the local pub, a group of elderly men spill out onto the street. When they notice us and doff their caps, I greet them with a smile, wanting nothing more than to be accepted by this out-of-the-way community in which Hector has deposited me. At least I'm of Welsh heritage, so that goes in my favour.

As soon as we've left the rows of terraces and small stone cottages behind us, I give Bluebell the signal and we're off. Beneath me, I feel her pedigree muscles working, and we almost fly through the Welsh countryside. Never do I feel so free as when I'm riding Bluebell at speed. Nothing beats the wind in my hair, the sharp tang of a crisp morning against my skin, and the way I suddenly feel alive again.

On horseback, the farm I'm looking for isn't as far as I thought, and I arrive before I intended. I direct Bluebell into a deserted yard and climb down, leaving her beside a trough of water where she takes a well-earned drink.

My first instinct is to try the farmhouse, but when I knock, there is no answer. Then a lively little Welsh terrier comes charging up to me, wagging its tail and shaking out its caramel and black fur. I crouch down and give it a scratch under its chin.

"Where is everyone?" I ask as the little dog licks my hand. It cocks its head, then runs over to a squat barn-like building. The dog barks twice, then it pricks up its ears, and goes darting into a field in chase of a poor unsuspecting rabbit. I cross the yard to the small building and pause in the doorway. What if the information Mr Banbury gave me about this woman is wrong? But then, why would he make up such a thing? *Stay true to your convictions, Ffion*, I tell myself. *Miss Williams is just the woman you need. Now step inside that building and get what you came for.*

Chapter Four

Angharad

I wipe a hand across my brow and stretch out my back, giving the cow in front of me a gentle pat to let her know she's almost done her duty for the morning. There are only a couple more cows to milk, then I'll head over to the farmhouse for a bite to eat before starting on Mr Stephens' laundry. He's been sullen all week, but that's only to be expected. Perhaps before starting the laundry, I'll take him a cup of tea.

The sound of horses' hooves in the yard doesn't trouble me. It'll be a local farmer come to do a bit of business. They all seem to have developed a code of hand gestures over the years to compensate for Mr Stephens' lack of hearing. I was amazed the first time I saw it in action, but it seems to work, and the Stephens farm continues to prosper.

I'm halfway through the next cow when I hear a sound so incongruous with the farm I wonder if I'm going mad. First, there is the tinkling of a woman's voice, and then the unmistakable click of heeled boots on the stone floor.

"It's Mrs Williams, isn't it?"

My head jerks up in what I know must be a most unladylike fashion and I spring to my too-large feet, causing the cow beside me to grumble in complaint. She scuffs her hooves against the stone below in impatience, but my attention is elsewhere, and she'll have to wait.

I can't help but gape at the beautiful woman standing in front of me. "It's Miss Williams, actually," I say, wondering how this woman knows my name.

"Oh, I am sorry. One should never assume a lady is married. People have a habit of calling me Mrs Hector Montgomery and I despise it. Mrs Montgomery alone sounds rather pompous, but Mrs Hector? It's bad enough having to take a husband's surname without being addressed by his first name, too. My name is Ffion, and it's a pleasure to meet you, Miss Williams."

"Angharad," I blurt out, in a voice so loud it echoes around the milking parlour. I swear silently. This is what happens when you rarely speak to people, you become out of practice and forget how to use your own voice. I lower my voice and try again. "My name is Angharad."

Mrs Montgomery, *Ffion*, smiles and takes my hand in a surprisingly firm shake. "Wonderful to meet you, Angharad."

There's no mistaking what class Mrs Montgomery belongs to. She is dressed in a single-breasted navy-blue riding habit with a green velvet collar, a full skirt, and bowler hat, and her riding boots are polished so well they reflect the light.

"Oh, I know," she says, removing her hat and following my gaze. "These skirts are most impractical on horseback. When I'm riding around the estate, I wear jodhpurs these days, but I don't want to scare the Welsh farmers when I'm out and about."

I flush. Mrs Montgomery must think me a simpleton. I close my mouth and pull my gaze away from her fine clothes. "Are you looking for Mr Stephens? He is most likely out in the fields, although you may find him in the farmhouse having his morning cup of tea."

Ffion's brow furrows. "Mr Stephens?"

"Mr Stephens owns this farm."

"Oh, yes." Mrs Montgomery tilts back a head of glossy blonde marcel waves and lets out a husky laugh, which startles the cow beside me. "I'm not after your Mr Stephens. I'm here to speak to you."

"Me? Whatever for?"

"I need your help."

"My help? I really don't think there's anything I can help you with, and I don't mean to be rude, but I really need to finish milking this cow so she can get back out into the fields."

"Oh, Angharad," says Mrs Montgomery, gripping my arm and laughing again, "you are a one."

The cow moos and flares her nostrils.

"Please, I really must finish this job. Would you like to wait in the yard? Or I'm sure Mr Stephens wouldn't mind you waiting in the farmhouse. There's tea in the pot."

"Actually, if you don't mind, I'd rather wait here. I've never seen a cow milked before and find the whole thing rather fascinating."

"Oh, I see. Very well then." I turn my back on Mrs Montgomery and resume my position on the stool. Aware of the lady's eyes on me, I pull too hard on the cow's teat, and she grunts in discomfort. What is Mrs Montgomery doing here? In the ten years I've lived on the farm, I have never had a personal caller other than Bryn, and sometimes Anne. And now, a glamorous young woman who I vaguely recognise as being something to do with the aristocracy or gentry has come into the milking shed, asked for me by name, and needs my help. If I wasn't so confused, I would be gaping like a fish.

With a deep, silent breath, I regain my composure and remind myself I know what I'm doing. My thumb and forefinger encircle the teat, milk squirts into the pail and the cow is released to her and my relief. I rub my hands on my apron, clear away the stool and suggest we head into the farmhouse.

"Lead the way," says Mrs Montgomery, her eyes twinkling.

"What can I do for you, Mrs Montgomery?" I ask once we're in the farmhouse kitchen and the tea is poured.

"Ffion, please. Well, Angharad, I need a driver, and a little bird told me you may be able to help?"

"A driver?"

"Yes, my usual chap, Stan, has gone off to that bloody war and left me rather in the lurch."

"I'm afraid I don't know any drivers."

Ffion tips back her head and lets out another husky laugh. "What a funny little thing you are," she says, dabbing her eye with a gloved finger.

I should probably be cross that this woman, despite being a member of the gentry, is addressing me so informally, but I experience a rush of pride that she's called me little. Silly, I know. "I'm very sorry I can't help you. Perhaps you could ask in Mr Jones's hardware shop? His eldest son couldn't join up due to breathing difficulties. I'm sure I've seen him driving his father's van before."

"I'm not after Mr Jones's son. It's you I'd like to act as a chauffeur."

"Me? But I can't drive you around."

Mrs Montgomery studies me through narrowed eyes. "I hope you're not going to pretend you don't know how, Angharad, as I've been reliably informed you're quite the devil behind the wheel."

Heat rushes up my neck. How could this woman possibly know about my driving? The lessons Eddy gave me were our secret. I'd ventured nowhere near the village. Oh, but what about the time I almost ran into Mr Banbury's flock of sheep after taking a corner too fast?

I'd hoped he had forgotten all about that incident many years earlier, but perhaps not. "I haven't driven for several years. I'm not sure I'd remember how."

Mrs Montgomery waves away my concerns with a gloved hand. "Driving is like riding a bicycle, you never forget, or so I'm told."

"But why me?"

"Because, if you must know, I've tried all other avenues and have drawn a blank. I'm rather at my wits' end."

"I see." For a moment Mrs Montgomery's visit had excited me, but the realisation I'm a last resort deflates me and brings me firmly down to earth. I am about to refuse her request when she interrupts my thoughts.

"Right, that's decided. Come to the house at two-thirty p.m. and please be punctual. We'll need to leave plenty of time to get there, and I don't want to be late."

"Where are we going? I'll need to be back on the farm by six to do the milking."

"I knew I could rely on you. I'll see you this afternoon. And, Angharad," says Mrs Montgomery, clutching my hand, "let's keep this between the two of us. You know how people like to gossip around here."

Before I can ask any further questions, she turns and marches out of the farmhouse, climbs up onto her horse, and canters away. As she disappears down the lane, all that remains of her visit is a lingering scent of perfume, and a whole host of questions I wish I'd had the confidence to voice aloud.

Chapter Five

Angharad

June, 1915

"Oh, Betty, what the heck am I doing?" I shake my head, scratch a bemused Betty under the chin, then with a sigh leave the comforting confines of my bothy and close the door behind me.

Since Mrs Montgomery's visit, my entire day has been spent rushing from one job to the next, trying to create a free couple of hours for whatever it is she wants me to do. I resent the intrusion into my daily routine, particularly as I feel I've been coerced into goodness knows what.

Between hand gestures and a note, I was able to explain to Mr Stephens that I need to pop out for a couple of hours, but he didn't look best pleased about it. Today there was no invitation to eat with him and he sat alone with his bowl of mutton stew. With no time to prepare a meal in the bothy, I've had to munch through a tin of kippers, which I hope hasn't left a lingering smell on me. If they have, hopefully the long walk to the Montgomery residence will rid me of any stink.

I know where Mrs Montgomery lives, but I have never set foot inside the gates. She must have wonderful views from her home. I've seen it from the shoreline several times when I've been walking Betty, and always wondered how someone ends up living in a house so grand.

The thought of servants tending to your every need sounds horrifying. What on earth would you fill your time with if not the basic chores of an ordinary life? Surely there are only so many books you can read or dinners you can host?

Perhaps my afternoon with Mrs Montgomery will be a window into a class of folk who've always intimidated me. As a minister's daughter and sister, I've always occupied a no man's land when it comes to social class. Whilst the Williams name commands a certain level of respect, as a family we've never been wealthy. Now I'm a spinster housekeeper for a local farmer, I'm even less sure of my position among the great and good of Llanfairpwll.

The driveway leading to the Montgomery residence must surely be a mile long and I worry I'll be late, but reach the grand old house with five minutes to spare. Mrs Montgomery is already waiting beside a motor car, wearing a long mink-trimmed coat and a wide-brimmed green felt hat in a shade that matches her eyes. Her understated glamour leaves me feeling even more like a fish out of water.

"Ready for the off?" calls Mrs Montgomery as I cross the gravel towards her.

During the walk I'd promised myself I'd speak up, confront the fact I didn't know where I was going or why, but in Mrs Montgomery's presence I am cowed, and simply nod a response.

"Wonderful. Hop in. I'll sit in the back, but we'll still be able to chat."

Chat? The last thing I want to do is chat. What could we possibly have in common? Besides, I'm bound to say the wrong thing and put my foot in it somehow. I open the door for Mrs Montgomery and she climbs in, tucking her long coat and dress neatly beneath her, and tilting her legs to one side.

"The Wolseley should give us a comfortable ride. Have you driven a Wolseley before?"

"No."

"Oh, well, not to worry. I imagine one motorcar is much like the next. What makes have you driven?"

In my mind's eye I picture Eddy's black Sunbeam, the pair of us jolted and jerked around as we tore through country lanes screaming and laughing, with tears of joy streaming from our eyes. "I'm uncertain of the make," I say, not wanting to share my precious memory.

"But you know how to start a car?"

I nod.

"Wonderful. The crank is in the boot."

For once, my size and strength come in handy as I insert the crank and use all my strength to turn it, fearful of the dreaded kickback I've experienced one too many times before. The Wolseley splutters into life and I remove the crank, jump into the driving seat, adjust the spark and throttle settings and finally the choke.

"What a treat," shouts Mrs Montgomery above the noise of the engine. "You are far more masterful starting this beast than my usual lad, or my husband, for that matter."

I force a smile, my hands gripping the steering wheel to stop them shaking. "Mrs Montgomery, you will need to tell me where we're going."

"Of course. We're heading to Bangor."

"Bangor? But that's miles away, across the Menai Strait!"

"I'm sure you'll manage. And besides, it's less than five miles, so really no need to worry. We could have walked it if we really had to."

My hands grip the wheel tighter, my knuckles white as rage sweeps through me. Why do I always let people do this to me? I could have said no, could have spoken up and demanded to know where and why I was going, but no, as usual, I kept my big mouth shut and now here I am, losing an entire afternoon to drive to Bangor of all places.

I channel the anger I am feeling and use it to loosen my tongue. "What will I do once we're in Bangor? I don't want to be home too late. As I told you, I have cows to milk, and I'll need to prepare Mr Stephens' supper."

"We shan't be too late home. I don't imagine the talk will last long."

"Talk? I assumed you were going to meet a gentleman friend."

"A gentleman friend?" A burst of Mrs Montgomery's laughter fills the car. "Perhaps you are not as old-fashioned as I thought. Whatever must you have been imagining, Angharad? Do you think me a scarlet woman?"

"No... I..."

"Goodness, if only my life were as exciting as you imagine it to be. I shall be meeting a friend in Bangor, but I assure you the Colonel is happily married and I'm certainly not having some illicit affair with him. Perish the thought! Aside from the obvious reasons, such a notion is preposterous. The Colonel's wife Jane is a very dear friend of mine. If you must know, Colonel Stapleton-Cotton has invited me to attend a meeting of the Agricultural Organisation Society."

"Oh, I see."

"Have you ever heard of a Mrs Arthur Watt, Angharad? Known to those in her inner circle as Madge?"

"I can't say I have."

"She's come all the way from Canada. Colonel Stapleton-Cotton has persuaded her to speak at Bangor University for the Agricultural Organisation Society on the subject of Women's Work in Agriculture. I shan't be taking part in the meeting, my position is only as an observer, but I have heard interesting things about Mrs Watt and I am looking forward to hearing what she has to say. It's a shame you won't be able to accompany me, Angharad."

Her use of my first name still shocks me. As a thirty-five-year-old woman, if people address me at all, it is always as Miss Williams. "It sounds as though it will be an interesting afternoon for you."

"Yes, and rather exciting to be visiting a university. Have you ever been to a university, Angharad?"

"No, Mrs Montgomery. The closest I've come to a lecture is listening to my father's sermons as a child."

"Ah yes, your father was clergy, like your brother?"

"A minister, at chapel, yes. Bryn took over when Father died."

"Oh, the great church and chapel divide. I'm afraid I belong to the former, and I am a lifelong Anglican. I hope that shan't sour things between us?"

"Of course not, Mrs Montgomery. I don't think folk around here are too worried about which denomination anyone belongs to."

"Are you a religious woman, Angharad?"

"Yes." No, if there is a god, I hate him. But I still go to chapel each Sunday, so give the expected answer.

"Poor you. I don't expect growing up in a religious household was much fun."

Fun? I almost laugh but swallow it just in time.

"You're not much of a conversationalist, Angharad, are you?"

"The engine is rather loud, Mrs Montgomery."

"I can hear perfectly well."

"Alright then, if you don't mind me asking, why did you ask me to drive you?"

Mrs Montgomery stares out of the window, and I wonder if she heard my question. A moment passes, but then she speaks. "It was true when I told you there were limited options with so many men at war, but I also chose you because I need a driver who won't tell my husband where I've been."

"Pardon?"

"Because I don't want my husband to find out where I've been!"

"Oh."

"It's not like that," she says, sounding exasperated. "He's not a cruel man, not all the time, at any rate. But he would disapprove of me attending a meeting at a university, never mind attending a talk by a woman. Dear old Hector can't stand women who think for themselves. He's still living in the Dark Ages and is staunchly against women being allowed to attend university. His views are extremely old-fashioned. Luckily, he spends much of his time in London, so most of the time I'm free to do as I wish. But he's home next week, and if a loose-lipped member of our staff tells him what I've been up to, it will cause the most almighty row. That's a very long-winded way of saying I asked for your help to keep my activities hush hush and give me a tranquil life. I'm sorry I bullied you into coming with me, Angharad, but I was so worried you'd say no."

"But you're attending with friends. Couldn't you have travelled with them, and won't they tell your husband?"

"They are overnighting in Bangor. And no, they won't tell Hector. They're rather progressive in their views. In fact, I'm not sure any of them are fond of my husband, or perhaps it's purely coincidence that they organise their dinner parties when he is away."

Mrs Montgomery chuckles to herself, then slips into a merciful silence. At last, I can concentrate on navigating the narrow country lanes in an unfamiliar vehicle. I can't remember the last time I'd ventured out of Llanfairpwll, and the thought of crossing the Menai Strait causes my legs to tremble.

Much as I resent Mrs Montgomery's coercion, I can't deny part of me is excited to leave the island of Anglesey. Butterflies dance in my stomach as I pull onto the Britannia Bridge. I'd forgotten what a joy it is to be behind the wheel of a motor car. After Eddy, I'd given up hope of ever driving again. *Oh, Eddy, if only you could see me now!*

Chapter Six

Ffion

"I really am sorry you shan't be able to come in with me. In all honesty, I probably shouldn't be here either and it was extremely kind of the Colonel to invite me." I glance at Angharad, who, if anything, seems relieved rather than disappointed to be waiting with the car.

"I quite understand, Mrs Montgomery. Do you know how long you will be?"

"Oh, I'm not attending the full meeting, so I don't suppose I shall be very long. I'll stay to listen to Mrs Watt speak, then excuse myself to come and find you."

"Alright, well, you know where I'll be waiting."

Angharad taps the car and I squeeze her arm in thanks. She jumps slightly, as though unused to human touch. Here is a woman who intrigues me greatly, but there is no time to dwell on Miss Williams' character, as I have a meeting to attend.

I walk with purpose up to a building which looks more like a cathedral than a place of learning. This is not my usual habitat, and the first tingling of nerves flutters deep within my stomach. Mother was a firm believer that a lady should never appear awkward or out of her depth, so with this advice in mind, I push back my shoulders, lift my head and place a smile on my face.

Limestone walls seem to encroach in on me as I try to find the entrance. It is no surprise the university intimidates me, given the bulk of my education was to prepare for a good marriage. Give me a piano and I'll play you a sonata, pile books on my head and I'll walk around the room without dropping a single volume. Gosh, I can even hold a decent enough conversation in French or German, but university? Well, that's quite a different matter.

"Mrs Montgomery!"

I turn and see the welcome sight of Colonel Stapleton-Cotton sitting in his bath chair beside an arched entrance.

"Good afternoon, Colonel. Thank you so very much for inviting me."

"That's quite alright, my dear." He turns to the gentleman beside him. "Mrs Montgomery recently moved to Llanfair PG with her husband and has expressed an interest in helping with the war effort. I thought it might prove valuable for her to attend this meeting and listen to Mrs Watt speak, as I'm sure our Canadian friend will have plenty of suggestions for the role women can play in this war."

"I'm sure she will," says the gentleman, raising an eyebrow at the Colonel. He smiles and turns his attention to me. "John Nugent-Harris, General Secretary of the AOS, a pleasure to meet you."

"Likewise," I say, shaking the outstretched hand.

"Nugent-Harris is a forward thinker and shares my view that women have much to offer at this difficult time for our country."

Before I can establish the precise role Mr Nugent-Harris plays in the AOS or what his forward-thinking views entail, a smartly dressed elderly gentleman appears and informs us our meeting will be held in the Council Chamber. I have no idea what one of those is, but smile as though attending a meeting in a Council Chamber is a regular Tuesday afternoon occurrence.

"Well," says the Colonel, clapping his hand against one of two legs that no longer hold any feeling. "Good sir, I don't suppose you can find some kind gents who can help get this blasted contraption inside, can you?" He taps the sides of his bath chair and the gentleman who greeted us scurries off to find some assistance.

Five minutes later, two thickset men in smart suits appear and each takes one side of the Colonel's chair. Mr Nugent-Harris and I follow behind, making our way up a wide staircase onto the first floor.

As we step into a long, elegant, wood-panelled room, I realise my hands are shaking and can't decide whether the cause is nerves or excitement. A long walnut table surrounded by high-backed chairs takes up the entire room. As an observer, I am seated in a chair beside the door as the men take up their positions around the table. Sun streams in through large windows and, to avoid squinting, I turn my attention to the intricate domed ceiling above us.

"It's a rather remarkable space, isn't it?" asks the Colonel.

"It certainly is, Colonel."

"I've requested that we hear from Mrs Watt early in the proceedings, and once she has finished her talk, you are welcome to slip out."

I smile at the Colonel, grateful for how he makes it sound as though the duration of my stay in the chamber is a personal choice. The truth is, the gentlemen are unlikely to want me hanging around as they discuss the finer details of their business.

"Thank you. I shall make sure I'm discreet when leaving the room and shan't disturb the important work you're doing here."

"Good woman," says the Colonel, patting my hand before one of his assistants wheels him away to his place at the table.

There are several minutes of chatter as suited men greet one another and make themselves comfortable. Then the door opens and in walks Mrs Alfred Watt. I'm not sure quite what I was expecting, but the woman in front of me is not it. She is short and stout with an unsmiling face, and her walk is a strange, purposeful shuffle.

The men in the room fall silent and after the meeting is formally opened, Mr Nugent-Harris gets to his feet.

"I have the great pleasure of welcoming Mrs Alfred Watt to our meeting today. Mrs Watt has previously held the position of Secretary to the Advisory Board of Women to the Department of Agriculture of British Columbia and holds a Humanities degree from the University of Toronto.

"I first heard Mrs Watt speak back in February at the Agricultural and Horticultural Union conference and her speech left a great impression on me. I realised we share an ambition to allow women a greater role in our society. Mrs Watt has played a pivotal role in the Women's Institute movement in Canada, and I firmly believe after hearing her speak, you shall be of the same mind as I, that during this perilous time of war, our great country needs our women to step up as never before. We are truly honoured, that prior to our annual meeting in London next week, Mrs Watt has agreed to address us here in Wales. Gentlemen, please give a warm welcome to Mrs Alfred Watt."

There is muted clapping from the gentlemen around the table, and I feel a shiver of excitement as Mrs Watt gets to her feet. I have never met a woman with a university education before, and I am intrigued to hear how she intends to win around a room full of men.

Nugent-Harris takes his seat beside the Colonel and leans close to him. "If Mrs Watt can persuade the Welsh a Women's Institute is a good idea, she can persuade anyone."

Nugent-Harris glances behind him to check his words remain private. I avoid his gaze, pretending to be oblivious to the comment I just heard, although it takes every ounce of control not to smile. Mrs Watt does indeed have a daunting task ahead of her, but by the looks of her, she is unfazed by the challenge.

"Gentlemen," begins Mrs Watt in her Canadian drawl, "it is my honour and privilege to be addressing you here today. As I'm sure you can tell from my accent, I am a Canadian born and bred. Yet over the past few years, I have developed a fondness for your United Kingdom, and now consider it my adopted homeland."

There is muted clapping from the assembled gentlemen, polite rather than enthralled. Mrs Watt nods in acknowledgement and continues her speech.

"There is much that unites our nations, not least, the war raging on the Continent. Indeed, Canada's response would not have been so successful, but for the fact we had at the head of military affairs in Canada, a Welshman in the temperament and genius of the Celt."

"Hear, hear." This time, the gentlemen's response is exuberant. Some slap their palms against the table, while others clap so loudly it hurts my ears.

"But I digress," says Mrs Watt, silencing the applause with a raised hand. "As grateful as I am to those young lads fighting for our freedom, it is not men I am here to talk about, but women. The women of this great land have a vital role to play in this time of war. I have seen first-hand all that can be achieved when women join under the banner of the Women's Institute to serve their community..."

As Mrs Watt speaks of her Canadian experience of Women's Institutes and the varied roles women play in their community, a strange thing happens. It's as if the room becomes brighter, the colours sharper. All eyes are on Mrs Watt, and something about her enthrals us. She speaks of practical matters and yet captures us with the fervour of an evangelist.

I begin to imagine a different life for myself, one where I have a purpose, beyond counting the days until my children come home to relieve my boredom. It has never occurred to me I might have skills to contribute to the world. But the women Mrs Watt speaks of are not all educated, goodness, it sounds as though they are not even rich. She is describing ordinary women working together to make their corner of the world a better place. Is it possible I could play a small role in this new movement? From the moment my father arranged my marriage, the only expectations of me have been as a wife and mother. But what if I could be Ffion, if only for a short while? Would Hector approve?

I lean back in my chair and let Mrs Watt's words wash over me. My skin tingles and my mind sparks with ideas. Whether Hector approves of my newfound sense of purpose suddenly seems of little matter, for with Mrs Watt on my side, I believe anything is possible.

Chapter Seven

Anghared

June, 1915

W hen Mrs Montgomery returns to the car, she is bright-eyed, and her brisk movements burst with excitement.

"Oh, Anghared, I have had the most marvellous time."

"The meeting went well?" I open the back door of the Wolseley. Mrs Montgomery seems desperate to tell me all about it, but time is running out before the cows need milking, so I need to get her in the car.

"The meeting was a revelation. Oh, how I wish you could have been there."

I nod and close the door, get the car started, and climb in. "I'm pleased you enjoyed yourself."

"Oh, Anghared, I did, I really did. And you'll never guess what."

"What?"

"Colonel Stapleton-Cotton is going to ask Mrs Watt to come and speak at Llanfairpwll tomorrow. Isn't that wonderful? Oh, I do hope she agrees. What a boon it would be to have a woman like her addressing our little village."

I nod and do my best to smile.

"You'll come to the meeting, of course."

"We'll see," I say, knowing I won't. I can't imagine anything worse than spending an evening in a room full of villagers.

"Well, if the meeting goes ahead, I insist you come."

I bristle at that. It's one thing being dragged along to one meeting as a temporary chauffeur, but gentry or not, Mrs Montgomery is not my master, and I will not put myself through the torture of attending a village meeting on her say-so.

Mrs Montgomery prattles on and I try to keep my attention on the road. I half listen as I drive, trying to nod or murmur in what I hope are the right places.

"And," she is saying, "I heard from someone who knows these things, that Mrs Watt's reasons for coming to Britain may not have been purely altruistic."

"Oh?" I ask, out of politeness more than curiosity.

"Yes, according to my pal, Mrs Watt brought her sons over here to avoid the scandal of her husband's suicide."

Her words hit me like a ton of bricks to the chest. I only take my eyes off the road for a second, but in that time a deer darts out in front of us. The car swerves, the steering wheel loose between my fingers. Mrs Montgomery screams, clutching on to the door handle and shouting at me to brake. Tears stream down my face as I try to regain control of a vehicle whose tyres screech as it skids across the road. A cry like that of a wild animal escapes my lips. I can just about see through my tears as the car swerves this way and that. My hands grip the wheel and against all odds, I manage to steer us onto a verge. The car splutters and slows, disaster averted. The deer is nowhere to be seen.

Without a word to Mrs Montgomery, and with the engine still running, I climb out of the car and stagger along the bank. As I bend over and retch, I hear the passenger door opening, then slamming shut, but I don't look back.

"Angharad? Miss Williams? What on earth happened back there? Are you ill?"

Am I ill? I nod, for surely, I am ill in the head. I crouch down on the grass and wipe a hand across my mouth, mortified at creating such a scene in front of a woman like Mrs Montgomery.

I can't bear to look up but hear her soft footsteps on the grass and feel a shift in the air as she sits down beside me. A cold hand presses against my forehead, and she makes a small humphing noise.

"You don't have a fever as far as I can tell. Here." She holds out a monogrammed handkerchief and when I don't take it, begins drying my cheeks herself. "Miss Williams, I really am rather worried about you."

"I'm alright now. I'm sorry for losing control of the car. A deer ran out in front of us. I must have lost concentration for a moment, then there it was. The incident has shaken me up, that's all." It is true I am shaking. Every muscle in my body twitches, and every bone seems to shake beneath my skin. Goose pimples cover my skin and I shudder.

"Have a little sip of this," she says, pulling a hip flask from her bag. "And please don't get the wrong impression of me. I only keep it in my bag in case of emergencies, which seems rather sensible of me, given the circumstances."

I take the hip flask and sip from it. It isn't often I touch alcohol, especially not since I signed that blasted temperance pledge. Even without the pledge, I don't trust the effect alcohol might have on me. I am walking a tightrope through life, and even a small glass of wine might send me toppling off into the abyss.

"Better?"

I nod. "Please forgive me, Mrs Montgomery. If there is any damage to the motorcar, I will cover the cost, and I am sorry to have ruined your afternoon."

"Not at all. The car is still intact, and you haven't ruined my afternoon. But you will ruin my mood if you don't start calling me Ffion." She grins at me and somehow, I return the smile.

My tears reduce themselves to occasional embarrassing hiccups and I suspect after my recent performance, Mrs Montgomery will steer well clear of me in the future. "Shall we get going Mrs... Ffion? I need to get back to the farm, and I'll take more care behind the wheel from now on."

"Those cows of yours can wait an extra half an hour if needed. Let's sit here for a while. You've had a nasty shock, and it would be better to allow a little more time to calm down. Tell me about yourself, Angharad."

"I'm sure you already know everything about me."

"And how would that be possible?"

"I'm spoken of frequently enough in the village, or so my brother tells me. *Strange Miss Williams, scary Miss Williams, ugly Miss Williams.*"

"Good Lord, surely not! And ugly? What tosh! You are a very fine-looking woman, although you'd look finer if you stood up straight instead of hunching all the time."

"That's very kind of you to say."

"Oh, Angharad, you'll soon learn I only ever speak my mind. I never pay compliments where they are not deserved. Ask my husband if you don't believe me. He says I'm a liability at his dinner parties."

Of course I don't believe her, but she makes me smile nonetheless.

"You still haven't told me anything about yourself. Did you grow up in the village?"

"Yes, my father was minister of the Wesleyan Chapel."

"And how lovely that your brother should choose to continue his legacy."

"Yes."

"You never married?"

I shake my head.

"Lovers?"

I spin around and look at her in horror. What a question to ask!

"I'm sorry if I have offended you. As I said, I have a bad habit of speaking my mind, which includes speaking before I think. Let's head on home, shall we?"

I hand her the hip flask and make my way back to the car, my mind a scrambled mass of all that has occurred over the past few hours. There is nothing I want more than to be back at my bothy, Betty snuggled at my feet and a book in my hand.

Mrs Montgomery's questioning has come too close to the bone, and I don't like it. For much of the past thirty years, fictional characters have been my only true friends, and if this afternoon has taught me anything, it's that it is safer if it stays that way.

Chapter Eight

Angharad

June 1915

I've not been home long from the morning milking when I hear the crunch of stones on the rough track that leads to the bothy. My heart sinks. It must be Bryn, coming to do one of his regular inspections of my life. He claims them as brotherly support, but only ever seems to find fault. Even my chicken coop did not pass muster with Bryn, despite my pride in having built it myself.

I glance out of the window and jump out of my skin. The man approaching my home is a stranger, yet I know him by sight and reputation and never imagined our paths might cross. My sleeve catches a teacup on the table beside me, sending it spilling onto the floor. China smashes against the slate below, scattering tiny pieces of painted flowers across the floor. Before I have the chance to sweep away my mess, I hear him call out.

"Miss Williams? Are you there?"

Betty barks and I shush her. As I open the door, she bolts out in front of me, running to the bath chair and jumping up at the man inside, her tail wagging.

"Oh, hello there, dear fellow, and who might you be?"

"I'm so sorry, Colonel. My dog Betty has a habit of getting overexcited."

"Not like my dear old Tinker, eh, boy?" says the Colonel, stroking the head of the docile animal on his lap, who, other than a brief glance, is doing a sterling job of ignoring Betty's attempts at friendship.

"Is there something I can help you with, Colonel? Mr Stephens is out in the fields if you need him."

"After Mrs Montgomery told me you drove her to the meeting yesterday, I've been asking around about you, Miss Williams."

"Oh." My heart sinks. Is the Colonel here to warn me off spending time with Mrs Montgomery? All the previous night I'd tossed and turned, wondering what the heck I'd been doing gallivanting off to Bangor with a member of the gentry. If Bryn ever finds out, he'll have a fit. If the Colonel has come about Mrs Montgomery, he needn't have bothered, for I have no intention of seeing her again, not after the show I made of myself on our way home.

"Don't look so worried, Miss Williams. I was intrigued, that's all, and I was delighted to discover this little bothy belongs to you."

"Oh, no, the bothy belongs to Mr Stephens, not me."

"But you're the present occupant?"

"Yes, Colonel, I am." What interest could the Colonel have in this tumbledown bothy in the middle of nowhere? A wave of fear runs through me. Am I going to be evicted? I have nowhere else to go.

"Oh no, I seem to have worried you, Miss Williams. My interest in your bothy and its surroundings is purely horticultural. I drive down the nearby lane most days on my travels with Tinker, and I've long been admiring your vegetable patch from a distance. Many a time I've been tempted to come for a closer look, but as I wasn't sure who owned it."

"You have?" It seems in the Colonel's presence, I cannot utter more than two words at a time.

"Yes, do you mind if I take a closer look? I promise not to trample any of your veg with either my donkey or bath chair."

I can't stop my eyes travelling to the Colonel's legs.

"It's alright to ask, you know."

"Ask what, Colonel?"

"Why I'm confined to this blasted chair. I'm surprised you don't already know. I thought the story had passed into local legend."

"I try not to listen to local gossip."

"Good woman! I think we shall get along very well. It was lightning that stole my legs from me, or their feeling from the knees down, at any rate. 1879, while I was fighting in the Zulu War, a bolt of lightning struck my tent and my legs were goners. It turned out there was no need to fear the enemy after all, just Mother Nature. What do you make of that then, Miss Williams?"

"It sounds like terrible luck, Colonel."

Colonel Stapleton-Cotton barks out a laugh and slaps his thigh. "Bad luck, I'd say so, Miss Williams. But it hasn't stopped me, and I firmly believe one should seize the day."

"Quite right," I say, despite not having seized any day for the past five years.

"So, these veg. Show me what you've got. I take a very keen interest in such matters and spend a great deal of my time trying to persuade people to do just what you've been doing of your own accord. You must be quite the enterprising young lady to have created such a garden out here in the wilds. Do you have help?"

As he talks, the Colonel pulls on the donkey's reins, and I walk beside the bath chair as he guides it around the side of the bothy and into the garden.

"No, I manage the garden by myself. Mr Stephens has no use for this land, so is happy for me to do with it what I will."

"And you work for Mr Stephens, I hear?"

"That's correct, sir. I have been Mr Stephens' housekeeper for the past ten years."

We reach the allotment, where I have separated the land into different beds to give to my planting.

"This garden must take up a lot of your time, and what with the work at the farmhouse, I'm curious how you find the time for social engagements."

"Social engagements?"

"Yes, don't you young ladies enjoy a game of bridge or a dance?"

"I'm not that young, Colonel." I wonder if the lightning has affected the man's eyes as well as his legs. "And I can't say I'm much of a fan of bridge or dancing."

"You're young compared to me, Miss Williams. So, you have no interests other than your work and your garden?"

"I like books, Colonel."

"Ah yes, reading is a wonderful pursuit, and aside from travel itself, the best way of broadening one's mind. Now, are those turnips I see?"

"Yes, Colonel."

The Colonel wheels his way between the beds, talking to himself as if checking items off a list. "A good crop of carrots, yes, and looks as though those marrows are ready to harvest."

"I harvested my first crop of potatoes last week."

"Wonderful, that is music to my ears, Miss Williams. Do you own my book on cottage gardens?"

"No, Colonel, I'm afraid I don't."

"Then I shall have to get you a copy, not that it looks as if you need my advice."

The tour around my allotment takes the best part of half an hour. The Colonel is keen to impart his wisdom, and I am happy to receive it. Not only is he knowledgeable, he is easy company, and despite my best efforts, I find myself relaxing in his presence. It is only when he makes to leave that my calm is shattered.

"I expect Mrs Montgomery told you I have persuaded a certain Mrs Alfred Watt to speak in the village this evening."

"She mentioned it, yes."

"You'll join us at the meeting, I hope?"

"Oh, no, I don't think so, Colonel."

"Why ever not?"

"I... I..." Before I can think of a suitable excuse, the Colonel continues.

"It would be most disappointing were you not to come. Mrs Watt is doing us a great service by coming to speak in the village and I would like as many local women as possible to be present. You know how it is, Angharad. Not only are we divided by church and chapel, ordinary women are afraid not just to mix with different social classes, but to step out from their menfolk's shadows and use their own voices. I believe much can be achieved by taking on some of Mrs Watt's ideas, but nothing will be achieved should she turn up to speak to only me, my wife, and Tinker the dog. We need local women. We need you, Miss Williams."

"But, Colonel, I really don't think I should be mixing with the likes of Mrs Stapleton-Cotton and Mrs Montgomery. I'm a housekeeper and milkmaid."

"You father was a minister at chapel, was he not?"

"Yes, that's correct."

"And your brother too?"

"Yes."

"And now here you are, an expert on the ways of rural life. You are just the type of woman we need, Miss Williams."

"I've cows to milk this evening."

"I'll have a word with Mr Stephens. We know each other of old and I'm sure one of my workers could step in to help if you are not finished in time."

"No, it's alright. I'll start a little earlier than usual."

"Very good, very good. I shall see you at seven o'clock sharp at Graig, the home of Mrs W.E. Jones. Do you know it?"

"I know of it," I say. I've walked past the grand house many a time but would have no reason to ever join the set who meets Mrs Jones regularly for afternoon tea.

Colonel Stapleton-Cotton bids me farewell and sets off in his donkey-driven bath chair. For a moment I stand leaning against the bothy wall, confused by the strange events of the past twenty-four hours. My insides are churning at the thought of attending a meeting at Graig. Who else will be there? Despite the Colonel's assurances, I'm certain my presence will not be welcome. But what am I to do? I've told the Colonel I will go, and it is too late in the day to come up with a believable excuse. There's nothing for it but to go. With a deep sense of dread, I return to my work.

Chapter Nine

Ffion

June, 1915

For the past hour, I've been like a cat on hot bricks, staring out of the window for any sign of my distinguished guest. At last, I hear an engine and run to the front door, not even bothering with my coat. As the black motorcar appears through the trees guarding the driveway, I take a deep breath, lift my chin, clasp my hands in front of my waist and smile.

Sun reflects against the car's windows, so I miss seeing Mrs Watt's reaction to the house. I hope she approves and likes what she sees. A chauffeur climbs out of the car, tilts his hat to me and walks around to open the passenger door.

"My dear, what a welcome this is."

My hands drop to my side, and I feel suddenly foolish, not to mention terribly disappointed. It only takes a second for me to pull myself together. "Hector dear, what a surprise. I wasn't expecting you home until Friday."

"Business concluded early, my dear. But if you weren't expecting me, who are you out here waiting for?"

"Come inside and I'll explain," I say, linking arms with my husband and giving him my best smile.

Susan scurries towards us as we step into the entrance hall, flustered by her master's sudden appearance. Without a word, Hector throws his coat at her as though she is a hat stand, and without turning his head, shouts, "tea in the drawing room, as quick as you can."

I give Susan a smile of apology and follow my husband through to the grand drawing room which houses beautiful yet uncomfortable furniture and, as it's north facing, always holds a chill in the air.

"I'd forgotten how cold this blasted house is," says Hector, throwing himself into a chair and crossing one leg over the other. "Come, sit on my knee."

"Hector, no, Susan will be in with the tea any moment."

"So? Come here."

I cross the room and perch uncomfortably on Hector's bony knee. He buries his face in my neck, spreading saliva across my skin with his kisses. There is an unfamiliar smell on him and with a start I realise what it is – a woman's perfume.

"Did you come straight from London?" I ask, trying to ignore the way his fingernails are digging into my shoulder.

"What? London? No, I overnighted at an inn just north of Shrewsbury. Why, do you want me well rested?" He tilts his head back and looks at me, his eyes black as coal.

Susan walks into the room carrying a tray and I jump off Hector's lap and straighten out my skirt. "Thank you," I say, as she sets the tray down on a table. "Don't worry about pouring, I can do that."

"Thank you, madam."

"Fetch Hargreaves and tell him I want this fire lit," barks Hector. "This room is like an icehouse."

"Yes, sir." Susan rushes from the room and for a moment, silence descends, punctuated only by the ticking of a clock on the mantel.

Hector ignores the tray of tea and pours himself brandy from a glass decanter. "Who were you waiting for out there?" he asks.

"I'm sorry, my dear, but as I wasn't expecting you home for a few more days, I agreed to host a friend of the Stapleton-Cottons."

"I see. And who is this friend? Not some do-gooder the Colonel's taken pity on, I hope. Honestly, I don't know why he bothers with all his lame ducks. A fellow should concentrate on his own business, first and foremost."

"From what I've heard, the Colonel's businesses are thriving."

Hector's glare comes as a warning. I've overstepped my place, and kick myself for speaking out.

"So, come on, who is this mystery guest? Male? Female?"

"Our guest is a distinguished Canadian lady, one Mrs Alfred Watt."

"I see. And what is she like, this Mrs Watt?"

I know the question my husband is really asking. He wants to know if Mrs Watt is young and attractive. It takes all my effort not to laugh. "She is a fascinating woman, by all accounts. The Colonel knows her through his work with the Agricultural Organisation Society."

"I see. And will her husband be accompanying her?"

"Mrs Watt is a widow."

"Right."

A sly smirk folds his lips, and I can almost see the cogs turning in Hector's mind. He'll be picturing a young, distressed woman in need of a man's shoulder to cry on. My poor husband doesn't know what's about to hit him.

The doorbell sounds and I rush to answer it.

"Leave it," calls Hector. "What's the point of me paying servants if you're going to do all their work for them?"

With a bout of frustration, I pace the room, knowing it will irritate my husband. I glance over at him and try to remind myself of his redeeming features. At almost twenty years my senior, Hector is not a man I would have chosen for myself, but as soon as he was through the respectable grieving time for his first wife, my father had invited him to supper, his intentions abundantly clear to everyone around the dinner table.

Our marriage had taken place four months later, and in one fell swoop I had become a wife to a man I barely knew, and a stepmother to two children who despised me from the off. I had hoped when I had my own children, Hector and I would form some sort of bond, but seventeen years into our marriage, I'm still not sure he even likes me for anything other than my appearance.

Voices reach us in the hall, and I resume the position I took earlier on the driveway. When Mrs Watt enters the room, I feel a surge of satisfaction as Hector's face falls.

"Mrs Watt, it is wonderful to see you again. I so enjoyed your talk yesterday afternoon." I could kick myself as, from my peripheral vision, I notice Hector's eyes narrow.

"The pleasure is all mine," says Mrs Watt, in her Canadian drawl.

Hector frowns, an outward sign of his inner suspicion of all things New World.

"Would you like a cup of tea, or would you rather be shown straight to your quarters?"

"A cup of tea would be grand, if it's not too much trouble."

"None at all."

Hector stands abruptly and nods to Mrs Watt. "I'll leave you ladies to it." As he passes me, he mutters under his breath, "we'll talk about this later."

As someone who frequently suffers bouts of loneliness, with Mrs Watt and Hector in the house I know I've nothing to complain about. But as Hector leaves the room filled with barely concealed aggression, and Mrs Watt makes herself comfortable in the chair Hector just vacated, I can't help but wish I had the house to myself once more.

Chapter Ten

Anghared

June, 1915

The sun is sinking lower in the sky as I cross the fields towards the village. June is one of my favourite months. Anglesey comes alive with a burst of spring flowers, and if we're lucky, even a glimpse of sunshine. This June day is no exception. The air is still, humid, and I can already feel beads of sweat forming beneath my clothes.

Nature, unaware of the war raging over on the Continent, parades its rainbow of colour to a backdrop of birdsong. As the hills of Snowdonia loom on the horizon and the Menai Strait glistens through the trees, I try to focus on the beauty around me, rather than the terror of what I'm about to do. I breathe in the floral scent hanging in the still air, smile at the sheep guarding their growing lambs, and run my fingers along the hedgerows brimming with life.

I've left Betty at home, a decision she was most unhappy about. The Colonel's dog Tinker will probably attend the meeting, but I can't risk Betty getting overexcited and drawing attention to herself, and therefore me. The village appears beyond the fields, the Marquis of Anglesey's column watching over it.

As I turn a corner, I see a group of ladies in smart jackets and even smarter hats walking up the road towards Graig. I push myself against the hedgerow in the hope they've not seen me.

"Good evening. My name is Angharad." No, that isn't right. I try again, muttering under my breath. "Good evening, my name is Miss Williams and I'm here by invitation of Colonel Stapleton-Cotton." No, this time it is too formal, and my voice sounds as if there's a frog caught in my throat. I cough and have another try. "Good evening. My name is Miss Williams. Pleased to meet you." Yes, that should do it. My hand reaches to my head to check my hat is in place. I own nothing so fine as the ladies I've just seen, but my Sunday best will have to do.

If there is one thing that could make this evening worse, it would be turning up late. With this in mind, I leave my place of hiding and try to walk with confidence down the road towards Graig, and the women I fear.

To my surprise, as I approach the house two ladies are coming towards me and I recognise the younger as the woman I've seen at chapel. Unlike the group I saw before, these ladies, whilst smart, are not as expensively dressed. As I draw closer, I realise they must be mother and daughter, for they share the same short, slim stature and mousy flyaway hair.

We coincide at the gates in a moment that would be awkward were it not for the warm smiles on their faces. Their hair may be unexceptional, but both women have the most extraordinary hazel eyes, and their cheeks crease in dimples as they greet me.

"Good evening," the older woman says. "My name is Mrs Ambrose, and this is my daughter, Miss Carys Ambrose. Are you here for the meeting?"

"Yes, I am. Miss Angharad Williams, pleased to meet you." I hold out a shaking hand, grateful that the frog has now left my throat, and I've made it through my first introduction.

The older of the two women takes my hand and gives me another warm smile. "Are you local, Miss Williams?"

"Yes, I live up on the Stephens' farm."

"I think I've seen you at chapel," says the woman I now know to be Carys Ambrose.

"Yes, my brother, Bryn, is minister there."

"Is that right? We are in good company," says Mrs Ambrose to her daughter.

My cheeks flush. Oh goodness, do they think I'm some pious woman who'll be judging their words and deeds? I mutter something inaudible about being grateful for their company.

"We'd best make ourselves known to our hosts," says Mrs Ambrose, opening the gate.

I hesitate, staring up at the grand whitewashed house in front of me. Miss Ambrose waits with me and whispers, "a bit intimidating, isn't it?"

"Just what I was thinking."

"At least you're a minister's daughter. My mother has delusions of grandeur but we're a farming family, not used to associating with the likes of Mrs Jones or Mrs Montgomery. I worry we'll not be welcomed."

The relief at meeting someone who shares some of my fears is so great I could cry. Before I can offer Miss Ambrose any reassuring words, Mrs Jones comes bustling down the driveway towards us.

"So good of you to come, ladies. We're meeting in the summerhouse as it's such a fine evening. Follow me and we'll make our introductions once we're all gathered."

It turns out Mrs Jones' summerhouse is at the top of her garden, and rather than the wooden structure I had pictured, it is stone built with a tiled roof. Lush creepers cover its frontage and remind me of the entrance to a secret garden I read about in my latest novel. The summerhouse is at least three times larger than my bothy, and I struggle to understand why anyone would need such a structure in the grounds of an already impressive home.

"Crikey, this is grand," mutters Miss Ambrose as we walk up the grassy slope.

A group of smartly dressed women are milling around the entrance to the summerhouse and I hang back. Mrs Ambrose joins them without batting an eyelid, recognising several ladies and engaging them in conversation. Miss Ambrose follows her mother, then must realise I'm no longer beside her as she turns back and comes to stand beside me.

"What's wrong?" she asks.

"I shouldn't have come. I need to go home."

"Home? But you only just got here!"

"I... I..." I turn and begin striding back down the slope. Miss Ambrose runs after me and pulls my arm.

"Miss Williams, please, stop and tell me what is the matter."

"I don't belong here."

Miss Ambrose surprises me by tipping her head back and laughing. "Don't belong here? And you think I do?"

I'm ashamed of my behaviour. Only yesterday I lost control of my emotions in front of Mrs Montgomery, and here I am doing the same in front of Miss Ambrose, who is little more than a girl.

"You're shaking," says Miss Ambrose, leading me to a wooden bench with views out to the Strait. "Sit here a moment."

I shake my head, unable to still my trembling limbs. "Whatever must they all think of me, running away like a frightened schoolgirl?"

Miss Ambrose turns and looks up at the summerhouse. "No one has noticed anything at all. From what I can see, they're all too busy enjoying a gossip and a cup of tea."

"You're sure?"

"Yes. I'm no liar, Miss Williams."

"Angharad, please."

"Then you must call me Carys." She smiles at me and my heartbeat slows.

"I really think I should head home. This isn't the place for me."

"And leave me on my own? Surely you're kinder than that, Angharad?"

I can't tell how serious she is. Her eyebrows are drawn close in indignation, but there's a lightness to her tone which suggests she might be teasing me. "You won't be on your own. Your mother is here with you."

Carys bats away my words. "Mami? You think she's going to pay any attention to me when surrounded by the great and good of Llanfairpwll? She hasn't even noticed I'm not by her side. Look."

I turn and follow Carys's gaze. She's right, Mrs Ambrose is locked in conversation with Mrs Jones, who seems to be trying to inch away from the confident farmer's wife. "I suppose I could sit at the back?"

"And I'll sit there with you."

"You will?"

"Of course."

"Thank you."

"Come on."

I follow Carys's lead and we walk back to the summerhouse. We're almost there when I hear someone calling my name.

"Miss Williams!"

I turn and see Mrs Montgomery walking towards me, accompanied by the Colonel, Tinker the dog, his wife, and a short stocky woman with beady eyes. My entire body begins to shake, and Carys must notice, because she takes hold of my hand and gives it a firm squeeze. With a nod of thanks, I walk over to meet the group.

Eddy always laughed at the way members of the upper classes turn me into a shrinking violet and would often tell me it was because of the authoritarian rules my father imposed on me as a child. Whatever the cause of my deference, as I sidle up to Mrs Montgomery and her posh friends, I want the ground to swallow me whole.

"Mrs Watt, this is Miss Angharad Williams."

"Nice to meet you," says Mrs Watt.

"It's an honour to have you visit our village," I mumble, my dry tongue feeling large in my mouth and getting in the way of my words.

"The Colonel is a hard man to refuse," says Mrs Watt, raising an eyebrow in the Colonel's direction and shaking her head.

The Colonel's cheeks are pink, and a broad smile sits beneath his moustache. "Good evening, Miss Williams. I'm so glad you could attend this evening's meeting."

"Jane, this is my new friend I was telling you about, Miss Angharad Williams. Angharad, this is Mrs Stapleton-Cotton."

The lady holds out a hand, but I take a moment to notice as I'm thrown by Ffion's description of me. Friend? Friend is too generous a term, too presumptuous.

"A pleasure to meet you, Miss Williams," says Mrs Stapleton-Cotton.

"Likewise."

"Angharad Williams? The daughter of David Williams, I presume?"

I nod mutely. It's impossible to tell how association with my father will be received, but given all the people in front of me are Anglican, I can't imagine Father would have been cordial in his dealings with them.

That's the tricky thing about being one of the Williams clan. Father still casts a long shadow over my life, despite being gone almost twenty years. His reputation still follows me, for good or ill. To some in the village, he's remembered fondly as the revered reverend who guided his flock with a steely conviction. To others, he was known as a tyrant, a thorn in the side of those wanting any sort of progress in the village. Although I'd never admit it publicly, I adhere to the second school of thought. When the Stapleton-Cottons add no further comment on my father, I can only assume their opinion is closely aligned to my own.

An awkward silence descends. It only lasts a couple of seconds, but I know I am the cause. As I tower over the assembled group, all I want is to shrink and disappear.

"Shall we get going, Colonel?" asks Mrs Watt.

"What a good idea, but first, let's find ourselves a cup of tea."

Chapter Eleven

Angharad

For the past five years, I've carved out a carefully curated existence that limits my social interactions to the most minimal as possible. Now, I find myself among the most intimidating group of people anyone could put me with – women. But not just women, upper-class women. I consider myself a reasonably intelligent woman and have given myself an education of sorts through all the books I read, but I've never learned the intricacies of social interactions women like Ffion Montgomery are taught from a young age.

The chatter around me assaults my ears. It is a far cry from the peace of my bothy. I wish this meeting could have happened in winter, for I could have worn a thicker hat to dampen some of the sound. A strange ringing grows louder in my ears, and I wonder if I am about to pass out. My hand reaches out and rests against the stone wall. The touch of cool stone brings me to my senses. I can't collapse here, not in the middle of so many people. It won't do to make a show of myself on my first public outing in years.

Mrs Montgomery appears to know everyone here if her greetings are anything to go by. She treats everyone as an old friend, and I can't help but admire her for it. I've lived in the village all my life and haven't even said good morning to most of the women here. Ffion has lived in Llanfairpwll for what, eighteen months? And yet an observer would think it is she rather than I who grew up here.

As Ffion engages two women in easy conversation, I hang back, a head taller than everyone here, but desperate to disappear. She catches my eye and beckons me over, but I shake my head. With my back to the wall, I am safe enough, so long as I keep my eyes to the ground.

If I'd known it would be like this, I would never have come, social niceties or not. In that moment, I hate Mrs Montgomery and the Colonel for dragging me into whatever scheme this is. They are no better than any of the other bullies I've encountered, only with a better vocabulary and more stylish wardrobes.

"Are you alright?" whispers Carys.

In my panic, I've forgotten she is beside me, and turn to her and shake my head. "No, I shouldn't be here. I don't want to be here."

Ffion walks over to us and smiles. Any animosity flees my body. There is something disarming about her smile, and her eyes twinkle with excitement.

"Isn't this a hoot?" she says, wiggling her eyebrows until I can't help but smile.

"I'm not used to things like this," I mutter.

"Me neither," agrees Carys.

"Believe me, Angharad, neither am I. The most excitement I have in my life is attending the occasional Mother's Union meeting, and given my children are away from me more often than they're home, I struggle to even think of myself in a mothering role."

Her candour catches me off guard and for a moment, intrigue re-places fear. As she speaks of her children, I recognise something in her voice. I take a moment to identify what it is, then with a jolt of surprise,

I realise. Mrs Montgomery is lonely. Another lonely woman in a man's world.

Mrs Montgomery leans in closer to us and reduces her voice to a whisper. "Who'd have thought a little old lady from Canada could cause such a stir? These women of Llanfairpwll won't know what's hit them. What a good idea of the Colonel's to invite Mrs Watt here. Isn't he a gem? Jane too, such a kind, thoughtful woman."

"They both do a lot for folk around here," says Carys.

"They certainly do."

Before we can continue our conversation, the Colonel is wheeled to the front of the room where he claps his hands together three times. The women around us hush and all eyes turn to him.

"Ladies, we are very honoured to have Mrs Alfred Watt with us this evening. Her time is precious, so I suggest we commence with our meeting, and of course, there will be plenty of time for tea later."

Women around us scurry to secure one of the limited seats, and Ffion makes her way to the front of the room with Mrs Stapleton-Cotton and Mrs Jones.

"Where shall we sit?" asks Carys, who seems as uncertain as I am.

"There are too few chairs for all of us, by the looks of things. Shall we stand at the back?"

"Just what I was thinking."

We position ourselves in a dark corner at the back of the summer-house close to the door. Knowing I have an escape route calms me a little.

"Right," says the Colonel, clapping his hands together again and commanding the room once more. "If we're all settled, I think we should make a start. But before I invite Mrs Watt to take the floor, I'd like to thank Mrs Jones for kindly providing a venue for tonight's meeting, and Mrs Edwards for providing the cake. Now, without further ado, may I present to you, Mrs Alfred Watt."

Mrs Watt takes her place at the far end of the narrow room. It's lucky we're standing, for she is so short, if we were seated, the sea of hats in front of us would block our view.

"Good evening, ladies..." she begins, and from that moment on, I am lost in her words.

Mrs Watt takes my breath away. It is a moment before I work out why and then it strikes me like a hammer to the chest – she reminds me of Eddy. Not in appearance or accent, of course, but in her manner. She speaks in clipped sentences, as though not wanting to waste time with unnecessary words when getting her point across. She is certain, oh, so certain, just like Eddy. But above all, it is her uncompromising belief in herself that stands out. A wave of jealousy sweeps through me. What must it feel like to be so comfortable in one's skin? To ignore the outer appearance in favour of what lies within? To stand in front of a room full of sceptics in the complete belief she can bring us around to her own way of thinking?

Beside me, Carys stands enthralled. Her rosebud mouth is slightly open, her hazel eyes sparkling, her thick lashes barely blinking. Her dainty round cheeks are flushed, and her hands lie clasped in front of her, as though she dares not move for fear of missing one of the many pearls of wisdom old Mrs Watt is sharing. She's even more enthralled than when she hears my brother speak in chapel, and that's saying something.

"Isn't she wonderful?" whispers Carys, when Mrs Watt pauses to take a sip of water. "I've never heard a woman speak like this."

I nod, for my throat is thick and dry, taut with longing as I wish Eddy could be here with us.

For the rest of Mrs Watt's lecture, I try to pinpoint what it is about her that creates the electricity among her rapt audience. Nothing she speaks of is particularly daring, certainly not compared to the likes of Pankhurst and Fawcett, and yet she sparks a feeling of possibilities, that women can sit alongside men and contribute an equal share to society, and that their hard work should be equally rewarded. I picture Bryn sitting in this summerhouse and don't know whether to laugh or cry. All evening I've been watching the door, wondering if Anne will make an appearance, but mercifully she seems that either she has not been invited, or has chosen to stay at home.

"What we have achieved in Canada can be replicated here. Is Llanfair PG ready to put itself on the map and forever be known for starting the first Women's Institute to grace our shores and the great nations of the United Kingdom?" Mrs Watt stops speaking and the summerhouse is so quiet you could hear a pin drop, then with a suddenness that makes me jump, the women around me break out into rapturous applause.

When the commotion has died down, Mrs Wilson gets to her feet and proposes that a society just as Mrs Watt has described be established in Llanfairpwll. The motion is seconded by Miss Watts, of Aber Braint. When Colonel Stapleton-Cotton puts the motion to the rest of us, I find my hand raising in tandem with every other woman in the room. It feels as though we are on the brink of something momentous, something exciting.

But as quickly as my excitement arrives, it fades. Anne may not have attended tonight's meeting, but there is no doubt she and Bryn will get to hear of it. Before the meeting has reached its conclusion, I whisper my goodbyes to Carys and slip out into the night.

Chapter Twelve

Carys

June, 1915

"What did you make of that then?" asks Mami as we walk through the dark, quiet village. We were some of the last to leave, so keen was Mami to catch up on local gossip with other farmers' wives and make herself known to the great and good of Llanfairpwll.

"It was a very interesting evening."

"Interesting? Interesting? Revolutionary, more like!"

"Come on, Mami, I can't see where the revolution lies in a group of women drinking tea and discussing knitting."

Mami stops walking and takes hold of my arm. "Never underestimate the power of a group of women getting together and finding their voice, *cariad*. Yes, our power may be disguised beneath cups of tea and handicrafts, but it's power, nonetheless."

"Yes, Mami."

We continue walking and Mami drifts away into her thoughts. When she speaks, her voice is quiet and takes me by surprise. "Us women have been overlooked for too long."

"I thought you disapproved of the suffrage movement, Mami?"

"Pah, that nonsense? Of course I do. Those women chaining themselves to things and committing violence do more harm than good, if you ask me. It's not the way of us rural women to create such a fuss."

"Wouldn't you like the chance to vote?"

"That's neither here nor there, and as the saying goes, *cariad*, there's more than one way to skin a cat. Townsfolk think us villagers are soft in the head, inbred, unworldly, but they couldn't be more wrong. Who do they think is responsible for feeding our great nation? The men? Lord, give me strength. It's the women who run the show on all these farms."

"I don't think Dadi would like to hear you speaking like that."

"Your dadi knows which side his bread is buttered."

"Still, I can't see him going for this idea of Women's Institutes, can you?"

"So long as his dinner's on the table and it doesn't interfere with our work, how can he object?"

By now we've left the village well behind us and are relying on moonlight to find our way down the winding lanes.

"That Angharad Williams is an interesting one."

"How do you mean, Mami?"

"Bit odd, that's what I mean. I don't want you getting too friendly with her, you hear?"

"Why not? I don't think she's odd. She's shy, that's all."

"Hmm, she looks strange enough."

"No, she doesn't. She's tall, but not deformed, and she has a rather handsome face."

"Handsome indeed. More like a man than a woman, that one."

"That's unfair, Mami. The poor woman can't help her size."

But there's no stopping Mami when she's on a roll. "She's a loner too, never comes down into the village from what I've heard. And goodness knows what her brother was thinking sending her to the Stephens farm. It isn't right, a single woman living up there with a widower."

I can't help but let out a splutter of laughter. "Mr Stephens? Surely you're not suggesting any impropriety between the pair of them? He's deaf as a post and old enough to be her grandfather!"

"That's as may be, but there's something unnatural about their arrangement. You know she lives in an old bothy designed for shepherds, no doubt. What's a minister's daughter doing living like a hermit?"

"Perhaps it's to avoid nasty gossip."

Mami doesn't get the hint. "I remember her when she started school. She's a good few years younger than me, but even as a little child, she was strange. Never had any friends to my knowledge and always had her nose in a book. Her parents were pillars of the community, and it must have shamed Mrs Williams to have born such a daughter. And what a worry for them. There was never any chance of finding a suitable match for Angharad Williams. What man wants a woman on his arm who's a head taller than he is? No one around here, that's for sure."

"She can't help her height."

"Perhaps not, but she could make more of an effort to engage herself in the community."

"What do you think she was doing this evening?"

It's a relief when we reach the farm and Mami stops her whinging. I liked Angharad very much and hate to hear such nasty words spoken about my new friend. When we walk into the house, we find Dadi dozing in front of the fire.

"You pair took your time," he says, his eyes snapping open as we walk into the room.

"Not that you'll have noticed," says Mami, kicking Dadi's feet off the table and shaking her head at the empty ale glass beside him. "Where's Peter?"

"In bed. What was it all about then, this meeting?"

"We heard from the most interesting woman from-" I say, before Mami's glare stills my tongue.

"The meeting was held in Mrs Jones's summerhouse, and was arranged by the Stapleton-Cottons," says Mami, name-dropping as if she's suddenly one of the gentry. "We've decided to set up a Women's Institute in Llanfairpwll."

"Have you now, and what's one of them when it's at home?"

"It's just like the farming meetings you attend, but for farmer's wives."

"Mrs Jones isn't a farmer's wife, nor is Mrs Cotton."

"Mrs Cotton might disagree with you there," says Mami, "but I never said it's just for farmers' wives. It's for all respectable women in the village and its surrounding farms."

"Well, I can't see what you'll need a meeting for. What on earth have a group of women got to talk about for hours?"

Mami looks over at me and rolls her eyes. "The idea is that we do good works in the community and educate each other in the ways of rural life."

"Educating? Now I've heard it all. So how often will these meetings happen? You know we're entering our busiest time of year?"

"Which is precisely why the next meeting is not scheduled until September. By then, the harvesting will have happened and there'll be more time to spare."

"Time to spare? You need your heads examining." Dadi heaves himself up out of his chair. "I'm off to bed." As he leaves the room, we hear him muttering under his breath, "a club for women, now I've heard it all."

"I'm going to make a cup of cocoa to take up to bed, Mami. Would you like one?"

"No, I'll go straight up. Your dadi can never get to sleep if I'm not beside him. Don't be too late yourself. You'll need plenty of energy for tomorrow."

"I'll be up as soon as I've made a drink."

"Good girl."

I'm stirring milk in the pan when a sound behind me makes me jump.

"I am very sorry, Miss Ambrose. I didn't mean to startle you."

"That's quite alright, Mr Jansen. What are you doing up at this time?"

"Lina woke up with another nightmare. I said I'd fetch her some cocoa."

"Poor little mite. I thought the nightmares would have stopped by now."

"We are coming up to the anniversary of her mother's death. I suspected it would be a difficult time for the girls, and it seems I was right."

"You're wonderful with them."

"Thank you, Miss Ambrose, but you and your family must take much credit for their happiness. Not everyone would want a family of Belgian refugees taking over their home."

"Hardly. You take up one room, and with my brother away, we've room to spare."

"Have you heard from your brother William lately?"

I shake my head. "No, I expect he is far too busy making a new life for himself to think of us. Here," I say, pouring the warm milk into a cup and stirring in some cocoa powder. "Why don't you take this up to Lina?"

"But that is yours."

"Lina needs it more than I do. Besides, I should get to bed."

"Thank you, Miss Ambrose, you are most kind."

Mr Florian Jansen smiles and fixes me with his startlingly blue eyes. My heart leaps and my cheeks redden as I hand him the mug of cocoa.

"Good night, Mr Jansen."

"Good night, Miss Ambrose."

When I reach my bedroom, I close the door behind me and lean against it. What kind of woman am I? My thoughts should be with my sweetheart Dai, off risking his life for King and Country, not with a disabled, widowed refugee twice my age. But it seems the harder I try not to think of Florian, the more I do. In the end, I pull the last letter I received from Dai from under my pillow, hug it to myself and close my eyes, praying it will be him who fills my dreams.

Chapter Thirteen

Anghared

June, 1915

I'm busy hanging sheets and shirts up on the line in the garden when I hear his voice.

"Sister, dear."

I spin around and there he is, a bible clutched to his chest. Bryn's usual day for visiting Mr Stephens is Wednesday, but today is Friday, and what's more, Anne is by his side. She rarely comes up to the farm, so worried is she by the thought of mud on her shoes.

"What a pleasant surprise," I say through gritted teeth.

"Perhaps you could leave your work," says Anne. "There is something important we'd like to discuss with you."

My heart sinks. I drop the sheet I'm holding back into the basket and follow them into the farmhouse. They sit at the scrubbed table, but I stay standing. "Tea?"

They both shake their heads. "Sit down," says Bryn.

I do as I'm told and look into their grim faces. "Is everything alright? Are the children well?"

"This is not about us," says Bryn, "it is you we are worried about."

"Me? I'm quite alright, thank you."

"We've heard a troubling rumour about you and hope you can clear the matter up."

My hands shake and I wish I had a teacup to hold on to. Have they heard about me driving a motor car? Is that it? I wait, knowing they'll want to prolong my agony for as long as possible.

Anne glances across at Bryn and nods her head. He returns the gesture and lays his hands flat on the table. "The problem is this, Angharad. News has reached us you are getting above your station."

"Pardon?"

"Are you going to deny you attended a meeting at Graig, the residence of Mr and Mrs Jones, yesterday evening?"

"No, of course not. I was there by invitation."

Anne lets out a sigh of disappointment and hangs her head. "Oh, Angharad," she says under her breath, shaking her head once more.

"Dear sister," says Bryn in a kindly tone. "Whatever possessed you to think it was acceptable to socialise with the likes of the Joneses, Montgomerys, or Stapleton-Cottons?"

"The Colonel asked me to attend."

"A mistake on his part, I'm sure," says Anne. "Don't you see, dear, it really wasn't your place."

"Has someone said something?"

Bryn and Anne exchange a glance, as though trying to decide whether to protect my feelings with a lie or tell the truth.

After a long pause and a deep breath, Bryn says, "it seems there was some disquiet among the participants of the meeting. Some attendees thought that your being there was an act of arrogance, that you no longer know your place."

"But there were other farmer's wives there," I say, hating the shake in my voice.

"But you are not a wife, dear, are you?" asks Anne.

"No."

"And you do not own any property," Bryn reminds me. "In fact, you are of no higher position in society than the maids who work at the houses of the gentry. What were you thinking, Angharad?"

"I'm sorry." My voice is a whisper, stolen by shame. The idea that some women I met the previous evening would have resented my presence is horrifying. They had all been so kind to me. I had done my best not to stand out or say the wrong thing. But clearly, I had got ahead of myself, been carried along in the excitement. What a terrible fool I am.

"Perhaps we could pray together?" asks Anne. "Ask the Lord for his guidance and repent of your arrogance?"

My eyes focus on the table, and I will myself not to cry. Anne and Bryn each take one of my hands and close their eyes in prayer. I follow suit, not to concentrate on the words they say, but to stop the well of tears from falling from my eyes.

As Bryn launches into his conversation with God, a conversation of my own plays in my head. *Stupid, stupid, stupid woman*, it says. *Whatever possessed you to think you would be welcome at Graig? Stupid, stupid, stupid, stupid.*

Bryn finishes his prayer with a loud Amen, and Anne and I follow suit. Anne continues to hold my hand and looks me straight in the eye.

"I'm so pleased we have cleared up any confusion," she says in the sweet voice I recognise from years before when she was new to the family.

"Yes," agrees Bryn. "From now on, it's probably best you stick to the farm and leave village matters to the villagers."

"Yes, I shall."

"Well," says Bryn, "you had best be getting on with your work. We shall see you at the chapel on Sunday."

"Yes. Goodbye."

As soon as I hear the front door close, I retreat out into the garden and back to my basket of washing. Tears slip down my cheeks as I work, and a feeling of shame cloaks me. It's hard to pinpoint quite what I am crying for. It could be embarrassment, shame, or the loss of a future I had envisioned that involved company, and if I was lucky, friendship. But there is no chance of that now.

I wish I'd never met Ffion Montgomery. It was she who started all this. Was I a project to relieve her boredom? Help the village idiot and make herself feel worthy in the process? Did she have a good laugh about me with her friends after the meeting yesterday?

But even if Ffion has been using me for her own amusement, it doesn't explain why the Colonel came and insisted I attend the meeting. I've heard nothing but kind words about him and his wife and can't imagine his motivations being anything other than good.

With all my morning tasks complete, I head back to the bothy. Mr Stephens is away at market so there's no need to prepare his dinner today. The sun is bright in the sky, and I should take Betty for a walk, but can't face it. Instead, once I'm inside the safety of my four walls, I open the chest where I keep my precious books and pull one out. The real world may be cruel and frightening, but the imaginary world is a place of safety, where the unkind get their comeuppance and the downtrodden win the day. If only life was really like that.

Chapter Fourteen

Anghad

June, 1915

I wake to a hammering on my front door and a hammering inside my head. My mouth is dry and feels full of fluff, my throat so sore I can barely swallow. I turn my head to the clock on the wall, shocked to see it is already nine in the morning.

Before I have the chance to pull on my dressing gown, I hear the unmistakable creak of the door, followed by my brother's heavy footsteps.

"Anghad? Where are you? There's no point in hiding. You'll have to come out sooner or later."

I stagger from my bed into the middle of the room, dizziness threatening to knock me to the ground. "I... I..." My attempts at speech are hampered by whatever is stuck in my throat.

"There you are. Why didn't you answer the door, and why are you not dressed at nine in the morning?"

"I... not... well."

My brother takes a step back but stares at me with narrowed eyes. "Isn't it rather convenient that you come down with a mystery illness mere days after our talk? I thought Anne and I dealt with you as gently as we could have given the circumstances, but you repay our thoughtfulness by hiding away in here and not showing your face at chapel. Have you been drinking away your sorrows? Is that it?" He turns and begins rummaging through my dresser, searching for bottles I know he won't find. I stagger after him, supporting myself against the wall. My body swings wildly from hot to cold, my headache so acute I can barely see. I make it as far as the rocking chair before my legs collapse beneath me.

My brother towers over me, shaking his head. "Look at the state of you."

"Bryn, I have an illness. I've not touched a drop of alcohol for years. I signed the pledge, just as you did."

He frowns, trying to weigh up whether I'm telling the truth. "Why should I believe you, eh? After all you've done in the past, all the lies you've told..."

"Bryn, I'm not lying."

"Then tell me," he says, "why were you not at chapel yesterday? I thought I made it clear the need to repent of your sins."

I swallow down a wave of nausea, wondering what on earth is wrong with me. The idea I've been drinking alcohol is laughable, and if I had the energy, I may have been tempted to smile. "I was... too unwell... to attend... chapel."

"A likely story. Are you sure this isn't an excuse to avoid the consequences of your actions?"

"What? I don't understand."

"You couldn't bear to face the village women after the fool you made of yourself attending that meeting last week, so came up with some cock-and-bull story about being ill."

"The..." Each word I speak is sliced by the knives in my throat and I struggle to hold on to any one thought. "I..."

"As I feared," says Bryn, "you've no defence for your behaviour. You are a disgrace, Angharad, and I shall not tolerate it. Do you want everyone in the village to know what you are, what you've done?"

I shake my head, the first of what I suspect will be many tears escaping my eyes. Bryn rests his arms on my chair and looms over me. Even in my befuddled state, I can tell he is enjoying this rare opportunity to be larger, stronger, than the sister who has long since outgrown him.

"You're going to have to face the world sooner or later." He straightens, then marches out of the bothy, slamming the front door behind him.

The noise of the door sends pain searing through my skull, and I close my eyes, wondering if this is the end and I am dying. When I open my eyes, I am still in this world, although the way I am feeling, death would be a relief.

Desperate for water, I inch myself up from my chair, wait for the room to stop spinning, and try to take a step forward. My limbs won't work, and I drop to the ground, crawling across the cold stone floor. I pull myself up against the table and grab a glass to fill. The water jug is half full, and I pray my energy will return to refill it from the well before it runs out. The thought of dying alone, from thirst of all things, is one humiliation too far.

With my glass filled, I slump down against a cupboard and force myself to take small sips. The water brings some relief, and I allow my heavy lids to close for just a moment. As I fall into a fevered slumber, the thought crosses my mind that I may never wake up.

When, much to my relief, I do wake, my clothes are damp and the bothy is dark other than a single candle flickering in the centre of the kitchen table. I am still lying on the floor, but someone has placed a cushion beneath my head and a blanket over my body.

I try to sit up, but the room spins as much as it had when Eddy used to waltz me around it. "Hello?" The word comes out as a squeak. I reach for my glass of water, take a swig, and try again. "Hello?"

By now I am sitting and have a clear view of the door. When Anne walks through it, I could cry in despair. A memory flickers in my mind of the pair of us sitting at my table many years ago nurturing what I thought was a fledgling friendship. But then came her betrayal, and any closeness we once shared was wiped out in an instant.

"Oh, good, you're awake. Bryn told me you'd imbibed too much last night. Honestly, Angharad, a woman of your age should know better."

"All I drank last night was tea."

Anne folds her arms and gives me a smile I'd learned long ago not to trust. "Tea? Drinking away your sorrows, more like."

"Anne, use your common sense. I have a fever, and you don't get one of those from the drink."

Anne's cheeks flush, but she quickly recovers herself. She folds her arms and sneers. "Then this sickness must be a punishment from God for your arrogance last week."

"I... was invited to that meeting... I didn't... even want to go. I've promised I won't go again," I say, but Anne ignores me.

"Women meeting without their men present? It's not natural. And as for a lady sitting beside a milkmaid like you, well, what on earth is this country coming to? I'd understand that sort of behaviour coming from a place like England, but Wales? Llanfairpwll? No, it won't do. Something must be done to stop this foolish nonsense."

Not for the first time, I wonder whether the words Anne speaks come from her or Bryn. I've seen enough bruises on her skin to know he has his own methods of controlling his wife, and I can't imagine her ever standing up to him. But Anne seems as indoctrinated in her old-fashioned puritanical views as Bryn is.

"The Women's Institute is nothing to fear, and I've promised I'll play no part in it," I say again, reaching for my glass, only to find it empty.

"On this occasion," says Anne, "I'm inclined to believe you. I think you've learned your lesson."

"Can you help me?"

"If I must. But please don't get too close to me as the last thing I need is to be taken from my duties by illness. It's no wonder you've fallen ill, given the people you've been consorting with lately. There's no doubt this is a punishment from the Lord. He sees all we do and knows where you were last week. You want to be careful you're not slipping back into your old ways."

Even if I'd had the energy, there would have been no point arguing my case. Anne has taken Bryn's view as gospel. And as much as it would have done my sister-in-law good to broaden her mind by listening to Mrs Watt speak, I would never try to convince her. Whatever I say to Anne will be reported back to Bryn and I've learned from bitter experience it is better to say nothing at all.

Before Anne leaves, I ask her to tell Mr Stephens that I am too unwell to attend to my milking. She says she will, and I believe her, for if Mr Stephens thinks I'm shirking my duties, he will throw me out, and I will become Bryn's problem once more.

As she reaches the door, Anne mutters something about quarantine, and the last thing I'm aware of before I slip out of consciousness is the sound of the Lord's Prayer being recited.

Chapter Fifteen

Angharad

June, 1915

I t's been seven days since I first fell ill and only now am I beginning to feel better. The water Anne drew up from the well for me is almost finished, but locked inside my useless body, I have no way of fetching more. By my calculations, today is Sunday. Will I be missed at chapel? Will someone come to find me and let me out of my prison?

Neither Bryn nor Anne has stepped inside the bothy since that first day, but they slipped a stale loaf of bread through my small window, along with a note telling me that under no circumstance was I to leave the place until my fever had gone and I was no longer infectious. So delirious was I when the bread arrived that by the time I discovered it, a corner of it had been eaten by one of the rodents who seek shelter in the bothy on cold evenings.

Every limb creaks and clicks as I try to pull on my clothes. By the time I've done up the buttons on my blouse, the cotton is soaked with sweat, not from any fever for that, mercifully, has subsided, but from the effort of moving after so long lying in bed. A week of fever has stolen my appetite and as I do up the button on my skirt, it sits loose against my hips. My lips are dry and cracked, for I've been sweating out liquid quicker than I can replenish it.

In the corner of the bothy, I've placed the bucket, which has been my makeshift privy for the past few days. I've covered it in a thick blanket, but the smell still reaches me, even with my blocked nose.

It takes all my energy to cross the room and wipe condensation from my small window. Outside, the day is bright, and after so long inside, I have to squint against the sunshine. My eyes adjust to the light, and I step back in shock, wondering if this is another hallucination. A figure is crossing the field towards me. It's not Bryn, nor Anne, for I would recognise their gait. I scrub harder at the glass and press my nose against it. Could it be a visitor for Mr Stephens who's got lost on their way to the farm?

With a cry of horror, I realise what is missing from my immediate surroundings. On a normal day, a stranger only needs to get within a mile of my home before Betty barks in excitement, but today the bothy is silent. Where is Betty?

"Betty? Betty, where are you?" It hurts my throat to speak, but I'm consumed by panic and don't care. When did I last see Betty? Five? Six days ago? Has she been shut outside all this time? What if a fox has attacked her, or she's starved to death? I run to the bothy door and use all my remaining strength to try to force it open. Despite the loose hinges, after a week of no use, the wood has expanded against the frame, and it is stuck fast. Perhaps if I had more energy, I could force it open, but I'm too weak. With a sob, I stumble back to my bed, pull my knees up to my chin, and let my tears fall.

A knock on the door puts an end to my self-pity.

"Miss Williams? Angharad? Are you in there?"

I walk to the door and steady myself against the frame. "I'm ill. I've had a fever. I've been shut in here for the good of others."

"The good of others?"

The door shudders as Ffion tries to open it. I step back. "No, don't, I could infect you."

The door stays shut, and a tentative voice asks, "How long have you had the fever?"

"Five days, maybe six, but it's gone now."

"Then I'll take my chances."

The door rattles in its frame, and after much huffing and puffing it opens and Ffion Montgomery stands panting on my doorstep. She's dressed in all her finery, an overexcited, yet thin Betty jumping around her ankles. Ffion takes a step forward, but I hold up a hand to stop her.

"No, please don't." I glance at the bucket in the room's corner, at the dishes piled on the table waiting to be washed. "Why are you here?"

Ffion bends down and scratches Betty beneath her chin. "I found this one trotting around the village in some distress. Given it's a Sunday, I thought she must have slipped her lead, so I carried her over to your chapel, but when I popped my head around the door, there was no sign of you."

My eyes open wide at the thought of Mrs Montgomery appearing at chapel. "Did you speak to anyone?"

"No. Your brother registered my appearance, and I rather fear I put him off his stride, but I slipped out before my presence could cause too great a disturbance. I know you'd never miss chapel without good reason, and that combined with this little lost pup led me to the farm. Mr Stephens made it clear by way of a note that you were unwell and drew me a rudimentary map so I could find your cottage."

"Goodness, that's a lot of trouble to go to."

"You did me a great favour when you drove me to Bangor, and I've been wondering how to repay it. It seems I've found my chance."

Betty runs into the bothy and jumps up, licking me and wagging her tail. "I've missed you," I say, picking her up and letting her lick my cheeks.

"Miss Williams, who shut you in here and why has no one been to help you sooner?"

My cheeks flush and I set Betty down. "It was for my own good and the good of others."

Ffion steps inside the bothy and wrinkles her nose. I could die from embarrassment. "Who left you here to fend for yourself, Angharad?" She reaches across and places a hand on my arm.

"My sister-in-law Anne. She didn't want me wandering off and infecting others with my fever. She told me to stay here alone until I'm fully recovered."

"I see," says Ffion, but her eyebrows are drawn into a frown. "And has Mrs Williams been back since to check on you?"

"She dropped off some bread through the window."

"Through the window?" This time, Ffion's eyebrows raise, and she takes a closer look around my bothy. "It's dreadfully stuffy in here, Angharad. The air won't be doing you any good."

To my horror, she walks towards the covered bucket. "No, please, don't look in there."

"I've had several children, Angharad. I'm not some prude."

"Yes, but you also have maids to deal with the more intimate details of life. Let me sort that out, please."

"Are you sure you're up to it? You're very pale."

"Please."

"Very well, but while you're doing that, I'll get the kettle going."

"I'm sorry, but I don't have any milk."

"You have little of anything, by the looks of things," says Ffion, opening and closing my cupboards. "Right, I'll be back shortly."

Before I can ask where she's going, she is striding off across the field. Betty wriggles in my arms, jumps down, and sets off in pursuit of her new friend. Despite the weariness that wants to pin me to my bed, I carry the bucket to the privy and empty it, rinse it in the stream, then give myself a bracing wash with the cold, fresh water.

On my return to my home, I see it through Ffion's eyes and experience a rush of shame. Whatever must she think of me? The small bed, built against one wall, is unmade and the sheets are yellowing with age. A lone rocking chair is positioned beside the fire that is my only source of heat and stove. Crumbs from the stale loaf cover the table, and other than the chest that holds my books and a small wardrobe, the bothy is little changed from the days when seasonal farm hands or shepherds would have occupied it.

Fighting the urge to sit down, I run a damp cloth over all the surfaces, collecting plenty of dust as I go. I prop open my two small windows and create a through draught which expels some of the mustiness. But this is all I can manage, for the effort exhausts me and I flop back onto my bed, frustrated by my weakness.

When Ffion returns with Betty at her heels, she is carrying a basket.

"What's that?"

"I explained your situation to Mr Stephens and gave him a piece of my mind for leaving you in such a state. Oh," she adds on seeing my expression, "don't worry, he won't have heard me. Nevertheless, I persuaded him to show me into his pantry and I have brought you some supplies. Do you feel up to eating anything?"

My throat still feels as if it's on fire, but my stomach rumbles at the thought of food. "I could probably manage something small."

"Good." Ffion pulls milk, bread, butter and cheese from her basket. She is quiet as she works, and it is only when she hands me a plate of food that she speaks again. "Angharad, I really am struggling to see how shutting you in here and not returning to care for you could be for your own good, or anyone else's, for that matter. What if you'd required medical attention? Now, I don't know your sister-in-law and I know it's probably not my place to say it, but her actions speak more of a punishment than protection. What reason could Mrs Williams have for punishing you, Angharad?"

I ignore her question and take a bite of my food. "Thank you very much for looking after me, Mrs Montgomery, but I am exhausted."

"Of course, I must leave you to rest. Take care of yourself, Angharad, and if I were you, I'd shave a little wood from that door before it jams again."

"Thank you again for your help."

With a smile for me and one last stroke of Betty's fur, Ffion leaves the bothy. A punishment? Of course, she must have been right. I thought by living out here on my own I'd be free from guilt and judgement, but it seems there is no escape for a woman like me.

Chapter Sixteen

Ffion

T he day is hot and sticky, but the railway station is mercifully quiet. An old gentleman in a tweed jacket is the only other person waiting. He stands in the shade of the iron bridge, lazy plumes of smoke spilling from his pipe. I've heard tales of the station's heyday when the construction of the Britannia Bridge brought hundreds of workers through its gates, but those days are long gone. Whether genius or madness, creating the longest place name in Europe doesn't seem to have brought the droves of visitors that the committee who dreamt up the scheme might have hoped. But at least the name provides some distraction for me as I wait.

The black and white sign attached to a wooden fence stretches almost as far as a train carriage. The sight of it draws a smile, then a determination that I must master the name to be considered a true local. My heels click against the platform as I walk the name one step for each syllable, trying to master the unfamiliar pronunciation as I go. "*Llan fair pwll gwyn gyll go ger y chwyrn drob wll llan tys il i o go go goch.*"

I pace back and forth beside the sign, in an effort to rid the nervous energy and excitement at the thought of seeing my children again. How many months has it been since I last saw them? I try to count back through the weeks but quickly lose track. In the distance I see a puff of smoke and stand on my tiptoes, trying to glimpse the train. As the train comes into view, nerves flutter in my stomach. Will the children be pleased to be home? Will they be pleased to see me? I jolly well hope so, as the past few months with only a brusque Hector for occasional company have been intolerable.

With a squealing of brakes and a hiss of steam, it's here at last. My brood of children emerge from a carriage joking and jostling with one another. They haven't seen me yet, so I enjoy a moment just watching them, trying to get used to how much they've grown and changed since I last saw them.

I wave and they spot me. Wait, there are only four children. There should be five arriving today. Hector's older two sons are both off fighting in the war, but my eldest, John, should be home for the summer holidays.

"Lovely to see you, Mother," says Michael, my second born, who now towers over me. He bends down and kisses my cheek.

"It is lovely to see you too, my dear, but where is your brother? Where is John?"

Michael's cheeks turn pink, and he can't meet my eye.

"Michael? Where is John?"

My daughter Mary steps forward and announces, "he's gone off to fight in the war."

"What? But he can't! Surely he can't sign up without my permission?"

"He can easily pass for eighteen, so I presume he lied about his age."

"Did you all know about this?"

Mary and Michael nod, whilst my youngest children, Rebecca and Henry, shake their heads.

"I tried to talk him out of it," says Michael, "but he wasn't having any of it."

"Whatever will your father say when he finds out? Oh, good Lord, I don't feel terribly well."

Michael steps forward and catches me as I fall. My head is swimming, and he leads me to a wooden bench and sits me down. Vomit rises in my throat, and I swallow it down, knowing how much it would embarrass the children should I cause a scene.

"John will be fine, Mother. And don't worry about Father, there's not much he can do about it now, is there?"

"But why hasn't the school contacted us?"

"Because he waited until the last day of term to enlist."

"Here, Mother." My youngest daughter, Rebecca, hands me a glass of water. Goodness knows where she got it from, but that's Rebecca to a tee: beautiful, kind, and unnervingly sensible. If there's a problem to solve, she will be the one to do it. I reach out to pull her close, but although she obliges, her small body is stiff, unwilling. Another sign that our former closeness is being chipped away, bit by bit, term by term.

"And how are you, my darling?" I ask her once I've recovered myself.

"Very well, thank you, Mother."

"You've been enjoying school?"

"Of course."

Her voice is flat, monotone, and I catch the quick glance she throws to Mary, who answers with a shake of her head. Something is afoot with those two and I pray there is no bullying involved. Cheltenham Ladies College has a wonderful reputation, but by the looks on my girls' faces, they are less than keen on the place.

"Can I help you with your bags?" asks an elderly porter.

"Thank you, that would be most kind. We've a car waiting outside."

"You bought the Wolseley?" Michael's eyes light up.

"Yes, and your father is driving it."

"Father?"

"All our usual chaps are away fighting, so he's had to get his hands dirty for once. I wish he'd teach me to drive. It would save me an awful lot of trouble."

"Don't be silly, Mother," says Michael. "Ladies don't drive."

I open my mouth to tell him about my new friend Miss Williams, then promptly close it again. Besides, with Hector around more than usual and already cross about having to host *that godawful Canadian*, I don't want to push my luck with further unusual friendships.

The children sprint out of the station and clamber into the back of the Wolseley.

"Get out and do that again with some decorum," barks Hector.

Cowed, the children do as they're told. I climb into the passenger seat and place a hand on Hector's knee to calm him, but he pushes it away.

"I know you're not happy about having to drive yourself, but please don't take it out on the children. They've only just arrived and have been so looking forward to seeing you."

"I pay good money to have manners instilled in my offspring. From what I've just seen, those girls won't know what's hit them when they go off to finishing school."

Boarding school, finishing school, then marriage. How cruel that a mother should only be allowed her children until the age of eleven. What a cruel world to fill a heart with so much love, and then rip away the objects of one's affections. What a cruel husband to want his children banished. I turn my head away so Hector can't see the hatred in my eyes.

Chapter Seventeen

Carys

August, 1915

The skin on the back of my neck is turning chapped and crispy beneath the hot summer sun, despite the shade from my wide-brimmed hat. Everything around me looks as though it is covered in fine gold thread, leading a trail to the distant mountains, which are almost purple under the soft summer light.

A sweet scent of newly cut hay hangs in the thick air, while insects buzz an angry hum at being disturbed, their raucous wings competing with the rhythmic swishing of our scythes. I allow myself a moment to catch my breath, wiping a hand across my forehead and leaving a dusty trail behind on my skin. My shoulders roll back and click, and I raise my arms above my head to stretch out my aching muscles.

"Here," calls Mami, throwing a flask of water over to me. I drink in greedy gulps, but am careful to leave enough for her.

"*Diolch*," I say, throwing the flask back to her row.

I return to my work and catch Mami's nod of approval. Years of practice have perfected the movements of my wooden pitchfork. I stab the forks into the hay, my muscles straining as I lift it, then scatter it evenly across the parched ground below. A gentle breeze catches the strands, but there is no time to stop and watch them dance. Instead, I step forward and repeat the process, again and again and again. We must make sure every inch of the hay is turned, for mould is our greatest enemy, and this is Wales, after all.

Along the edge of the fields, Florian guides the horse-drawn rake, the leather harness creaking and the horses' hooves pounding out a drum beat onto the dry ground. I reach the end of my line as he is passing, and he throws me a smile.

"You are doing a good job here, Miss Ambrose."

"Thank you, Mr Jansen. How is your head holding up?" I know since losing the sight in one eye, he's suffered from terrible headaches, and hope the sun hasn't made them worse.

Florian knocks his knuckle against his skull and says, "it hasn't fallen off yet."

"I'm pleased to hear it."

He laughs and continues on his way.

"Start on the next row," calls Mami. Her sleeves are rolled to the elbow, the summer sun turning her skin chestnut. No doubt she'll be cursing those tan lines later, praying they will have faded before our next meeting with ladies whose only experience of summer sunshine is to be hidden beneath a parasol.

With my back turned to Florian, I begin on the next row, my muscles now crying in complaint as my pitchfork moves up and down, up and down. My feet kick up dust as I move along the line, my boots crunching dry grass beneath them. Dust tickles my nose, and I sneeze.

There is not a cloud in the sky, and I send up a prayer of thanks for the unusually fine weather we are having, praying it holds until the hay is gathered in. We must get the field finished today, for it will bring Dadi such relief. He'll be pacing the floor of his bedroom, no doubt cursing his bad chest for keeping him away from the work.

My path draws level with Mami's, and she pauses her work, leaning against her fork. Sweat stains her cotton dress, and strands of hair which have escaped their pins stick to her damp forehead.

"That man is a godsend," she calls, pointing to where Florian is working the far edges of the field. "With Peter away at market today, there's no way we could have finished this field without Mr Jansen."

"No, we're lucky alright. I heard quite a few of the migrants in Porthaethwy have left for England in search of work."

"Let's hope our Mr Jansen doesn't follow suit. We'd never be able to keep the farm going without his help."

"Peter's still here, and Dadi will get better soon."

"I hope you're right, *cariad*, I really do."

Mami frowns and I try to think of something that will take her mind off Dadi and his hacking cough. "Lina's been having nightmares again," I call.

"It's no wonder, the poor little mites. Mind you, I've had a fair few nightmares of my own worrying Peter may join up and whether William's alright over in Canada."

Mami's words surprise me, for she rarely mentions my brother Will, or anything to do with the war.

"I'm sure Peter will stay here running the farm. Have you heard anything from Will lately?"

Mami ignores my question and turns her attention back to the work. "Once you've finished this row, go back and start stacking into cocks. It doesn't look like we'll be getting any rain, but you never know."

I do as I'm told, and once the rest of the line is tossed, I return to my previous rows and begin stacking the hay into cocks, their tips pointed to shed any rain which may fall on them. After all, you can never trust the weather to behave itself here.

The sun is setting when we finally finish our work. We meet Florian at the edge of the field, and all take a moment to enjoy the fruits of our labour. Neat cocks of hay stand proud against the sky, monuments to our sweat and aching limbs. They gleam like golden statues, casting long pools of shadow in front of them.

"You've been hard at it today," calls a voice behind us.

We all turn to see Dadi crossing the field with the aid of his stick. He stops every few steps as a coughing fit overtakes him. A leather bag is slung over one shoulder, and he is sweating with the effort of reaching us.

"Whatever are you doing out here, you fool!" cries Mami. "The air is full of dust. This will make your chest so much worse!"

"I hate to be idle," says Dadi, reaching us and dropping his bag to the ground. He looks at me and points to the bag, "open it, *cariad*. You've all earned a rest."

I open the leather bag and pull out four bottles of ale.

"This is most kind, Mr Ambrose," says Florian, "but I should get back to the girls."

Dadi bats away Florian's concern. "They're off feeding the chickens for me. They'll not be in for a while."

"They've been behaving themselves?"

"Good as gold," says Dadi. "When I came downstairs, I found the dishes washed and dried and all the floors swept. Those girls could teach my Carys a thing or two about keeping home."

"Oi, Dadi, that's not fair," I say, but I can see his eyes twinkling and know he is joking.

"This should cheer you up," says Dadi, pulling an envelope from his pocket and handing it to me.

"Oh," says Mami, leaning over to see the writing on the front, then clapping her hands together. "A letter from Dai. How exciting."

I stare at the letter, feeling none of the usual excitement I would at hearing from my sweetheart. Instead, I resent how Dai has broken into our evening. When I lift my head, I realise Florian is staring at me. He catches my eye and looks away.

"Thank you for the ale, Mr Ambrose," he says, "but I'd better get back to the farmhouse and get myself cleaned up."

"Right you are."

"So," says Mami, pointing to the letter, "what has he got to say for himself? Is he coming home on leave soon?"

"I'll read the letter later," I say, pushing it down into the pocket of my apron. Sometimes I wonder if Mami loves Dai more than I do. Perhaps I should ask him to address the letters to her instead. "I'm going to head back to the house. You two enjoy a moment of peace to yourselves. I'll start on supper, so there's no need to rush back."

As I walk through the field to catch up to Florian, I glance behind me and see Dadi spreading his jacket on the ground and sitting down with Mami beside him. She rests her head on his shoulder and the sight of them together brings tears to my eyes.

"Miss Ambrose," calls Florian, and I turn my head and try to smile away my tears. "Is there something you need?"

"No, I thought I'd give Mami and Dadi a few moments to themselves."

"You received a letter from your sweetheart."

He says it as a statement, and I don't know how to respond.

"You should read it."

"I'm going to once I've cleaned myself up and won't cover the paper in hay dust."

"Ah, I see."

The corner of his lip turns up in a smile, then he strides off ahead of me. After a day working in the fields, my legs are like lead, so rather than run to keep up, I let him go. Mr Florian Jansen has a habit of leaving my mind in a scramble, and allowing a bit of distance to form between us seems no bad thing.

Chapter Eighteen

Angharad

September, 1915

C arys tries to catch my eye again and I look at the floor, but not before I see the hurt in her own. I feel terrible for rebuffing her attempts at friendship, but without even checking, I know Anne is watching me like a hawk and one misstep could end in disaster. So far, I've had no further interactions with either Ffion or the Colonel and count my blessings. But summer is at its end, and there'll be no escaping them soon enough.

Bryn has even more fire in his belly than usual today, and the service has dragged on. Betty will be getting fed up tied to her railing, and by the time we reach the final hymn I'm as tense as a coiled spring.

With my usual nod to Anne, I slip out of the dour stone building and rush to Betty, who barks her frustration at me but wags her tail nonetheless. As I'm untying her, I hear the chapel door slam and see Carys walking towards me.

Head bowed, I grab hold of Betty's lead and stride off down the lane. With legs twice as long as Carys's, I know I can outpace her, so I'm surprised when she appears beside me, out of breath and with red cheeks.

"Angharad, please slow down," she says.

I pretend not to have heard and cast an anxious glance back towards the chapel. Has Anne seen me? The final hymn is still in full flow, but I wouldn't put it past her to slip out and spy on me.

"Angharad, please."

"I'm sorry, Miss Ambrose, but I really can't stop. I'm needed back at the farm."

"Very well then, *Miss Williams*, I shall walk with you if you're in such a hurry."

There is no way Carys can match my strides, and must run to keep pace. We round a corner and, reassured we can no longer be seen, I stop and turn to her. "Is there something you wanted from me?"

"A hello would be nice." Carys places her hands on her hips and glares at me.

"Hello."

"Do you know, Miss Williams, I had hoped we could be friends, and despite all I've heard about you, I chose to form my own opinion. But it seems others were right. You are not only strange, but damned rude if you ask me."

"There you are then. You'd best leave me be."

But Carys will not do as I ask. As I walk, she continues trotting beside me.

"I was kind to you, wasn't I, Angharad? I didn't have to stand by your side at that meeting, but I could see how scared you were and wanted to show some compassion."

"And I seem to remember I thanked you at the time."

"What has changed between then and now?"

"Nothing."

"I don't believe you."

"Believe what you like."

"Does this have anything to do with your brother?"

"My brother? No, of course not."

"Because I've seen the way he and his wife look at me, look down on me, I should say. Perhaps they think I am not suitable company for a member of their family? Well, Miss Williams, I come from fine farming stock and my family runs one of the most successful sheep farms on this island. So, you can put that in your pipe and smoke it!"

The burst of laughter surprises me as it leaves my lips. My cheeks flush red. "Goodness, I am so sorry."

But instead of being cross Carys's eyes are twinkling, then her lips twitch, and before we know it, the tension is released in a fit of giggles. "Why are we laughing?" she asks eventually, wiping her eyes.

"I really couldn't say. Perhaps it was the shock of hearing such stern words spoken from such a young mouth?"

"I am sorry, Angharad. I'm not usually so bold or rude."

"You were right, though. And please believe me when I say I haven't wanted to ignore you these past few months."

"Then why have you?"

"It's not something I can talk about."

"Goodness me, will you please stop walking so fast?"

With a sigh of defeat, I sit down on a grassy bank beside a hedgerow and let a delighted Betty off her lead. The day is clear, the distant mountains stark against a blue sky. Carys sits down beside me and wipes her brow with a handkerchief.

"Thank you. This is the opposite direction to my farm and at the speed you were going, I thought I'd have to retrace my steps for miles. So come on, what's happened this summer to turn you into foe, not friend?"

Rather than answering her question, I pick blackberries from a cluster growing in the hedge beside me. Carys sighs and I drop the blackberries to the ground and turn to look at her. "My brother wasn't best pleased I attended Mrs Watt's talk at Graig. He's made it plain he'd rather I have no more to do with any women's movements in the future."

"What right does he have to say that?" Carys's brow is drawn into a frown and I can tell she doesn't understand.

"He's my brother."

"But not your keeper, from what I gather. I've never got the impression the pair of you are close." She stretches her legs out on the grassy bank and tilts her face towards the warm autumn sun.

"No, but he's still family."

"Of course, but what skin is it off his nose? Why does he care who you associate with?"

I shrug, for how can I possibly answer truthfully? I turn from her and collect the blackberries into a handkerchief, my fingers staining purple. "How have you been? I noticed you've not been coming to chapel as regularly as before."

"No, it's not been the easiest few months. The harvest has been very busy, as I'm not sure if you're aware, but there's something not right with my dadi." Carys draws her knees up to her chin and hugs her arms around them.

"In what way is he out of sorts?"

"Aside from being tired all the time, there's something wrong with his chest. It's like he can never get enough breath for what he needs to do. We've a family of Belgian refugees lodging with us and if they hadn't been there during the harvest, I'm not sure what we'd have done. Poor

Dadi hates being so tired all the time, but when we asked the doctor about it, he seemed at a loss for what to do."

"Couldn't his tiredness just be because of the season and all the work you've had going on? And perhaps all the pollen and hay dust in the air has affected his chest?"

"Maybe, but Dadi's always been as strong as an ox. I'm worried about him, and there's been no one to talk to about any of it."

"What about your family?"

"One of my brothers scarpered to Canada a few years back, and although my brother Peter stayed on the farm, sometimes I wish he hadn't. He's grumpy all the time and I wouldn't be surprised if he joins up to fight. Mami is burying her head in the sand and keeps saying Dadi will get better soon, she won't hear any different. I used to talk to Dai, of course..."

"Dai?"

"My sweetheart." Carys gives me a strange look, half smile, half grimace, then her face falls. She picks at the grass beside her, her fingers urgent, pulling up large tufts. "Dai is away at war. Goodness, Angharad, what a lonely summer it's been. With Dadi under the weather, there's been no singing, no laughing. My brothers used to drive me mad, but now I'd do anything to hear them shouting at each other across the yard or wrestling each other in the barn. Peter hasn't been himself since Will left. Will was always the more jovial of the two and the only one who could bring Peter out of his shell."

"What about the family of refugees? I'm guessing they don't speak Welsh, but what about English?"

"Mr Jansen, Florian, speaks very good English, but we don't talk often. I think he's ashamed not to be away fighting, but aside from the fact he's a widower with two young girls to care for, he lost the sight in one eye in the attack which took his wife's life. I don't wish a disability on him, of course, but the fact he can't fight in the war is a blessing, as we can't spare another worker with Dadi so unwell."

"I'm sorry you've been lonely, and it's been a hard few months for you, and I'm sorry I've ignored you all summer." I surprise myself by taking Carys's hand and giving it a quick squeeze. She smiles and nudges me with her shoulder.

"Apology accepted. You'll be coming to the meeting next week, I hope?"

"What meeting?"

"You know, the meeting at Graig. Everyone's welcome. I'm hoping the decision to start our very own Women's Institute will be formally set in motion. Wouldn't that be exciting?"

I try my best to smile, but it's hard. Bryn and Anne have made their feelings plain, and I can't go against them. "I may be busy that evening."

"Oh, really? That is a shame. Can't you make an exception just for that one evening? I'm sure whatever plans you have can be altered. Come on, Angharad, we started this adventure together and I'd like to continue it with you."

"I'll see what I can do," I say, not meaning it. "I'd better be getting back as I need to get Mr Stephens his dinner."

"Of course. Well, I will see you on the eleventh of September at Graig. Shall I wait for you outside the gates?"

"No, I'll see you in there if I'm able to make it."

"You make sure you do," says Carys. She climbs to her feet, then with a cheerful wave sets off toward the village.

I walk a few steps, then pause. "Carys?" I call, turning and running back to her.

"What is it?"

"Bryn... Bryn said... he suggested some ladies don't want me at the meetings. Do... do you think it's true?"

Carys straightens her back and places her hands on her hips. "Given your brother is a minister, I'll assume he wasn't lying, but he must have misunderstood whatever it was he heard. Of course you're welcome at the meetings. Don't be so silly."

"Thank you. Goodbye."

As I walk, I ponder Carys's words. She seems so sure Bryn is wrong, but whatever the truth, I'm not sure I've the courage to find it out.

Chapter Nineteen

Angharad

"I'm sorry, Betty, but I can't trust you not to bark. Yes, I know Tinker will be there, but he's older and calmer than you, my lovely little pup. I promise I'll not be long. I'm only going for a look."

Betty stares at me from beneath her bushy eyebrows. She cocks her head and lets out a small whine.

"Here," I say, giving her the bone I've been saving for emergencies. "That should keep you happy for an hour or two."

Before Betty can pull on my heartstrings any further, I close the bothy door. Before leaving, I peep in through the window, pleased to see Betty engrossed in her bone and oblivious to my absence.

All day I've been trying to decide what to do about this evening. Bryn has made his feelings on the matter plain, and I'm in no position to go against his wishes, but there's no harm in going for a little look, is there? I'll not go inside. Heck, no one will even know I'm there.

I time my walk carefully to ensure I arrive on Lon Graig five minutes after everyone has arrived. Once I'm certain I'll not bump into any latecomers on the street, I walk as far as the Graig driveway and peer around the gates. It's a damp evening, drizzle hanging in the air, so there is no socialising on the lawn as there was at that first meeting back in June.

The weather suits me well, for with everyone distracted up in the summerhouse, there is far less chance of me being spotted. Through the open door, I spot Carys waiting with her mother. They are in conversation with Mrs Jones and Miss Roberts from the post office, but Carys seems distracted. She keeps looking around as if searching for someone, and I whip my head back. Is she looking for me?

For a moment, I am tempted to march through the garden and defy my brother by attending the meeting, but I can't. Instead, I let my new friend down by standing my ground out in the cold, in both senses of the word. There seem to be even more women at this meeting than the last. From what I can see, the ivy-covered summerhouse is full to bursting. No doubt Ffion is in there along with the Stapleton-Cottons. With a flash of envy, I wonder how it would feel to have control over your life, where you go, who you speak to, what you do. But there's no point in dwelling on such matters, as my life will never be that way.

My fist meets the stone wall in frustration, and I suck on the ensuing graze, feeling even more sorry for myself than before. There is no way I can join the meeting. Instead, I hurry past the gates, hoping no one will notice me. At the junction, I turn left, away from the village but still in the opposite direction from the farm. The odd horse and cart clatters past but I keep my head down.

It is only when I reach a narrow lane that I lift my head. Confident no one will be around at this time of day, I can walk tall with no fear of recognition. The lane slopes down towards the shoreline, St Mary's spire reaching up into the cloud-filled sky. The gate creaks as I slip through into the churchyard.

Neither Bryn nor Anne has visited either of my parents' graves since the day of their funerals. The churchyard is enemy territory as far as

Bryn is concerned, but what did he expect us to do, bury our parents in his garden?

I skirt around the edge of the church, a beautiful stone-built building, elegant, graceful with its pointing spire. From my years of Sunday school lessons, I know a building itself should be of no importance, but I can't help but wonder if it's easier to worship surrounded by beautifully carved walls and colourful stained glass, than square walls and an interior as grey as the weather.

Whatever Bryn may feel about this place, I'm glad Mother and Father have such a beautiful final resting place. Their graves sit side by side at the farthest reaches of the churchyard, a mere stone's throw from the waters of the Strait. The tide is in, and as I crouch beside their headstones, I can hear waves gently lapping, and the tinkling of raindrops meeting the salty water below.

It is impossible to feel anything but peace in this churchyard. After a day of changeable emotions and indecision, here I can sink into the past and remember a different time, when life still held possibilities, before I had shamed and disappointed those around me.

Mother's headstone is green with moss, so I find a sharp stone and begin scraping it clear. "There's a meeting up at Graig tonight, Mami. If you were here, you would have been in your element organising and making your feelings known. It's a funny old thing, to have the likes of the Joneses and Stapleton-Cottons sitting beside farmers' wives and daughters. I can't think of anything quite like it that would have happened in your lifetime, and I certainly never expected it to happen in mine."

It's tempting to tell Mami about Bryn warning me off, but it would feel too disloyal, and I wouldn't want her to worry. A robin flies down and sits on top of the headstone, tilting its head and staring at me with knowing eyes. I turn my head away and hope it can't see into my soul, guess at the falsehood of my chatter.

For the truth is, I don't think Mami ever really liked me. She was beautiful, my mother, all neat proportions, trim waist and luscious auburn hair which sat perfectly in its pins and never seemed to stray. Mary Williams was a delicate woman, elegant, but with fierce intelligence that made her my father's equal, until I ruined it all, at any rate.

If I'd never mentioned seeing her out walking with our neighbour, Mr Evans, she and Father might have lived the rest of their lives in peace. Even all these years on, I don't think there was anything other than a warm friendship between Mami and Mr Evans. But my ill-chosen words one evening at the dinner table sparked a jealousy and fury in my father that no amount of protesting from Mami could quell. Given the years of beatings and accusations she suffered after my one innocent indiscretion, I can't blame Mami for hating me. It turned out Father was right, I shouldn't be seen or heard. If only I'd remembered his words when Eddy came along.

Mami must have had such high hopes for me when I was born. My hair was auburn like hers to begin with, but by the time I started school, it had faded to a dull brown and I was already displaying the broad-shouldered frame my father proudly displayed. I was clever enough with reading and writing, but could never get the hang of numbers, and what with that and my size, it didn't take long for me to become known as the class dunce.

I shake my head. That is all in the past. Lying beneath the ground, I can picture Mami as I'd like her to be, not how she was. She can be my friend, my confidante.

"Anyway, Mami, I'd best be getting back to my bothy. I'll come and visit again next week. Take good care of Father, won't you?" I kiss my fingertips and press them against the stone. The robin jumps to Father's headstone, then flies off into the trees, probably to tell his family about the strange woman he encountered talking to old mounds of earth.

Chapter Twenty

Ffion

September 1915

After one last scan of the summerhouse, I can't help but let out a sigh. This is now the third meeting Angharad has been absent from. She had seemed so keen to begin with and, given her apparent isolation, I assumed she would jump at the chance to be involved in such a unique opportunity for female camaraderie.

I double-check the notes in front of me, proud to see my name listed among the committee members. Jane Stapleton-Cotton quite rightly has been voted as our President, with Mrs Jones Vice-President and Treasurer. Mrs Wilson is our secretary, and I am counted alongside a rather distinguished group of local women who all volunteered to be committee members. Of course, being a member of the committee means additional meetings, such as the one I am currently attending, but it isn't as if I have any other calls upon my time.

"So," says Mrs Watt in the matter-of-fact way I have grown used to, "I'm assuming we are all happy to accept the minutes from last week's meeting? Thanks, by the way, to Mrs Wilson for writing them up and distributing them to everyone."

There are nods and calls of "hear, hear" in response. I check the minutes again, having only bothered with a cursory glance earlier.

1. Proposed by Mrs. Cotton, seconded by Miss Roberts, that we form a Women's Institute in Llanfairpwll, affiliated to the Agricultural Organization Society.

2. Proposed by Mrs. Cotton, seconded by Mrs W. E. Jones, that it be called the Llanfairpwll Women's Institute.

3. Proposed by Mrs Cotton, seconded by Mrs J. R. Williams, that regular monthly meetings, of an educational and social character, be held on the first Tuesday in each month, at 2 p.m., in the room kindly lent by Mrs W. E. Jones, until such time as the Women's Institute has its own building.

4. Proposed by Mrs Wilson, seconded by Mrs Jones, Bron Llwyn, that the membership fee be 2/-, paid in advance, at the annual meeting to be held in January of each year. That new members be proposed by an existing member. That members be not confined to Llanfairpwll parish.

"Now that's done," says Mrs Watt, taking a quick sip of her tea, "I suggest we get down to business. I've been talking with the Colonel about what our ongoing focus should be, and we're both in agreement that during this time of war, the food supply of the country should be a special subject for discussion. Now, I'm no expert on agriculture, but thankfully, we all know a man who is." Mrs Watt pauses and winks at the Colonel, prompting a blush from the man himself and titters from those not shocked into silence.

"I'm most willing to share any expertise I might have," says the Colonel.

"And as the only male member of any Women's Institute I've ever known," adds Mrs Watt, "you're going to have to earn your keep."

More giggling ensues and the Colonel's wife Jane claps her hands together as if this is the most fun she's had in a long time.

"Before we go any further, it would be prudent for me to remind you of the workings and principles behind a successful Women's Institute. By the way, Women's Institute can be a bit of a mouthful. I suggest we shorten it to WI, after all, as you're all from Llanfairpwllgwyngyllgoge-rychwyrndrobwllllantysiliogogogoch you should be used to shortening names."

A cheer erupts at Mrs Watt's remarkably accurate pronunciation of the village name. I've lived here almost two years and still struggle to get my mouth around such a tongue-twister.

"An Institute is not ruled," continues Mrs Watt, "but rules itself. In addition, four freedoms should be kept in mind: Truth, Tolerance, Justice and Fellowship. In my opinion, Fellowship is the most impor-tant of these. We must be grave and gay, explore the world together and educate ourselves in everything from growing roses, to trimming hats, to Darkest Africa, and Bolshevism. If you become dull, the young will not join you, and your numbers will decrease."

The meeting continues in a more serious manner, with the com-mittee's roles confirmed and a programme for the next three months decided on.

"Now the programme's organised," says Mrs Watt, "I suggest we turn to practical matters. Mrs Jones, you've been so kind to provide this delightful summerhouse for use by the Women's Institute, but if we're to attract the number of members we're hoping for, we're going to need more furniture. I propose we receive any gifts towards furnishing this place at our next meeting on the twenty-fifth. I'm sure between us all we can get the venue shipshape."

"I'm sorry we're rather lacking in chairs and tables," says Mrs Jones, her cheeks pink.

Mrs Watt waves away her concerns. "Mrs Jones, I very much doubt you thought you'd ever be hosting every woman from this village and roundabouts in your lovely summerhouse, did you? I'm sure twelve chairs seemed more than adequate when your summerhouse was used for garden parties and hosting friends. Poor Mr Jones must be wondering what on earth is going on at the end of his garden. But please be assured we are terribly grateful for this space, without it Llanfairpwll would not hold the title of the first Women's Institute on these isles. And if your husband gets fed up with us, tell him it will be our priority to establish a building of our own as soon as we're able."

"Thank you," says Mrs Jones with a smile, "but you're all welcome here as long as the space is needed."

"Right, I think Mrs Stapleton-Cotton would like to add a note about refreshments. Isn't that right, Jane? She and I have spoken about the matter and propose we serve tea, bread, and one kind of cake."

"That's right," says Jane. "In order to prevent these meetings becoming a burden to any one individual, I suggest we take it in turns to provide the cakes, and perhaps someone could draw up a rota? Tea and sugar will be provided by the Institute."

"And another thing," interrupts Mrs Watt, "it's my view that the December meeting should be purely social. We can arrange the programme at a later date, but I'd suggest inviting husbands along. Men are suspicious when us women strike out on our own, and there's nothing like throwing open our doors to put their minds at ease. Let them in to see we're no group of Bolsheviks, and they'll be on our side in no time."

"Hear, hear," we all agree.

Our attention turns to questions and Mrs Watt generously tells us she'll answer each and every question we may have. I raise my hand and am invited to speak.

"My question is about how we can help improve the food supply of our country at this critical time? Do you suggest we all begin digging up our lawns and turning them over to allotments?"

"That's one way. Have you ever wielded a trowel, Mrs Montgomery?"

"I can't say I have, but I'd be willing to try. And it's not as though we're lacking in outside space."

"Quite, and I'm sure the Colonel will be more than willing to advise any women on how to grow vegetables. Likewise, those of you on farms will have a vast knowledge of your own, so don't be shy in coming forward to share that expertise. This is what the Women's Institute is all about, sharing knowledge, teaching, learning, and working together for the greater good."

Miss Roberts from the Post Office raises her hand next. "Some of us are engaged in other occupations and have little or no land for growing vegetables. Is there any way we can help with our limited resources?"

"Limited resources? You have many resources at your disposal, my dear," says Mrs Watt. "It's not just about growing things, but also about eliminating waste. I'm presuming every woman here has a kitchen?"

Mrs Watt looks around the room and we all nod. For a moment, I'm pleased Angharad is absent, for having seen the tiny cottage she calls home, I'm not sure the open fire and rudimentary cupboards could count as a kitchen, and I fear she would be embarrassed.

"If a woman has a kitchen, she can learn to preserve any fruit or vegetable. In fact, I believe I am scheduled to give a demonstration at our next meeting. But beyond that, there are a myriad of other ways we can work together to improve the food supply.

"This Women's Institute is open to all, and thus we have a unique opportunity to educate our community in all kinds of skills that will help us see out this war. If someone has a particular skill such as bread-making or preserving, please volunteer your services to give a demonstration. We can also organise the distribution of resources so those in greater need have access to provisions. I'm sure the Agricultural Organisation Society can give us suggestions on how we can best be of use?"

"They'd be delighted to do so," says the Colonel.

The questions draw to a close and I make my way to the tea table where I have volunteered to serve. I am working alongside Miss Pritchard, a young woman I recognise from the village but have as yet had no dealings with. I introduce myself and we set to work laying out the cups and saucers.

"I've just seen Mr Jones leave the kettle by the door," says Miss Pritchard.

"Wonderful, I'll fetch it."

Mr Jones is walking back towards his house, and I call my thanks to him.

"Just following orders," he replies with a broad smile.

"We're very grateful," I say. "All that talking has left us parched."

"No doubt."

The kettle is heavy and I take care not to spill any boiling water as I cross the summerhouse. With the tea brewing in our motley selection of pots, Miss Pritchard turns to me. "Isn't it wonderful to have such a sense of purpose?"

"It is," I say, recognising the strange feeling that has been growing in me all evening. I haven't felt useful in a very long time, but as I pour tea into cups, I feel I may be finally finding my way back to the Ffion of old, before Hector, before the children. It seems I have a lot to thank Mrs Watt for.

Chapter Twenty-One

Angharad

September, 1915

Mr Stephens and I are finishing our dinner when, through the window, I see Ffion Montgomery riding into the yard. I must pull a face, for Mr Stephens turns, and on seeing we have a visitor grunts, pushes aside the remains of his food and leaves through the back door.

I've only just cleared the plates into the kitchen when Ffion knocks. "Coming."

"Oh good, you're home," she says as I open the door. Without asking, she marches into the farmhouse, unbuttoning her jacket as she goes. "It's still surprisingly warm out there. I think we're having an Indian summer."

"What can I do for you, Mrs Montgomery?" She glares at me, and I know why. "What can I do for you, Ffion?"

The glare is replaced by a smile. "What I need from you, Angharad, is to understand why you haven't attended the last few meetings of the Women's Institute?"

"I've been busy."

"We're all busy," says Ffion, blushing slightly at her lie. "Young Miss Ambrose has attended every meeting, and she has a similar workload to you."

"The meetings don't interest me," I lie, turning my back on her so she can't see the guilt on my face.

"What rot. I saw how engrossed you were in that first meeting. You were hanging on Mrs Watt's every word. What has changed between June and September, and don't try fooling me with more lies, I expect more from a minister's daughter."

"I don't feel it is appropriate for me to attend."

"Why not?"

"My brother says..."

"Your brother? What's he got to do with anything? Oh, I see, he's warned you off, is that it?"

"No, it's..."

"Perhaps I need to have a word with your brother and sister-in-law? I can explain the aims of the Institute, and once they hear what it's all about, I'm sure they'll be delighted if you attend."

"Please don't."

"Don't what?"

"Please don't speak to them about this. It's a matter between family and should stay within the family."

"Whilst that may be true, I am concerned about your welfare. First, I find you shut in your cottage and fending for yourself while dreadfully unwell, and now I hear you are forbidden from attending a meeting with the most respectable women in the area. What is going on here?"

"Nothing, as I said, it is between my brother and me, no one else."

"Well, I hope you can resolve matters, for we could really use your help at the Institute."

"I'm sure you have plenty of capable women already attending."

"But from what the Colonel says, your allotment is second to none. Our focus from now on is on the country's food supply during this period of war. You have knowledge and skills that could prove very useful to us."

"The Colonel knows far more about agriculture than I do, and besides, there are plenty of women from farms who'll know how to work the land."

"But you have set out to achieve something on your own. You've had no man guiding you, telling you what to plant or where. You show a feminine spirit that we should all aspire to. I honestly believe your contribution to the Institute could be extremely valuable. Please say you'll think about attending our meeting next Tuesday?"

"I'll think about it."

"Good, that's all I ask."

Later, as I walk to the well to draw fresh water, Ffion's visit plays on my mind. I hope I can trust her not to intervene where Bryn is concerned, but she's a woman used to getting her own way and won't understand the consequences such an intervention could cause.

How have I ended up caught between my brother and a woman like Ffion Montgomery? This isn't how my quiet life is supposed to be. I'm an expert in hiding myself away, not causing any trouble, and keeping my head down. I curse the day Mrs Watt ever came to the village with her grand ideas for a Women's Institute. Life was fine before she set all this in motion.

It's all very well for the likes of Mrs Montgomery and her pals to want another social occasion to brighten their dull lives, but why does it have to involve ordinary women like me? The natural order of things should remain – men speak and women listen.

"Oh, *cariad*, really?" I stifle a sob as Eddy's voice sounds in my mind. "Is that what you really think, my love? What about all I taught you? What about all those hopes and dreams you once had? Has it really come to this, that you're now Bryn in all but name? These thoughts you're having belong to him. Don't let him infect you like this. It would break my heart."

"Be quiet," I shout, "be quiet, be quiet, be quiet." I bang my fists against my head, trying to stop the voice I know isn't real. The pail in my hand clatters against the stone surroundings of the well and I realise I must have thrown it myself. "You did this to me!" I shout. "This is your fault, Eddy! You shouldn't have changed me; you should have left me be. Why did you have to open my eyes? Why? Why?" I collapse onto the ground, clawing at the grass like an animal, unable to draw in a breath through the sobs that hit me with violent force.

When I'm finally calm enough to stand, I dry my face on my apron. My legs are shaking as much as the hands that lower the bucket into the well. Thank goodness the only witnesses to my loss of control are the cows in the neighbouring field. "You should have left me well alone, Eddy," I whisper, as I draw up the pail and carry my water back to the house.

Chapter Twenty-Two

Ffion

September, 1915

Of all the ideas I've had in my life, this could be the worst. The clock chimes eleven, and I pace the drawing-room floor.

"You'll wear a hole in the carpet if you're not careful," says Hector without looking up from his newspaper.

Surely it will soon be time for him to return to London. He's been home a week already and each night I've had to endure his hands on my bare skin, his stale alcohol breath on my cheek. As he grunts and groans on top of me each night, it's all I can do not to empty the contents of my stomach into the chamber pot. And the thought of conceiving another child strikes fear into my heart. To have another child ripped from me and sent away as soon as it reaches school age is more than I can bear.

"Aren't you listening to me?"

"Pardon?"

"I sometimes wonder if you're in your right mind," says Hector, throwing down his newspaper and getting to his feet. "I was asking what possessed you to invite the village idiots here for tea and cake?"

"I'm trying to get to know members of the local community, that's all."

"That's what you call it, is it? I can see right through you, Ffion, and I know when you're lying. It's that blasted Women's Institute putting ideas into your head, if you ask me. That Canadian has a lot to answer for."

"It's just tea and cake with two upstanding members of the community, nothing more."

"Whatever you say, my dear. I'm sure you'll be pleased to hear I'm off out."

"Oh? Where are you going?"

"You know very well I'm due to meet the Marquis for a spot of shooting. It's why you arranged your little tea party for eleven o'clock. You can't fool me, my dear, so it's best not to even try."

"Honestly, Hector, I had quite forgotten about your engagement with the Marquis. You'd better be going, as you don't want to be late."

Hector chuckles to himself and leaves the room. As soon as he's gone, the air seems cleaner, the room less oppressive. But the doorbell sounds, and my momentary peace is shattered. I take a seat on the settee and pick up some needlework, as though I have not been watching the driveway for their arrival.

A knock sounds on the door, and my maid, Susan, enters. "Reverend and Mrs Williams are here to see you, madam."

"Thank you, Susan, show them in, and please bring us a pot of tea and three pieces of fruitcake."

"Of course, madam."

I stand as Reverend and Mrs Williams enter the room and put on my best smile. "Good afternoon, it is a pleasure to meet you properly at long last." I reach out my hand and they each take it. Mrs Williams has a firmer handshake than her husband, who takes my hand in his own limp, clammy one. It takes all my resolve not to wipe my palm against my dress. "Do sit down," I say, pointing to the opposite sofa. The fire is raging in the hearth, and the room is too warm.

"We were rather surprised to receive your invitation," says Reverend Williams. "You are a parishioner at St Mary's church, if I am not mistaken?"

"You're quite right, Reverend. But coming from a different denomination doesn't prevent a friendship between us, I hope?"

"Of course not," says Mrs Williams.

My eyes settle on her, and I experience an irrational burst of distaste. She doesn't notice my gaze, her own eyes too busy sizing up the expensive furniture and ornaments with unadulterated envy all over her face.

Susan comes in with a tray of tea and I thank her. "Do have some tea," I say, pouring out the cups and handing them to my guests. "Tell me, do you have children?" I address the question to Mrs Williams, who I'm finding the harder of the two to get the measure of.

"Yes, four."

"I see. Boys and girls?"

"Four girls, more's the pity," says Reverend Williams.

"Really? And why's that then?"

"Because none can follow me into the ministry, of course. We've a long-held tradition of ministers in our family, and I mourn my lack of an heir greatly."

"I'm sure your girls will make you proud in other ways," I say.

"They will if they marry well," says Mrs Williams. "And I have great hopes that they will."

I smile, but my heart sinks. It's not that I can sit in judgment. I'm sure my own parents would have said much the same thing about me, and Hector certainly shares the Williamses' sentiments when it comes to our daughters, but I can't help but want more for them.

"Do you have children yourself, Mrs Montgomery?" Mrs Williams smiles, but it doesn't reach her eyes.

"Yes, I have three boys and two girls, and my husband Hector has two older sons from his first marriage."

"First marriage?" There is a coolness to Mrs Williams' tone that makes my skin crawl.

"My husband's first wife died, sadly."

"Our condolences," says Reverend Williams.

"Thank you, but it was a long time ago now. At least your daughters shan't be going off to fight in the war. Our three eldest boys have all joined up and I can't tell you what a worry it is."

"I'm sure," says the reverend, taking a sip of his tea.

"Anyway, you might be wondering why I invited you here today?"

"I doubted it was for spiritual guidance," says Reverend Williams. Mrs Williams gives him a sharp look, but he just raises an eyebrow and continues drinking his tea.

"No, quite. I've invited you here in your capacity as one of our local spiritual leaders. Many times I've been told of the wisdom of your sermons, and you are highly regarded among my acquaintances who attend your chapel."

Reverend Williams' chest puffs out and he does his best to hide the smile playing on his thin lips. I swallow down my distaste, not just at how predictable men can be, but at how such an ineffectual weasel of a man can maintain such a firm hold over Angharad's life.

"You may have heard," I continue, "that we are forming a women's group to improve village life and assist the war effort in any way we can."

"I may have heard a rumour."

Reverend Williams sets his teacup down on the table and peers at me over the top of his spectacles. Mrs Williams has her hands clutched so firmly in her lap I wouldn't be surprised if one of her fingers snapped off. Her mouth is squeezed into a thin line and her eyes are narrowed.

"It is to be called the Women's Institute and really is a wonderful organisation."

"I can't say I see much need for such an organisation in our village," says Mrs Williams. "I would have thought most women around here have better things to be doing with their time."

"Oh, Mrs Williams, but that's just it. I knew you'd understand. The Women's Institute is aimed at helping in the community, especially during this time of war. Of course, us women always have more jobs to do than time, but we feel in these exceptional circumstances, with so many men away, there is nothing to do but to step up."

"Step up?"

"With the war effort, yes. Our primary focus will be on securing the food supply of our nation. Speaking of growing food, I believe we have a mutual acquaintance."

"We do?" Mrs Williams frowns, her curiosity stirred.

"Yes, your sister-in-law, Angharad Williams. She's a wonderful woman, I'm sure you'd agree."

Reverend Williams chokes on his tea and tries to hide his reaction behind a handkerchief. "You know my sister?"

"I certainly do, Reverend. You must be very proud of her."

"Proud?"

"Yes, Mr Stephens seems very happy with her work up on the farm and her allotment is rather wonderful. As you can imagine, Reverend, your sister will be most helpful in all matters agricultural."

"I really don't think..."

"And Colonel Stapleton-Cotton is most keen she joins our merry band."

"Colonel Stapleton-Cotton?" asks Mrs Williams, her interest piqued.

"Yes," I smile at her, knowing a social-climbing snob when I see one. "I understand you have your reservations about the setting up of an Institute, but I'm sure the Colonel, not to mention his relation, the Marquis of Anglesey, would be most encouraged to hear we not only have your blessing, but that a member of your family is joining the fold."

"The Marquis of Anglesey is behind this new venture?"

"Oh, yes, it has his full support."

"I see." Reverend Williams looks at his wife, but she ignores him and returns her attention to me.

"I don't know what gave you the impression we are opposed to the setting-up of this institute, Mrs Montgomery. And as for Angharad, she is free to do as she pleases. She is a grown woman, after all."

"I knew I could rely on you," I say, giving them my most charming smile. I'm about to invite Mrs Williams along to our next meeting, but instinct stops me. I wouldn't trust the woman as far as I can throw her, and fear she'll only make trouble for my new friend should she choose to attend. Instead, I ring the bell, and Susan comes hurrying into the drawing room. "Take the tray away now, would you, Susan? My guests are leaving. I'm sure you have plenty to be getting on with, and I've taken up enough of your time."

Mrs Williams casts a longing glance at the slices of cake which remain untouched on the tray.

"I shall inform the Colonel and Marquis of your support for the new Institute. I'm sure they will be delighted to hear it has the backing of the local clergy, particularly from a family as well regarded as your own."

"Thank you," says Reverend Williams, his chest puffing out again as he stands.

It is a relief to close the door on the dreadful couple. As soon as they have rounded the corner on the drive, I open the drawing-room windows, wanting to banish any memory of them from the room. It is too late to worry now whether I've done the right thing, but I pray my actions will not rebound on Angharad. At least she'll be able to attend the next meeting without them standing in her way, but something tells me I'll need to keep an eye on Reverend and Mrs Williams from now on.

Chapter Twenty-Three

Carys

September, 1915

"Off on your own again, are you? Our chapel not good enough for you?" Peter hauls a bale of hay into the barn, then comes back into the yard, wiping a dusty hand across his brow.

"At least I'm going to chapel."

"Rather be here baling hay, would you?"

"Chapel is one of the few times I leave this farm, Peter, and you can't say I don't pull my weight around here."

"I'd swap you for a man any day."

"Perhaps you would, but I don't see any of those queuing up to help, do you?"

Mami comes out into the yard looking smart in her Sunday best. "Stop bickering, would you? Surely we can set our squabbles aside on the Sabbath."

"Sorry, Mami," I say.

"Are you still insisting on walking all the way to Llanfairpwll?"

"Yes."

Mami shakes her head. "I don't know what's got into you, girl. Anyway, I'd best be off, and so had you, Carys, if you don't want to be late. Peter, check in on your dadi from time to time, would you? He's had a dreadful night."

"Alright."

Peter's scowl follows me as I set off down the lane. What neither he nor Mami understand is that I'm thinking ahead. When me and Dai wed, we'll be setting up home in the village, and the sooner I get accepted as part of the community, the better. Dai will no doubt be addled from fighting the war, but if I go into our marriage armed with local knowledge, it will be all the better for him. I may even secure us a tenancy before he gets home if I speak to the right people. What a homecoming that would be!

Pleased to have yanked my thoughts from Peter back to Dai, I sing as I walk, enjoying the freedom of using my voice before I return to the silent farm. It wasn't so long ago the house was full of song. Wherever you went on the farm, Dadi's tuneful voice would follow you. These days, all you hear from him is a hacking cough that casts gloom around the place.

When I reach the chapel, I greet fellow members of the congregation I have got to know over the past few months. It is a welcoming community here, and I know they will prove a useful support to me and Dai as he eases back into civilian life. Some women were at the meeting with Mrs Watt, and we smile at each other in recognition. Angharad isn't here yet from the looks of things, not that I expected her to be. I find my usual place on a pew and wait for the service to start.

Going to chapel does me good. I knew it would. As ever, Minister Williams is a little hard to follow, but I listen as best I can. I sense Angharad has arrived, and turn to catch her eye. I thought we had cleared the air, but perhaps I was wrong. She can't even bring herself to look at me and keeps her eyes fixed on the hymn book in her lap.

Minister Williams draws his sermon to a close and we bow our heads in prayer. I try to follow along and pray for the men away fighting, but thoughts of Angharad crowd my mind. She's a funny one, and despite the glimmers of friendship I've seen, I still can't work her out. She scuttles in and out of that chapel as though she is scared or ashamed and I'm blowed if I know which it is.

As ever, my favourite part of the service is the hymns. Oh, the chance to sing again. Not my usual quiet whistle as I work, but a kick-in-the-guts kind of sound. I'm hoping God hears my singing all the way up in heaven and will look kindly on me and my prayers. After months of foolish thoughts about Mr Jansen, once Dai returns safe and sound, all will be well. We can be married, and it will wash away my sins.

The service draws to a close and I take my leave. After our conversation last week, I wonder if Angharad may wait to greet me after chapel. She slunk out during the last hymn as she always does, but she might have waited out on the street. But when I step outside, there is no sign of Angharad, or her little dog, and by the looks of things, she is long gone.

I turn toward our farm with a sigh, the calmness chapel provided me leaving as quickly as it came. The thought of returning to the farm leaves me tired, and I groan as I remember all the work waiting for me. I've been doing at least the work of two people since Dadi fell ill.

The farm appears all too soon and I pause the song I am humming. The barn door is open, and I can see Peter hard at work with the shearing.

"I'm home, Peter. Where's Mami?"

"Not yet back from chapel."

"How's Dadi?"

Peter grunts, shrugs and continues his work. Inside the farmhouse, which is too still, too quiet, I fill the kettle and place it above the fire. Peter will not have stopped since I left and will have forgotten to drink or eat, no doubt. While the water heats, I run upstairs to change out of my Sunday best. There have been no new clothes since Dadi fell ill. Even if I ask Mami for money to buy material to make them myself, I know the answer I'd get. Now I'm promised to Dai, Mami sees no need for pretty frocks.

Will there be new frocks once I marry Dai? I try to picture my life with him but can't. I can barely even picture the man himself and feel terribly ashamed. He's off risking life and limb, and I can't even remember the colour of his eyes. What kind of woman does that make me?

Before I change out of my Sunday clothes, I go to check on Dadi. The powerful man I knew has vanished in the past couple of months, replaced by a skeleton who lies hacking away in bed, unable to get a decent breath into his lungs.

"Dadi, I'm back," I say, perching on the edge of his bed and running a hand across his thinning hair. "Is there anything I can get you?"

"Water." His voice comes out like a croak.

I fill a glass from the jug and hold it to his chapped lips. He tries to take it between his shaking hands but doesn't have the strength. It's terrible to say, but at night I sometimes pray that God will put an end to his suffering, although I dread to think what will become of us all when the moment arrives.

Dadi falls into a deep sleep, and I make my way downstairs. I make a fresh pot of tea and scrub a kitchen I've not tackled yet this week, what with all the extra work I've taken on. I hear Peter call me and I carry his tea outside.

"You'll need to help me get through these sheep this afternoon. You can start off the skirting once you've made us something to eat."

"Peter, it's the Sabbath. What will people say if they see us working?"

"I couldn't care less, Carys. With Dadi taking to his bed, we have to work all the hours we can or we'll fall behind."

"You make it sound as though Dadi's in bed through choice."

"That's not what I'm saying, and you know it."

"Have you asked Mr Jansen to help? I think he's back from visiting his friends in Menai Bridge."

"Mr Jansen has his uses, but he hasn't yet mastered shearing. You'll need to help me with the sheep."

"Alright." My heart sinks at the thought of skirting. Picking all those bits of manure and goodness knows what from the fleece is a stinking job.

As I walk back to the house, Peter calls out. "That Colonel was round here again yesterday, trying to get me to increase production to help with the war. How does he think we can do that with no manpower? I'm reliant on a weak sister, an aging mother, a half-blind refugee, and two old codgers from the village who are well past their prime. He lives on another planet, that man."

"I'm sure you're right, Peter." From what I saw of the Colonel when I went to that talk by Mrs Watt, he seems a real gent, but Peter has a thing about those of a higher class to him, so it's best I keep quiet.

Thinking of the Colonel leads me into thinking of Mrs Watt, which in turn leads me on to Canada. Thank goodness me and Mami had the sense not to mention where Mrs Watt came from. Canada is a dirty word in our household since my oldest brother got tempted by some offer of free land out on the prairies. He jumped on the first boat he could find, and we've seen neither hide nor hair of him since. At least it got him out of fighting in the war, so we should be grateful for small mercies. Not that I'd ever say that to Dadi or Peter.

Chapter Twenty-Four

Angharad

September, 1915

My fingers feel for the note inside my pocket. When I read it, I felt a simultaneous rush of excitement, fear, and anger. On the face of it, Ffion persuading Bryn and Anne of the Women's Institute's merits is a good thing, but I know it will come at a price. From the jolly tone of Ffion's note, she thinks the matter is settled, but I know otherwise.

There has been no visit from my brother since he was invited to the Montgomery residence, and this in itself is troubling. I know my brother, and he would have left Ffion's house furious. I also know that he doesn't have the self-control to sit on that fury. Either he has taken his frustration out on Anne, which is a possibility, or he's saving it up, ready to hit me with it when I least expect it.

"You're here!" shouts Carys, leaving her mother's side and rushing up the street towards me.

"Yes, here I am."

"I'm so pleased you changed your mind. This will be my third meeting and Mami has deserted me at each one so far and tried to get in with ladies well above her station. She's miffed she's not on the committee, but goodness knows how she would have fitted it in with all her work had she been chosen."

"I'm sure you're right."

A horse-drawn carriage clatters up the road towards us, interrupting our conversation.

"That'll be the soldiers," says Carys.

"What soldiers?"

"Three wounded soldiers from Bangor."

My heart thuds in my chest. I find men easier to deal with than women, but I can imagine Bryn's reaction if he finds out I've been associating with soldiers. "Why are there soldiers here? I thought these meetings were for women only, except for the Colonel, of course."

"They are, but the committee decided to make an allowance for our guests. Our focus will be contributing to the war effort with the food supply, but there are other ways we can help too."

"Will wounded soldiers really want to attend a women's meeting?"

"They'll probably think they've died and gone to heaven," says Carys with a raised eyebrow.

I flush and turn my attention to the carriage. The Colonel has wheeled his bath chair down to the road to greet them. As the men step out of the carriage, I try to hide my shock. Their faces are grey, their eyes slightly glazed. One man is missing a leg, another an arm. The third soldier seems to have all his limbs intact but is twitching as though surrounded by a swarm of bees.

"Let's go up to the summerhouse," says Carys. "I doubt they'll want us staring at them as they try to get up the slope."

She takes my arm, and I let her guide me through the Joneses' garden, fear deadening my legs. This meeting feels even harder than the last I attended. Ffion may be convinced I have Bryn's blessing to attend, but I'm more sceptical and can't help but feel I'm walking into some sort of trap.

Ffion is sitting at the front of the room with Mrs Stapleton-Cotton and Mrs Jones. Her face lights up when she sees us walk in and she gives us a quick wave before continuing with her conversation.

"Want to sit at the back again?" asks Carys.

"What do you think?"

She rolls her eyes at me, and we take our seats. Mrs Watt is here again and gets to her feet once everyone has sat down and caught up on the latest gossip. She begins by welcoming our male guests, apologises that before we start we have to get through the formalities of reading and accepting the minutes from the previous meeting, then gets down to business.

Hearing the minutes read is an uncomfortable experience, a reminder not just of my previous absence, but of the risk I am taking in attending at all. I picture Bryn and Anne as sleeping lions lying just out of sight, ready to attack when I least expect it.

"I like the sound of a Christmas social," whispers Carys. "They said you can bring man friends or husbands, so that means if Dai is home on leave, I can bring him along with me."

I smile at her, already dreading the occasion. There is nothing worse than turning up to a room full of couples alone, or so I imagine.

"And now we move on to the important matter of fruit and vegetable preserving," says Mrs Watt. "I've brought along some examples."

Carys and I strain in our seats to see the table groaning with glass jars of every colour and size. "Waste not want not," Carys whispers, and I nod.

Mrs Watt's talk is as entertaining as the woman herself. Even the wounded soldiers seem interested, their faces lighting up when she invites them to taste some samples she has brought along.

"So, as I'm sure you all know, ladies, preserving is a skill we all must learn and share to ensure nothing goes to waste, and we have plenty of nutritious food to see us through the long winter months."

As Mrs Watt's talk and demonstration draw to a close, everyone in the summerhouse applauds.

"Now I'd like to invite Miss Thomas up to play for us."

A young lady gets to her feet and sits beside a harp. She settles down and begins to play. As her fingers gently pluck the strings, the most beautiful music fills the room. Miss Thomas picks up the pace, filling the surrounding air with a cheerful *cwydd*.

"This *cwydd* reminds me of a hornpipe Dadi used to play," whispers Carys.

Miss Thomas finishes the tune she is playing and begins another that causes my heart to ache. I close my eyes as I am transported to my bothy.

My hands are interlinked with Eddy's as we waltz around the bothy, singing 'Ffarwel i Aberystwyth' at the tops of our voices. Eddy's delight in having mastered the Welsh lyrics is infectious. Our singing becomes faster in tandem with our feet, and we become dizzy, bumping into chairs, the table, laughing so hard we can barely push out a tuneful note. We collapse onto my bed, out of breath and beside ourselves with joy. Eddy leans forward and kisses me firmly on the lips. The room stills, the air thickens, and time stands still.

"Angharad, you're crying."

I open my eyes and find Carys frowning at me, holding out a handkerchief. My fingers reach up to find cheeks damp with tears. A quick glance around the room tells me no one has noticed, and I take the offered handkerchief with thanks.

"Do you need to leave?" Carys whispers.

I shake my head. To leave now would be to succumb to the cowardice that has tainted the past five years. Eddy would never leave a gathering before the end, and neither should I.

Chapter Twenty-Five

Ffion

September 1915

I could burst with happiness. The meeting is proving a tremendous success. I'll admit I had been sceptical whether the poor chaps from the military hospital in Bangor would gain much from an afternoon in a room of rural women, but they seem to be enjoying themselves as much as the rest of us. Their feet tap along in time to Miss Thomas's delightful tunes.

When the recital is over, we all get to our feet to thank the shy young woman still sitting behind her harp.

"Thank you very much, Miss Thomas. I'm sure we can all agree what a fine young musician you are."

Another round of applause erupts, and Miss Thomas's cheeks turn scarlet.

"I'd say we've all been sitting still for long enough," says Mrs Watt. "If you'd like to make your way to the back of the room, Mrs Cotton and Mrs Jones have refreshments ready for us. If we could be back in our seats in half an hour, that would be wonderful."

Around me there is the hum of conversation and the rustling of skirts as we jostle for a much-needed cup of tea.

"Good afternoon, gentlemen. I'm Mrs Montgomery and it is a pleasure to meet you. Can I get you any refreshments?" I smile at the soldiers who are still in their seats in the front row.

"A cup of tea would be grand, miss."

"A slice of cake wouldn't go amiss neither."

"And you?" I ask the third soldier. His legs are twitching, and the muscles in his face spasm every few seconds. In the end, one of the other soldiers answers for him.

"Best not give a hot cup of tea to Fred, but I'm sure he'd enjoy a piece of bread and butter and a slice of cake. Isn't that right, Fred?"

Fred gives a brisk nod, but his eyes remain fixed on the ground. My heart twists at the sight of these men, broken in ways we can't understand while fighting for our freedom. We owe them so much, and yet can give back so little. A couple of cups of tea and a few slices of cake suddenly feel woefully inadequate.

"I'll get your refreshments and bring them to you," I say, overwhelmed by the men's presence and needing to escape.

I find Angharad and Carys standing by the door, cups of tea in hand.

"Hello, Mrs Montgomery," says Carys with a warm smile.

"Good afternoon, Miss Ambrose. How is your father?"

"Not too good, I'm afraid, Mrs Montgomery."

"Ffion, please. I'm sorry to hear that. If there's anything I can do to help, you must let me know. And how are you, Angharad? It really is marvellous to see you here."

Angharad answers me with a smile and a nod of her head. There is a red tinge around her eyes that suggests she has been crying. Her head is bent, and her shoulders are hunched over. I want to tell her to stand up straight and let the world see her handsome face without shame, but this is not the place, nor the time.

"I've promised those poor soldiers tea and cake," I say, "so I'd better not keep them waiting, but I'll come and find you after the meeting if you don't have to rush off?"

"I'll need to get back to the farm," says Carys, "but dragging Mami away from her new friends is another matter, so I'm sure I'll still be here long after the meeting draws to a close."

Angharad says nothing and doesn't catch my eye. Did I do the wrong thing in speaking to her brother, I wonder? At least she is here, but her manner is not exactly friendly, and I fear she resents my interference. Hector always says I should keep my nose in my own business and perhaps he is right.

At the tea table Mrs Cotton greets me with her usual friendliness and when I explain I'm fetching refreshments for the soldiers, cuts them extra-large slices of fruit cake and spreads their bread with a thick layer of butter. "Those chaps need feeding up," she says.

"I couldn't agree more, Jane."

It is quite a job carrying my tray through the room. The summer-house is narrow and with all the newly acquired chairs, not to mention members, it is a wonder I reach the soldiers with any tea left in their cups.

"Thank you," say the two more talkative chaps and I hand over the cups and plates.

"Where are you all from?" I ask.

"I'm a Bangor lad," says one. "Tommy is from Llandudno, and Fred there is from Carmarthen."

"And how long have you been at the hospital?"

"Too long," says Tommy. "Me and John have been there two months already. We were in the same battalion, and both got our injuries at

Ypres. Fred only joined us a month ago. It may not look it, but he's improved a lot since he's been at the hospital."

A quick glance at the shaking and shivering Fred makes me wonder just how bad he must have been when he arrived if this is considered an improvement.

"Are you local, Mrs Montgomery?" asks Tommy.

"Yes, I live on the outskirts of the village, only a few minutes' walk from here."

"It's quite something you've started here," says John. "I'd never heard of anything like it when the Colonel told me about it. I'm sure my own mami would love something like this in her village."

"You should tell her about it," I say. "We hope that before long there will be Women's Institutes all over Wales, not to mention England, Scotland and Ireland. With Mrs Watt at the helm, I've no doubt that ambition will be achieved."

Our conversation is interrupted by the lady in question, who asks us to take our places ready to sing.

"We're going to sing 'Land of My Fathers'," says Mrs Watt, "and I hope you don't mind, but despite the final line telling us the author hopes the old language is preserved, I shall have to sing in English, as my Welsh is confined to place names. Feel free to sing in whichever language you wish, though, ladies."

I smile at the memory of Mrs Watt saying the full name of Llanfairpwll as though she were a native Welsh speaker. Since we've lived in Llanfairpwll, my understanding of Welsh has increased, but I'm still very much a novice and it is a relief to know I don't need to attempt 'Land of my Fathers' in a language that still sits uncomfortably on my tongue.

'Land of My Fathers' is swiftly followed by a rendition of 'God Save the King' and it warms my heart to hear the soldiers proudly singing along despite all they have lost in their service to King and Country. As the voices in the summerhouse rise, I can't help but marvel at how far we've come in a few short months.

What would we all be doing if we were not here? Cooking? Cleaning? Filling our time with needlecraft or endless lunches? The difference in the soldiers' demeanours speaks of the possibilities lying before us. As individual women, there is only so much we can achieve, but together, we can accomplish so much more.

Chapter Twenty-Six

Anghared

December, 1915

C hapel passes by as usual, but on my way out, instead of her typical curt nod, Anne grabs hold of my sleeve and hisses under her breath, "go to the house, your brother wants to speak with you."

Before I can ask why Bryn wants to see me, Anne gives me a nudge which causes me to stumble out of the door.

"I'm sorry, Betty, but we're to go to Bryn's house," I say as I kneel to untie her from the railings. Betty gives me a whimper and widens her eyes. I can't help but laugh. "You're a clever one, aren't you, girl? I'd like to go straight back to the farm, too, but we've been summoned and there's little I can do about it."

Betty resists with every step I take, pulling hard on the lead and trying to force me to turn toward the farm. In the end, I give up and hold her squirming body tight to my chest. She calms down and I kiss her on the forehead. "I don't know what I'd do without you, *cariad*."

We arrive at Bryn's house, and I pause a moment to look at it. It may be Bryn's home now, but it was mine too, for the first twenty-five years of my life. It has changed little since my parents' day and is as uninviting today as it was back then. The stone frontage contains only two mean windows, leaving the rooms inside dark and dingy. It is a level above the cottages opposite, being semi-detached rather than one of a terrace, but with four children and two adults, it must feel claustrophobic at times.

There is no front garden, and as I walk up to it, I can see into the sparse and gloomy parlour where Bryn, just like in my father's day, conducts his prayer meetings. A wooden cross sits on the windowsill, just in case anyone is unsure to whom this house belongs.

I let myself and Betty in through the side gate and walk to a bench to wait for the family's return. The house is always left unlocked, and if I'd wanted to, there is nothing to stop me walking in and waiting inside. But the house hasn't been my home for a very long time, has never been my home, if determined by the true sense of the word. And besides, I could never muster the courage to find out what would happen if I opened the door of my own accord and waited inside.

I let Betty off the lead, and she scampers away to explore the small back garden. If Anne finds the dog loose on her lawn there will be hell to pay, but the Williams are creatures of habit, and I know we have at least forty minutes before any of them will return. From my position on the bench, I survey the house once more. Bryn and Anne may have far more home comforts than I do in my bothy, but nothing on earth would make me want to swap with them. I remember when I moved to the bothy it was as if I could breathe freely for the first time in my life.

By the time Bryn, Anne and their four children arrive home, drizzle has soaked through my woollen jacket, and Betty's fur is looking decidedly dishevelled. I walk to the back door and knock. Anne answers, shaking her head at the sight of my dog.

"I don't know why you insist on taking that wretched creature everywhere with you, Angharad. It's not the done thing for a lady to be seen out and about with such a scruffy mutt."

"Perhaps, Anne, but Betty is good company."

"Company?" Anne gives her tinkling laugh, which fooled me in the early days. Now I hear the harshness of that sound, the shards of glass hidden in her tone. "Why can't you find yourself a husband and children like every other woman in this village has done?"

I look at the floor and shrug, hating the way my default position is to hang my head and not meet her eye. Anne knows as well as I do that any prospect of the motherhood I once longed for is long gone.

"That dog needs to stay outside."

"It's raining." I can't defend myself, but I can at least try to defend Betty.

"Fine, but if I catch him anywhere near the stairs, he'll be out on his ear in the garden."

"I promise *she* won't go upstairs."

I follow Anne through the back door and step straight into the kitchen.

"Your sister's here," calls Anne, as though my arrival is a surprise, and I haven't been summoned.

Bryn is in his usual seat in the parlour. At first the closed curtains surprise me, but then I notice the glass in his hand and understand why he won't want anyone from his congregation looking in. He's already working his way through his first whisky of the day, despite his public claims of temperance.

Even now, after so many years have passed, I expect to see Father in the seat Bryn now occupies. If Father were here, he'd be horrified to see my brother drinking, but would probably find some way to lay the blame at my door.

"Did I see you at chapel?" barks Bryn, glaring at me over the top of his spectacles.

"I was in my usual pew."

"Is that so?"

"Anne saw me."

Anne glances from me to her husband, not wanting to take my side, but not wanting to tell a sinful lie, either. "I think I might have done, at the end of the service."

"How would I have known to come here otherwise?"

"I'll not have you taking that kind of tone in my house," says Bryn. Anne smiles at the rebuke.

"How are my nieces?" I ask, to redeem myself, not that I care a jot about the answer. My nieces are too much like their parents, in my opinion. I have next to no experience with small children, but even I can tell they are pious and spiteful. On days I mourn my lack of motherhood, I picture Bryn and Anne's children and sometimes convince myself I had a lucky escape.

"I'm sure you're aware we were invited to the Montgomery residence not that long ago," says Bryn.

I shake my head as my insides turn to ice. The passing months have lulled me into a false sense of security that I'd receive no retaliation from Ffion's interference, but I shouldn't have been so complacent. "I wasn't aware of that, no."

"If the idea of you having any sort of influence over a woman like Mrs Montgomery wasn't so ridiculous, I might not believe you," says Bryn. "The thing is, Angharad, as your brother, I feel I can hide my concern no longer. I am worried about you. Why do you think a woman such as Mrs Montgomery is showing an interest in you?"

"I don't know, brother."

"Well, I do. As much as I hate to upset you, it is for your own good that you hear the truth. It is plain as day that Mrs Montgomery sees you as a project to relieve her boredom. All that talk of your horticultural skills is little more than a ruse to butter us all up. I've heard rumours about that husband of hers, and they are not the type of people you should consort with. Besides, you're making a fool of yourself trying to ingratiate yourself into Mrs Montgomery's circle. Surely you see that?"

I nod, forcing a smile as my stomach lurches and a cry forms in my throat. Perhaps Bryn is right and I'm nothing more to Ffion than a project to keep her entertained? The stale air and darkness of the parlour are closing in on me and I need Bryn to get to the point before I scream. "Is that why you wanted to see me, brother?"

"Partly, but there is also another matter we must discuss. Anne was in the post office yesterday and heard Miss Roberts talking about the December meeting of the Women's Institute. According to her, members are being encouraged to bring along a husband or... or..."

Anne steps in to help her faltering husband. "Or a *man friend*."

She spits out the last words and my blood runs cold. They are going to forbid me to attend the WI again, I know it.

"As much as I respect Mr and Mrs Jones, and the Stapleton-Cottons, I am deeply troubled by the direction in which I fear this women's group is going. Mrs Montgomery assumed my support without giving me a chance to investigate the idea fully."

"I assure you, brother..."

Bryn holds up a hand to stop me from speaking. "Anne and I have decided, given several members of my congregation have joined this organisation, and in order to put my mind at rest, that I should attend the Christmas meeting."

"You? You want to come to the WI?"

"I believe each member can bring a guest to the December meeting. You are a member, are you not?"

"Yes." My voice comes out as a croak.

"And I presume you have no husband hidden away, or any *man friend*?"

"No, but..."

"Good, then that is decided. I suggest you meet me here at the house ten minutes before the meeting begins on the fourteenth of December. We can walk to Graig together, and I can see for myself what this Institute is all about, and whether it's something I can support my congregation in attending, or whether they are being led astray."

I am too stunned to speak. Bryn lights his pipe and picks up a newspaper. Anne stands and motions to the door. With a nod, I stand on shaking limbs. Anne shows me to the door, and as I am leaving with Betty leaving, places a cold hand on my arm.

"Thank you for calling, Angharad, and for the invitation. I'm sure my husband will find the evening most informative."

Somehow, I force out a thank you.

Anne smiles at me with knowing eyes. Of course, I'd never take Bryn with me if it was up to me, but I have no choice. My family's hold over me is something I am powerless against. They know too many of my secrets for me to risk ever trying to break free.

Chapter Twenty-Seven

Ffion

December, 1915

"Hurry up, darling, or we'll be late for this damned meeting of yours."

"It's not a meeting," I say, making my way down the wide staircase. "It's a social event. If it were a meeting, you wouldn't have been invited."

"Charming."

"The clue's in the name, darling. It's a *Women's* Institute."

"Perhaps they should have stuck to that rule today. Don't these women realise us men have better things to be doing with our time than listening to gossip over a cup of tea?"

I try to hide my disappointment at Hector's blatant lack of enthusiasm. As a committee, we've worked extremely hard to make our first Christmas celebration the best it can be. There was much debate over whether to invite men to join us. I'd been one of those in favour of the idea, so the thought of turning up with a miserable husband on my arm isn't appealing.

"Please, darling, you will make an effort for me, won't you?"

"There's no need to put on that simpering voice. You know how much it irritates me. I'd rather pull teeth than attend this darned meeting, but I've been brought up with good manners, so you don't need to worry about me embarrassing you in front of your friends."

"Thank you." I lean across and kiss Hector's cheek, leaving a red lipstick mark behind. Pulling a handkerchief from my bag, I try to rub off the stain, but Hector pushes me away and tells me to stop fussing. Fine, if he wants to go out looking like he's wearing rouge, so be it.

I'm wearing my favourite fur coat and a handsome new hat I treated myself to on my last visit to Bangor. Hector either hasn't noticed the effort I've made with my appearance or doesn't approve of my choices.

"You're looking rather dashing," I say, admiring the new tweed suit which arrived from the tailor's just in time.

"It's a little tight," says Hector, straining his shoulders.

My husband is not always an easy man to love, or like for that matter, but there's no denying he's a handsome man. Even now in his late forties, his grey hair gives him a distinguished look, and he still retains the trim figure of a much younger man. If only his personality were as pleasing as his appearance.

"Come on," he says, as I check my appearance one last time in the mirror. "I've got the car ready."

"The car? It's only a few minutes' walk."

"In those?" asks Hector, pointing at my new button boots.

"These are actually rather practical."

"They don't look it."

I glance down at the new boots I'd been so excited about when I saw them in Dickins & Jones. The lower sturdy black leather is complemented beautifully by a softer green upper, and the heel, though delicately shaped, is actually rather sturdy. "Fine, if you've got the car ready, we'll drive."

Despite the foolishness of driving less than half a mile, it's important to keep Hector on side, important to make today a success. Despite his occasional jaunts shooting with the Marquis and his friends, the opportunities to socialise as a couple are few and far between with Hector away in London for so much of the time. I want him to make a good impression on my new friends.

We arrive at Graig in under five minutes, and Hector pulls the Wolseley into the driveway. Mr Jones emerges from the house and strides over to greet us.

"I hope you don't mind us leaving the car in your driveway, old chap," says Hector, shaking Mr Jones' hand.

"Not at all, not at all. It's a pleasure to have you here."

"And it is most generous of you to give up your summerhouse on so many occasions," I say.

"That's quite all right. It was all my wife's idea, of course. I must say, I'm rather intrigued to attend the event today and find out just what has been going on at the end of my garden for all these months."

"Gossip and tea drinking, I expect," says Hector. If he's hoping for an ally in Mr Jones, he doesn't find one.

"Oh, no, I think these women are actually onto something. From what my wife has told me, they're coming up with some rather ingenious ways to assist with the war effort. And any venture that has the support of Richard Stapleton-Cotton is a worthy one in my eyes. Have you met the Colonel yet, Hector?"

"Only in passing."

"Then I must introduce you. Excuse us, Mrs Montgomery, we shan't be long."

"Take as long as you like," I say, grateful to Mr Jones for taking my husband off my hands.

"Mrs Montgomery."

My heart sinks as I recognise the voice calling my name. What on earth is that man doing here? I turn around and force a smile onto my face. "Reverend Williams, this is a surprise."

"My sister invited me, and it would have felt churlish to refuse."

I try to catch Angharad's eye, but she has her gaze fixed firmly on the ground. She is wearing even dowdier clothes than usual and at a good foot taller than her brother, is finding all sorts of ways of trying to shrink herself including bowing her head, rounding her shoulders, and even bending her knees, if I'm not mistaken.

"It's good of you to come," I say, turning my attention back to Reverend Williams. "I'm surprised you could find the time. It must be a very busy period for the clergy in the run-up to Christmas."

"I'm more than happy to make time for my sister." As Reverend Williams pats Angharad on the arm, she flinches.

"Why don't we show your brother up to the summerhouse, Angharad?"

Angharad nods and Reverend Williams links arms with her. They look like such an odd pair. If anything's going to make Angharad self-conscious about her height, it will be walking arm in arm with her stunted brother. I ease my way in between them and, thanks to my new button boots, find that even I am a good few inches taller than this smarmy man.

"I should probably warn you, Reverend Williams, that the summerhouse we meet in is rather rustic. We have hopes to have a WI hall in the village one day, but in the meantime, it is very kind of Mr and Mrs Jones to make their summerhouse available to us."

"I find there is too great an emphasis on luxury these days," says the reverend in his reedy voice.

"I'm sure you're quite right," I say, "but it would be nice to have a heat source when we meet in the winter months. We have to come in so many layers it's sometimes hard to recognise each other."

My joke falls flat and Reverend Williams turns his attention to his sister. "I'm sure you have no need for extra layers, sister."

Is he suggesting Angharad is overweight? I certainly hope not, not only because it would be unconscionably rude, it is also untrue. Angharad shrinks even further into herself, and I want to slap this weaselly little man.

We enter the summerhouse, and I lead them straight to the refreshment table. "Perhaps once we've a cup of tea, you would like to join the men?" I suggest. "They seem to be huddling together over there in the corner. Strength in numbers, and all that."

"I'd prefer to stay with my sister," says Reverend Williams. The hope I'd seen on Angharad's face when I made my suggestion disappears.

I try to think of some other way I can get Angharad away from her awful brother. Never have I seen her so uncomfortable, not even during that first meeting. We are rescued when a member of Reverend Williams' chapel spots him and comes rushing over.

"Reverend, how wonderful to see you here."

"Thank you, Mrs Grant. My sister invited me, and I took up her invitation to see for myself what all the fuss is about."

Angharad seems to shrink even further into herself. She still hasn't met my gaze and pulls on a loose thread from a jacket that has seen better days.

"And your wife, she is well, I hope?"

"Yes, Anne is in good health, thank you."

"She's not tempted to join our ranks here at the WI?"

Angharad winces at Mrs Grant's words. Clearly, Mrs Williams is no better prospect for Angharad than her brother.

"She is far too busy with her duties to our congregation. Since my parents died, there has been much work fallen on our shoulders."

"Oh, the poor thing," says Mrs Grant. "If there's anything I can do to lighten her load, I'd be delighted to help."

"Thank you, Mrs Grant. You are most kind."

Mrs Grant shuffles away and a silence stretches between us as I struggle to think of a single thing more to say to the man in front of me.

"Ffion?"

"Oh, I am sorry, that is my husband calling me. Thank you for coming, Reverend Williams, and I hope you enjoy the evening."

As terrible as I feel about leaving Angharad alone with her brother, I can't deny it's a relief to escape him and walk away.

Chapter Twenty-Eight

Carys

December, 1915

"Are you sure you're alright there, Dadi?"

My father nods, his bony hand clinging to my arm as I help him down from the cart. Mami tethers the horse to a post in the Joneses' drive, then comes and takes charge of Dadi. I wish she hadn't insisted on him coming. He needs to be in bed, not at a Christmas celebration. His suit is hanging off him and his teeth look too big for his mouth. We take the garden at a snail's pace, Dadi stopping every few steps to catch his breath.

"Why don't you go ahead, Mami? I'll help Dadi up the slope."

"You're a good girl, Carys," says Mami, then with a smile she is off in search of her friends.

"Would you like to stop for a moment, Dadi?"

He nods, and I lead him to a bench. After collapsing into the seat, Dadi throws me a brief smile and pulls a metal hip flask from his breast pocket.

"Dadi, you sly old dog."

"Want some?"

"Are you sure you should have that?"

"It helps my chest, clears the old airways. Just don't tell your mother." He laughs, but it turns into a hacking cough.

"We should probably get you into the warm. This cold air won't be doing you any good."

"Let's sit for a moment, *cariad*. I'm not sure I'm up to facing a room full of cackling women just yet. Here."

Dadi hands me the flask, and after checking no one is watching us, I take a quick sip.

"So, what will happen this afternoon, then?"

"What do you mean, Dadi?"

"I mean, are you women going to lecture us men and put us in our place?"

With a laugh I tell him, "Of course not. There'll be songs, games, and plenty of tea and cake, no doubt."

"Songs?"

"Yes, I expect so."

"Will you be singing?"

"I hadn't planned on it."

"Please, Carys," says Dadi, his bony hand gripping my arm. "Let me hear you sing."

He doesn't say *one last time*, but the unspoken words hang between us.

"Alright, Dadi. If there is the opportunity, I shall take it. Is there any particular song you would like me to sing?"

"'Dafydd y Garreg Wen'."

"Your favourite. I'll talk to the ladies when we get inside and see if they'll let me do a turn."

"You're a good girl, Carys. I hope you know how proud I am of you."

"Thank you, Dadi. Now, how about we go inside where it's warm?"

By the time we reach the summerhouse, the windows are steamed up and the chatter, although polite, is noisy and excitable. Mami is in the corner of the room surrounded by a group of her friends, and hovering near the refreshment table are Angharad and her brother, of all people.

"Come and meet my friend, Dadi," I say, taking his hand and leading him across the room. I'm aware our time is limited before he'll need another sit down, but I'm so curious to see Reverend Williams here, I can't resist making my introductions.

"Miss Ambrose," says Angharad with a quick nod when we reach her. I'm confused by her formality until I catch her worried expression as she glances to her left. "This is my brother, Reverend Williams."

"Pleased to meet you."

"You look familiar, Miss Ambrose. Have we met before?"

"You'll have seen me at chapel," I say with as warm a smile as I can muster, faced with a gaze which seems to linger on my chest. "This is my father, Gwilym Ambrose."

"Pleased to meet you, but I don't think I recognise you from chapel, unless I'm mistaken?"

"I've not been in the best of health," says Dadi, "but when I am, me and Carys's mother attend the chapel at Porthaethwy. It's marginally closer to our farm, and my family has been members there for generations. Our Carys here has broken the mould by attending your chapel at Llanfairpwll. You must give a good sermon for her to walk to Llanfairpwll each Sunday."

"Thank you, Mr Ambrose. I like to think my flock are satisfied with my Sunday messages, after all, I am simply a messenger for the Lord."

"Your sermons are indeed most instructive." Reverend Williams smiles at the compliment, but a look crosses Dadi's face that I know means he's in pain and will need to find a seat soon. "Have you sampled any of the refreshments yet?" I ask, pointing to a table groaning with mince pies, fruitcakes, and steaming cups of tea. The scents of nutmeg, cinnamon, and fresh-baked bread drift towards us, mingling with the pine fragrance of the small Christmas tree placed just inside the door.

"It all seems rather extravagant given the country's at war," says Reverend Williams, wrinkling his nose.

"It would be a shame to waste the food though, wouldn't it? Reverend Williams, if you'd be so kind as to find my father somewhere to sit, Miss Williams and I will bring you both some refreshments."

Dadi throws me a look of panic, which I pretend not to see. Before Reverend Williams can refuse, I give him my best smile, link arms with Angharad, and almost drag her away.

"What is your brother doing here?" I whisper as soon as we're out of earshot.

"He didn't leave me any choice."

"You didn't invite him?"

"He invited himself."

Angharad looks so downcast I want to either hug her or give her a good shake. Before we can talk further, a spontaneous burst of song erupts from a group of men huddled in the corner of the room.

"Goodness," says Ffion, rushing towards us, "look at poor Hector. He doesn't know what to do with himself."

We follow her gaze to where her husband stands among the throng of singing men, studying the inside of his cup as if he's reading his tea leaves.

"Doesn't he know the song?"

"He doesn't speak Welsh."

"Ah, I see. Yes, that could be a problem."

As we watch Ffion's rather pompous husband trapped among the singers, Angharad is unable not to smile.

"Oh, ladies, I suppose I should rescue him. It's very tempting to laugh, but if I do, it will come back to bite me, no doubt."

Ffion bustles off, and Angharad turns to me. "Will you sing a song, Carys?"

"Would you like me to?"

She nods. "I hear you singing in chapel and it's so beautiful. It would bring a little joy into what is proving to be quite a tricky afternoon."

"Your brother?"

Angharad nods, but says no more.

"Well, you're in luck, as I've already promised Dadi I'll sing his favourite song for him."

We fill plates with food from the wonderful spread and carry them over to where Dadi and Reverend Williams are sitting. Dadi glares at me as I approach and I get the impression he has not been enjoying Reverend Williams' company. The men finish their song, and I seize the opportunity to make Dadi smile.

"'Cariwch,' medd Dafydd, 'fy nhelyn i mi,
Ceisiaf cyn marw roi tôn arni hi.
Codwch fy nwylo i gyrraedd y tant
Duw a'ch bendithio, fy ngweddw a'm plant.
"Neithiwr mi glywais lais angel fel hyn,
Dafydd, tyrd adref a chwarae trwy'r glyn,
Delyn fy mebyd, ffarwel i dy dant,
Duw a'ch bendithio, fy ngweddw a'm plant."

When I finish the song, I barely notice the applause, my attention caught by Dadi, whose eyes and cheeks are damp with tears. With some difficulty, he pushes himself up from his seat and steps towards me. His hands hold my face, and he stares into my eyes.

"*Duw a'ch bendithio, fy ngweddw a'm plant*. Widow and children, God's blessing on you," he says, his voice little more than a whisper.

Over Dadi's shoulder, I see Mr Williams frowning in disapproval at the emotion on display, but as Dadi embraces me, I realise Angharad is staring at us, not with disapproval, but something more like envy. She tears her eyes away from us, casts a look at her brother beside her, and sinks further back into her chair.

"Time for a game of charades," calls Colonel Stapleton-Cotton.

Dadi releases me and without another word, sits back in his seat. Just as I'm about to sit down, Reverend Williams stands up.

"I think we've experienced enough for one afternoon, don't you, sister?"

Angharad nods mutely and stands beside him.

"Won't you stay to finish your food?" I ask, pointing to their still full plates.

"I think it is better we leave. I have no intention of being drawn into such childish games as charades."

"Then at least take the food with you. As I said earlier, it would be a shame for it to go to waste."

Mr Williams narrows his eyes at me, then turns to Angharad. "Say your goodbyes. I shall wait outside."

"It was lovely to meet you, Mr Ambrose," says Angharad. "*Nadolig Llawen.*"

"*Nadolig Llawen a Blwyddyn Newydd Dda*," says Dadi, ever the gentleman.

"Can't you stay a little longer?"

She shakes her head. "My brother wishes to leave."

"But couldn't you stay anyway? The games are only just starting."

"It's best I do as he says. Will I see you at chapel on Christmas Day?"

My plan was to attend Porthaethwy chapel with Mami on Christmas Day, but on seeing the naked hope in Angharad's eyes, I change my mind. "I'll be at the Plygain service. Will I see you there?"

Angharad nods and smiles. She briefly takes my hand. "*Nadolig Llawen*. Merry Christmas, Carys."

"*Nadolig Llawen* to you too, Angharad."

From the door, Mr Williams calls her name, and with a sigh she turns and leaves the gathering.

Chapter Twenty-Nine

Carys

December 1915

"What is it you're doing here, Miss Ambrose? Is there anything I can help you with?"

"Oh, Mr Jansen, you startled me."

"Sorry."

I smile at Florian and wipe a hand across my warm forehead.

"You've got..."

I rush to the window and see a streak of white flour across my face. When I turn back, Florian is laughing.

"It's all part of the Christmas traditions," I say. "You know, I was wondering how you'd feel about letting your girls stay up later than usual this evening?"

"And why is that, then?"

"You remember how we all shared in your Sinterklaas Day tradition?"

Florian smiles. "Oh yes, that was such a wonderful day, and the girls were thrilled with their gifts."

"Then they're easily pleased," I say, thinking back to the socks I had knitted them. "Tomorrow, before the sun rises, there is a Plygain service to be held at chapel. Usually, it's me and Dadi who attend the service at

Porthaethwy, but he's not well enough to go this year, so I'm going to the one at Llanfairpwll instead."

"And you'd like my girls to come?"

"I'm not sure they'll be able to stay awake. We stay up all night, then walk to the service by candlelight. In normal times, we bake treats, make toffee, play games. With less food around, thanks to the German U-boats, we're a little stretched for ingredients, but I'm sure we'll manage. I wondered if the girls would like to join me in some baking, and then we could play a few games? I know this must be a difficult time of year for them without their Mami."

"You are very thoughtful," says Florian, "and of course they can stay up a little later than usual. But tell me, if your father is too ill to accompany you to chapel, does that mean you'll be walking there alone?"

"Yes, it does."

"In the middle of the night?"

"Well, very early in the morning, to be exact."

"That doesn't sound right to me. How would you feel if I were to accompany you?"

"You?"

"It is a bad idea. I'm sorry."

"No, it's a good idea, I mean, so long as you don't mind. All the carols will be in Welsh."

"I'm sure that will make them even more beautiful. If there are carols, does that mean you'll be singing?"

"Perhaps."

"In that case, I insist on accompanying you, for I'd hate to miss the chance to hear you sing."

My cheeks burn red. "How do you know I can sing?"

Florian laughs. "You sing all the time without even realising you are doing it."

"I do?"

Florian nods. "I'll fetch the girls, and you can put them to work."

An hour later and the kitchen table is covered in flour, a pan with what sugar we could spare is bubbling on the stove, and the air is full of children's laughter. Across the table from me, Lina and Emma smear each other's faces with flour. When Florian tries to scold them, they turn their attention on him, emptying a handful of flour into his thatch of brown hair.

"Don't encourage them," he says, when he catches me laughing.

"You look like Sinterklaas," I say, and the girls burst into noisy laughter.

"What on earth is going on here?" asks Mami as she walks into the kitchen. She is smiling, but the skin around her eyes is grey and sagging and her appearance is sobering to us all.

"We're making treats for Christmas," says Emma, the bolder of Florian's girls.

"Is that right? Well, I hope you save some for me and Mr Ambrose."

As the girls become engrossed once more in their creation, I cross the room to Mami and ask under my breath, "how is Dadi?"

"Not good, not good at all."

"Should I fetch the doctor?"

"There's no point, *cariad*. A visit to him will cost us more than we can afford, only for him to tell us there's nothing he can do."

"I was going to go to the Plygain service later, but I can stay here and take a turn with Dadi if you need me to."

"Why don't you both go," says Florian, "I can sit with Mr Ambrose while you're out."

"No, that is very kind, Mr Jansen, but I'd rather stay with my husband. I hear you're going to the service with Carys?"

"I was planning to, but I can stay here if you'd rather?"

"Good Lord, no. I'd much rather Carys had someone with her when walking the lanes in the dark. The girls will be fine here with me."

"If you're sure."

"I'm sure so long as you bring us up some Welsh cakes and toffee when they're ready, and a nice hot cup of tea wouldn't go amiss either."

"I'll make the tea now."

"Thank you, you're a good girl, Carys."

By two a.m. the house is quiet, other than the occasional bout of coughing from Dadi's room. Florian is sprawled in an armchair beside the fire, his mouth open and his eyes closed. It feels cruel to wake him, but if we're to make it to the chapel by three, I must.

"Mr Jansen," I say, gently shaking his shoulder.

"Huh?" His eyes flicker open and for a moment, we're locked in each other's gaze. With a cough, I turn myself away and hand him his jacket.

"I'm sorry to wake you, but we need to set off if we're to make it to chapel in time."

He stretches his arms above his head and yawns. "How long have I been asleep?"

"A couple of hours, I should think."

"No, but we were supposed to play games in front of the fire!"

"Yes, well, I wouldn't worry about that. I was quite content sitting beside the fire with a few hours' peace."

Florian stands and pulls on his jacket. I hand him a large glass jar with a broad-based candle lodged inside. "To light our way," I explain, "and the jar should ensure the flame doesn't go out. The weather is fine, so it should be alright, but I've got some spare candles in my coat pocket just in case."

"How long is the walk?"

"It usually takes me half an hour, but it will be longer in the dark."

"Then we'd best get going."

Outside, the air is crisp and still. Our candles light our way, casting strange shadows as the wicks flicker within the glass. I'm glad to have Florian by my side, as there's an eeriness to being out in the countryside in the middle of the night.

"Look up," says Florian.

I lift my eyes to a blanket of stars against a navy sky.

"It is one of the most beautiful things I have ever seen," he whispers, as though even his voice could shatter the beauty of the night.

Our breath pours out in creamy clouds around us, and we stand gazing at the sky until our necks grow stiff and sore.

"Let's keep walking, or my feet will turn numb."

"Mine already are," he says, pointing to a pair of boots which have seen better days.

As we walk in silence, I wonder what it must feel like to leave your home with little more than the clothes on your back. The Jansens have been luckier than some finding a home on our farm, but there are plenty in Porthaethwy and Menai Bridge less fortunate.

The cold bites through my gloves and I shiver. Florian stops walking and begins unbuttoning his jacket.

"What are you doing?"

He removes his jacket and places it over my shoulders. "You look cold."

"Not as cold as you'll be in just a jumper and shirt. I can't take this." I try to hand the jacket back but he refuses, marching off ahead so I have to run to keep up. When I do, he smiles at me and it is a smile which warms me more than any item of clothing. The jacket's wool holds his smell, and as I pull it tighter around myself, it is almost like being held in his arms.

Chapter Thirty

Angharad

December, 1915

The sun has not yet risen, and the air is so cold it's almost painful to breathe. For a moment I stand and stare up at the chapel, and perhaps for the first time in my life I see beauty in the solid stone building. Pale yellow light softens its stark windows, tugging at something deep inside me and drawing me up the path.

As I step inside, the only light comes from candles, flicking their muted glow against the whitewashed walls, and casting shadows across the faces of the assembled congregation. Most of the pews are full, and there is no chance of sitting in my usual place. I spot Carys and she waves me over, shuffling to make room for me. She smiles, her eyes glassy, as though filled with tears.

"Are you alright?" I whisper.

She nods her head and slips an envelope across to me. My hands shake as I open it and tears spring to my own eyes. It is the first Christmas card I have received since Eddy. Surprise is swiftly followed by shame. So used am I to being alone, I haven't even thought about giving cards this year. As the thick paper shakes in my hand, I realise it is the greatest gift I have been given in a very long time.

"I'm so sorry," I whisper. "I don't have one for you."

Carys places her small hand on my large one and smiles at me. "There's no need to apologise, Angharad." She turns her head to the man sitting beside her. "Mr Jansen, this is my friend, Miss Angharad Williams."

The man reaches a hand across Carys for me to shake. "A pleasure to meet you, Miss Williams." His foreign accent is thick, but his English is perfect.

"I've explained to Mr Jansen the service will be in Welsh."

"Do you speak Welsh, Mr Jansen?"

"Not a word," he says with a laugh. "But I don't mind."

He has a kind face and even kinder smile, but there is no further chance of conversation, for Bryn stands and opens the service with a series of prayers and a reading from the Gospel of Saint Luke.

Bryn claps his hands together and announces, "Plygain is open."

A group of men walk to the front of the chapel and strike up a song. Their music cloaks me with a peace I haven't experienced before. They are halfway through their carol when Carys pulls a battered leather-bound notebook from her pocket.

"What's that?" whispers Mr Jansen.

"It's our family book of Plygain carols."

"Do you know what you'll sing?" I ask.

"Not yet."

"You've not decided?" asks Florian, eyebrows raised. "When is it your turn?"

Carys smiles, shakes her head and whispers, "that's not how it works. People go to the front to sing as the mood takes them. Once everyone who wants to has sung, we start again, keeping to the same order as before."

"Oh, I see. Will you be singing, Miss Williams?"

I smother a laugh with my scarf. "I wouldn't impose my singing on anyone, Mr Jansen."

He grins and leans back against the pew. When the first group of singers finish their carol, Mr Jansen lifts his hands to clap, Carys catching them just in time.

"No clapping," she whispers.

Next up is a married couple, known for singing the same two carols year on year. Their voices blend beautifully, and despite their advancing years, the love between them is plain to see and hear. I feel a flutter of envy at their closeness.

As the couple draws their carol to a close, Carys gets to her feet and walks to the front. I hold my breath as she turns the pages of her old song book and settles on a page. She closes her eyes, sings a note, and I release the breath I've been holding. She is utterly captivating. Her voice soars up to the high ceiling, and you could hear a pin drop. Lit by candlelight, she looks and sounds like an angel. When I turn my head to see if the rest of the congregation is as enraptured as I am, the look on Mr Jansen's face stops me short. His eyes are glistening, his lips parted. He is sitting as still as a statue, and it is as if Carys has cast a spell over him.

Her carol is over too soon and as she takes her place back on the pew, there is a noticeable murmuring of appreciation from the congregation.

"You were absolutely wonderful," I tell her.

"That was the most beautiful thing I have ever heard," says Mr Jansen.

Carys flushes, and looks relieved when a group of singers step forward and the focus is no longer on her.

**

"Merry Christmas," I tell Carys and Mr Jansen as we leave the chapel.

"Merry Christmas to you, too, Miss Williams. I must say, despite not understanding a word of what went on in that service, it was one of the most pleasant evenings I've ever had."

"Mornings, you mean," says Carys, pointing to the sun rising slowly from the horizon.

"Come on, we'd best be getting home. No doubt your girls will be up early on Christmas morning."

"Goodbye, Miss Williams. It really was a pleasure to meet you."

"Goodbye, Mr Jansen, and likewise. Have a wonderful Christmas, and send my love to your mother, Carys."

"I will. Merry Christmas, Angharad." She surprises me with a quick hug, then she and Mr Jansen head off towards their farm.

As I make my way home, I'm grateful they didn't ask about my plans for Christmas Day. Carys probably assumes I'll be spending the day with Bryn and Anne, but that couldn't be further from the truth. It may be Christmas Day, but the cows still need to be milked. At least it gives me something to do.

The day is crisp and bright, a low mist hanging over fields coated in frost. As I follow the line of the hedgerow towards the farm, spiders' webs glint like jewels in the low winter sun and my breath swirls around me in wispy clouds. I pull in a deep breath of cold air, determined to enjoy a day that never fails to be a painful reminder of just how alone I really am. At least I got to share a wonderful Plygain service with friends. That's a significant improvement on previous years.

Betty rushes to greet me when I reach the yard, and once I've given her a good deal of attention, I look up and notice Mr Stephens has already moved the cows into the lower field. This must be his Christmas present to me, as it is usually my job.

"Good morning, girls, and a very merry Christmas to you," I say, opening the gate to the field and leading the first cow out.

The cow takes no notice of Betty as we cross the yard, so familiar with her scampering excitement it no longer registers. We enter the milking parlour and with its stone walls and uneven, muddy floor, I wonder at its likeness to the stable in the Christmas story. I get the cow settled, lower myself onto the stool, and begin my work.

As we fall into a rhythm, I sing 'Ar Gyfer Heddiw'r Bore' in recognition of the day. The cow lets out an amused grunt at my deep-throated growl that counts as singing. Betty raises her bushy eyebrows at me, then settles down, her head resting on her paws.

With the first cow empty, I fetch the second. My singing has reduced to a quiet hum, memories filling my head as I work.

"Teach me a carol, in Welsh," says Eddy.

"In Welsh? Are you sure, *cariad*?"

"I can't live in Wales and not learn at least a bit of Welsh, can I?"

"Fair enough. Let's start with my favourite, 'Ar Gyfer Heddiw'r Bore'. "

"An Gyfer Heddiw'r Bore'... did I say that right?"

I try so hard not to laugh at Eddy's terrible pronunciation. Instead, I say, "We'll make a Welsh speaker out of you yet. Here, I'll sing a line, then you copy me. *Ar gyfer heddiw'r bore 'n faban bach, faban bach.*"

"You what? I think you're going to have to say that again for me."

With a start, I return to the present and realise tears are dropping from my cheeks into the bucket below. With my apron, I scrub them away. These memories should be precious, they should bring joy, not sorrow, especially on a morning such as this. Will they ever stop hurting? I tilt my head back to stop my tears contaminating the milk and sing again.

"*Ar gyfer heddiw'r bore 'n faban bach, faban bach,*

Y ganwyd gwreiddyn Iesse 'n faban bach;

Y Cadarn ddaeth o Bosra,

Y Deddfwr gynt ar Seina,

Yr Iawn gaed ar Galfaria 'n faban bach, faban bach,

Yn sugno bron Maria 'n faban bach."

Betty has lifted her head from her paws. As my singing grows louder, she shuffles back.

"Sorry, *cariad*," I say when I've finished. "But I had to get that out, for Eddy. You understand, don't you? You may not say it, but I know you miss Eddy as much as I do."

As I'm leading the cow back across the yard to the field, Mr Stephens appears from the cottage and gives me a wave and those rarest of things – a smile. "*Nadolig Llawen*, Angharad," he calls.

"*Nadolig Llawen*," I call back. He won't hear me, but he'll know what I'm trying to say.

With a nod, Mr Stephens mounts his horse and sets off in the direction of his cousin's farm, where he will spend the day with what family he has left.

"Even Mr Stephens has someone to spend Christmas with, Betty," I say, as we fetch our next cow for milking.

Once the milking is finished, we head back to the bothy. "Thank goodness the fire is still going," I tell Betty, who wastes no time snuggling up in front of it to warm herself. "After that early start, I think we've both earned a rest, don't you? But first, let's exchange our gifts."

Betty lifts her head, her eyes watching me as I place an item wrapped in newspaper and tied in a bow in front of her. She takes less than a minute to tear the paper off with her teeth and reach the bone inside.

"There, I thought you'd like that," I say, turning my attention to the present I've bought myself on Betty's behalf. "Oh, *The Valley of Fear* by Arthur Conan Doyle. Just what I wanted. Thank you, Betty." I curl up in the chair with the book in my hands, thinking that despite my loneliness, there are probably worse ways to spend the day.

Chapter Thirty-One

Ffion

December, 1915

We walk along the shoreline, the rocks and stones beneath our feet glistening with frost, the snow-topped mountains of Snowdonia standing proud against a fierce blue sky. In the distance, Plas Newydd glows gold in the low winter sun.

"Can we stop for a moment to skim some stones, Mother?" asks Michael.

"I don't see why not. We're in no hurry today." It is a joy to see the boy behaving like the child he still is, rather than the man he will soon become. School seems to have aged my children prematurely, even little Becca speaks like a young lady these days. At fifteen, Michael now needs to shave several times a week, but occasionally, I still see the glint in his eye that he had as a young boy when up to mischief. My heart aches for the days when my children still depended on me, but I push the foolish thoughts aside. They are here now, so I must enjoy the moment.

"Mother, look at this one," says Becca, running to where I have perched myself on a flat rock.

"Goodness, I would think you'll get several skips from that one."

"Will you come and watch?"

"Of course." My heart swells as her small hand slips inside mine. I reach down and pull a small stone from beneath a pile of slippery seaweed. Before I can stop her, Becca grabs the dislodged green sludge and hurls it at her brother Henry. "Rebecca, what are you thinking?"

"It's alright, Mother," says Henry, grinning at me, before grabbing a rope-like piece of seaweed and retaliating.

"Both of you, stop it," I say.

"Sorry, Mother."

"So you should be. What would the good people of Llanfairpwll think if they could see what you're up to?"

"There isn't anyone around," says Henry, "only us."

"That isn't the point. Here," I say, handing Henry the stone I found. "Why don't you have a competition with Becca to see who can get the most skips."

"Only if you join in, too."

"Give me a moment to find another stone." As I scour the shoreline, I can't keep the smile from my face, despite the children's earlier disobedience.

We pass a happy half-hour skimming stones across the flat surface of the Strait. Absorbed in our game, we could easily belong to a time before war and school, and all the other nasty things that have come between us.

It seems a shame to put a stop to our fun, but the tide is creeping ever closer to the bag of gifts I have brought with me and the sun has sunk considerably in the sky since we set out from home. "Come on, we'd better keep going or it will be dark before we're finished."

"Where are we going first?" asks Mary.

"Susan's is the first cottage we'll come to."

"Can I give her the gift? I like Susan."

"Of course you can," I say, holding back the warning I want to give about not forming friendships with our servants. I have nothing against Susan but can imagine Hector's reaction should he discover the friendship.

The children chatter around me as we walk further along the shoreline. Eventually we reach a small harbour, a bubbling stream, swollen after all the recent rain rushing to meet the waters of the Strait. We turn our backs on the mountains and water and begin the uphill walk into the village.

"I wish John could be here," says Michael, falling into step beside me.

"So do I, Michael. So do I."

"He'll come back in one piece, Mother," says Michael, linking his arm in mine.

We each become lost in our thoughts, walking in companionable silence as the younger children chatter behind us. It doesn't take long for us to reach the row of small cottages where Susan lives. Mary steps forward and knocks on the door. When Susan opens it, she flushes at the sight of us all standing there. The other servants know to expect us, but given Susan has never spent a Christmas with us before, she seems unaware of our Boxing Day tradition.

"Merry Christmas," she stutters, despite having been with us the day before.

"Merry Christmas to you too, Susan," says Mary. "We've brought you a present to say thank you for all the work you do for us."

Susan's cheeks flare red, and she takes the box Mary offers with shaking hands. "This is very kind, but there was no need."

"It is something we do every year," I explain. "Our next stop is Mrs Edwards' cottage."

"I see. Well, thank you, madam, and thank you, children. This really is a wonderful surprise."

"Who's at the door, Sue?" comes a shout from inside the dark cottage.

Susan's cheeks go from red to purple and she pushes the door until only a sliver is visible. "I'd better get back to my mami," she says, "but thank you very much for calling round."

"You're most welcome. Enjoy your day off."

As we walk the short distance to Mrs Edwards' home, I listen to the chatter of the children around me. This is the first year I have brought them with me on my Boxing Day tradition and they can't hide their shock at how small and dark Susan's cottage was. I'm pleased they've seen how local people live. It does no harm for them to realise they are privileged to be born into our family.

Mrs Edwards' cottage is not much bigger than Susan's, but when she opens the door, the sound of laughter and the smell of cooking reach us. The only surprise she expresses about our visit is the fact the children have accompanied me this year.

"Would you like to come in for a cup of tea?" she asks, as Henry hands over her gift.

"That is very kind, Mrs Edwards, but you make enough cups of tea for us when you are at work. Besides, we had better be getting back, for it will be dark soon. Enjoy your day off with your family."

"I will do, and thank you, Mrs Montgomery. The gift is much appreciated, as is the day off."

"I wouldn't mind having Mrs Edwards as my mother," says Henry as we walk away, "then I could eat all the cakes I like."

"Don't be so unkind," says Rebecca, taking my hand again. "I'm glad you're our mother."

"Even if I can't bake cakes?"

"Even then."

We walk home through the village, our progress far quicker than when we walked along the shore, but a lot less picturesque. The rows of terraced homes and run-down cottages remind me of the dark days we are living in, and the struggle so many families face. I remember to count my blessings, despite any downsides to being married to a man like Hector.

"You go into the house," I say as we walk up the drive. "I'm just going to say a quick hello to Bluebell."

The children run off ahead and I make my way around the back of the house to the stables. I can't let a day go past without at least saying hello to my precious mare. In my pocket are four carrots and an apple, a secret gift, as I know I should conserve our resources for humans rather than animals in these uncertain times.

As I step into the stables, the familiar smell of straw and sound of snorting horses brings a smile to my face. But then unfamiliar sounds greet me. It is a grunt, but not one anyone of the horses has made. I'm tempted to call out, but instinct stops me. From a hook on the wall, I grab one of my riding whips. If there is an intruder, it is best to be prepared. With my arm raised, I tiptoe deeper into the stables, only pausing to give Bluebell a quick rub on the nose and a whispered promise that I will return.

The deeper into the stables I go, the louder the grunting becomes. By now I'm convinced the sound belongs to a man, but then I hear a woman moan and stop in my tracks. The sounds have a familiar rhythm to them and my heart beats so fast I can hear it in my ears. I take one more step and look over the top of the wooden barrier. My hand flies to my mouth. Hector is naked from the waist down, moving back and forth on top of a young woman. No, not a woman, a girl. Her shiny blonde hair is fanned out around her head, matching the colour of the straw they lie on. She turns her head and sees me. I hold my breath. Her eyes widen, then a small smile crosses her lips, before she grips my husband tighter and moans with pleasure in his ear.

My legs are numb as I leave the stable as quickly as I can without making a sound. I don't even acknowledge Bluebell as I pass, too ashamed am I by what I have just witnessed. The carrots and apple sit heavy in my pocket as I reach the stable entrance and begin running toward the house.

Tears fill my eyes, but as I step inside, I blink them away.

"We've decided to play charades," says Henry, running up to me, grabbing my hand, and pulling me toward the drawing room.

"Lovely," I say, pinning a smile on my face and trying to forget all about what I have just seen.

Chapter Thirty-Two

Angharad

January, 1916

The day is awful, even by January's standards. The surrounding air thunders with the sound of torrential rain pounding the ground below. I pass a corrugated shed and for a moment, it sounds as though I am under attack from a slew of bullets. My woollen cloak, which is usually so useful against the weather, is soaking in water like a sponge. My boots splash through unavoidable puddles, the water reaching my stockings below.

The cold is biting, and each drop of rain that pummels and stings my cheeks feels more like ice. I pull the hood of my cloak so far down over my face it's hard to even see where I am going. As I approach Graig, the familiar nerves return, but thanks to the weather there is no time to dwell upon them.

Despite my recent loneliness and my eagerness to see some familiar faces, the thought of spending an hour in a cold summerhouse wearing drenched woollen clothing seems foolhardy. If I make it back to my bothy without having caught a chill, it will be a miracle.

The surprise of walking into a summerhouse that is warm almost brings me to tears. Steam is rising from the outer garments hung on the backs of chairs and I try to work out why the summerhouse is not its usual damp self.

"Oh goodness me, you are soaked to the skin!" Ffion rushes towards me in her characteristic style and begins removing my cloak.

"Why is it so warm in here? I was expecting to freeze to death."

"A happy New Year to you too," says Ffion with a smile.

She seems surprised and amused by my directness. I blush. "Sorry, Ffion. *Blwyddyn Newydd Dda* to you."

"The source of our heat is a belated Christmas present from our dear friend Colonel Stapleton-Cotton. Come and see."

Ffion takes my hand and leads me through the crowded room. I fight my shyness to smile and nod to the women we pass, most of whom are warming their hands on cups of tea usually saved for the end of our meetings.

"Here, isn't it wonderful?" Ffion stands in front of a stove, holding out her hands to warm them. "It's an oil stove, the latest in technology and most kindly donated by the Colonel."

The stove is not only a thing of beauty with its wrought iron cut-out design, but also a thing of wonder. I step closer and feel my muscles relax as warmth meets them. "This is such a generous gift!"

"Isn't it? I'm not quite sure how we ever thought we'd manage without heat, especially not in this rotten weather."

"There seem to be a lot of new faces here today."

"Yes, word is spreading about what we're up to. Isn't it wonderful to see our numbers flourishing?"

I smile and nod, while looking around the room in dismay at the unfamiliar faces. More ladies I'll have to talk to.

"How was your Christmas, Angharad?"

"Fine, thank you. And yours?"

"I had the children at home, which is always a treat. Did you spend the day with your brother and sister-in-law?"

"No, they were busy entertaining Anne's family, who visited from the mainland."

"Oh." Ffion frowns. "So you spent the day with Mr Stephens?"

My cheeks flush. "No, he had an invitation to spend the day with a cousin."

"Angharad, are you telling me you spent Christmas day alone?"

Ffion is holding on to my arm, her eyes wide with pity. "I wasn't alone, I had Betty with me, and I saw Carys at the Plygain service."

"But what about the rest of the day? The Plygain service finishes around six in the morning, does it not?"

"Well, yes, but it was seven before I arrived home, and then I had to milk the cows, and attend to a few jobs around the farmhouse, so really, it was rather a full day."

"Angharad, as someone I hope you now consider a friend, I would like to offer a sincere apology."

"Whatever for?"

"For allowing you to spend Christmas alone. Did you even have a decent meal?"

"Of course I did. There was plenty of left-over cawl for me to heat up."

"Oh good God, Angharad, left-over stew for your Christmas dinner? Whatever am I to do with you? Next year, if you are in the same position again, I want you to tell me. A friend of mine spending Christmas alone? I don't think so. Promise me you'll tell me next time?"

With no intention of honouring such a pledge, and with only a tiny tinge of guilt at lying, I give Ffion my word.

"Good, now let's take our seats as we have several members of the Agricultural Organisation Society here to speak to us today."

Mrs Watt is the first to take the floor. She's known for her dry sense of humour, and I'm surprised to see her looking so solemn.

"Ladies, as I'm sure you're aware, a new Military Service Act is due to be passed this month, ushering in a dreadful new phase in the war. Soon, all men aged between eighteen and forty-one will be liable for military service. We can expect some exemptions for farm workers, but I would strongly advise us to err on the side of caution and plan to lose most of our able-bodied men from the fields of Anglesey to the fields of France and beyond.

"With this in mind, our work here at the Institute has never been so important as in this, our country's hour of need. It is now up to the women, us, to stand up and be counted. It is we who shall ensure our fellow countrymen do not go hungry, we who must take on the running of this great land.

"Ever since I arrived on these shores, I have been evangelising on the good that can come from Women's Institutes. In the few months since this, the first WI began, you have shown greater aptitude and imagination than even I could have predicted. Every woman here has a role to play in our community in service of the greater good. We have already set the food supply of the country as our priority, but we must also think of other ways we can serve."

After Mrs Watt, Mrs Nugent Harris, Mrs E. Jones, and Colonel Cotton all take to the floor to reinforce Mrs Watt's message of the pressing need for us to come together at this time. With a start, I realise that in the months since I became involved with the organisation, I have been thinking about everything backwards. For all my worries about what others may think of me, I haven't stopped to see the bigger picture, the greater good.

Perhaps, for the first time in my life, it occurs to me I may actually be useful. No men left to work in the fields? Give me a pitchfork or shovel and I can work as hard as any man. No men left to organise and mobilise a community? I'm sharp-minded enough to be put to good use. My physique, so long a source of angst, can now become my power.

As the meeting draws to a close, I lean over to ask Ffion a question I never thought I'd have the courage to utter. "Do you think it would be a completely ridiculous idea for me to put myself forward as a member of the committee?"

Ffion's face spreads into a wide grin. "I think that is the most wonderful idea I have heard so far this year."

I laugh and remind her we are only eleven days into 1916, but she simply smiles and pats my hand. For a moment, in my mind's eye, I picture Eddy leaning against the back wall, watching our interaction.

"About time too," mouths Eddy, with a smile. "About time too."

Chapter Thirty-Three

Carys

February, 1916

We all gather in the yard, even Dadi making it out of his sickbed for the occasion. Mami stands beside me sobbing.

"Mami, please stop crying. It won't help Peter to see you so distressed."

"But it might be the last time I see him," she cries, blowing her nose into her hanky.

"Yes, but he's bound to be nervous, and the sight of you crying your heart out isn't going to fill him with much confidence, is it?"

Mami nods, blows her nose once more, then pockets her handkerchief. Beside her, Florian has his arms around his girls, drawing them close to him. They seem confused by what is happening, and I hear him trying to explain what is going on in their mother tongue.

Dadi leans against a fence post, coughing and trying to catch his breath. I run inside to fetch him a chair. "Here, Dadi, sit yourself down."

"Thank you," he says, reaching up and squeezing my fingers, until another coughing fit forces him to let go.

Peter walks into the yard, a canvas bag slung over one shoulder. "Well, I think I'm all set. I don't need you all out here seeing me off. It's bloody freezing. Get yourselves back inside."

"Oh, my boy," cries Mami, throwing herself at Peter and clinging on to his shirt. I look away. This is not the Mami I've always known. Since Dadi became unwell, she's been like a different woman. She's so nervy she jumps as the slightest sound, and her emotions swing wildly between calm and distraught. Her favourite saying has always been 'there's no point crying over spilt milk', and yet now even spilling a drop of tea onto a saucer can set her off.

Dadi inches his way across the yard, leaning heavily on his stick. "You take care of yourself, boy."

"And you, Dadi."

Dadi gives Peter a slap on the back, before prising Mami away from her son and leading her back toward the farmhouse.

"Good luck over there," says Florian, stepping forward and shaking Peter's hand. "I only wish I was joining you."

"We need you here taking care of the farm," says Peter. "Look after them all for me, won't you?"

"Of course."

Finally, it is my turn. Peter turns and smiles at me. "Come here, trouble." He pulls me over to him and kisses the top of my head. "Don't get too comfortable here, will you? Your big brother will soon be back, ready to annoy you again."

"I look forward to it."

With one last wave, Peter marches off through the yard and out onto the lane beyond.

"Are you alright?" asks Florian as I dab my eyes with a handkerchief.

"Oh, yes, I've just got a little dust in my eye." Given the amount me and Peter fight when he's here, it's silly to be upset about him leaving. But with Dadi so ill, I have a bad feeling about what's to come.

Back inside the farmhouse, Mami is sitting at the kitchen table nursing a cup of tea. "I don't feel much like going to the meeting this afternoon, Carys."

"I'm not surprised, Mami. I don't suppose anyone will mind if we give it a miss this month."

"You could go though, couldn't you? Represent the family and send them my apologies."

"I think it would be best if I stay here with you."

"No, please go. I don't want them thinking we're shirking our duties."

"No one will think that. They know what's happening today."

"Even so."

"Alright, I'll go."

"You'd better leave now, else you'll be late."

With a sigh, I pull on my coat and head back out into the yard. As much as I love our new Women's Institute and all the friends I have made there, I could really do without attending a meeting today.

By the time I reach Graig, the meeting has already started, and heads turn as I squeeze into the room and find a place to stand beside Angharad at the back.

"Are you alright?" she whispers. "It's not like you to be late."

"Peter left today."

"He's joined up?"

"He didn't have a choice, but even if he'd been given an exemption, I think he would have joined up, anyway."

"Is your mother alright?"

I shake my head. "What have I missed?"

"The man at the front is Mr Jones from Llangefni. He's come to talk to us about the Board of Agriculture's poultry scheme."

"Teaching grandma to suck eggs?"

Angharad raises an eyebrow and tries not to laugh.

I realise the small man at the front is looking at us and it suddenly feels very hot in the Graig summerhouse. "Do you have something you wish to add, ladies?"

I look at Angharad in horror, knowing my cheeks will have turned puce. She looks just as uncomfortable as I am, but to my amazement, steps in to save the day.

"We were remarking on how interesting the poultry scheme you've been speaking about sounds," she says, throwing me a rather panicked look.

"In what way?"

Goodness, this man is worse than any headmaster I've come across and seems determined to show us up for our gossiping.

"Um... well..." With all that's happened today, my mind is a muddle, and I lose my train of thought.

"We were wondering if we could get involved in some way," says Angharad, coming to my rescue yet again. "Both Miss Ambrose and I are experienced in raising and caring for poultry. Perhaps we could offer some classes or demonstrations to local women who currently feel daunted by the thought of having chickens in their gardens?"

"What a splendid idea," says Colonel Cotton, grinning broadly at us. His enthusiasm seems to give Angharad confidence, and she continues.

"One barrier for local women may be the need to build a chicken coop. That is also something we could assist them with."

"Oh, really?" says Mr Jones, glancing around him with an amused smile. "Have experience of building chicken coops, do you?" As he lets out a laugh, I notice Angharad square her shoulders.

"Actually, Mr Jones, I do. I built my chicken coop with my own hands, and without the assistance of any man."

The Colonel barks out a laugh and claps his hands together. "That's put you in your place, hasn't it, Mr Jones? I warned you not to under-estimate the ladies of Llanfairpwll."

Mr Jones turns a deep shade of purple and I reach across and squeeze Angharad's hand.

"Are there any other women here who have experience with poultry and would be willing to offer their expertise to those less experienced?" About ten hands raise in the air and Mr Jones coughs and studies his notes. "It seems I'm rather preaching to the converted."

"In that case," says the Colonel, "perhaps we should move on to questions? Then I can begin my brief talk about buying good seed... unless, of course, Miss Williams and Miss Ambrose have anything else they'd like to add?"

Angharad and I shake our heads, giggles burning my throat as I try to quell them. Who'd have thought timid Angharad could put someone in their place like that? Several women put questions to Mr Jones, and by the time he has finished answering them, it seems some of his self-esteem has been restored. I risk a glance at my friend and notice her cheeks are still pink, her eyes downcast. Yet despite these signs of unease, there is evidence of a stronger woman emerging. Gone is the stoop of her back and she stands at full height, her chin jutting out as though daring the world to take her on.

Chapter Thirty-Four

Angharad

March, 1916

I'm guiding the cows across the yard and into the barn when Colonel Stapleton-Cotton appears in his bath chair. The donkey's feet scuff in surprise as the Colonel yanks on its reins and the metal-rimmed wheels slow. He pulls back the fabric hood and leans against the high-backed seat, sniffing the air and smiling.

"Colonel, good afternoon. This is a pleasant surprise."

"Good afternoon to you, Miss Williams. Nothing beats the smell of a farmyard, don't you agree?"

"Um, I suppose not, Colonel. Are you here to see Mr Stephens?"

"No, I'm here to speak to you, but I can see you're rather busy, so I'll wait over there until you're done."

"Thank you. The weather's turned so cold again, I want to get the cows into the barn before nightfall."

"Very sensible."

Betty, who has been some help in shepherding the cows, abandons her work and snaps at the heels of the donkey pulling the Colonel's bath chair. He doesn't seem to mind, so I return to the job at hand, conscious of the Colonel's eyes on me as I work. But when I glance behind me, the Colonel is not looking at me, but at Betty, who has jumped up onto his lap and is enjoying a firm tickle beneath her chin.

"I do so love Welsh terriers," he calls. "So full of personality."

That's one word for it, I think, laughing to myself as the final cow enters the barn.

"You say personality, I say mischief," I call as I close the barn door and walk over to meet him. "What can I do for you, Colonel?"

"I've been putting together my talk for the next WI meeting. The title is Women's Labour on the Land, and I thought you might help me with it."

"Oh, I'm not sure about that. I'm a voracious reader, but I've never tried my hand at writing."

"I don't need you to write it, my dear. I'm quite capable of doing that. What I'd like is for you to share some of your expertise. It's all very well me talking about women's labour on the land, but as you may have noticed, I am a man. We've had quite a few new members join our merry band recently, most of whom do not come from farming families. I thought it would be interesting for them to hear from you."

"Me? Oh no, you wouldn't want that. I'm no public speaker, Colonel."

"You could have fooled me last month when you put our distinguished guest in his place."

"I'm very sorry about that, Colonel. Only, my friend Miss Ambrose had had a trying day, and I didn't want her told off in front of everyone for talking. I was trying to protect her, that's all. It wasn't my intention to embarrass Mr Jones."

"I'm sure it wasn't. But you spoke well, Angharad. And you have plenty of experience working the land with your marvellous allotment. Not only that, you have taught yourself everything you know. You don't come from a family of farmers, and that makes you the perfect candidate, in my eyes. I presume your allotment didn't exist prior to your arrival on the farm?"

"No, it didn't."

"Precisely. You started from scratch. You know what is required to get started in those early days. In short, you are just the woman for the job."

"Colonel, I'm flattered, of course I am, but you know my reputation in the village. The women at the Institute have been mostly kind, I'll grant you, but even there I'm an outsider. No one is going to want me lecturing them on growing fruit and veg."

"I wouldn't always assume the worst of folk, Angharad. You know, my dear, I have a favourite saying which I feel is well applied here – look up, not down; look out, not in; and lend a hand."

"Wise words, Colonel."

"They are, even if I say so myself. And you, Angharad, always seem to be looking down. You are always stooped, hunched, and whatever for? You have much to offer our institute, my dear, and it is time you started looking up and out."

The Colonel's rebuke, however kindly given, leaves me feeling like a small child in front of the headmaster. What's worse is I know he is right. "What precisely would you like me to do, Colonel?"

"That's the spirit, my dear! Let's go into the farmhouse and get out of the cold, and then we can make a plan."

**

Two days after the Colonel's visit, I find myself sitting at the front of the summerhouse, with Mrs Jones on one side, and Mrs Cotton on the other. Both have surprised me with their friendliness and ease of conversation. I feel disloyal leaving Carys at the back by herself, but having explained what I've been roped into, I hope she understands.

"It is very good of you to address us today, Miss Williams," says Jane Stapleton-Cotton. "I don't suppose my husband left you with much choice?" She raises an eyebrow above her glass eye and gives me a mischievous grin.

"He is a very persuasive man," I say, returning her smile.

"That he is. We get ourselves into all kinds of schemes thanks to his exuberant enthusiasm."

"No doubt," I say as the warmth from the woman beside me lightens me and somewhat calms my shaking limbs.

The meeting begins and my nerves return with full force, my limbs shaking so greatly it's a miracle I don't fall off my chair. After Mrs Jones has read the minutes from the last meeting and they have been adopted, the Colonel takes his position at the front of the room.

"Now, ladies, I have prepared a detailed talk for you on the Women's labour on the land question, as nothing can be more important at this current time. But before I begin, I have asked one of our number to recount her own experience. Please join me in welcoming Miss Angharad Williams to the floor."

As the round of applause assaults my ears, I walk to take my position, concentrating on putting one foot in front of the other for fear my legs will give way.

"G... g... good afternoon," I say. My voice quivers and it's a wonder anyone can hear me, and my throat is so dry I don't know how I'll be able to slip more words through it.

"Here," says the Colonel under his breath, handing me a glass of water. My hands shake so badly as I take it, water spills out onto my dress, and I have to discreetly wipe my chin.

"The... the Colonel asked me to talk to you about my experience of working my allotment." It's not a bad start, but my voice is wavering so badly I'm certain others in the room must hear. Betty, who I have brought with me for support, must sense my terrible nerves, for she runs along the side of the summerhouse and with a bark, comes and sits beside me. Her sudden appearance causes the assembled ladies to laugh. I join in the laughter and feel some of my nervousness slipping away.

With a deep breath, I stare out over the top of a sea of hats, focussing my attention on the back wall, where Carys gives me an encouraging smile. And there, beside Carys, in my mind's eye, is Eddy.

"You can do this, darling," Eddy says. "I know you can. Just remember, you know more about tending an allotment than anyone else in this room bar the Colonel. You are the expert, you are in control. And if all that isn't enough to encourage you, remember why you are doing this. Picture the brave men away fighting for your freedom. Imagine what a difference these assembled ladies can make if every one of them grows their own food. Small acts can move mountains, *cariad*."

"So," I say, forcing my voice out with a confidence I don't feel. "I will give a brief description of how I created my allotment, how I secure the right seed, and I shall finish with an overview of the yearly cycle of planting and harvesting."

To my surprise, the women seem interested in what I am saying. With a start I realise this is my chance to put to bed rumours of madness, dumbness, cruelty, and everything else said about me.

"The first thing I did when choosing a site for my allotment was to study the soil. Within Llanfairpwll alone, we have several soil types..."

When I reach the end of my prepared speech and have passed some of my produce around the assembled ladies, I almost don't hear the applause. I take my seat in a daze, my mind strangely blank. My limbs still tremble and twitch, but I am also filled by a glow of achievement.

"That was marvellous, dear," whispers Mrs Jones, as the Colonel begins talking. "Truly marvellous." She pats my hand, and I sink back into my seat, wondering if the past half an hour is simply a dream.

The Colonel finishes speaking and invites me back to the front, taking me by surprise. It is probably best I didn't know he would do such a thing, for I would only have spent the duration of his talk fretting. Together we field questions from women who seem inspired to turn their gardens over for growing food.

"I propose," says the Colonel when the question-and-answer session ends, "that a canvass of the village be taken as to potential help." With this proposition agreed by all members, the Colonel draws our contribution to a close. "My thanks again to Miss Williams for assisting me today. And now, I believe Mrs Clegg is going to demonstrate bread making, the results of which, I very much hope, we shall be able to sample with our tea."

Chapter Thirty-Five

Carys

April, 1916

This is the last thing I want to do today. All night I was kept awake by the terrible sounds of Dadi struggling for air, and Mami's frequent trips up and down to the kitchen to fetch him more water. Today isn't even an actual meeting of the WI, but Mami insisted I come. It's almost as if she wants me out of the house, and I can't bear to think why that might be.

As I approach the post office, I see a group of women already gathered, huddling under the shelter of several large umbrellas.

"A lovely day for it," says Ffion, as I approach them. "I wasn't sure you'd be able to come, as I know how busy you are on the farm."

"Mami wanted me out of the way, I think."

"Oh dear, getting under her feet, were you?"

"Something like that," I say, but tears fill my eyes and a sob sticks in my throat.

"Goodness, come here," says Ffion, taking my elbow and pulling me a distance away from the group. Before we get too far, she turns and calls over her shoulder, "Miss Williams, can you come with us, please?"

We form our own huddle a few doors down from the post office, and I'm filled with embarrassment at having taken them away from the group.

"What's happened?" asks Angharad.

I try to answer, but can't seem to get the words out.

"Something at home, I think," says Ffion, as though I'm not here. She turns back to me. "Is it your sweetheart or brothers? Have you had bad news?"

I shake my head. "No, it's... it's..."

"Is it your dadi?" asks Angharad. Contrary to her appearance, Angharad has a sensitivity to her, deeper than any I've come across before. It's as though she can read people's minds sometimes.

"How did you know?"

Angharad shrugs. "You talked about his illness a lot at first, but more recently, you've been avoiding the subject. At first, I wondered if he is better, but there's a sadness cloaking you which suggests otherwise."

Ffion looks at Angharad with a mix of admiration and envy. "You picked all that up from a few conversations?"

Angharad shrugs again, then turns to me. "Am I right? Is it your dadi?"

"Y... yes. He's not been able to get out of bed so far this week and last night was the worst yet. I think he's... I think he's going to... but I want to be there..."

"I'm sure your mother knows best," says Ffion. "If she's sent you out of the house, it will be to protect you."

"But I don't want protecting, I want to be with Dadi!" I must be shouting, for the women nearby turn and look at us with interest.

"And what about your dadi? Do you think he'd want you to see him struggling for his final breath, or for you to remember him as he was?" Angharad speaks the words softly, her large palm placed gently against my back. "In my experience, however difficult, it's important to remember someone at their best, and that can be hard enough without seeing them in their final moments."

She must be talking about her own mother and father, for I don't think she's lost anyone else.

"Of course," she continues, "we might all be getting ahead of ourselves. Perhaps your mother just wanted to catch up on some sleep with no one around, or wanted a quiet house so your dadi can get some rest. We all know what you're like, singing all the time." She smiles at me, and I'm grateful for her attempt to lighten the mood.

"I thought you liked my singing."

"Oh, I do, very much. But I imagine it's less welcome if you're trying to sleep and someone is singing their way around the house."

I smile. Of course, I don't believe her alternative version of reality. If Mami only wanted a quiet house, she would have sent Florian and his girls out too. But if I'm to make it through the next few hours without making a show of myself, it's in my own interests to go with this version.

"Oh look," says Ffion, "the Colonel's motor car is here. Shall we let the other ladies go first? I don't think we'll all fit in there together."

We walk back to the post office where women are climbing into the motor car. Just like me, some of them have never been inside a vehicle like this, and their shrieks and squeals speak of their excitement.

"I'll not be long," the driver tells us. "Are you ladies alright to wait here for me?"

"Of course," says Ffion. "We came prepared." She points to her umbrella and gives the old chauffeur such a warm smile it makes him blush.

While we wait for the motor car to return, my friends try to distract me with their chatter.

"Isn't it kind of Mrs Cotton to invite us for tea at her house?" says Ffion.

"It is," agrees Angharad. "Have you been there before? From what I've heard, it's a mansion."

"Yes, to both questions," says Ffion. "But whilst the house is lovely, it's the gardens which make it extra special. The Colonel's planting really is a work of art."

"I'm looking forward to seeing it," I say, doing my best to join in with their enthusiasm.

It isn't long before the car reappears. With the confidence of someone who has ridden in a motor car many times before, Ffion takes her place in the front, while Angharad and I climb in the back. Poor Angharad's legs are so long, they bump against the driver's seat, causing her knees to ride up to her ears.

"At least it's not a long journey," I say, and she laughs.

"I'd rather be the driver than the passenger."

This makes me laugh, but when Ffion turns to give Angharad a knowing look, I wonder if there is something I'm missing. Of course, Angharad doesn't know how to drive. The idea is ridiculous.

Being in the car is quite something. The hedgerows blur as we race along the road, and I grip the door handle, my knuckles white.

"Carys, we're only travelling at fifteen miles an hour," says Angharad. "You're quite safe."

"Safe? Safe is travelling on my own two feet, not in this noisy machine."

Angharad laughs and points as we make our way up a long drive. "Look, there's the house. Goodness me, it is grand."

I forget my nervousness about being in the car and instead marvel at the beautiful limestone-fronted house in front of us. You could fit twelve of our farmhouses into it, and not for the first time, I wonder why the upper-classes need so many rooms.

The driver helps us climb out of the car and shows us to the front door, where we are greeted by a maid in a smart black-and-white uniform. I find all this special treatment embarrassing, for the maid must be around my age and her work is no more menial than mine, it is only the setting which is different.

"We should invite people like her into the WI," I whisper to Angharad as we're shown into a grand, high-ceilinged drawing room.

"I can't see it, can you?" Angharad whispers back. "We're as lowly as they'll go, but never say never."

"But the work we do is no better than the maid's, and at least she stays warm and dry."

"It's not about work though, is it? For right or wrong, it's a matter of class."

Whilst the idea of class doesn't sit right with me, there is no time to dwell upon it, as Mrs Cotton greets us with her usual warmth and pours us each a cup of tea.

"I know the weather isn't in our favour," she says, "but I would still like to show you the grounds, if you are willing. The daffodils are currently at their best."

"That would be wonderful," I say. "Thank you."

"And we have our umbrellas to keep us dry," adds Ffion.

"Is the Colonel at home?" asks Angharad.

"No," says Jane. "He and Tinker are at the egg collection depot today. He will be sorry to have missed you all, but as I'm sure you are aware, he is an impossible man to keep in any one place for any length of time. Instead of the man himself, we shall have to satisfy ourselves with the fruits of his labour. Are you ladies ready to see the bulb fields?"

"Yes please," we all agree.

With our brollies up and holding off the rain, we venture out into the grounds of Plas Llwynon, which stretch on for miles. The ground is soggy underfoot, and I am beginning to wonder if I shouldn't make my excuses and head back to the farm when we turn a corner, and I see it.

"Oh my goodness." Angharad bumps into me as I'm stopped in my tracks by such beauty as I've never seen. Ahead of us stretch fields and fields of flowers, their sweet scent carrying on the breeze. Against the grey sky, a rainbow of colour emerges from the ground; yellows, pinks, blues, purple. My eyes don't know what to look at first.

"We have hyacinths, daffodils and tulips all currently in bloom," says Jane. "I wanted you to come and see them today for in a matter of days they will be cut ready to be sold. My husband realised that whilst cut flowers are not profitable on a small scale, grow them in a great enough volume and you can make a penny or two. Unlike some of his hair-brained schemes, this is one I fully endorse."

Something about the burst of colour before us gives me a sense of hope. Perhaps, when I return to the farmhouse, Dadi will be on the mend, Mami will smile again, and all will be well with the world.

Chapter Thirty-Six

Angharad

April, 1916

When you live on a farm, you soon learn that death is an inevitable part of life. For all my years of chapel teachings about the afterlife, I've seen enough animals die to know that nothing supernatural occurs in those seconds between life and death. One moment a creature is living, the next they are not. But regardless of the mechanics, losing a loved one tears at us like a knife, leaving an open wound that weeps and stings for many months or years before it can heal.

I have only experienced such a loss once in my life, and although all that is left of my old wound is a scar, it still stings and itches more often than I'd like. And so, armed with this knowledge, I make my way to the Ambrose farm to be by my friend's side.

As I walk up to the farmhouse, the yard is unnaturally quiet. All the curtains and blinds are drawn, and a piece of crêpe holds the brass knocker in place. I remember Carys once telling me this was one of the greatest sheep farms on the island. Whilst that might once have been true, with sons away and the head of the house ill for so long, the farmhouse and surrounding buildings have seen better days. A barn door hangs drunkenly on its one remaining hinge. Several tiles from the farmhouse roof are missing, and the windowsills are in a worse condition than my own.

With a quiet knock on the front door, I open it and step into a musty hallway. The place smells of decay and death, or perhaps it is just because I know what has occurred here.

It takes a moment for my eyes to get used to the gloom, so I stand and listen. I have never been inside Carys's home before, but the layout of the building seems much like Mr Stephens's. To my left is the kitchen, and from behind a door on my right I hear weeping, so assume this must be the parlour.

The door opens with a creak and as I step inside, Carys flings herself into my arms. "You came," she says, dampening my shoulder with her tears.

"Carys, have some decorum," scolds her mother.

"Sorry, Mami." Carys gives my hand a squeeze, then crosses the room to take her place beside the coffin, which occupies a table in the centre of the room.

It is several months since I last saw Mrs Ambrose and the change in her is shocking. Her hair has lost most of its colour, her cheeks are sunken, and the skin around her eyes is chapped and sore. The weight of grief in the room is suffocating and is so familiar I wonder if I have the strength to stay. But then Carys gives me a watery smile and I know I can't leave her side. I'm indebted to her stubborn insistence on a friendship between us, and this is my opportunity to repay what I owe.

"It is good to see you again, Miss Williams. I only wish it was in happier circumstances." Mr Jansen steps forward and takes my hand. I'd forgotten how handsome he is with his square jaw and thatch of brown hair.

"Good morning, Mr Jansen."

He smiles at me and the skin around his eyes crinkles so deeply I know he must be a man who has spent much of his life smiling, despite the hardships he has faced. "It is very good of you to come. Please, let me introduce you to my daughters, Lina and Emma."

Two little girls, both dressed in black, smile shyly at me. They keep casting glances at the coffin, and for their sakes, I am glad the lid is firmly on.

"I'll go and ready the cart," says Mr Jansen, momentarily placing a hand on Carys's lower back. I notice a look pass between them, which tells me more about their feelings than any words could.

"We're taking Dadi to the chapel on the cart," says Carys. "It's too far to carry him, especially without my brothers here to help."

At the mention of her sons, Mrs Ambrose collapses into a chair, her shoulders heaving in silent sobs. Carys rushes to her mother, and the girls' faces betray the worry they are feeling.

"Lina and Emma, shall we go into the kitchen and get you a glass of milk before we go to chapel?"

The girls jump at the chance to leave the room, and Carys gives me a nod to signal I am doing the right thing. We retreat from the room, the sound of dignified mourning following us.

"Our mother died," says Lina. "And now Mr Ambrose is dead, too."

"Oh, I am so very sorry to hear that."

Lina shrugs and Emma frowns at me. "Why are you so big?"

Despite the circumstances, I can't help but laugh. "I don't know, Emma. I suppose it is just the way God made me."

"Oh."

My answer seems to satisfy the girls, and they are happy to let me pour them milk from the jug whilst issuing a barrage of questions about what they can expect from the day.

"We shall walk behind the horse and cart to chapel, then there will be a service to remember Mr Ambrose, and his coffin will be buried in the ground, and then we may come back here for a cup of tea to share fond memories of him."

"Were you his friend?" asks Lina.

"No, I only met him once, but he struck me as a very kind man."

"But if you didn't know him, why are you here?" asks Emma.

"Because Carys is my good friend, and I want to support her on what I'm sure will be a difficult day."

Lina takes Emma's hand and looks at me with solemn eyes. "Emma is my best friend. I look after her."

"I'm pleased to hear it. Friendship is a very important, precious thing." As I realise what I am saying, I grab hold of the kitchen table to steady myself.

"Are you alright, Miss Williams?"

"I am quite well. Thank you, girls." It was Eddy who taught me not just how precious but also how precarious friendship can be. For so long, I've protected myself from it, but all the while I've been looking at things in the wrong way. I'm ashamed it has taken so long for me to understand. As precarious as friendship may be, the risk of losing it is worth it for the chance to have it in the first place.

"We are ready," says Mr Jansen, walking into the kitchen and kissing each of his girls on the tops of their heads.

"We don't want to come," says Lina, still gripping tight to her sister's hands.

"Girls, remember what I said about friendship?"

They both nod.

"Well, I hope you are both friends to Carys, just like I am?"

They nod again.

"Then we must look after our friend today, yes?"

Lina shuffles closer to me, pulling Emma along with her. With a shy glance and rosy cheeks, she whispers, "will you be our friend, too?"

Her simple request brings tears to my eyes. "Of course I will."

Satisfied, Lina slips her small hand in mine. "We will look after each other?"

"We will."

Amidst this surprising statement of solidarity, we leave the kitchen and prepare to face the day.

Chapter Thirty-Seven

Carys

April, 1916

I t's only when we're halfway to the chapel that I look behind me and
realise just how many have joined the procession. Psalms fill the air
as around me voices rise. Out in front, Florian keeps a tight grip on the
horse's reins, guiding us all along the narrow lane at a respectful pace.
The slow speed we're moving at may be out of respect, but I'm not sure
any of us could walk faster even if we wanted to. The past few days have
taken a toll on us all.

Mami's hand sits cold in mine, her thick black shawl doing nothing
to ease the chill. Her tears have all been shed and in their place is a
hollowness that scares me. I don't recognise this version of Mami, and
fear what will become of us with Dadi gone and the boys away.

The sound of Florian's voice reaches me and brings unexpected tears
to my eyes. He may be getting most of the Welsh words wrong, but
to even try means so much. Florian is one of the few men to join the
procession. There are a couple of aging farmers among the group, but
mostly it is women and children from neighbouring farms.

Ours has always been a close-knit community, but now more than
ever, we lean on each other in our grief. The letters I wrote to my
brothers and Dai have all gone unanswered, but I hope they are taking

a couple of moments to remember Dadi today, wherever in the world they are.

Boots crunch against gravel as the chapel comes into view. Florian pulls the horse to a stop, and we all follow suit. The minister walks up the path to greet us and takes both my and Mami's hands in his own, expressing his condolences.

Florian walks to the cart and without needing any signal, the elderly farmers join him. Somehow, despite their age and failing muscles, they get the simple wooden coffin onto the bier, and with one fluid movement hoist it so it rests on their shoulders. Arms locked against their opposite number's shoulder, the men take faltering steps forward, until they find their slow, mournful stride.

The minister stands in front of the coffin, the pages of his open bible fluttering in the light spring breeze. He begins to sing, and we join him in Psalm 23.

The chapel comes into view, perched on the edge of a hillside, its grey stone stark against the green surrounding it.

"Why are so many people standing outside?" I whisper to Mami as we draw near to the chapel.

"I've no idea. They should have taken their seats by now."

We were expecting only the usual congregation to be present, and with so many men away fighting, that congregation is far less than it once was. It is only when we are mere yards from the chapel doors that I realise what has happened.

"Mami, look, they are all from the WI."

"Surely not?"

"It's true, Mami. Look, there is Mrs Jones, the Colonel and his wife, Mrs Montgomery, Mrs Roberts and goodness knows who else."

I turn to Mami, and her face mirrors my own, streaked with tears, eyes wide in disbelief.

"But most of them are Anglican," she says in almost a whisper.

"That may be, but I suspect that doesn't matter to them today. If I'm not mistaken, they are not here as members of any congregation, but as our friends."

"Our... our... friends?"

"Yes, Mami."

"But they didn't know Dadi."

"Maybe not, but they know us."

"Oh, *cariad*," she says, collapsing into my arms, "such great kindness is too much for me today."

I stroke Mami's hair just as she did for me when I was little. "These friends of ours will help us through the next months and years, Mami."

With her hand clutched in mine, we blink tears away, lift our heads, and walk through the gate and along the stone path toward the chapel. Those waiting outside bow their heads, hats either raised or clasped to their chests. Ffion catches my eye and gives me a sad smile. I suspect she is the brains behind this surprise turnout of WI members, and her kindness is almost too great to bear.

As we enter the chapel, it is soon clear why a crowd waited out in the cold. There is not a spare space on any pew other than those at the front reserved for Dadi's family. The sight of so many mourners steals my breath.

With Mami sitting on one side of me, and Angharad on the other, both holding my hands, I ready myself for the service to begin.

Time is not behaving as it should. The service feels at the same time endless and over all too soon. As though in a dream, I let Angharad help me to my feet, and only as I turn do I realise the rest of the congregation are standing, heads bowed, waiting for us to follow the coffin outside.

As we process towards the churchyard, the scene around me is blurry, sounds muffled as though by a thick scarf. The only thing I'm aware of is Angharad's strong arms holding me and Mami up as we shuffle along the path.

It should be only men at the grave, but with so many away, and none of Dadi's sons present, we break with tradition and follow Dadi's coffin to the graveside. A thick black cloud slips in front of the sun and I shiver as both light and temperature drop. The minister reads from his bible.

Ashes to ashes, dust to dust...

We each take a handful of earth, which lands with a thud on the lid of Dadi's coffin. The thought of him lying there in the dark is unbearable, and I fight the urge to rip off the lid, pull him out, and hold him in my arms. Angharad, with that sixth sense she seems to possess, places an arm around me and pulls me close. Her coat holds a musty farmyard smell that is so comforting it brings about a wave of fresh tears. Her grip tightens as my shoulders shake and I draw strength from her embrace. The torrent of tears fades to a trickle, and I pull away. She lifts a hand to my face and brushes my cheek with her thumb.

"It will be alright," she says, and despite where we are standing and all the day has brought, I believe her.

Chapter Thirty-Eight

Angharad

May, 1916

"Are you sure it is alright to visit them unannounced?" Ffion asks.

I can't help but laugh at her question. "I thought that was the only way you visited people?"

"Oh, Angharad, don't be like that. It's just as well I have visited you unannounced, or we would never have become friends, and you would never have become such a valued member of the Institute. Of course, I can't take all the credit, the Colonel played his part."

"He certainly did, but you're right, Ffion. I'm not sure I've ever thanked you for forcing me out of my hermit-like existence."

"You're most welcome, but it still begs the question whether we should have warned Carys in advance of our visit."

"I'm sure she won't mind. If anything, she may be glad of the distraction." It's strange seeing Ffion so unsure of herself. She is a woman who always seems to know her own mind, a quality I have long since admired in her. But ever since Christmas, I've sensed her wavering, as though something happened to shake her self-belief. "What's brought on all this uncertainty?"

Ffion blushes. "If you must know, I have little experience of bereavement. I'm rather worried I shall say the wrong thing."

"It is better to visit and say the wrong thing than not visit at all," I say, remembering the lonely weeks and months after Eddy when the only caller I received was Bryn, who had only come to gloat.

"Is that how you felt when your parents died?"

I shrug. "I can't say I felt all that much after their deaths, other than disappointment that things couldn't have been different between us while they were alive. And they both died peacefully in their sleep at the natural end of their lives."

"Really? But I've always gotten the feeling you've suffered a great loss in your life, Angharad, and after what happened on our way back from Bangor, I wondered whether one of your parents had..."

"Nothing like that," I snap, then regret my harsh tone. "There have been other losses in my life besides my parents, but not everything needs to be spoken of."

"Sorry."

"No, I am sorry. I shouldn't have snapped at you. Right, here we are."

"The curtains are still drawn. I'd have expected them to be open by now."

"Ffion? Angharad?" Carys walks out of a nearby barn and stares at us. "I wasn't expecting a visit from you today."

"See," whispers Ffion, "I told you we should have sent a note."

"We wanted to come and see you, to see how you are. Several members of the WI have been baking for you," I say, lifting the wicker basket I'm holding.

"That is so kind of you all," says Carys. She walks over to us and I notice how thin she has grown. Her hair could do with a wash, and although she is still wearing black, her dress is stained and muddy in places.

"How have things been since the funeral?" asks Ffion, taking Carys's hand. "I hope you don't mind me saying, but you don't look all that well."

Tears glint in Carys's eyes. "Would you like a cup of tea?"

"That would be lovely," I say, "but we don't want to intrude if you've work to do."

"I'm due a break," says Carys. "I was up in the night with a difficult lambing. There seemed little point going to bed, and it's now... goodness, I don't even know what time it is."

"It's one o'clock," says Ffion, studying her smart wristwatch. "Are you telling us you've not stopped to eat or drink anything since the early hours of this morning?"

"Nothing other than a quick swig of water from a flask."

Before we can scold Carys for not looking after herself, Mr Jansen emerges from the barn looking just as tired as Carys. The cotton shirt he wears rolled up as far as the elbows has streaks of blood across it and a sheen of sweat sits against his forehead.

"I think that's the last one for today," he says, giving Carys a weary smile.

"Thank goodness for that. We're nearing the end of the lambing season," she explains, "but there are still a handful of ewes who are clinging on to their unborn lambs."

"How many workers do you have helping?"

Carys laughs and shares a wry smile with Mr Jansen. "You're looking at them. Florian's girls have been doing their best to help with work in the house, and they're now expert keepers of hens. Between us, we're trying to muddle through as best we can."

"What about your mother?" asks Ffion.

A shadow crosses Carys's face. "Mami hasn't been too good lately. She tries her best, but it's a worry. She's asleep more than she's awake these days."

"Why don't you sit down," I say, "and I'll make the tea, and find you something to eat."

"Oh, no, I don't want you going inside the farmhouse," says Carys, her eyes wide. "It's not that I don't want your company, but as hard as the girls try, they're little and I've had no time for cleaning of late."

"Carys," I say, placing a hand on her arm. "You've not seen where I live, have you?"

Ffion smiles at me. "It's very quaint, your little bothy."

I laugh. "Quaint is a polite word for it."

"You live in a bothy?" asks Carys, her eyes wide.

"On Mr Stephens' land, yes. Obviously in polite company I refer to it as my cottage, but it is a single-roomed dwelling in the middle of a field, so bothy is the most accurate term. What I'm saying, Carys, is you don't need to be house-proud around me. I can see how hard you're working, and if there is a little dust around the place, I'm not going to hold it against you."

"And you certainly don't need to worry about me," says Ffion. "The only reason my house is clean and tidy is I have servants to do it all for me."

"Even so," says Carys, "perhaps you could wait out here with me, Ffion."

Ffion frowns and seems a little offended, but Mr Jansen steps in to save the day. "Yes, Mrs Montgomery, please stay here to keep Carys company. I need to check on my girls, so will help Miss Williams with the tea while I'm at it."

"Very well. Do you have any lambs I can see?" asks Ffion, brightening at the thought.

"I've a lamb you can feed, if you want to. Her mother is struggling to produce enough milk, so I've taken over the feeding for a while."

Carys leads Ffion over to the barn and I walk with Mr Jansen toward the farmhouse.

"How is she, really?" I ask him, when we are out of earshot.

"I'm worried about her," he says. "There is far too much work for the two of us, and I fear the hours she is keeping will send her to an early grave. Added to that is the worry over her mother..."

He stops talking as we enter the farmhouse and make our way to the kitchen. There is no sign of Mrs Ambrose, but regardless, it doesn't feel right speaking about her in her own home.

"Why don't you fill the kettle and put it on the stove while I cut some bread and gather whatever I can find to go with it? Do you mind if I call the girls? They were very taken with you when you met at the funeral and have been talking about you nonstop ever since."

"Me? Are you sure?"

Mr Jansen laughs. "Quite sure, Angharad. Sorry, do you mind me using your first name?"

"Not at all."

"Then you must call me Florian. I'll fetch the girls, but I shall also make sure they leave you in peace when you are with Carys. It will do her good to spend some time with her friends. Oh and, Angharad?"

"Yes?"

"Children are excellent judges of character. My girls have taken a shine to you, and that tells me a lot about the person you are."

"Thank you," I say. After a lonely childhood and even lonelier adult years, the thought of anyone liking me is still so novel my hand shakes as I fill the kettle with water from the jug.

"Angharad!" Lina and Emma race into the room and throw their arms around my legs.

"This is a lovely welcome."

"Will you come and see the chickens?" asks Lina. "We are in charge of looking after them."

"So I hear. I'd love to come and see your chickens, but I need to make a pot of tea first."

"I'll do that," says Florian.

My eyes open in surprise and he laughs.

"I know you women can have a low opinion of us men, but some of us are capable of making a pot of tea." His voice is light, and I can tell he's teasing.

"Alright then, come on, girls, lead the way."

"I've heard Angharad is an expert on keeping hens, girls, so let's hope you pass her inspection with flying colours."

The girls square their shoulders and push their chins into the air. "We are experts too, Papa."

"Don't listen to your papa," I tell them. "You seem to know exactly what you're doing. Come on, let's go and see these hens."

Lina and Emma each take one of my hands and drag me out of the farmhouse towards the chicken coop. *Children are good judges of character.* Isn't that what Florian said? As the girls chatter away, my concerns over my friend are momentarily forgotten, and I feel so happy I could cry.

Chapter Thirty-Nine

Ffion

May, 1916

The barn is full of dust, which dances among streaks of sun coming in through gaps in the wood. My nose wrinkles at the smell of hay and animals. It is not unpleasant, but I'm not used to such rustic scents and my nostrils tingle with the prospect of a sneeze.

"Come in here," says Carys, leading me into a small fenced-off enclosure. "Sit on that bale there and hold on to this." She hands me a glass bottle full of milk with a rubber teat on the end. With expert hands, she moves aside clumps of hay to reveal a small black lamb quivering in a corner of the pen. She lifts the lamb and holds it tight to her chest as it squirms in her arms. "It's alright," she says, before singing softly. The lamb grows still, and she carries it to where I'm sitting.

"Do I need to hold it?"

"No, it's best off standing to be fed. I'll sit behind it as they have a habit of backing up. Just make sure you hold the bottle above the height of the lamb's head as we don't want it swallowing any air bubbles."

"Goodness, it's more complicated than I first thought."

"It's fine once you get the hang of it." Carys kneels down in the hay and sets the lamb between her legs, facing me.

"How old is it?"

"Only two days. There, that's it," she says as I ease the teat into the lamb's mouth. It starts sucking, yanking with surprising force on the bottle in my hands. "You're a natural."

"A natural sheep?" I ask, and Carys laughs.

"We'll make a farmer out of you yet, Mrs Montgomery," says Carys.

"Actually, I have begun an allotment, thanks to Angharad's guidance. We decided to use some of my gardens as a training ground for local women."

"With Angharad as the instructor?"

"Yes, she's only led one session so far, but it went very well."

"It's hard to believe she's the same woman we met less than a year ago."

"I know, and that awful brother of hers seems to be leaving her alone for the time being."

"Long may it continue."

We fall into a comfortable silence, the only sounds the suckling of the lamb and the rustle of hay beneath its hooves. There are so many questions I want to ask Carys, not least about the handsome Belgian she lives with, but I hold my tongue and keep my patience, waiting for Angharad to arrive.

"I think she's had enough," says Carys, kissing the lamb then patting it on the bottom to send it further into the pen. "Thank you for helping."

"It really was my pleasure."

We climb out of the pen and pull two bales of hay together to create a makeshift seating area.

"Carys, you know I wouldn't have judged you if I'd seen inside the farmhouse?"

Carys's cheeks turn pink. "I'm aware of the class difference between us. I'd be a fool not to be."

Shame causes my cheeks to match Carys's in colour. "Do I give the impression of being a snob?"

"Oh no, not at all!"

"But I must do, for you to feel I would judge you. Carys, I may have been born into the upper classes, but growing up, my family had no money. My father gambled away what inheritance he had, hence I was married off to Hector."

"Your parents married you off for money?" Carys looks horrified.

"Status too, but money was the driving force behind the match. So, you see, I may live in a big house and with all the trappings that come with a rich husband, but I'm not so different from you, and in fact, you probably have a lot more freedom."

Carys laughs. "I've told you about my sweetheart, Dai?"

"Yes, I think you mentioned him."

"He's the son of the neighbouring farmer. He's a lovely lad, but our parents engineered the match, intending to combine our acreage in the future."

Before I have a chance to respond to Carys's revelation, Angharad walks into the barn carrying a tray filled with a teapot, cups, and slices of thick bread and cheese. She sets the tray down on a spare bale, and before she's even finished pouring the tea, Carys has demolished a hunk of bread and cheese.

"Sorry," says Carys, wiping crumbs from around her mouth. "That was greedy of me, but goodness I was hungry."

"I'm not surprised. Thank you," I say, as Angharad hands me a cup and saucer.

"I can't take any credit. The girls dragged me off to look at the chickens, so this is all Florian's work."

"Florian?"

"Mr Jansen."

"Ah, yes, your Mr Jansen is rather dishy, isn't he, Carys?"

Carys's cheeks burn scarlet. "I hadn't noticed."

I hold the back of my hand to her cheek and pretend to be scalded. "You could have fooled me."

"He's a widowed refugee, and I'm promised to Dai. Whether I've noticed Mr Jansen's good looks counts for nothing."

"Just because the love between two people doesn't conform to what society expects of us doesn't mean it's wrong."

Carys and I stare at Angharad. We wait for her to say more, but she quickly changes the subject.

"How have things been since the funeral?"

"Not good. Not good at all. Dadi's death couldn't have come at a worse time, what with lambing in full swing. It would have been hard enough with Mami helping, but without her, it's been near impossible."

"Is there anything we can do to help?"

Carys looks at me with thinly veiled amusement. "That's a very kind offer, but I can't imagine you with your hand up a ewe's... never mind."

"No, I don't fancy the thought of that, but there must be other ways we can help. What about a rota of meals? I'm sure other members of the WI would be happy to muck in."

"I couldn't ask that of folk, especially not with food so scarce. And besides, Mami is a proud woman. She'd not feel comfortable accepting charity."

"We're worried about you," says Angharad. "There must be something we can do?"

"You've both got your own lives to lead, and I can't see Mr Stephens being happy for you to neglect your duties in favour of another farm."

"Maybe not."

"Your friendship is enough," says Carys, "it means an awful lot that you've taken the time to come and see me."

"Of course we did. We hate to think of you struggling alone."

"I've got Florian to help me, and the girls."

"And thank goodness for them," I say, sharing a look with Angharad. Carys isn't in a mood to be teased about it, but it's obvious there's more to her feelings for Mr Jansen than simple admiration and gratitude.

"Will you be coming to this month's meeting?" Angharad asks. "It's set to be an interesting one. Miss Antonia Williams is coming to tell us how their institute is getting on up in Holyhead, and Mrs Hunter Smith from Bangor University is going to demonstrate the easiest and most humane way of killing a fowl."

"The what?" says Carys, spluttering with laughter.

"It's important we're all resourceful," I say, trying and failing to keep the amusement out of my voice.

"Some of those ladies won't know what's hit them. Is Mrs Hunter Smith actually going to dispose of a fowl at the meeting?"

"Yes, I think so."

"Goodness. Well, it would be a shame to miss that one. I bet there'll be a few green faces in the room with all that going on. It's good they've established a WI up in Holyhead, though, isn't it?"

"Yes, and from what Jane Stapleton-Cotton told me, they're beginning to pop up all over the place. Not just in Wales either."

"Who'd have thought us Anglesey ladies would be such innovators?" says Carys, taking another bite of bread.

"It's Mrs Watt who deserves the credit."

"Yes," I say, "but from what I've heard, she'd been trying to set up the Women's Institute here in Britain for several years without success. The fact it was our band of merry women who got it going for her is something to be very proud of. Our names will go down in history, I shouldn't wonder."

"I'd be happy for my name to be kept out of it," says Angharad, true to form.

"Don't be silly," says Carys. "Whether you like it or not, you're one of us now."

"I'll drink to that," I say, holding my teacup aloft. "To the ladies of Llanfairpwll."

"To the ladies of Llanfairpwll," say Carys and Angharad, clinking their teacups against mine.

Chapter Forty

Angharad

May, 1916

I'm helping young Miss Prichard from the village harvest the spring cabbages and early turnips when a familiar voice makes my heart sink.

"What's going on here, then?"

I spin around and force a smile onto my face. "Good afternoon, Bryn. I wasn't expecting to see you today."

"You know it is my day for visiting Mr Stephens."

"Yes, but you haven't been up here to see me for a while."

"Should I have? Do you need spiritual guidance?"

"I get plenty of that at chapel on a Sunday," I say, hoping to appease him.

He ignores the compliment. "Word reached me you are inviting villagers up here and I felt it was my duty to see what was going on and check you aren't leading anyone astray."

I swallow my frustration. Will I ever be able to shake off the many labels Bryn has attached to me? "I assure you everything we're doing here is very much above board."

"I see you're using a lot more of Mr Stephens' land than you were before. Does he know about this? Are you paying him fairly for your use?"

"Mr Stephens is not only aware of what I am doing, but fully supports this scheme. I have extended my allotment to be able to provide extra food for those in need in the village, and to give guidance and experience to those hoping to begin a vegetable patch of their own. Take Miss Pritchard here. She only has a small parcel of land behind her cottage, but it is big enough to grow a few staple crops. It was all Colonel Stapleton-Cotton's idea."

"I see."

Bryn clasps his hands behind his back and begins striding up and down the grid of plots I have created. He pauses occasionally, inspecting a shoot, or to pick out a weed, as if he has any idea what he is looking at.

"Isn't it marvellous what your sister is doing?" says Miss Pritchard when he reaches the area she is working.

"It all strikes me as rather unnecessary," says Bryn. "As far as I'm aware, there is still plenty of food to go around."

"Not as much as you'd expect, Reverend Williams. And the Colonel has warned us there is likely worse to come. Targeting our food supplies could give the Germans an advantage, and we must be prepared for that eventuality. The work Angharad and others are doing could make a big difference to the outcome of the war."

Bryn tips back his head and laughs, then catches Miss Pritchard's eye and realises she is not joking. He clears his throat, wanting to keep up appearances. "Let's hope the Colonel is wrong in his gloomy prediction. From what I've heard, this war will be done and dusted before we know it."

"I certainly hope you're right, Reverend Williams," says Miss Pritchard, "but I rather think the Colonel..."

"Why don't you come and look at the bed over here?" I interrupt, knowing how much it will anger Bryn should Miss Pritchard continue her sentence. "The carrots are doing very well in this soil and should be ready for harvesting by next month."

Bryn walks to where I'm standing, turns to check Miss Pritchard is a good distance away, then lowers his voice. "I don't know what you think you're doing here, Angharad, but I consider it most unwise. What do you think Miss Pritchard's mother would think about her daughter being up here alone with you if she knew the truth? You are supposed to keep yourself well away from members of our community, not try to ingratiate yourself into their affections. You're playing a dangerous game, Angharad. All it would take to put a stop to all this is one word from me in the right ear. You remember that, dear sister."

I nod, unable to reply. Over the past months, I've been questioning Bryn's view of me and how I see myself. But there is no denying on one matter he is right. One quiet word in the ear of a respectable member of the village, and I would become a pariah.

"Tread carefully, Angharad," says Bryn, as he prepares to leave. "Tread very carefully indeed."

"I'm going to make a cup of tea," I tell Miss Pritchard once Bryn has disappeared down the lane. "Would you like one?"

"No, thank you, I had better be getting home."

"Make sure you take those cabbages and turnips with you."

"Are you sure? Why don't I leave some for you?"

"I've plenty here to keep me going," I say with a smile.

"You are very kind. Is it alright if I pop up here again next week? I should like to help you plant out the swede."

"Of course, you are welcome any time, Miss Pritchard."

"Do you know," she says, surveying the allotment, then turning to gaze at the distant mountains, "this is quickly becoming one of my favourite places to be."

"I'm glad to hear it."

Miss Pritchard takes her leave, and I retreat into my bothy, still shaken from Bryn's visit. Perhaps it was a mistake to invite anyone to come to the allotment. The plan had been to teach my classes in the grounds of Ffion's grand home, but when a couple of the younger ladies asked to see my allotment, relief at some extra pairs of hands outweighed any shame at admitting to my humble abode. That's not to say I didn't choose wisely. Miss Pritchard and her friend Miss Ross are both kind souls, unlikely to judge me for my bothy, or report my circumstances to others as gossip.

I pour myself a cup of tea, carry it to the door and lay it down on the front step. Unable to stop my hands from shaking, I indulge in a rare treat. From the back of a cupboard door, I pull out a tin box, carry it back to the front step, and open it. Eddy's pipe. So afraid am I of breaking one of the few items of Eddy's I still own, that it rarely comes out of its box, but today I need a reminder of how things once were.

With the pipe between my lips, I hold a match to the tobacco and take a series of quick sharp puffs. The tobacco catches and I push a long plume of smoke out from my lungs. It swirls around me, the sweet scent of the burning tobacco carrying me back through my memories, to a happier time.

Chapter Forty-One

Ffion

May, 1916

H ector is angrier than I think I have ever seen him.

"It's a disgrace, an utter disgrace, I tell you!"

"I know, darling, but what can we do? The law has changed, and unless you intend to become a conscientious objector, there's nothing for it but to comply."

"Conscientious objector? Pah, I'd rather die in the fields of France than have my good name sullied by all that nonsense. What about my business, eh? It's all very well dragging every man under the age of fifty off to war, but the country will collapse in our absence. What's the point of fighting for our country if there's no one left to run it? We'd be better off letting ourselves be taken over by the Germans."

"You don't mean that."

"Don't I? This country is going to pot, and things are only going to get worse."

"You may find you're given a role on home soil. Surely it's unlikely a man of your status will fight on the front line."

"And what's that supposed to mean? Are you calling me a coward? You think it's fear that's stopping me from heading off to fight, is that it?"

"No, that's not what I'm saying."

"I need a drink." Hector crosses the room and pulls out the stopper from a cut glass bottle. He fills a glass to the brim with whisky and downs it in several gulps. He refills the glass, and the alcohol has the desired effect of calming him a little.

Now might not be the best time to put an idea to my husband that has been brewing in my mind, but if I don't try now, it will be too late. "Hector, I've been thinking about what to do with the house while you're away."

"What are you talking about, woman? You want to lock it up and return to London? That's fine by me if you do. I'm beginning to wish we never came to this godforsaken island."

"No, I'm happy to stay here."

"Really? I thought you hated it?"

"My work with the Women's Institute is proving rather fulfilling."

"That so? Well, if knitting, flower arranging and piddling about in the garden keep you busy, who am I to complain?"

"As I was saying, about the house, darling... With so many soldiers returning home with ghastly injuries, there is a growing need for con-valescent homes."

"You want to go off and play at nursing, is that it?"

"No..." I stand beside him and place a hand on his arm. "I was thinking we could offer the house, for a limited time, of course."

"This house? You want to turn this house into a hospital?"

"Not a hospital, no, a convalescent home."

"Do what you like with the place," spits Hector, his earlier frustra-tion back with full force. Spittle gathers on his moustache, and his face is a deep red. "It's not as if I'm going to be here to enjoy the place, is it?"

As Hector storms from the room, I can't help but smile. Of course, I hope he doesn't come to any harm, but the thought of being free of him for months, possibly years on end, fills me with a rush of pleasure. Once I would have dreaded being alone for so long, but thanks to the WI, I am no longer lonely. If it weren't so late, I'd head straight to the Red Cross and offer our house to them.

I can hear Hector stomping about in his study, no doubt muttering to himself about the unfairness of his situation. He'll be in there for hours, no doubt, so I use the opportunity to wander the house, visualising what it could become.

"Oh, madam, anything I can help you with?" asks Mrs Edwards as I wander into the large, well-equipped kitchen.

"Well, perhaps there is. I've had an idea about the house. Is Susan nearby? It would be good if she was here to hear my idea."

"Did you call me, madam?" asks the maid, scurrying into the kitchen.

"No, but I'm glad you're here. You may have gathered from all the shouting that my husband has been called up to fight in the war. With the children away at school, it seems silly keeping a cook, maid and butler all for myself."

Mrs Edwards and Susan exchange a worried glance.

"Oh, goodness, I'm sorry. I'm not talking about letting you go. Why don't we sit down and perhaps, Susan, you could make us a pot of tea?"

"Of course, madam."

"Are you hungry, madam? I have some Welsh cakes not long out of the oven."

"That would be lovely, thank you."

The two women fuss around, and from the looks they keep throwing my way, I can tell they are uneasy. Nerves tremble in my stomach, for if Mrs Edwards and Susan are against my idea, it will leave me in quite a pickle. From what I've heard, there is already a shortage of nurses and volunteers to run the many hospitals and convalescent homes popping up, and if my staff refuses to offer their help, the idea will be scuppered.

"Thank you," I say, as Susan lays a cup and saucer in front of me. "Please, both of you, take a seat." Mrs Edwards and Susan sit at the far end of the table, and I laugh. "Move closer, please. I don't bite, and this isn't an interview."

They each give me a nervous smile and carry their own cups to the seats either side of me.

"What I wanted to discuss with you is an idea I've had to turn this house into a convalescent home for wounded soldiers. But I would need your help to do it."

"Blimey," says Mrs Edwards, "I thought you were going to give us the heave-ho!"

"Of course not, Mrs Edwards. I don't know what I'd do without the pair of you. How do you both feel about my proposal?"

"Would it be just the two of us helping you?" asks Susan.

"I shouldn't think so. There are so many bedrooms, and we'd have to open up all the rooms that are currently out of use. We'd need reinforcements."

"I'm not sure how I feel about strangers taking over my kitchen."

"As permanent members of my staff, you'd obviously still be in charge of your own areas, but there's no doubt you'd need some help if we fill this house."

"Like a kitchen hand?" asks Mrs Edwards.

"Precisely."

"Well, if that's the case, I'm all for the idea. My son James was injured only last month. He lost his right eye and is in a hospital somewhere over in England."

"I'm so sorry to hear that," I say, shocked that I've been oblivious to the weight Mrs Edwards has been carrying on her shoulders.

"And my brothers and father are all away fighting," says Susan. "If any of them get hurt, I'd like to know they had somewhere as lovely as Plas Llanfair to stay while they get better."

"Wonderful," I say, "then it's decided. I shall approach the Red Cross tomorrow with my offer, and then we'd better get started opening up the rooms and getting this place shipshape!"

Chapter Forty-Two

Angharad

June, 1916

Unlike the early days of meetings, now I enjoy arriving early with enough time to greet my fellow members before the meeting begins.

"You've stopped hunching," Ffion whispers in my ear, as she comes to join a conversation I'm having with Mrs Francis and Mrs Ross. "It's wonderful to see."

I smile at her, recognising just how far I've come. Amongst these women, I no longer feel a freak. No one notices my unusual height, extra-enormous feet or dinner-plate hands. When these women speak to me, they look me in the eye, as if concentrating far more on what's inside rather than out. Of course, each time new members join, as they frequently do, I get the same old stares and whispers, but those moments pass quickly enough.

"Look," says Ffion, "there's Carys."

"Oh good, you're here," I say, as a tired-looking Carys squeezes around groups of chattering women to join us.

"Yes, I'm sorry I couldn't make it to last week's meeting. I'm sure the Colonel was well intentioned organising an extraordinary meeting, but it's hard enough getting to one meeting a month, let alone two. Did I miss anything important?"

"Mrs Hobbs from the Agricultural Organization Society gave a lecture on the conserving and bottling of fruit. It was very interesting, but we can pass on all her tips, if you'd like them?"

Carys shakes her head. "I know how important preserving food is at the moment, but I've already got too much on my plate to add anything else. I'll mention it to Mami, though. It might do her good to have something to occupy her time."

"She's still not too good?" I ask, but before Carys can answer, we are asked to take our seats.

Mrs Jones reads the minutes of the previous meeting, and we all accept them, and then a rosy-cheeked woman in an apron who is introduced as Mrs Edwards gets to her feet, and a table groaning with food is carried over and placed in front of her.

"Mrs Edwards works for me at the house," whispers Ffion. "We've had to get very creative with making cheap meals since the convalescent home opened, so I asked if she'd come along and give a demonstration."

"What a wonderful idea."

"Yes, but she took a bit of persuading. She was certain it was a waste of good food, but I convinced her to think of the greater good if every woman is armed with her skilful recipes."

"You could charm the birds from the trees," I tease, before turning my attention back to Mrs Edwards and her table of food.

We are treated to an explanation on how to make cawl, a dish so familiar to me I lose interest, but then Mrs Edwards moves on to a variety of ways to use the herring and mackerel so abundant in our waters and my interest is piqued. She then demonstrates how to make Bara Lawr, which I've never been able to master, despite collecting copious amounts of seaweed to try. By the time Mrs Edwards reaches her final dish, leek and potato soup, I feel armed with a selection of recipes sure to put a smile on Mr Stephens' face. Carys, too, seems enthralled by Mrs Edwards, the ability to make cheap meals never so important to her as now.

Mrs Edwards takes her seat to a round of noisy applause. Ffion gives her an approving nod and Mrs Edward's cheeks flush an even deeper red at the praise.

"And now," says the Colonel, "Miss Dickenson will speak to us on the subject of Child Welfare."

I'm ashamed to admit Child Welfare isn't a topic I've ever given much thought to. Children have always seemed an alien race, free from the social niceties that adults possess to spit their barbed insults freely. And with no children of my own, my experience of them has been limited to the recent affection of Lina and Emma, and I suspect they are the exception, not the rule, when it comes to kindness.

"Thank you for inviting me to speak on Child Welfare," begins Miss Dickenson. "It is a topic close to my heart and one I feel we should all be taking time to consider, particularly in these dark days of war. Often, the children most in need are kept out of sight, and therefore out of mind. In some of the worst instances I have seen in my work with The Children's Society, children are abandoned by parents who, through no fault of their own, no longer have the means to support their offspring."

Several women in the room tut, and Miss Dickenson frowns.

"I would suggest that rather than judgement, these parents should be shown some compassion."

That shuts the tutting ladies up.

"You'd probably be surprised just how easy it is to fall into poverty. Even before war broke out, if the man of the house was injured, he would be unable to work, and a family who until that point had been getting by, would suddenly find it impossible to feed every mouth in the house. Now, with so many of our men going off to fight in the war, households are struggling more than ever. Women, as you know, are doing a valiant job of taking over the roles men previously occupied, but with children to look after, homes to run, and less earning capacity than their male counterparts, more and more families are falling into abject poverty.

"Now, you might think you know of no such cases? I shouldn't imagine you would. Poverty is often considered taboo, a dirty word. The women and children who find themselves in this situation are no different from you or me. They are proud people, who will often struggle through until it kills them before reaching out for help. We at The Children's Society do all we can for such families, but until the issue is more widely acknowledged, and the shame attached to such circumstances is removed, these cases will persist, and with the way the war is going, they are also likely to increase.

"So, that is a little background and a glance over at some of the root causes. Now, I would like to address one of the most pressing issues facing these poor little souls. Access to medical treatment. In peace time, these families often cannot afford any form of health care, so what would be quite minor ailments for children of wealthier families can often lead to infant mortality in the poor. For these children, there is no early diagnosis to prevent the development of serious conditions, and even with a diagnosis, parents are unable to afford the medicine their children might need.

"Since conscription was brought in, many of our local doctors have been called into service, and any women with nursing training are enlisted in helping the many wounded soldiers returning from the front line. This has put an enormous strain on our local healthcare provision, and the poor families of which I speak have slipped even further down the pecking order.

"Am I right in thinking that the Women's Institute was the brain-child of one Mrs Adelaide Hoodless in Canada, who had lost an infant due to contaminated milk, and who wanted to educate rural families on basic hygiene principles?"

A murmuring of agreement ripples around the room.

"Good, then I cannot think of a better organisation to take up our concerns of child welfare right here on Anglesey, and in wider Wales. As a group, you have already demonstrated a formidable ability to fundraise and mobilise and educate the local population into increasing food production, and I have no doubt the same principles can be applied to the subject of Child Welfare. I am not here to suggest any solutions, for this is a most complex problem. My role in addressing you today is to begin a conversation, to focus minds, and to partner with a most inspirational group of women, and by that, I mean you."

Laughter fills the summerhouse as we bask in Miss Dickenson's praise. Already pockets of conversation have broken out around the room as Mrs Cotton thanks Miss Dickenson and announces it is time for tea.

Ffion, Carys and I turn in our seats to join a conversation between Mrs Roberts, Mrs Thomas, and Mrs Jones.

"That was a most thought-provoking talk," says Mrs Roberts. "I'd love us to find ways to help those poor little mites."

"I quite agree," says Mrs Jones. "Something which has been on my mind for a while is whether in the future we might enlist the help of a nurse."

"Oh, what a wonderful idea," says Ffion, clapping her hands. "I'm all for that. It is all very well meeting once a month for lectures and drinking tea, but it is when we put our minds to practical matters that we make the most difference."

"As is apparent in the Colonel's drive to get us increasing food production," says Mrs Thomas.

"Quite," agrees Mrs Roberts, "I don't think there's a back garden in Llanfairpwll that hasn't been dug up for growing carrots."

We are all still laughing when Mrs Jones turns to me. "What about a tea party for some children being housed by The Children's Society?"

I've no idea why she's looking at me, but as she is, I feel I must answer. "That sounds like a wonderful idea, Mrs Jones."

"I knew I could count on you, Miss Williams."

"I'm sorry. I'm not sure what you mean?"

"Well, with all the skill you've shown teaching the locals about vegetables, you seem the most natural fit to organise something for the children."

"I'm sorry, Mrs Jones, but I think vegetables are rather different to children. Surely Mrs Montgomery would be better placed, given she has children of her own."

"I'm far too busy getting the convalescent home up and running," says Ffion. "And besides, I think Mrs Jones is right, you have such a calm manner with the villagers you've been helping, I'm sure you could apply that same approach to a group of children in need."

"And look at how much the Jansen girls love you," says Carys.

As our gathering breaks up and we all head to the back of the room for tea, I can't shake the feeling that my friends have somehow set me up. It's one thing helping the women of the village to grow a few carrots and turnips, but children? The thought of spending an afternoon in a room full of children puts the fear of God into me.

Chapter Forty-Three

Angharad

July, 1916

I t takes all my effort to hide my reaction to seeing the children. They arrive at the summerhouse accompanied by Miss Dickenson and two of her colleagues, and it is impossible to guess their ages, as they are all so small. Their clothes hang from frames so bony and fragile a stiff breeze might snap them in half. In fairness to The Children's Society, those under their care are at least clean, but those who have come from elsewhere have faces smudged with dirt, and all have a hollow look in their eyes.

"Now, children," says Miss Dickenson. "We are very fortunate to be here with Miss Williams and Mrs Jones, so I expect you all to be on your best behaviour. These kind ladies have laid on a special tea for you, so if you'd like to find a seat at one of the tables, we shall eat and afterwards play some games."

The children rush to find a place at one of the tables hastily donated from various village homes. When I'd arrived earlier to set everything up, Mr Jones had greeted me with a shrug of resignation that his summerhouse was being taken over yet again. Given we had both limited time and resources, I can't help but feel that Mrs Jones and I have done a rather good job.

The tables are covered in white sheets, with crockery begged and borrowed from WI members, who have also contributed various dishes to the meal. I still can't quite get used to the generosity of the women I have come to know, especially in these times of war. In the centre of each table sits a small glass jar filled with wildflowers that I collected during my walk into the village.

"Angharad," says Mrs Jones. "I've left one of my water jugs down at the house. Can you get the children settled and explain to them what will happen with the food? I think it's easiest if one table at a time comes up and selects what they want, although we must be careful with portion sizes, as we don't want to run out."

"Me? You want me to speak to the children?"

"Yes, you've had plenty of practice speaking to a group since you joined the WI."

I nod, not wanting to admit how much these small people scare me. Some of them will no doubt have either heard things about me, or drawn their own conclusions if they've spotted me walking through the village. They terrify me, with their unfiltered thoughts, and stinging tongues.

"I shan't be long," says Mrs Jones. "Best talk to them now before they get too wild." With a pat on my arm and a fleeting smile, she leaves me alone with Miss Dickenson and her many charges.

With my feet slightly apart and my head held high, I take a deep breath. "Children," I say, waiting for them to be quiet. "Children?"

Miss Dickenson claps her hands together three times and the children are quiet. She turns to me and gives me a reassuring nod. "Best give your instructions in Welsh," she tells me. "Not all the children here speak English."

"*Yn sicr*, Miss Dickenson," I say, trying to rid the shake from my voice as I switch to my first language. "Now you have each found a place to sit, I shall explain a little of how this afternoon will work. Mrs Jones and I have laid the food out on a table at the back of the room. We shall call one table at a time to come and make their selection, but please do not be greedy, as we must make sure there is plenty to go around. Once you have finished your meal, please make use of the games we have left out on the tables, but stay in your seats until everyone has finished eating."

Mrs Jones enters the summerhouse, and I breathe a sigh of relief. We take our positions at the table covered in various plates of food, and Miss Dickenson sends the first group of children up to us.

The children are an interesting mix of nervous, confident, polite and rude. One boy demands extra potatoes and is quite rude to Mrs Jones when she refuses. Another boy won't even look me in the eye and gives the tiniest nod of his head when I ask if he would like a slice of bread and butter. A little girl with pigtails, wearing a dress so old it has almost worn through, begins every request with 'please', and ends them all with 'thank you'.

We are onto our third and penultimate group of children when a small boy with matted red curls stops in front of me and looks up. "Why are you so big?" he asks.

My cheeks flush and I prepare myself for the taunts of those around him, but instead of insults, they stare at me with curious eyes. "Well," I say, "my father was a very tall man, so I suppose I take after him."

The boy nods as though satisfied by the answer, but then cocks his head to one side and looks puzzled. "Do you think I shall be as big as you one day?"

"I should think so," I say, guessing this is the answer he wants to hear. "Is your dadi a big man?"

The boy frowns. "I don't know."

"You don't know? Well, is he as tall as me?"

"I've never met him."

The boy's matter-of-fact tone is startling.

"I met my dadi," says the little girl beside him, "but then he died in the war."

"Mine went away to England to find work."

"I know my dadi," says another, "but Mami is dead."

"I don't have a mami or a dadi," says an older girl who has just joined the queue, "so you lot can all shut up with your moaning."

"How are we all getting on here?" says Miss Dickenson, appearing by my side to save the day.

"Very well," says Mrs Jones, giving me a quick wink.

"What games will we play after dinner?" asks one boy.

"We're going to play Blind Man's Buff to begin with," I say.

"Then can we play Cuddio a Chwilio?"

"Hide and seek? I don't see why not."

"Dal a Rhydd?"

"Hmm, I'm not sure. How do you feel about this lot playing tag on your lawn, Mrs Jones?"

Mrs Jones smiles at the children. "Dal a Rhydd is allowed, so long as no one tramples across any of my flowerbeds."

"We won't," promise the children in front of us.

The little boy with the matted red curls hangs back at the table as the others go to take their seats.

"Is there something else you need?" I ask him.

"I... if... well..."

I walk around the table and crouch down in front of him, shocked that even on my knees I'm still towering over him. His small pocket is bulging and his legs are shaking.

"Is there something you'd like to tell me?" I ask, pointing at his pocket.

The boy flushes, and tears pool in his eyes. "I know I shouldn't have... but..."

I hold out my hand and as he pulls a bread roll from his pocket, a single tear drops from his eye to the floor. "What's your name?"

"Samuel."

"Samuel, my name is Miss Williams and I'm not very happy about this." I'm trying to sound cross, but it is very hard when faced with the boy's tears. "You know stealing is wrong, don't you, Samuel?"

"Yes," he says, another tear falling to the ground. "But I was worried I'd get hungry later."

"I see. Well," I say, lowering my voice to a whisper, "you did the right thing admitting to the theft, so how about we say no more about it? And if there's any food left over, perhaps you can take a few items home with you?"

Samuel nods, and his cheeks flush slightly. "If... if..."

"What is it, Samuel? You don't have another bread roll hidden on your person, do you? How about inside your shoe?"

This puts a small smile on his face and shakes his head. "If... if we play any team games, will you be on my team?"

"You want me to play with you?"

He nods and his cheeks grow redder. "I'd... I'd like to be your friend. You're so big," he says, "but not in a scary way. You're like a kind, pretty giant."

I can't help but laugh, taking his words as the compliment they are meant. "I'd be honoured to be on a team with you, Samuel. But if we're to be teammates, you'd better eat your dinner up or you'll have no energy to play."

"Alright. Thank you for my food, Miss Williams."

"You're most welcome, Samuel."

When I look up, I see Miss Dickenson and Mrs Jones watching me. Have I done the wrong thing by talking to the little boy? Should I have scolded him more for stealing the bread? It is with apprehension that I return to my position behind the table.

"What did he say to you?" asks Miss Dickenson. I try to hear a rebuke in her tone, but find none.

"He asked if I'd be on his team for games, and if I'd be his friend."

"There's something you should know about Samuel," says Miss Dickenson. She sighs and, in that moment, I can see how exhausted she is. "He was placed in our care two months ago, after his mother could no longer cope. She's struggled by for seven years, but since war came and prices for ordinary food have risen, it all became too much for her."

"She was raising Samuel alone?"

"Yes. They've been in and out of the workhouse most of his life. The thing is, Miss Williams, since Samuel arrived with us, he hasn't uttered a word."

"Really?"

"Not even yes or no. You're the first person he has spoken to since leaving his mother's side. Thank you, from the bottom of my heart. I don't know how you did it, but you've achieved more in five minutes than we have in eight weeks."

"I did nothing special."

"Well, whatever you did... oh goodness, someone has just knocked over their glass of milk. Please excuse me."

Miss Dickenson rushes off, and I struggle to untangle the feelings inside me. My new friend Samuel has put my own problems into perspective and I'm ashamed of what a coward I've been for so long. All that time I've been hiding away, trying to protect my reputation, I could have been doing good for others. For so long I've blamed Bryn for my small, narrow life, but now I realise it has been my fear holding me captive.

"They say children are excellent judges of character," says Mrs Jones with a smile.

This is the second time someone has said this recently. Perhaps it's about time I started believing the truth in those words and trusting the judgment of Samuel, Lina, and Emma rather than my own.

Chapter Forty-Four

Ffion

July, 1916

"Oh my goodness, Ffion. You've transformed this place."

It's impossible not to feel a surge of pride at Angharad's words.

"Was this your drawing room?" asks Carys.

"It was," I say, turning to look around a room that is now unrecognisable. All the previous furniture has been removed and stored in one of the bedrooms upstairs; in its place are five beds lining each of the long walls. "This seemed like the most logical place to set up the main ward, as many of the soldiers who come to us are so immobile, stairs would prove too great a challenge."

"You're not using the rooms on the upper floors?" asks Angharad.

"Oh, we are. Some of them are being used as private rooms for soldiers whose symptoms are... different."

"Different?" asks Carys.

"A lot of the soldiers coming to us have as much wrong with their minds as their bodies," I say, lowering my voice so the patients won't hear me. "The most extreme cases go to specialist hospitals, but we still take some men who need peace and quiet. They are housed in the rooms upstairs at the back of the house, where there are fewer sudden noises and more peace. We also use some rooms up there for staff quarters. Some of the Red Cross volunteers come from the mainland, and it's easier for them to take a room here than go back and forth each day."

"And you're running things?"

"I'm in charge of the overall management of the house," I explain, "but with no small amount of help from the Red Cross. I'm not medically trained, so there's a limit to what I can do, but I know this building like the back of my hand, and it's funny how transferable party organising skills are." I laugh, trying to downplay my involvement, but my friends aren't fooled by my modesty.

"You are quite something," says Carys, turning full circle to take in all we have built.

"Are you pretty ladies going to come and say hello?" calls one of the wounded soldiers.

"Private Macky, I hope you're not trying your luck with my friends?"

"Come with me," I say, leading Carys and Angharad over to Private Macky's bed.

"Charlie," he says, holding out a hand.

If Carys and Angharad are shocked by the flat sheet where his legs should be, they don't show it. They each take his hand in a firm shake and introduce themselves.

"So how do you girls know Mrs Montgomery?" he asks.

"From the Women's Institute," says Angharad.

"Oh yes, I've heard all about it," says Charlie. "Bloomin' good work you're doing up there, from what I hear."

"We try to do our bit," says Carys.

"I've always thought women were overlooked in this world," says Charlie. "If you met my mami, you'd agree. Put her on the front line and we'd have won this war months ago. She's that bossy, she'd have had the Germans laying down their guns and cleaning up the mess they've created in no time."

We all laugh, and it warms my heart to hear Charlie so cheerful. His charm and jollity hide a man damaged not only physically but from what he has encountered in the fields of France. Each night since he arrived, nightmares have woken him, and most of those nights, I've had to sit by his side until he drifted back into a fitful sleep.

"If you don't mind, Private Macky, we'll love you and leave you. My friends here work on farms, so can only spare an hour to visit us at this time of year. They're keen to see the rest of the home."

"Of course," says Charlie, his face dropping in disappointment.

It is Angharad who picks up on his change of mood. To my great surprise, she reaches across and takes his hand. "It has been our pleasure to meet you, Private Macky. I wonder if you would mind if I visited you again? I bet you've some tales you can tell about that strong mother of yours, and I for one should love to hear them."

Charlie's eyes light up and I notice tears glistening in his eyes. "Would you? As grateful as I am to have landed up in Mrs Montgomery's fine home, it gets boring lying here all day."

"Perhaps the next time I come, we could borrow a bath chair and take a turn around the grounds?"

"A pretty woman offering to take me out for a spin? How could I refuse?"

I notice Angharad blush and wonder how many men have noticed her beauty before. From her reaction, I'm assuming it's not many.

"I'll liaise with Angharad and the nurses and we'll find a time in the next few days for her to visit again. You'd better make sure you follow all Matron's orders though, Charlie, or she'll not be letting you out of that bed."

"Matron scares me far more than Mami ever did," he says in a stage whisper.

"It was lovely to meet you," says Carys, taking his hand again.

"I'll see you soon," says Angharad, waving as we leave the drawing room.

"That was kind of you," I tell Angharad when we are back in the entrance hall.

She shrugs and says it's nothing.

"Let me show you the beating heart of the home," I say, leading them down a passage and into the kitchen.

"Oh, hello there," says Mrs Edwards. "Mrs Montgomery giving you the tour, is she?"

"She certainly is," says Carys. "It's so impressive what you're all doing here. It must be quite the job to feed all these hungry mouths."

"It keeps me on my toes," says Mrs Edwards.

"Without Mrs Edwards, this place would fall apart."

"I can imagine," says Angharad. "Oh, by the way, we tried out quite a few of the recipes you showed us when we hosted a children's gathering earlier in the month. All the dishes went down a storm."

Mrs Edwards puffs out with pride, and I wonder if Angharad has any idea what a gift it is to read exactly what people need after only a brief interaction. Whether it's poor old Charlie, Mrs Edwards, or the great and good of Llanfairpwll, Angharad's sensitivity is hard to miss.

"Can I get you ladies a cup of tea?" asks Mrs Edwards. "I may even rustle up a piece of cake."

"Don't tempt me," says Carys. "I need to be getting back to the farm, but I'd love to try your cake another time."

I hide my disappointment at Carys's early departure, knowing how much she has on her plate at the moment. "Do you need to rush off as well?" I ask Angharad.

"I've plenty of work to do back at the farm, but the offer of tea and cake is too hard to refuse, and besides, I'd like to see the rest of the set-up here, if that's alright?"

"Of course it is."

"Why don't you ladies go off and explore, and by the time you're done, I'll have some tea and cake waiting for you."

"Thank you, Mrs Edwards. Shall we?" I lead Angharad back along the corridor and upstairs, her obvious enthusiasm for the house filling me with confidence that I have in fact done the right thing. All I can hope is that when Hector next comes home on leave, he feels the same way.

Chapter Forty-Five

Angharad

September, 1916

The change I've noticed in myself over the past year is undermined by the nerves I feel in attending my first committee meeting. It is one thing attending meetings as a bystander, but quite another being part of the committee. The women here are of a different class to me. All are wealthy, some are well educated, and they have the kind of power and influence I can barely imagine.

Unlike our usual meetings, I walk in to find a large table filling the middle of the room with chairs positioned around it. There is nowhere to hide, and I'm tempted to turn on my heel and head straight back to the farm.

"Miss Williams," says Ffion, "you remember Mrs Watt?"

"Of course," I say, crossing the room and accepting there will be no escape now. "It's a pleasure to see you again. Are you staying with Mrs Montgomery?"

"I didn't think Mrs Watt would fancy bunking in with a room full of soldiers," says Ffion with a smile.

"Trust me, I've had worse," says Mrs Watt, with her usual dry delivery and sparkling eyes. "Colonel and Mrs Stapleton-Cotton are hosting me, which is most kind of them."

"It is. And how long are you staying in Llanfairpwll?"

"Only one night, unfortunately. I've grown rather fond of this part of the world, but duty calls. I'll be at the anniversary meeting later on today, then tomorrow I'm off to meet with some fellows at Bangor University."

"Gosh, you are busy."

"Well, Miss Williams, as Lord Chesterfield once said, 'idleness is the only refuge of weak minds, and the holiday of fools'." With a chuckle, Mrs Watt wanders off to take her position at the table. I watch her and wonder at her confidence and unusual drive. It is impossible not to be inspired by her, particularly knowing what she went through with her husband's suicide. She puts my behaviour to shame, and not for the first time, I regret the self-imposed isolation I endured for so many years.

Ffion pulls out a chair for me and we sit beside each other at the table. The Colonel opens the meeting with a vote of thanks for Mrs Watt's attendance and then his wife takes charge. Jane Stapleton-Cotton seems frailer than usual, and I wonder if she has some illness she is trying to conceal. But suffering or not, she continues with the matters of business undeterred. First, she proposes fourteen new members, which Mrs Roberts seconds, and we agree.

The recruitment of new members no longer holds the fear for me it once did. I've now been in the WI long enough to feel settled, and if new members find me strange, or keep their distance, I know I can rely on Ffion and Carys to remain by my side.

"I propose," says Mrs Cotton, "that programmes for one year be drawn up, in both English and Welsh."

There is a general murmur of support for this motion. I can switch between English and Welsh comfortably, but I still remember the days of trying to teach Eddy my native language and know that several of the Welsh speakers struggle in just the same way with English. I've come to realise the Women's Institute is keen on tolerance, and using both languages feels like a sensible step.

Other suggestions are put to the committee, all of which, thankfully, I fully support. Although my first experience on the committee is going well, I wouldn't like to disagree and draw attention to myself. We accept proposals for a War Loan Association to be formed, a Suggestion Box to be used, and a Roll Call to be tried, among other measures.

"We've two hours before the anniversary meeting starts," says Ffion. "Will you go back to the farm?"

"By the time I get back there, I'll have to come out again."

"Why don't you come to my house then? I'm sure Private Macky would be glad to see you."

I smile at the thought of my new friend. "And I him."

We leave Graig together and begin the short walk to Plas Llanfair.

"How did you find your first committee meeting?" asks Ffion.

"Better than I expected."

"And what did you expect?" asks Ffion, laughter in her voice.

"I don't know, I suppose I wasn't sure I'd fit in, but everyone was very welcoming."

"Of course they were. Haven't you realised by now that the WI runs by working collectively? We look for what unites us in a common purpose, not that which divides. You've more than proved yourself over the past year, Angharad. You deserve a place at the table, and I was very glad to see you there."

"I'm looking forward to the anniversary meeting later."

"So am I. Isn't it strange to think we've had our WI now for over a year? It doesn't feel possible."

"Perhaps, but then just look at how much we've all changed. You running your hospital, Carys almost singlehandedly keeping her farm afloat."

"And you stepping up and doing your bit rather than hiding away like the timid mouse you once were."

Ffion nudges me to show she's joking, and I smile. She is wrong, of course. It wasn't shyness that kept me hidden away from society. Sometimes I forget the threat of Bryn and Anne as the keepers of my secret. Sometimes I can pretend I have moved on from those days of fear and secrecy, but however much I try to convince myself otherwise, my downfall is only one word away, and I'll do well to remember that.

Chapter Forty-Six

Ffion

November, 1916

"Are you sure it's alright for me to pop out for a few hours?"

"Of course," says Matron, "the place won't fall down in your absence."

I nod, irritated at how somehow Matron has assumed the role of my superior, despite the convalescent home being in my house, with me supposedly managing it. I haven't yet mentioned to her that Hector is due home on leave soon. His reaction to the change at Plas Llanfair doesn't bear thinking about. An image comes to mind of Hector and some unknown woman in the stables, and bile rises in my throat. I shake my head and fix a smile on my face. I'm sure it was a one-off. Hector has never strayed so close to home before, and I like to think he wouldn't be so foolish as to do so again.

"You off out somewhere nice, Mrs Montgomery?" Charlie asks, descending the stairs on his bottom.

It's impossible not to smile at the sight of him bumping his way down, one step at a time.

"I hope you're not laughing at me, Mrs Montgomery?"

"Of course not, Private Macky. I'm smiling with pride. It's amazing how far you've come in a few short months. You'll be leaving this place before we know it."

A shadow crosses Charlie's face, and I could kick myself for being so insensitive.

"I hope you won't be getting rid of me just yet," says Charlie.

"Of course not. You're welcome here until you're good and ready to leave."

"Thank you, Mrs Montgomery. Anyhow, you didn't answer my question. Are you off somewhere nice?"

Matron frowns, tuts, and shakes her head before marching off. She disapproves of my friendliness with the soldiers in our care, but after all they've been through, I can't see how a little friendship can hurt.

"I'm off to the Women's Institute."

"Oh, yeah, of course. Funny though, isn't it, how you let the Colonel join in?"

"And don't forget Tinker, the dog. They're the exception, not the rule," I say, "so don't think about trying to wangle an invitation. As far as I'm aware, no other Women's Institute in the land has ever admitted a man to their ranks, or probably ever will."

"I guess the clue's in the name. Oh, while you're there, can you tell Angharad I've finished the book she gave me and am ready to move on to the next?"

"Of course I will. I'm sure she'll be glad of an excuse to visit." The blossoming friendship between Angharad and Charlie is a joy to behold. As far as I'm aware, there are no romantic feelings on either side, but they seem to have found an affinity with one another, which warms my heart. "I'd best get going. Do you need any help to get back into your chair?"

"Nah, all part of my rehabilitation, Mrs Montgomery. If I'm ever to find work when I leave here, I'll need to get around by myself."

"Of course." I pull on my coat and let myself out of the house, but as I walk along the drive, my thoughts remain with Charlie. Even if he gets the hang of prosthetic legs, it's hard to imagine what employer will take on a man with so great a disability. And Charlie will be one of many broken men once this war is over and done with. As I reach Graig, I push the thoughts from my mind. The Institute is a hope for the future, especially since the Colonel's remarkable donation of one hundred and fifty pounds towards our building fund.

"Oh, Angharad," I say, running to catch up to my friend. She turns and smiles a greeting. "Charlie asked me to let you know he's finished the latest book you brought him and has asked for a replacement."

"Goodness, he needs to slow down, or I'll run out of books!"

"Is it too much, your visits to him, I mean? Only I know how much work you have up at the farm, not to mention your allotment and all the help you're giving to the Institute."

"Not at all. Visiting Charlie doesn't feel like work. He's a friend. Actually, I've been thinking about him quite a lot lately. Not like that," she adds on seeing my eyebrows raise, "I mean, I've been thinking about what will happen to him when he leaves your place. Perhaps we could find a time to talk through my ideas?"

"Yes, any bright ideas you have on that subject would be most welcome. But right now, we've a meeting to attend, and if I'm not mistaken, it looks as if it's about to begin."

Today, the Colonel is not the only man in the building. He is joined by men he introduces as Mr W. Jones of Llangefni, and Mr Hughes of Llangaffo, both here to talk about a new War Savings scheme. I know all about the scheme, having attended a committee meeting only a week previously to discuss it, but I'm interested to see how the idea sits with those who've not yet heard of it. Times are hard, and I'm sceptical about how many will be willing to part with their hard-earned money, but as the men begin speaking, they receive a warm reception.

"Have I got this right," whispers Angharad, "we invest any savings we have into the scheme and our money is used to help fight the war, then the government returns it, plus interest in the future?"

"That about sums it up."

"Sounds like a good idea to me."

Angharad's reaction pleases me, but I wonder whether she actually has any savings to invest. Money is not a topic we discuss, although by the looks of Carys, who arrives late and looking flustered, I guess it is something that dominates my friend's thoughts. It can't be easy for Angharad as a single woman, and Carys seems to carry the world on her shoulders as she tries to keep the farm afloat.

At the end of the meeting, I find the Colonel grinning broadly beside a table where he is gathering names and subscriptions.

"I'd like to add my name to that list, please."

"Marvellous. Thank you, Mrs Montgomery. With you added, we've reached thirty-three subscriptions. How much would you like to deposit with the scheme?"

"I'll begin with ten pounds, then I may add more, but I'd need to discuss that with Hector first."

"Quite right too."

As the Colonel adds my name to the piece of paper, I can't help but notice that Angharad has agreed to one pound, which, knowing her circumstances, must be a significant amount of money.

"It's a wonderful group we've gathered here, Mrs Montgomery," says the Colonel. "I'm not sure I've ever thanked you for helping get things off the ground."

"I'm not really sure I did much."

"Nonsense, you and your friend Miss Williams are the backbone of this institute, and don't you ever forget it. By the way, I hope I'm not speaking out of turn, but I couldn't help notice your friend Miss Ambrose is looking a little wan. Is everything alright there?"

"To be honest, Colonel, I think things have been a struggle for them since Mr Ambrose died. You'll have noticed Mrs Ambrose hasn't attended any meetings for a while."

"Perhaps I could send Jane round for a visit. What do you think?"

I picture Carys and her reluctance to let even me inside her home. "Perhaps a note would be better, Colonel. That way, if Mrs Ambrose isn't up to hosting a visitor, she will still know you and Jane have her in your thoughts."

"A splendid idea. I shall do just that. Thank you, Mrs Montgomery."

"Not at all, Colonel."

Chapter Forty-Seven

Angharad

December, 1916

"Welcome to the madhouse," says Ffion as she opens the door. "Things are that bad?"

"No," she says, laughing. "I just have a house full of soldiers, four confused children wondering what's happened to their bedrooms, and a grumpy husband insisting he is entitled to peace and quiet while on leave, something which around here is scarce."

"Are you sure you want me here on top of all that? I can head home and leave you to it if that would be best."

"Believe me, Angharad, one more body is not going to make any difference, and we are all delighted you could make it. Everyone is gathering in the library if you'd like to come through? It's one of the few spaces in the house that doesn't smell like a hospital."

"If it's alright, I'll quickly pop in to see Charlie, then come through and join you all?"

"Of course, take as long as you want. I know he's been looking forward to seeing you."

"Have you said anything to him about my idea?"

"No, I thought I'd leave that up to you. Are you sure Mr Stephens is in favour of the plan?"

"Oh yes. Anything to ease the pressure a little, and given his lack of hearing, he's more open-minded than some men would be when it comes to disability. Why, do you think I'm being rash?"

"Perhaps a little, but on balance, I'd say your plan makes sense. There will be challenges, given Charlie's physical condition, but I'm more than happy to give him a character reference, and you've got to know him well enough during your recent visits."

"That's true. He strikes me as a hard worker, and you can't fault his determination when it comes to recovering from his injuries. I think he'll be an asset on the farm."

"Wonderful. Well, I'd better get back to the family, but come and find us when you're ready."

Ffion rushes off and I climb the stairs to where Charlie now shares a room with just three other men. His progress has been remarkable, and it was his own idea to move to a less accessible room in order to improve his mobility.

From behind the door comes the sound of men's laughter. I knock and push the door open.

"Your fancy woman's here," says a one-armed soldier sitting on a bed in the far corner of the room.

"Ignore him, Angharad," says Charlie. "He's just jealous."

Despite a lifetime to grow used to taunts, the soldier's jibe still hurts. The joke isn't that Charlie and I are in a romantic relationship, the joke is that he'd ever be in such a relationship with someone like me. It hurts, even though there is nothing going on with Charlie beyond friendship. I suppose I've grown too used to being accepted at the WI, I'm no longer on guard, and this is a timely reminder not to let down my defences.

Taking Charlie's advice, I try to ignore the other men in the room and pull up a chair beside his bed. I hand him a small parcel wrapped in newspaper.

"You didn't have to bring me anything. I've not got you a gift."

I smile. "Charlie, you're recuperating, buying gifts should be the last thing on your mind. And besides, it's not really a gift, just a novel to replace the one you've finished, and seeing as it's Christmas, I thought I'd wrap it for you."

Charlie grins and tears the newspaper. "*The Valley of Fear* by Arthur Conan Doyle. Hang on a minute, this doesn't look like the other books you've given me. This one looks new."

I feel heat rise up my neck and into my cheeks. Despite my attempts to dog-ear the pages, and bend the spine a little, I've been caught out. "It's Christmas," I say with a shrug.

To my enormous surprise, when I can bear to lift my eyes I see a lone tear run down Charlie's cheek. "Thank you," he says, his voice gruff. "This is the kindest thing anyone's done for me in a long time."

"Got any gifts for us?" calls a soldier from across the room.

"Shut up," says Charlie. "You can read this once I've finished with it."

"There's something I want to talk to you about," I say, lowering my voice. "But maybe not here?"

"Alright, let's sit on the landing, shall we?" Charlie wriggles to the edge of the bed, and with some difficulty eases himself into his three-wheeled chair. I fight the urge to offer to help, knowing it's important he does this himself. "Come on," he says, inching the chair through the room.

From the look on his face, I can see the cumbersome chair is heavy and difficult to move forward, but still I stay quiet and allow him his independence.

When we reach the landing, Charlie pulls his wheelchair up beside a wooden chair and we sit beneath paintings of Montgomery ancestors, while cries of pain, the chatter of patients, and the occasional Christmas carol fill the air.

"Go on," says Charlie. "What's all this about?"

"I wondered if you've thought what you might do when you're well enough to leave here?"

Charlie frowns, his cheerfulness gone. "Go home and burden my mami seems the most likely option. I've been working so hard to get my independence back, but the truth is, Angharad, I'll never be able to work like a man again. I'll never see the inside of another mine or be able to earn my keep. Sometimes I think it would have been better if I'd died in battle, instead of surviving as half a man."

"Don't say things like that, and I didn't ask to upset you. I want to make a suggestion, but if it sounds like the worst thing in the world, please say so."

"Go on."

"We are very short of labourers on our farm. Mr Stephens, who owns the farm, lives alone in the farmhouse. I wondered how you would feel about working for us, for a small wage, plus board and lodgings? Mr Stephens is deaf, and it would be reassuring to know someone is in the home with him, should anything happen."

"Angharad, that's such a kind offer, but look at me. What could I possibly do on a farm?"

"Right, here's what I was thinking..."

Half an hour later, I've left a smiling Charlie upstairs and have navigated the warren of rooms to find the library. When I walk in, a game of charades is in full flow. Ffion introduces me to her children, who look at me with naked surprise, then turn back to their game. When she introduces me to her husband, he reacts with an amused grunt, before turning his attention back to the newspaper spread across his knees. It is a greater humiliation than the children's surprise. The grunt says everything. I am an unattractive woman, and not worthy of his time or attention.

"Come and join our game," says Ffion. "Would you like a drink?"

"No, thank you." I perch on the edge of a sumptuous leather armchair. "I'll watch for a while, if that's alright?"

"Don't you know how to play charades?" asks a young girl, who is the spitting image of her mother.

"I can probably get the hang of it, but it isn't a game I've ever played before."

"But what does your family do at Christmas?" she asks, wide-eyed.

"Rebecca," says Ffion, "don't be so rude."

"It's alright," I say, trying to find a suitable answer to her question. It's been a long time since I spent Christmas with my family, but I can't imagine Bryn has strayed far from the traditions of my father's day. There were certainly no charades played in the Williams household. Instead, it was a day of even greater religious observance than normal. "My brother is the minister of a chapel, so much of his day is taken up with services."

"But they must play some games," says Rebecca, unperturbed. "And what about food and presents?"

"They'll eat a special meal in the afternoon," I say, "and then will give each other a small gift."

"Why don't they want you there?"

Ffion's cheeks redden at her daughter's question, while Hector snorts from behind his newspaper.

"They're very busy on Christmas day with all their church services," I say. "It isn't convenient for them to host me today."

Rebecca frowns, but before she can ask any further questions, Ffion places a hand on her arm and shakes her head. Two young women rush into the room in a cloud of perfume and giggles.

"This is my daughter Mary, and her friend Eleanor, who is staying with us over Christmas. We're about to play charades, girls."

"Oh good," says Mary, sitting down cross-legged beside the fire. She pats the ground for her friend to sit beside her. As Eleanor takes her place on the carpet, I glance up and see the look in Mr Montgomery's eyes. He's staring at Eleanor with what looks like hunger, his eyes wide, his pupils dilating as the girl's skirt rides further up her legs. I turn my head away in disgust, and see Ffion's gaze moving between me, her husband, and Eleanor. We catch each other's eye and her cheeks grow pink.

"Right," she says, clapping her hands together and forcing jollity into her voice. "Hector, you can be timekeeper. Now, who is going to start?"

Chapter Forty-Eight

Carys

December, 1916

When Angharad answers the door, I can tell she is in a panic. She is wearing what looks like a man's shirt, half tucked in, half hanging out of a long woollen skirt.

"You didn't have to come so far out of your way," she says, standing aside so I can enter the bothy.

"I knew you'd be nervous at the thought of tonight."

"You're very kind, Carys, but I would have been fine."

I nod, not believing a word she is saying. There's no question her confidence has grown over the past year, but in an unfamiliar setting, or large group of strangers, she reverts to the Angharad of old – stooped, hunched, unable to meet anyone's eye.

Angharad moves to a trunk and begins pulling items of clothing from it, then throwing them back with a sigh of frustration. Betty, lying beside the fire, watches her mistress, gives a disgruntled whine, then lays her head back on her paws. I know how she feels and, in that moment, long to take her place.

"I think perhaps it would be best if you went without me."

"Why?"

"Because all the ladies there will look so pretty, and I…"

As tears fill Angharad's eyes, I put an arm around her shoulder. "You'll what, Angharad? You're a handsome woman, you've nothing to be ashamed of. Besides," I say, unbuttoning my coat to show my patched shirt and thinning skirt, "look at me, I'm not exactly wearing a ball gown. Tonight isn't about what we look like. It's to raise money to help the Red Cross, which has two unpaid bills and not enough money to pay them."

"I know, and I want to support the cause, but I don't understand why I need to attend to do so. You can take a donation from me instead."

"You need to be there because it is our WI who are putting this event on. It is one of the few occasions we've had to show the village what we're made of, a public display of all the work we've been putting in to help with the war effort."

"There'll be plenty of other members there."

"But if you're not there, you'd be missed."

Angharad laughs. "I shouldn't think anyone would notice."

"Charlie will notice, Ffion will notice, I will notice."

"Charlie's going?"

"Yes, several soldiers from Ffion's home are going, those that are well enough, that is. You're standing here worrying about looking out of place, but how do you think Charlie feels? There's no hiding his injuries, is there?"

"I suppose not. I'm sorry, Carys, it's just I've grown used to attending WI meetings and mostly I've grown comfortable among the women there, but others from the village have long-standing opinions of me I'd rather not face."

"And those opinions will be upheld if you choose to hide away like a hermit, as if you've something to hide. If you won't come for your own sake, come for the sake of your friends."

"Will my Sunday best do for something to wear?"

"Of course it will," I say, trying to keep my patience. It's been a long week and every muscle in my body is aching. I'm not sure how much more cajoling I've left in me. Angharad must notice, for she takes my hand.

"I'm sorry for being so difficult about this. Here I am getting worked up about going to a fund-raising evening, and you've got no end of real worries. I'm sorry."

"Don't be silly. I'll wait outside while you get dressed, then I'll help with your hair."

"Thank you."

By the time Angharad is ready and looking her best, all light has faded from the sky and in its place is a blanket of stars. Breath swirls from our mouths as we begin the long walk into the village, the ground soggy underfoot from all the recent rain.

"We'll turn up covered in mud at this rate," I say, as the earth tries to swallow my boot.

"Don't worry, we'll meet the path soon enough, and I know these lanes like the back of my hand. It won't take us too long."

Angharad is right, and we arrive at the school building far quicker than I thought we would. Noise from inside spills out through the open windows, and already the sound of a fiddle fills the air.

"I can't dance," says Angharad, and I realise this is what her reluctance has really been about.

"Of course you can dance."

"No, Carys, I really can't. My feet are so big I'll crush other people's, and what man will want to dance with a woman taller than him?"

"Didn't you enjoy the Twmpaths the village used to hold when we were children?"

"Father disapproved of such traditions. We never went."

My mind drifts back to those warm summer evenings when we'd join in the traditional dances out in the fields. They were carefree days before death, war, poverty, and grief sank their teeth into our family. I'd often wondered why there were no longer Twmpaths held, and now wonder if Angharad's father might have had something to do with the end of the tradition.

"Angharad, have you ever been to a dance before?"

Her silence speaks volumes.

"Angharad?" I say, as gently as I can.

"Father always said I'd show the family up if I went to a dance with them and Mother felt the same way."

"But that's awful."

"They were probably just trying to protect me."

Protect her, my foot! I keep my thoughts to myself. Instead, I say, "just because there will be some dancing tonight, doesn't mean it's compulsory. Plenty of people sit in chairs around the room enjoying the music and talking with their friends."

"Really?"

"Of course. You don't think poor Mrs Cotton, with all her recent ailments, is going to be flinging herself around the dancefloor, do you?"

"No."

"And what about Charlie? He's doing a good job with his new chair, but I can't see him joining in a set dance, can you? And besides, dancing is only one part of tonight's event. There are going to be various people performing."

"Will you be singing?"

"If you must know, yes, I have been roped into giving a song or two."

"Why didn't you say?" Angharad throws her hands in the air and lets out a long sigh. "Goodness me, Carys, I've been dragging my feet about coming, making you late for an important night. If you'd said you were involved, I'd have been there like a shot."

"It's only a couple of folk songs."

"Have you sung since your dadi died?"

"No."

"Precisely. This is important to you, and therefore, it is important to me. Come on, let's make our way inside."

As Angharad marches along the path to the entrance of the school building, I shake my head. She's a funny one, but no one can doubt the fierce loyalty she has to her friends.

Chapter Forty-Nine

Angharad

December, 1916

The school room is full of people. Long tables are positioned to allow space at the front for a small dancefloor and stage. Along the back wall, a series of trestle tables groan with food, everyone bringing what they can spare to add to the feast.

From my bag, I pull out the cheese wrapped in a cloth, a jug of milk, and the loaf of bread I made that morning.

"Thank you, Angharad. This bread smells delicious," says Mrs Jones.

Knowing my small contribution is welcome puts me slightly more at ease. But then I see them, at a table near the door and before I can turn and run, Bryn spots me and waves me over. At the same moment, I see Ffion, Charlie, and five wounded soldiers at a table on the opposite side of the room. Carys has joined them, along with Florian, Lina and Emma. Ffion calls my name and for a moment I stand in the middle of the room, torn between friends and family.

In the end, I let my head rule and my heart sinks as I walk towards Bryn, Anne and their four daughters. All wear clothes in brown or grey, the girls' long hair hanging down their backs in braids.

"Good evening, Angharad," says Anne, as I reach them.

"Good evening, Bryn, Anne, girls."

My three eldest nieces acknowledge me with a nod of the head, only the youngest risking a smile. Why are they here? They hate this kind of event.

"We wanted to come and show our support for the Red Cross," says Bryn, answering my unspoken question. "I trust you will sit with us."

"Actually..."

"Of course she will," says Anne. "Who else is she going to sit with?" She shakes her head and gives the tinkling laugh I detest.

I pull up a chair and try to engage my nieces in conversation, but none seems interested in anything I have to say. On second thoughts, the way they cast glances at their parents makes me wonder if they've been warned off speaking to me.

"I trust you had a good Christmas, brother?"

Bryn launches into a monologue about all the good work he did among his congregation during the festive period. Anne looks on adoringly, but the girls fidget, whispering and giggling.

"Show some decorum, girls," spits Anne, and her girls turn their eyes to the ground, folding their hands in their laps.

"I think I'll fetch myself a cup of tea," I say. "Would anyone else like one?"

"No, thank you."

"I'd like a piece of fruitcake," says my youngest niece.

"No, you wouldn't," says Bryn. "I can't have my daughters growing fat."

I give the scrawny girl in front of me a sad smile and resolve to sneak her a piece of cake later. It is a relief to join the queue for refreshments and I don't notice Charlie wheeling his chair up beside me.

"Who are those people you're sitting with?" he asks me. "No offence, but they look like they've swallowed a few wasps."

I can't help but laugh, then immediately glance behind me to check if Bryn has noticed. Thankfully, his attention is on the front of the room where a harp player is setting up.

"That's my brother, his wife, and my nieces."

"Oh, I'm sorry. I was rude."

"No, you were quite right. They're the most miserable people I've the misfortune to know." I slap my hand across my mouth, shocked at my candour.

Charlie laughs. "You can always come and join our table."

If only. "Best not. How are you?"

"Very well, actually. My wounds are all healing and even scary Matron seems pleased with me. In fact, she seems keen to get rid of me to free up a bed." Charlie looks up at me with the lopsided smile I've grown so fond of.

"Does that mean you're considering my offer?"

"It means I'd like to accept, if your offer is still on the table?"

"Of course it is."

We reach the front of the queue, and I'm served my tea. I also buy a slice of fruit cake, which I wrap in a napkin and slip into my pocket, ready to sneak to my niece later.

"I'd better get back to my family. I'll come and speak to you about arrangements in the next few days. Enjoy the evening."

"Hey," says Charlie, grabbing my sleeve. "Does that mean I won't speak to you again tonight?"

I look around and see Bryn now watching me. "It's probably best I stay with my family," I say, unable to look at Charlie as I trudge back to the table.

"Who was that?" asks Bryn as I take my seat.

"One of the wounded soldiers from the convalescent home at Plas Llanfair."

"How do you know the likes of him?"

"The likes of him? You mean a war hero?" My nieces gasp and look at me, wide-eyed. "Sorry, brother, I just mean those poor fellows have been through an awful lot."

"You haven't answered my question."

I swallow down a sigh, wondering how to answer in the least inflammatory way. "I occasionally volunteer at the Plas Llanfair convalescent home. Also, I assist with their allotments, so it's inevitable my path may cross with some soldiers from time to time."

"As long as you remember your place, Angharad," says Anne. "It's not just your own reputation you've to think of, but ours as well."

"Are you suggesting I shouldn't volunteer my services to help with the war effort?"

"Of course not," snaps Bryn, squeezing Anne's hand.

A hush descends as the harpist takes to the stage, but as all heads turn, I notice my youngest niece giving me a look that seems suspiciously like admiration. With everyone distracted, I slide the wrapped fruitcake from my pocket and drop it into her hands.

Chapter Fifty

Angharad

Feb 1917

"I 'd best be off," I say, collecting up the empty dishes.

"How come the Colonel's the only chap allowed at these meetings then?" asks Charlie.

"If you're angling for an invitation, you'll be waiting a while. The Colonel is the exception, not the rule."

"But why is he the exception?"

I shrug. "Because he's the Colonel. I rather suspect he's the exception in everything he does. I for one have met no one quite like him." I can't help but smile as I think of the man who, in no small way, is responsible for broadening the horizons of my previously narrow world.

"Fair enough, but I reckon I'm quite exceptional myself," says Charlie, waving his hand in the space where two legs should be. "And not that different from the Colonel in some ways. In fact, loan me Betty for the afternoon and find me a donkey to pull my chair and none will tell us apart."

"Away with you," I say, shaking my head. Mr Stephens watches our exchange with an amused look on his face. He seems to enjoy the new lively atmosphere in the farmhouse, even if he's unable to hear any words spoken.

"Right, some of us have work to do, hey, Geraint?" Charlie mimes shovelling, and Mr Stephens nods and stands up, pushing back his chair. As Charlie follows him out of the room, he throws me one of his dazzling smiles.

When I invited Charlie to the farm, I truly believed it would be me helping him, but the light he's brought to our usually sombre mealtimes, and the ease of another body to carry some of the workload has improved things on the farm immeasurably. Yes, Charlie may be limited in the work he can do, but given his determination not to let his disability hold him back, so far he's exceeded all our expectations.

After scraping the remaining scraps into a bowl for Betty and washing the dishes, I pull on my coat and make my way to the meeting. By the time I reach Graig, I'm still smiling at the thought of our strange makeshift family up at the farm.

"Someone's full of the joys of spring," says Ffion as she meets me on the street.

"Spring is optimistic," I say, shivering and tapping my feet against the frosty ground which hasn't thawed.

"Don't worry, I'm sure they've got the stove going inside the summerhouse. It's going to be a busy meeting today. There's a lecturer from the university giving a demonstration on fruit pruning, a talk on vegetable culture, then Dr Williams is speaking on a nursing and maternity scheme."

"Goodness, let's hope the stove can hold out long enough for all that."

"Come on," says Ffion, linking arms with me as we walk up through the garden.

The summerhouse is packed with bodies and a quick scan of the room reveals at least forty members and friends present. With so many people looking for seats, I opt to stand at the back where Carys joins me halfway through the fruit pruning demonstration.

"Sorry," she says, "I couldn't get away any earlier. A ewe birthed three lambs just as I was getting ready to leave."

"Isn't that a bit early?"

"Yes, she certainly took us all by surprise. The girls were delighted, of course, but it was an unwelcome reminder of all the work that lies ahead of us over the coming months. I honestly don't know how we're going to manage this year."

As Carys turns her attention to the demonstration at the front, I study her from the corner of my eye. She is pale and far too thin for my liking.

"Now I've Charlie helping with the milking, I might be able to spare a few hours to come and help you."

"Really? Are you sure?"

"Yes. I can't offer much, but I'm sure I can spare a few hours a week."

"Thank you," Carys whispers, the strained muscles in her face softening a little.

I should ask after her mother, but Carys's appearance tells me everything I need to know. Instead, I turn my attention to Dr Williams, who has taken the floor.

"In 1915 alone, there were close to ninety thousand deaths in babies under one year old in England and Wales. People often cite the poverty experienced in our towns and cities, but the plight of rural women should not be ignored. Even in peacetime, residents of rural Wales often have to travel great distances to access any form of healthcare, and when coupled with an unreliable water supply and primitive sanitation, this can have disastrous results. I am reliably informed that when Mrs Adelaide Hoodless began this wonderful organisation in Canada in

1897, it was driven by the loss of her own infant son. I, and many others, believe the Women's Institute can continue this founding mission of contributing to better hygiene and sanitation in the home, and a greater understanding of the root causes of infant mortality."

"A decent water supply in the village would be a good start," Carys whispers.

Overall, it is a very enlightening meeting. Dr Williams, although a little dry in his delivery, is nonetheless well informed and gives us plenty of food for thought.

As I say my goodbyes and begin the walk home, Dr Williams' words echo in my mind. With such a strong focus on helping the war effort, I'm not sure any of us have thought much beyond it. But now I realise our work will not cease the moment peace is declared. There will be a country in need of rebuilding and problems such as infant mortality won't be solved by the laying down of guns.

"You look deep in thought," says Charlie, as I walk into the kitchen and place the kettle on the stove.

"Goodness me, Charlie. You gave me a fright."

"Sorry. Good meeting?"

"Interesting. We had a doctor speaking about a nursing and maternity scheme. I had no idea how great a need there is for such a scheme, not being a mother myself."

"So what did he have to say, this doctor?"

"He spoke at length about infant mortality."

"A cheery subject for a Tuesday afternoon."

"Charlie, it was important background information to help us understand the need for the maternity scheme."

Charlie holds his hands up, palms out. "I'm sorry, I know from experience it's no laughing matter."

"What experience? Oh dear, I am sorry. I didn't mean to pry."

"It's alright. I'd like you to know. The thing is, I was married back in the day. We lost two sons when they were still babies and a few before they were born. We gave up trying to have a family in the end."

"That is so sad. What happened to your wife?"

"She ran off to England with a travelling salesman."

"What an awful thing to do!"

Charlie shrugs. "Perhaps, but losing all those babies, well, I think it sent my Rachel a bit loopy. I understand why she needed to run away. I suppose by joining up to fight, I was running away too."

"Do you ever hear from her?"

"No, and I think it's best that way. I hope she's happy, but more than that, I hope her new fellow has given her the family I couldn't."

"You are quite remarkable, Charlie Macky. Quite remarkable indeed."

Chapter Fifty-One

Ffion

March 1917

A s soon as Miss Antonia Williams from Holyhead begins speaking, I feel my muscles tense. She has the enthusiasm of youth, and the fervour of a preacher.

"In Holyhead, we have seen a wonderful response to our Girls' Club. It is easy to forget sometimes just how isolated rural women and girls can be. If they're lucky, girls leave school at fourteen, but the reality is most leave even younger, and some never attend at all. It is a sad state of affairs, but nonetheless true that girls' education is not valued in the same way as boys'.

"How can we expect these girls to grow into intelligent, capable young women if they are kept isolated from all outside influences? As we at the WI know, sharing knowledge is immeasurably valuable, and although not mentioned as frequently, I believe the camaraderie and support of meeting with one's peers is just as important.

"Besides providing practical skills and contributions, Girls' Clubs are also a way of opening youngsters' minds to some of the less desirable ways of the world. I am aware what I am about to speak of remains taboo, and I am also aware I may offend some of you in speaking of it, but I fear it is a matter that should not be ignored. Women and girls suffer abuse from men far more frequently than we like to imagine. I'm not saying that by operating a Girls' Club we can stamp out that abuse, but we can make girls more aware of the dangers they face in the world and provide a space for them to share any concerns they might have."

Around me there are mutterings that family business should remain private, and I must say these feelings resonate. Hector has turned his fists on me on more than one occasion, but I would never dream of sharing this experience with even my closest friends. As admirable as Miss Williams' little speech is, I can't help but feel the formation of a Girls' Club would open a hornet's nest. There are certain ways the world operates that we may not like, but will never change. One of those is men's physical superiority over women. What does Miss Williams want these girls to do? Fight back? In my experience, taking what you've got coming quietly is the most effective way of ensuring it ends as quickly as possible.

"Yes," continues Miss Williams, "I hear your concerns, but frankly, I disagree with the notion that educating girls in the ways of the world is a bad thing. Besides, the aim of our group is not to raise the next generation of suffragettes. It is as much about practical skills that can be used in the home as anything else."

"Can't these girls learn such skills from their mothers?"

"That would be the hope," says Miss Williams, standing her ground, "but the reality is the burden on women has never been so great as it is in these dark days of war. How many mothers have time to stop and teach their daughters when they've farms to run, or businesses to keep going in the absence of their men?"

Around me, many of the women seem to be coming around to Miss Williams' way of thinking, and it worries me. The nature of these Girls' Clubs worries me. As much as I support the right of women to use the skills they possess to help society, much as I have done with the convalescent home, there is still a natural order to the world, whether we like it or not.

Miss Williams' voice becomes muffled as I drift off into my own thoughts. I can't get the image of the young girl beneath Hector in the stable out of my mind. There was nothing innocent or unworldly about her. From the look on her face, she knew exactly what she was doing.

Miss Williams finishes speaking, and the Colonel stands up to give a lecture on our duty to our neighbour. It is a homely little talk, and his words are soothing, yet the idea of Girls' Clubs still plays on my mind, and I find it hard to focus on what he is saying.

The next talk, by one Mrs Drage, holds my interest more than the Colonel's. She gives a fascinating account of the wholesale market they have set up at Criccieth, and I wonder if we could attempt the same. I could happily have listened to her for far longer and find myself disappointed when the meeting draws to a close.

"Wasn't Miss Antonia Williams interesting?" says Carys as we sip our cups of tea.

"Interesting is one word for it. Personally, I preferred the talk by Mrs Drage."

"You don't like the idea of a Girls' Club?"

"Not particularly."

Both Carys and Angharad frown at me. "Why is that?" asks Angharad. "I thought the work they're doing up in Holyhead with girls sounds rather good."

"So did I," says Carys. "I left school at twelve and it was so lonely on the farm."

"Yes, but it sounds as though Miss Williams is promoting more than a social event."

"Oh, you mean warning girls what they can expect from the world?"

"Yes."

"But why is that wrong? Surely the WI is all about educating women?"

"Educating in the ways of domestic life and service to our community, not filling young ladies' heads with all this suffrage nonsense."

Angharad chokes on her tea, her cheeks turning purple as she struggles to catch her breath. "I don't think the purpose of Miss Williams' Girls' Club is to turn out mini suffragettes," she says when recovered.

"But so what if it was?" says Carys. "Don't you want equal rights to men?"

"There is a natural order of things. If we disturb that, who knows what will happen to society?"

Carys is staring at me open-mouthed. "I'm sorry," she says, "I don't think I'm quite understanding you. Are you suggesting we should remain subservient to men, that they should remain dominant over us?"

"Yes, I am," I say, trying to sound more confident than I feel.

"But what about your convalescent home? I don't imagine it was your husband's idea or that he was very happy about it. And what about all the work I'm doing on the farm? What about all the jobs women are doing now the men are away at war? Are you suggesting that when the war ends, we climb back into our boxes despite showing ourselves just as capable as they are?"

"And what if we don't? What will the men do when they return home from fighting for their country to find all their jobs taken by women?"

"I think you both have a point," says Angharad. "But I really don't think Miss Williams was suggesting anything as radical as you imagine, Ffion. I like to think of a future where men and women will be more equal than they currently are. After all, it is going to take a combined effort to build back the country after the war. But even so, there was no suggestion we start a Girls' Club in Llanfairpwll, any more than setting up a wholesale market, as Mrs Drage described."

"Let's hope you're right."

Chapter Fifty-Two

Carys

March, 1917

"How are you getting on?"

Florian is on his knees amid the hay and as he turns to me, he wipes a hand across his brow. Despite the cold day, sweat draws his shirt tight against his skin. "This one didn't go well. The lamb became stuck. I couldn't save it."

"Oh no. And the ewe?"

"I've been trying to bring her towards life for the past half hour, but she's lost a lot of blood."

I climb into the pen and kneel beside him, rubbing a hand across the ewe's warm stomach. "I'm sorry to have left you alone to deal with this."

"You've barely left the barn to eat and sleep this past week. It was good you get out for an hour or so. How was the meeting?"

A sigh escapes my lips and comes out in a cloud.

"That good?" laughs Florian, his blue eyes sparkling.

"There was a disagreement with Ffion."

"A disagreement? With you?"

"Yes. A lady came to talk to us about a Girls' Club the Holyhead WI is running and for some reason Ffion took offence. She implied girls should remain uneducated in order not to upset the applecart and keep them subservient to their men."

"Surely not the same Ffion who runs a convalescent home against her husband's wishes and throws herself into every opportunity the WI presents?"

"I know. It's as though her thinking hasn't caught up with her actions. I'm not saying I wholeheartedly support all the tactics the suffragettes employ, but I think us women have shown ourselves to be more than capable over the past few years, and the very least we should receive is the right to vote."

"But Ffion doesn't?"

"I really don't know. Her views took me by surprise, so I didn't have much time to form an argument against them."

"Remember, Carys, that Ffion has grown up in a very different world to yours. She was schooled in how to be a good wife and find a rich husband. Beauty and grace would have been favoured over intellect. Work is still a novelty to her, something she can play at. After the war, she will most likely go back to hosting dinner parties and attending to her husband's needs."

"Perhaps, but the work she does with wounded soldiers is more than playing. Her views irritated me, but I suspect she will find it hard to go back to her old life once this war is over."

"Tell me about this Girls' Club. Are there plans to start one in Llanfairpwll?"

"Not that anyone said, but once we'd got used to the idea, there was more interest in it. Do you think your girls would be keen to join a club?"

"I'm certain of it. They love the farm, but we're quite alone out here. It would do them good to make some new friends."

"You're a wonderful father to those girls."

Florian looks as if he's about to say something, then closes his mouth and holds my gaze. The air between us changes, the March chill banished in favour of warmth, and a tension that keeps us pinned to the spot. Florian shuffles forward until I can feel his breath on my skin. Then, beside us, the ewe grunts and opens her eyes. Florian laughs, the moment is broken, and we both turn our attention back to the animal.

"It looks as though this lady might be alright after all," he says. "I'll stay with her for a little longer. Why don't you go inside and warm up?"

If anything, after the moment we just shared, I'm too hot, but I nod, brush pieces of hay from my skirt and leave the barn. When I walk into the kitchen, I find Mami at the table drinking a cup of tea. Her eyes are as blank as the day Dadi died, but she has more colour in her cheeks than I've seen in a long while.

"Hello, Mami. It's good to see you up and about. How are you feeling this morning?"

Mami shrugs and takes a sip of her tea. In a way, having her up and about is harder than the days she takes to her bed. When she's downstairs, it's a reminder to all of us, including her, that we have one less worker but the same number of mouths to feed.

"We had a busy night with the lambing," I say, to fill the silence stretching between us.

Mami nods and takes a sip from her tea. I want to scream at her to stop being so selfish, that she isn't the only one grieving. What would the local women who've known her all her life think if they could see her now? Former friends have long stopped visiting. There are only so many times you can turn someone away before they give up altogether.

"Do you think you might help me clean out the barn later?" I ask, trying as hard as I can to keep my tone light.

"I'm not well."

Before I can reply, a knock comes on the front door and when Mami shows no sign of moving, I go to open it.

"Hello, Carys."

The sight of the young woman in front of me leaves me too shocked to speak.

"I'm sorry to turn up unannounced like this."

"What are you doing here, Gwynn?" The words stick in my throat. It may have been out of sight, out of mind where Dai is concerned, but seeing his sister on my doorstep turns my insides to ice. I may not love Dai in the way I should, but he's been my friend all my life, and the thought of him coming to harm in the war is dreadful.

"I've come to tell you Dai is home. Mami said I shouldn't say anything, but I thought you had a right to know."

"He's home? When?"

"Last week."

"I should go over there and see him."

"The thing is, Carys, he's not the same man who went off to fight. He's changed."

"Even so, we're engaged. Wait there, I'll get my coat."

Chapter Fifty-Three

Carys

March, 1917

Before Dadi, before the war, before Florian, the thought of marrying Dai made me happy enough. I pictured a life like Mami and Dadi shared, a team, working together for the good of the family. With our combined acres the work would be long and hard, but we'd have Peter, Dadi and Mami working the Ambrose farm, so me and Dai could concentrate on his. Love never really came into things. Mami and Dadi weren't a love match from what I've heard, and they'd grown to love one another.

Now, though, with everything changed, the thought of seeing Dai scares me. I'm not the same woman he left behind, and I'd be surprised if he's the same man. *Don't be silly*, I tell myself. *You've known him all your life. He's your friend, and friends pick up where they left off.*

The heavens open and water seeps through my coat, running down my back, legs, and into my boots. The fields I cross are boggy underfoot, and it isn't long before my boots fill with water. If this was any other meeting between sweethearts, my appearance would not go down well, but Dai knows me as a woman who works the land, so a bit of mud shouldn't unsettle him too much.

Dai's farm comes into view. It would be nice to stop and gather my thoughts, but the weather is relentless, icy drops of rain stinging my skin and the wind so fierce I fear it may knock me off my feet. I run the final distance, my legs aching as my boots fight against the mud beneath them,

Only once I'm in the yard do I stop to catch my breath. The farmhouse I'm in front of isn't as big as ours, but it looks better kept. With Dai's brothers too young to go off and fight, this family has not suffered from the lack of workers we have.

With a deep breath, I walk up to the front door and knock. Once I would have walked straight in, but there's a quietness to the house that unsettles me. Perhaps everyone is sheltering from the weather, and I'll find them all huddled in front of the fire?

The door opens and Mrs Jones' face falls. "What are you doing here?"

"Gwynn told me Dai's home."

"The silly girl, I told her not to. You shouldn't have come. Please go home."

"But I'm sure Dai will want to see me."

"You don't understand."

"Don't understand what?"

Mrs Jones sighs and shakes her head. "Please, Carys, please just go home. I can come and visit you tomorrow to talk about Dai, but now is not a good time for you to visit."

"I'll only be a few minutes. Just let me say hello then I'll be on my way."

"You need to go home, Carys." Her voice is steely, her arms folded tight across her chest as she blocks the doorway.

"No."

"I beg your pardon?"

Mrs Jones looks at me with horror and only now do I realise just how much I must have changed. Whether it's running the farm or my meetings at the WI, since war broke out, I've found my voice, and Dai's mother no longer intimidates me as she once did. "I've walked all this way in the pouring rain. I'm not going back out in this weather without speaking to Dai first."

"He doesn't want to see you."

"Why not?"

"That's none of your concern."

"Have you forgotten he asked me to marry him before he went off to war?"

"No, of course not, but things change."

"Then he can tell me himself."

"Let the girl in," comes a deep voice from somewhere in the house. "She'll find out, eventually. It's best she sees with her own eyes."

Mrs Jones purses her lips, but stands aside to let me in. I walk into a tidy entrance hall, boots and coats lining one wall. "This is a mistake. Dai isn't a well man."

"As I said, I'll not keep him long."

Mrs Jones screws up her face and I can't tell if she's angry, or if she's trying not to cry. Her face softens, and she raises her hands in a gesture of surrender. "He's in the parlour. If you have any trouble with him, his dadi and me will be in the kitchen and we'll come if you shout."

"Trouble?"

Instead of answering, Mrs Jones turns her back on me, and I follow her into the kitchen. Mr Jones is sitting at the table filling a pipe and greets me with a nod of his head. Mrs Jones pulls out a chair and sits beside her husband. It surprises me when he reaches out and takes her hand.

"Go careful with him," says Mr Jones. "And remember, we're just the other side of the door if you need us."

The strange behaviour of Dai's parents leaves me unsettled, and my hand rests against the latch to the parlour as I summon the courage to open the door. Aware of Mr and Mrs Jones watching me, I click the latch and slip around the door, closing it quietly behind me.

The room is dark, the curtains drawn. It takes my eyes a moment to adjust to the gloom. The only light comes from a fire, blazing and crackling in the hearth. Every chair is empty, and I wonder if Mrs Jones was wrong about Dai being in here.

I step further into the room and then I see him. If I passed him in the street, I'm not sure I'd recognise him. The man shaking in the corner of the room is all skin and bone. His once fine head of hair is gone, replaced by stubble and weeping scabs.

"Dai?" I say, taking another step closer. "It's me, Carys."

Dai looks up at me, but his wide eyes are empty, as if he doesn't recognise me. I step closer again and his shaking intensifies. High-pitched yelps escape his lips, and he pulls his knees even closer to his chin. The shirt and trousers he is wearing hang loose from his bony arms and legs. His feet are bare. Long toenails, black with dirt, claw at the carpet beneath them.

"Dai?" Slowly, I sit on my knees until we are at the same level. "It's me, Carys." This time, he doesn't even raise his head. I reach out my hand and lay it gently against his arm. He flinches, and his whimpering grows into a whine.

Suddenly, from the kitchen comes the sound of something being dropped against the stone floor. The noise makes me jump, but my reaction is nothing compared to Dai's. He scrambles to his feet, leaps across the room and lies flat on his stomach beneath the settle, hands over his ears, eyes searching wildly around the room.

"*Cymryd y ffordd! Cymryd y ffordd*! Go away! Leave me be!"

I try to climb to my feet and back out of the room, but before I'm fully standing, Dai crawls out from beneath the settle and launches himself at me with a roar of anger. I'm thrown back onto the floor and scream as he claws at my face. His full weight is on me and I'm pinned to the ground. "Help!" I scream, "please, help me!"

The parlour door opens with a bang and strong arms pull Dai off me. Mr Jones is sweating, Dai's determination to free himself giving him greater strength than his weak body would suggest.

"Come here, *cariad*, come here, my darling." Mrs Jones rushes forward, stroking Dai's face until his wild expression calms. All the fight leaves him, and he flops into his mother's arms, crying like a baby. "It's alright, my boy, it's alright. Come on, let's sit you down beside the fire."

Mr Jones takes my arm and leads me back into the kitchen. He points at the table, and I sit. There is no explanation, no tea offered. My legs are trembling beneath the table and all I want to do is run away and never come back, but I wait.

After what feels like an age, Mrs Jones appears from the parlour, closing the door so gently I can barely hear the latch click. "He's asleep," she whispers. With a sigh, she sits at the table and fixes her eyes on me. "I told you not to see him."

"I had no idea he was like that! What's wrong with him?"

"His mind's gone," says Mr Jones, his voice gruff.

"Shouldn't he be in a hospital?"

"No hospital!" says Mrs Jones, her tone a challenge. "What my boy needs is to be in his home with his family. Not some soulless hospital with hundreds of other men."

"Has he seen a doctor at least?"

"What good would a doctor do? You can't bandage up his mind. I'll fix my son myself. All he needs is feeding up and a bit of love, and he'll be right as rain in no time."

"Sarah," says Mr Jones, placing a hand across his wife's. "Better to be honest with the girl."

"What do you mean?"

"Sarah is convinced she can make Dai well again, but he's been like this ever since he got back and has shown no improvement. He was in a hospital for a while, but it didn't help. You know I was in favour of your match with Dai as much as your own dadi, but we need to be honest with you, Carys. Your betrothal to Dai is over. There will be no wedding."

"But..."

"No, Sarah," says Mr Jones, scolding his wife. "Stop it. We must be honest about things. It could take years for our son to be well again. Carys deserves to know the truth."

"Thank you," I say, standing up on legs that feel they could buckle at any moment. "I appreciate your honesty." Then, as much as I don't want to, I feel I owe it to Dai to ask, "should I visit again?"

"I think it's best you don't," says Mr Jones.

"I understand." I walk out of the farmhouse as steadily as I can, fighting the urge to run with every step. As the door closes behind me, I feel I can finally breathe again.

Chapter Fifty-Four

Angharad

April, 1917

B ryn is unusually cheerful this morning, which means I'm immediately on my guard.

"Good morning, sister. I trust you were expecting me."

"Of course, brother, it is Wednesday, after all. Mr Stephens is waiting
for you in the parlour. Would you like a cup of tea to take through with
you?"

"That would be most kind, thank you."

I set about making the tea, wrong-footed by the fact that Bryn is
whistling a cheerful tune. Not only have I never heard him whistle
before, he's so rarely cheerful. In the end, curiosity gets the better of
me. "You seem very happy today, brother."

"That I am, Angharad, that I am. I read a story in the newspaper
recently that amused me."

"Oh?"

"Yes, it was several weeks ago, but I've been saving it to show you."

My body tenses with suspicion. I turn around and Bryn throws a
newspaper down onto the table, an article circled in pencil.

"Sit and read, sister. The tea can wait."

I do as I'm told, and read. *The following story relating to the employ-
ment of women in agriculture has caused much amusement in Anglesey,*

and though doubted by some, it seems to have the merit of being true.
My heart sinks as I read on. The story describes a clueless woman who turned up at a farm claiming to know nothing about farming, fearing animals but still wanting to do her bit. According to the article, she gave up her folly after chasing a pig through the orchard and upsetting a beehive, which resulted in being stung across her face.

"Amusing, isn't it?" asks Bryn when I replace the paper on the table.

"Not for the woman who was stung."

"But that's the punchline. And doesn't it go to show how foolhardy you and the other ladies at that institute are, thinking you can solve the nation's food supply problems? Everyone is laughing at you, Angharad. You're up there at that blasted allotment thinking yourself as important as one of the lads on the front line, but don't you see? It's all a game. No one truly believes women can replace men. You are all figures of fun. Look, it's here in black and white!"

"Perhaps you are right, brother, but even so, I would rather do something than nothing at all."

Bryn shakes his head. "Oh, Angharad, don't you see I'm trying to protect you? Do you want to be laughed at even more than usual? That article could just as easily be describing you, couldn't it? I've said all along you are best keeping yourself to yourself, and this article proves my point. Anyway, where is that tea? Mr Stephens will be wondering where I am."

"I'll bring it through to you, shall I?"

"Thank you."

I take my time over making the tea, my mind brooding over the article Bryn has shown me. Perhaps the story is true, but even if it is, shouldn't a woman be commended for trying to do her part? And is that how folk see the rest of us? The thought is so depressing I try to push it from my mind.

With the tea laid out on a tray, I knock on the parlour door and walk into the room. It is a long time since I've seen my brother with any of his flock, and it is a surprise to see Mr Stephens so animated in Bryn's presence. My brother is reading from the bible, but he says the words slowly, enunciating clearly and keeping his face turned towards Mr Stephens so the man can lip read. On the table in front of him is a notebook, and I can see the two men have been communicating their thoughts on paper. This is a different side to Bryn, one I have only glimpsed over the years. Perhaps I have been too harsh in my opinion of him? Perhaps he really cares about me and protecting my reputation rather than his own? Could the article he showed me be a well-meant warning rather than an attempt to mock? As I serve the tea and leave the room, I find myself more confused than ever.

It is afternoon when I hear the unmistakable rattle of the Colonel's bath chair. I'm half-heartedly weeding the allotment and try to smile as the donkey stops the chair a few feet away.

"Good afternoon, Angharad. I hope I'm not disturbing you?"

"Not at all. What can I do for you, Colonel?"

"I wanted to pick your brains about the food supply."

I inwardly groan. The last thing I want to be doing is falling into Bryn's vision of a woman overestimating her abilities. "Wouldn't you be better talking to someone from the Agricultural Organization Society?"

The Colonel smiles at me. "I have done, don't you worry, but you're working at the coal face, so to speak. You'll have heard the news about these blasted German U-boat attacks?"

"I have."

"They've really ramped up since the New Year. It seems the Germans plan on winning this war by starving us all into submission. Well, I won't have it, not on my watch!" The Colonel is red in the face, his bunched fists banging against the legs he can no longer feel. "You've been doing a sterling job of educating our local women in food production, Angharad, but I wonder if there's still room to expand."

"Expand? I'm not sure I understand, Colonel."

"The voluntary rationing introduced last month won't touch the sides of the problem. I see compulsory rationing on the horizon, and we must make sure our community here on Anglesey is prepared for it. Clearly, we are in a better position than much of the country with all our agricultural land, but I think we should have a real push on getting people growing their own. I thought perhaps you could help me in completing a survey of the area, identifying any spare patches of land that could be given over to crops, or used for hens and other livestock."

"Of course I'd like to help you, but..."

"But what? What is it, Angharad?"

With a sigh, I pull the newspaper Bryn gave me from my apron pocket, and hand it to the Colonel. "Have you seen this article?"

The Colonel scans the page I am pointing to, then surprises me with a laugh. "Surely this hasn't worried you?"

"People are laughing at us, Colonel, and perhaps they are right to."

"Stuff and nonsense. Angharad, this is one light-hearted story designed to lift the spirits of a community living through a very hard time. Yes, some men may laugh at women's efforts, but more fool them, I say. What you ladies have achieved at the Institute so far is remarkable."

"But is it, though? Yes, we've learned to preserve fruit, cook simple meals, tend our gardens, but have we really made much difference to the war?"

The Colonel frowns at me and my cheeks redden. "Angharad, none of us in the WI can join our soldiers in the trenches, or risk our lives running over the top towards the enemy, but that doesn't mean we can't make a difference."

"I'm not suggesting you haven't made a difference, Colonel. The work you do with the Agricultural Organization Society is very valuable."

"As is our work at the WI. Change must begin with our own communities, Angharad. Just look at how word of the WI has spread since the ladies of Llanfairpwll put their shoulders to the wheel. You women risked ridicule and silenced the naysayers with your calm organisation. Think of all the families we have fed, the money we have raised for the Red Cross, and other worthy organisations. Think about the children, the nurses, the soldiers, whose spirits we have raised. These are not small things, Angharad. Think of them like the snow we get each winter. We cup a clump of snow between our palms, then we lay it on the ground and begin rolling. That one small piece grows until the size of a boulder. The work you have been part of has spawned similar projects across Wales and beyond. I would take it as a personal insult should that work be seen as unimportant."

"I'm sorry, Colonel. I didn't mean to offend you."

"You haven't, and you've nothing to apologise to me for, though I do wish you'd have more faith in yourself and your colleagues at the Institute. Instead of paying attention to ignorant opinions as expressed in this newspaper, look around you at all we have achieved. Mark my words, the ladies of Llanfairpwll have ignited a spark that will set the country ablaze. You will go down in the history books. But for now, let's put such grand thoughts aside and return our attention to allotments, shall we?"

"There's a disused paddock beside St Mary's church, which seems to have excellent soil. I've been eying it up for a while as a potential site for allotments."

We become so engrossed in our discussion that it is only after the Colonel has gone that I realise the newspaper must have slipped from his lap and fallen into the mud. As I walk back to the bothy, the article laughing at the woman lies face up. My boot lands on it, squashing it further into the ground, the words bleeding together until they are no more.

Chapter Fifty-Five

Angharad

July, 1917

F rom my position at the back of the milking parlour, I watch Charlie work. He mastered his three-wheel chair quicker than everyone expected and even the cows have got used to his unusual mode of transport now. Most days, Betty is assistance enough, but if any of the cows ever give Charlie the runaround, I make sure I'm only a shout away.

I turn as Mr Stephens comes and stands beside me, hands on his hips. From out of his pocket, he pulls a notebook and pencil and writes one simple sentence. *You were right.*

My mouth forms a wide O at the rare praise, and Mr Stephens scribbles again on his pad.

He's a good worker. Another lame duck to add to the fold, but a good worker.

Then, with a humph, as if giving a compliment is too much for one day, he turns and strides out of the barn. The sound alerts Charlie and he turns his head.

"Come to check up on me?" he asks.

"I know by now you don't need any checking up on. You've got this down to a fine art."

"Can you fetch me a fresh bucket? This one's almost full."

I replace Charlie's full bucket with an empty one and perch on a bale nearby, enjoying the chance to rest my legs for a moment.

"You know, Angharad, I don't think I've ever thanked you properly."

"It's me who should thank you. You've no idea how hard it was running this place between the two of us with a few doddery helpers from the village."

"You don't need to pretend. I know my being here gives you more work than I give back."

"Nonsense. Having someone else in the farmhouse with Mr Stephens brings me peace of mind, and now you're able to help with the milking, it frees me up to attend to the long list of other jobs."

"Maybe, but if it weren't for you, I'd be back in Llandudno, unable to work, burdening my mami with another mouth to feed, and keeping her up at night with my ranting and raving."

"The nightmares are still just as bad?"

"They're better than when I first arrived with Mrs Montgomery, but I still get them most nights."

"At least Mr Stephens is deaf, so you don't need to worry about waking anyone."

Charlie barks out a laugh. "That's very true. Honestly, Angharad, if I had any feet left, I'd say I'd landed on them. There's little use these days for a no-legged copper miner. God knows what would have happened to me had you not stepped in to help."

"That's what friends are for. And besides, it's not exactly charity when you milk our cows twice a day."

I feel a change in the atmosphere of the milking parlour even before I see her.

"This looks very cosy."

I spin around and see Anne, leaning against the wooden door frame, watching us with narrowed eyes.

"Oh, hello, Anne."

"Angharad." Anne walks further into the room, turning up her nose at the sweet smells of hay and warm milk.

"This is my friend, Mr Charles Macky. Charlie, this is my sister-in-law, Mrs Anne Williams."

"Pleased to meet you," says Charlie. "I'd shake your hand, only..." He nods his head to the udder between his fingers.

Anne ignores him, wrinkles her nose once more and turns to me. "I wonder if I could speak to you in private, Angharad."

"Of course. Come through to the farmhouse."

"This won't take long. I'll wait for you in the yard."

Anne marches out of the milking parlour and Charlie whispers, "My, isn't she a charmer?"

"You don't know the half of it," I say, my shoulders slumping as I go to find her.

The sun is low enough in the sky that I need to squint against it. Everything around me is bathed in a warm yellow glow, marred only by Anne in her drab colours, her face pinched and her foot tapping in impatience.

"What can I do for you, Anne?"

"Your brother is worried about you."

"Worried about me? Why?"

"We've heard what you've been getting up to, positioning yourself at the centre of village life. It's a dangerous game you're playing, Angharad. If folk find out the truth, it won't just be you who suffers the consequences. How do you think Bryn could stand up in front of his congregation if anyone finds out what his sister is, what she's done? It would ruin all our reputations."

"I understand and share your concerns, sister, but our country is at war. I can't just sit back when I have skills that can be used for the greater good."

"Skills? Don't make me laugh. Growing a few turnips isn't going to help us win the war."

"If what you've heard about me is true, you'll know I've been doing more than just growing turnips."

"Exactly! You're sharing a home with a single man, who you don't know from Adam!"

"I am not sharing a home with either Mr Stephens or Mr Macky. Charlie is living in the farmhouse, and I live in my bothy."

"You know how tongues around here wag."

"Please, Anne, it's nothing like you describe. I've provided a home and a job to a wounded soldier. If anyone in the village questions the propriety of our situation, I'd be happy to explain the arrangement to them."

"Hmph, well you want to watch your back, missy. But that's not why I'm here."

"Why are you here?" I ask, failing to keep the annoyance from my voice.

"Word has reached us that the Women's Institute is planning to start a Girls' Club."

"Not that I've heard. We listened to a talk by someone from Holyhead who runs one and all thought it sounded like a good idea, but no one has proposed we set one up in Llanfairpwll. But even if we did, I'm afraid I don't understand the problem."

"Don't understand the problem? It would completely contradict what we teach our members at Sunday school."

"How?"

"We teach our girls obedience, respect for their elders. You lot will fill young girls' heads with foolish notions of women being independent from men, and getting above their station in life."

"That's not what a Girls' Club is about."

"Oh, really? Well, Bryn and I have decided it's about time we find out what really goes on at these meetings of yours."

"What do you mean?"

"What I mean is I intend to join your Women's Institute and see what goes on there for myself. I've heard you need an existing member to propose a new one, so that will be your job, Angharad. You can come to the house before your next meeting and we shall attend together."

"I'm really not sure the Women's Institute would be your cup of tea, Anne."

"Trying to discourage me, are you? That makes me even more sure you've something to hide. It will be very interesting to see what goes on with my own eyes. When is your next meeting?"

"I'm not sure."

"Don't be ridiculous."

As much as I'd like to lie, I know there is no point. "The next meeting is on the eighteenth of September, but next month we have all been invited to tea by Lady Anglesey."

"At Plas Newydd?" says Anne, her eyes lighting up.

"Yes, but as you won't yet be a member, it's best you wait until the September meeting to join us."

"And miss the chance of tea at Plas Newydd? I don't think so! I shall come as your guest."

As Anne takes her leave, any joy seeps from my soul. Nothing will be the same with Anne involved. My every move will be scrutinized. I shall have to revert to the old Angharad I thought I'd left behind. Despite the warm sun on my skin and the golden light surrounding me, the world suddenly feels rather grey.

Chapter Fifty-Six

Angharad

August 1917

Today is one of those rare summer days where everything is soft. Golden light blurs the horizon with a slight haze, the Menai Strait glistening like a jewel around the neck of Plas Newydd. A hint of summer flowers floats on the air and a gentle breeze keeps the sun's heat at bay. The day would be close to perfect, if it weren't for Anne by my side.

"What a remarkable house," she says, as we emerge from the tree-lined drive to see the mansion in all its glory. For someone who professes not to covet material things, Anne's eyes sparkle with poorly disguised envy. "I've always wondered what it is like inside."

"It was kind of Lady Anglesey to invite us for tea. She recently became a patron of our WI and subscribed five pounds. I'm not sure that is entirely within the rules, but it was very generous of her and will contribute to our building fund." Nerves set my tongue wagging, and I regret even this small amount of information I have passed to Anne. I've grown so comfortable among the Institute members it is hard to revert to the cautiousness of my previous life.

"It sounds as though you're trying to ingratiate yourself into a class you don't belong to," says Anne, and I try not to laugh at the hypocrisy of her words.

"No, not at all."

"And it is rude to discuss money, especially in the context of someone such as Lady Anglesey."

"Sorry."

As I follow Anne along the gravel driveway, I notice her adjust her hat and straighten her jacket. But in contrast to the natural beauty around us, even Anne's best clothes look dowdy, her pretty face pinched, lines marring her skin across her forehead from frowning and around her mouth from the disapproval of pursed lips.

A maid greets us at the door and leads us through an ornate entrance hall.

Ffion's eyes widen in surprise as I walk into the grand room with Anne by my side, then she springs into action, introducing me to Lady Anglesey and explaining my work on the allotments. Anne's lips curl at the praise.

"And this is my sister-in-law," I say, "Mrs Anne Williams."

"Wife of Reverend Williams," says Anne, pushing me aside with her shoulder as she stretches out a hand in greeting. "It is a pleasure to meet you, Lady Anglesey, and thank you for the invitation to your beautiful home."

Ffion catches my eye and raises an eyebrow. Lady Anglesey appears not to care much for Anne's fawning ways as she hurries on to greet two new arrivals.

"Come and sit over here with me," says Ffion.

As we follow Ffion to a settee as big as a bed, I say, "Anne is keen to join the Women's Institute."

"Oh, I see. What's brought on this sudden interest?"

"There is nothing sudden about my interest," says Anne, her voice prim. "I've heard so much about the organisation from my sister-in-law,

I thought it was about time I came to see what it's all about myself. I hear you have a committee?"

"Yes, we do."

"Good, then I should like to be considered for membership."

"Of the committee?"

"Yes."

"I see. It might be best to attend a few meetings first, to make sure the Women's Institute is something you feel ready to commit to."

"I'll have you know, Mrs Montgomery, I have run the chapel Sunday school every Sunday for the past ten years. I have not missed a single week. That should give you an idea as to the level of commitment I am capable of."

Ffion's eyebrows raise, but she seems unable to come up with a response.

"I don't think we've been introduced," says Mrs Jones, sitting beside Anne. "I'm Mrs Jones of Graig, where we hold our monthly meetings."

"Mrs Williams," says Anne.

To my and Ffion's relief, Mrs Jones engages Anne in conversation, freeing us up to talk.

"Why is your sister-in-law really here? Why the sudden interest in the WI and the work we do?"

"I fear her only interest is to spy on me and gather information to take back to my brother."

Ffion frowns. "Surely not? Angharad, if that is true, it would be helpful to know why there is such a rift in your family. Why is your brother so keen to clip your wings?"

"That's family business."

"Not if it affects the WI. Is she serious about becoming a committee member?"

"If she is, it will only be to cause trouble."

"In that case, I'll do everything I can to stop it from happening. You know, whilst the WI is proud to be a broad church, I'm not sure everyone is suited to it."

"What do you mean?"

"Well, it's about building community and teamwork. Ladies with their own agenda are unlikely to fit in."

"I'm not sure what I can do, though. Anne seems adamant about joining."

"Leave it to me," says Ffion. "I'm sure I can think of something."

Chapter Fifty-Seven

Carys

September, 1917

"We're very lucky with the weather," says Angharad, carrying another two chairs out onto the lawn. She looks relieved to have escaped her sister-in-law for a minute. That woman has been glued to Angharad's side from the moment she joined the WI, and I don't like it, or her, one bit.

"How many people are we expecting?" I ask, fanning myself against the unusually warm day.

"Around fifty, I think," says Ffion. "A few chaps are coming from my convalescent home, but they're mostly coming from the military hospital in Bangor."

"Just soldiers?

"Soldiers and nurses."

My mind drifts to Dai. I've respected Mrs Jones' instructions not to visit again, but it leaves me with terrible guilt. Have I been keeping my distance for Dai's sake, or has it been for more selfish reasons? The way Dai went for me left me so shaken and I wish I could have told Mami, Florian, Angharad or Ffion about it, but it didn't feel right, it would be a betrayal of Dai.

"Carys?"

"Sorry," I say, looking up at Ffion. "Did you ask me something?"

"Yes, Mrs Cotton has suggested we serve the tea outside, given it's such a fine day. Would you help Angharad carry the tables out?"

"Of course."

"It will give her a few more minutes away from Mrs Williams," says Ffion under her breath, one eyebrow raised.

I meet her statement with a nod of understanding. Our friend seems to have retreated into her shell since the arrival of Anne Williams, and it will be up to us to prise her out of it again.

"Don't you have men to do that for you?" asks Anne as I enter the building and help Angharad select the tables we will need.

"We are called the *Women's* Institute."

"Only when it suits," says Anne. "The Colonel doesn't look much like a woman to me. If only you'd consider being more tolerant, my husband, Reverend Williams, could bring no end of expertise to the group."

I curse silently. Not this again. Ever since the blasted woman darkened our door, she's been trying to find a way to involve that husband of hers. If she didn't want to be part of a women-only organisation, she shouldn't have bothered coming along in the first place.

"You know the Colonel is the exception, not the rule, sister," says Angharad, her voice quiet, her eyes downcast.

"Yes, but Bryn is just as much a part of this community as the Colonel and..."

"Can we not have this argument again?" Angharad's words are sharp and loud, and several heads turn in our direction.

Anne steps towards us, glowering. "I'd watch your tongue, if you know what's good for you, sister." She spits the last word, as though naming some unmentionable disease. I wouldn't mind taking one of these tables and cracking it over the woman's skull.

"Come on, Angharad," I say, "there's work to do."

As Angharad picks up the table, I notice her entire body is shaking. I give her a reassuring smile and we set about our task.

An hour later and we're all set up. There is space on the lawn for physical games, and tables set up with chess and other board games for the soldiers whose injuries prevent them from joining in the sports. Three tables sit on the edge of the lawn, covered in all the food we could cobble together since restrictions came in. I'm often minded of the story of Jesus feeding the five thousand when I look at the spreads our WI puts together.

Excited chatter breaks out as a bus pulls up on the road. Soon, a stream of women and men are making their way towards us. Many of the men are pushed along in chairs by nurses, some walk with the aid of crutches. The last group of men to leave the bus appear to have no physical injuries, but huddle together, their eyes darting around them as though suspicious of their day out.

As the last group of soldiers make their way towards us, my breath catches. Dai. Nobody told me he'd been sent to the military hospital, but then why should they? And given what I witnessed at the Joneses' farm, it shouldn't come as a surprise that they couldn't cope with him at home.

At first, I hang back, unsure of what to do.

"Are you alright?" asks Ffion, coming to stand beside me. "You look like you've seen a ghost."

Given the unpredictable nature of my former sweetheart's condition, it seems honesty is the best approach today. "One of those soldiers is my sweetheart, Dai."

"What?" says Ffion, her eyes widening. "I didn't know your fiancé was back in Anglesey."

"Former fiancé," I say. "He's not the same man who joined up. The war has done terrible things to his mind."

Ffion nods her understanding. Of course, out of everyone she would understand, given her experience at the convalescent home. "Why didn't you say something sooner?"

"I suppose I wanted to protect Dai. It's the least I could do for him, given the circumstances."

"Which one is he?"

I point him out and we both spend a moment watching the man with the wild eyes, whose muscles twitch beneath his clothes and whose head keeps jerking up and down as though it has a mind of its own.

"He may well recover to some degree," says Ffion, "but it is likely to take quite some time. The military hospital is the right place for him."

"Part of me thinks I should have tried harder to stand by his side."

"He needs to focus on his own recovery. It sounds as though he has the support of his family?"

"Yes."

"Then that is a lot more than some men have. These injuries to the mind are unfamiliar and some find them hard to understand. There can often be unhelpful feelings among families that returning soldiers should just pull themselves together and everything will be alright, but I'm afraid that is not how these things work."

As if proving Ffion's point, Anne comes bustling up to us, shaking her head. "Just look at those soldiers over there. They are an embarrassment to their country. As I told Angharad when she was gloomy and pining over..." Anne's mouth clamps shut, her cheeks turn pink.

"You were saying?" says Ffion.

"Nothing. I just believe men should behave like men, that's all."

"You can't imagine what those poor chaps have been through," says Ffion, "particularly as your own husband didn't go off to fight."

"My husband was needed here, doing important work for the church!"

"They do have chaplains on the front line, you know," says Ffion, before marching off to help serve the teas.

I'm left with Anne, unsure of what to say. Before I can find an excuse to leave her side, Dai breaks away from his group and walks towards us. My heart sinks, not at having to speak to Dai, but at having to speak to him in the presence of Anne.

He is wearing civilian clothes, his shirt tucked neatly into his trousers. As he reaches us, he removes his cap and gives us each a nod.

"Hello, Dai. It's good to see you looking much better."

"Yes... I..." His face and head appear to spasm between each word, and he groans in frustration. "All... all... I... ugh." He places his hands on either side of his head to still it, and gets his words out in a rush. "I wanted to say sorry for my behaviour when you came to visit me."

"Dai," I say, placing a hand on the arm that is trying and failing to stop the jerk of his neck. "You have nothing to apologise for. I am glad you are home and wish you a speedy recovery."

"Thank you... Carys... and again... I'm truly sorry." Dai's eyes fill with tears, and I realise he is not just apologising for my experience at the farm. He is mourning the future we might have had should war not have crossed our paths.

"Right," says Anne, "I think a cup of tea is in order." She claps her hands, and the sound causes Dai to cover his ears and shriek. His body folds in on itself until he is half standing, half crouching, looking around him in terror.

As I wrap my arms around Dai's trembling body and lead him to a nurse, I glance back at Anne. At least she has the good grace to look embarrassed.

"I'm sorry," she calls after us, "I didn't mean to..." Her words fade as we walk away.

"He's had a shock," I explain as I hand Dai over to one of the nurses.

"You're Carys," she says, and although she smiles, she looks sad. "He dreams about you sometimes."

The nurse turns her attention to Dai and I walk away, my heart breaking not just at the nurse's words, but what the war has done to my friend. As the soldiers are corralled, ready to begin the games, I wonder if all our efforts are futile. After all, what is the point of a few games and a slice of cake after all these men have been through?

But as the more able-bodied soldiers are armed with spoons and hard-boiled eggs ready for their race, I change my mind. Even those not able to take part can't help but laugh as the men wobble their way along the course, eggs tumbling off spoons and rolling away down the slope. We won't win the war with an egg and spoon race, or by plying these men with cups of tea and fruitcake, but we can bring them some joy in a dark world. We can remind them what it feels like to smile. By inviting them here, we are telling them they are not alone. As I watch Dai's face transform into something resembling a smile, I see the power in the day. We are only ladies from a village in Anglesey, but today it feels as though we have made a big difference in our small corner of the world.

Chapter Fifty-Eight

Ffion

September, 1917

Matron is at her desk, looking as glum as ever when I enter the house. "Good afternoon, Matron. Is my husband at home?"

"Don't you think I've enough men to be keeping tabs on without worrying about your husband's whereabouts?"

"I only asked if you'd seen him."

"He's not down here," huffs Matron, before turning back to the notes she is studying. It's tempting to pop into the ward and offer words of encouragement to the soldiers in there, but Hector's reaction to arriving home to find his house overrun was bad enough without me neglecting him during his leave.

At the top of the stairs, I turn to my left where we have kept our private rooms and open each door, finding all empty. Matron must have been wrong, and Hector must be downstairs, after all.

I'm about to make my way to the staircase when I hear a cry from the servants' quarters above. It has always been my policy to keep the servants' quarters private, but the cry I hear unnerves me. For a moment, I hover with my hand on the rail beside the stairs, listening. Yes, there it is again, the unmistakable cry of someone in distress.

My immediate thought is that one of the soldiers has somehow found their way up here. The stairs are narrow and steep, so it must have been a man with less serious wounds. As I climb the stairs two at a time, I run through a list of all the men in our care and try to settle on a culprit.

"No!"

The cry causes me to break into a run, my boots clicking against the stone steps, my dress hitched up around my knees. Once on the landing, I pause, listening. Sounds reach me from a room at the end of the corridor and I run towards it.

"No, please, stop!"

My palm is sweaty as I grip the door handle, and I pause for a moment, terrified at what I'll find, then I shake some sense into myself. This is my house, and the people in it are under my care. The noises don't belong to a romantic tryst. The voice I heard sounds scared.

I push the door open, and it bangs against the wall. My hand flies to my mouth as I see Susan pinned to the bed, her skirt pushed up around her waist. A man is holding her down with one hand, while trying to force her drawers down with the other. His own trousers sit around his ankles, and he is panting as Susan struggles beneath him.

"Stop what you are doing immediately."

The man turns, and a second wave of horror strikes as I realise this is no demented soldier.

"Hector?"

As Hector's mouth drops open, Susan uses the moment to make her escape, pushing past my husband and running into my arms sobbing, her body trembling as she leans against me.

"What on earth is happening here?" It is the most foolish question I could ask, as it is plain as day what I've interrupted. The thought of what might have happened had I not arrived home when I did causes my stomach to turn. My disgust only intensifies as a lazy smile spreads across Hector's face.

"Ffion, darling, this is a surprise. I wasn't expecting you back so soon."

"Clearly not." Somehow, I force my voice to come out in a steady sound, despite my legs having turned to jelly. "What exactly do you think you were doing?"

"The maid and I were just having a bit of fun."

I glance down at Susan, whose sobs have reduced to hiccups, but whose body is still trembling violently. "Fun? *Fun?* This is your idea of fun?" The words come out as a shriek, causing Susan to jump and press closer against me.

"I'm sorry, madam," she whispers through her tears.

"You have nothing to be sorry about."

"This is all a lot of fuss about nothing," says Hector, pulling up his trousers and fastening his belt. "I thought I'd treat the maid to a good time. It's not my fault she's frigid as a plank of wood."

"The maid has a name, Hector. Susan is little more than a child. She's younger than your own daughter."

"Age is of no consequence with these country girls. Isn't that right, Susan?"

The poor girl lets out a whimper and buries her face in my neck.

"Look what you've done," I say, the hatred I feel clear in my voice. "You're a monster."

"A man has needs, my darling. And if a wife won't fulfil those needs, you can't blame a chap for looking elsewhere."

Hector strides across the room towards us, and both Susan and I flinch. He laughs, raises his hand, then tips back his head in mirth as we flinch again. "So pathetic, the pair of you," he says, before pushing past us and marching off along the corridor.

For a moment, Susan and I stand in a shocked silence. Then I try to move her back to the bed so she can sit down, but she starts to cry, batting away my hands and shivering in fear.

"You don't want to be in this room?"

Susan shakes her head so violently her hair falls out of its pins.

"Alright, we'll go down to the kitchen. It's only Mrs Edwards in there at this time of day. You can warm up and we'll get you a cup of sweet tea. You need something after the shock you've had."

Somehow, I keep hold of my anger as I wrap an arm around Susan and lead her along the corridor and back down the stairs. We pass Matron, who gives us a strange look. "Susan's feeling unwell," I explain. "Nothing to worry about. I'm just taking her to get a cup of tea."

Matron nods, despite her narrowed eyes showing she doesn't believe a word of my explanation. When we walk into the kitchen, Mrs Edwards drops the rolling pin she's holding and rushes towards us. "What on earth has happened here?"

"Susan's had a shock. Can you make her a cup of tea, and put some sugar in please, if we've any spare?"

"Lucky I keep some hidden in the pantry for emergencies."

I settle Susan on a chair beside the fire and by the time Mrs Edwards returns with the tea she is no longer shaking, but is staring into space, her eyes blank.

Mrs Edwards sits herself on a chair opposite and takes the girl's hands. "Is it the same as what happened before?" she asks. Susan gives a tiny nod, and I stare at them both.

"This isn't the first time? Oh, goodness, please say he didn't... has he..."

"Last time it was me that found them," says Mrs Edwards. The usual warmth is gone from her eyes, and she gives me a hard stare.

"I promise you, I had no idea anything like this was going on under my roof. Why didn't you say something before?"

Mrs Edwards laughs. "Say what, exactly? To whom?"

"You could've told me."

"And you'd have believed us, would you? Folk like Mr Montgomery think they rule the world. Susan has been luckier than some. At least she had the good sense to tell me about his remarks, his touching, so I could keep an eye on her and put a stop to it when he finally tried it on. It happens more often than you'd think, Mrs Montgomery. Girls get taken into service while they're still children, innocent to the ways of the world, and men like your husband take advantage of that innocence."

"I truly had no idea. I'm so sorry, Susan. What can I do to make this better?"

"You can keep your husband away from her, for starters."

"Today is the last day of his leave. He returns to base tomorrow."

"Then tonight Susan can come home with me. But will you be alright?"

Despite the circumstances, I can't help but laugh, even if it holds no mirth. "I think I'm a little old now for my husband's tastes. So many times, he's returned home from one of his business trips smelling of another woman's perfume, but never did I imagine he'd do anything like this."

"Well, if he's off tomorrow, Susan will be safe from him for a while."

"And I'll make sure this never happens again. I don't know how yet, but you have my word on that, Susan."

"Thank you, Mrs Montgomery. And I'm sorry for what has happened."

"You have nothing to apologise for. Now, why don't you stay in here with Mrs Edwards for the rest of the afternoon, and I'll make sure Mr Montgomery stays well out of your way."

I leave the two women finishing their tea. Unable to face anyone, I let myself out of the back door and walk down through the garden until I've reached the Strait. My husband is a powerful man, and I have little sway over him, but suddenly the idea of the Girls' Club I'd pooh-poohed makes sense. If we can teach young girls to find their voice and understand a little more of the world around them, maybe it will go some way in preventing the incident I witnessed this afternoon. Perhaps that is wishful thinking, but given what I've just experienced, anything is worth a try.

Chapter Fifty-Nine

Angharad

September, 1917

S omething is wrong with Ffion. Her skin is pale and there are purple shadows beneath her eyes. With Anne distracted by a conversation with Mrs Cotton and Mrs Jones, I am grateful for the chance to speak to Ffion free from Anne's watchful gaze. "Are you alright?" I ask her as we take our seats for the special meeting. "I wasn't sure you'd attend this meeting given your feelings about the Girls' Club." Ffion gives me a curt nod, and I notice her eyes fill with tears as she looks away. A minute of silence passes between us, then she speaks without turning her head.

"You were right about the Girls' Club. I shall support it fully."

"Oh, that's good. What's caused this change of heart?"

"I'd rather not say."

Ffion's hands wring in her lap and as she looks down, a lone tear spills down her face, resting on the end of her dainty nose until she brushes it away.

"Hello," says Carys, sitting down beside us with an exhausted sigh.

"How are you?" I ask.

"Fine, thank you."

I sit back in my seat, wondering what is wrong with my friends. As far as I can tell, there has been no falling out between them.

"Would you ladies have time for a brief stroll after the meeting?" asks Ffion.

"A stroll?" It's impossible to hide my surprise at the suggestion. Women like me and Carys don't stroll without purpose or destination, and neither does Ffion, since the convalescent home stole all her free time.

"It was a silly suggestion," says Ffion, twiddling her fingers with more intensity.

"No, it's a good suggestion. I can spare an hour after the meeting before I need to get back to the milking."

"So can I," says Carys.

Carys catches my eye, and I shrug to show I have no more idea what is happening than she does.

The meeting progresses well. Mrs Langlands proposes we set up our own Girls' Club and Mrs Sargent seconds the idea. The structure of the club sounds straightforward enough. It will be held each week on Tuesday, between six and eight-thirty p.m. When a subscription of one shilling is proposed, I suggest it should be payable either in advance or in instalments, to give flexibility for girls who might otherwise be unable to pay, and it is a relief when everyone agrees. I feel Anne's eyes boring into my back and wish I hadn't spoken up, for I will no doubt pay for it later.

It is agreed that girls must be aged over fourteen to join, and this seems sensible, as girls of this age will be out of school and often more isolated. Miss Margaret Williams volunteers to write to the school managers for loan of the school kitchen, and each week three or four ladies will be responsible for the smooth running of the evening.

We then enter a discussion on rules of the club, but I find it hard to concentrate on the chatter around me. My mind keeps straying to whatever it is upsetting Ffion, and the practical matter of how I can meet my friends without arousing Anne's suspicions, for if she finds out, she will insist on coming too.

"I'll walk home with Anne," I whisper to Ffion, "pretend I'm going home, and then come to meet you for that walk. Where will you be?"

"Meet me by Nelson's statue. You know where that is?"

"Of course I do."

The meeting draws to a close and I begin the short walk from Graig to Anne's house.

"You shouldn't have spoken up as you did," she says.

"About the subscription? Surely there wasn't anything controversial in what I said?"

"That is not the point. The point is, you were drawing attention to yourself, and I thought we'd agreed that is unwise. Do you really want those ladies finding out about your past? And while we're on the subject of getting too big for your boots, you had better not be thinking of volunteering to help at the Girls' Club. That would be expressly against your brother's wishes and I shan't be able to protect you from the consequences of such a betrayal."

"Of course, sister."

We reach Anne's house, and I bid her farewell. I sometimes wonder if she has a sixth sense for deception, for instead of walking up to her front door as she usually would, she stands at the front gate watching me walk away. It means I'm forced to walk a good half a mile in the opposite direction I want to be, and by the time I reach the Menai Strait, I am out of breath, and Carys and Ffion are pacing out their impatience beside Nelson's statue.

"We thought you weren't coming," says Carys as I reach them.

"Anne stood watching me, so I had to walk the length of the street, and didn't think I could risk doubling back on myself in case she was looking out for me."

"Do you think she's a witch?" asks Ffion, a smile playing on the edges of her lips. "What is going on between the pair of you, anyway? It's as if she's a spy, watching your every move."

"Oh, it's nothing. We're not here to talk about me. Come on, tell us what is going on."

"Can we walk?" Ffion asks. "I find it easier to talk that way."

"Of course."

We follow the line of the water, our boots kicking up salty spray as we go. I wonder if Ffion will speak at all, her eyes fixed on the distant mountains turned golden by the setting sun.

"Hector enjoys the company of young women."

A moment of shocked silence passes before Carys tries to lighten the mood. "Don't all men?"

Ffion takes a deep breath. "Hector enjoys the company of young *girls*." She slips on a patch of seaweed, and I grab her arm to steady her.

"You mean he has affairs?"

"Yes, and I've known about those our whole married life. What I wasn't aware of was how young he liked his women, or how determined he can be to get what he wants from them."

"You mean he attacks them?" Carys is unable to keep the horror from her voice.

"Not always, at least I hope not. At Christmas, I caught him in the stables with a girl from the village. He doesn't know I saw them, but she knew I was there, and it seemed to make her enjoy the experience even more."

"Hence your reaction to the Girls' Club."

"I'm sorry," says Carys, "I don't understand what the Girls' Club has to do with anything?"

"This is the part I'm most ashamed of," says Ffion. She walks up the beach and we follow her to a low stone wall where she sits, her right hand playing with the gold band on her ring finger. "I blamed the girls. I thought it was their fault. I tarred all the village girls with the same brush, refusing to see what was right in front of my nose. It wasn't for the girls to refuse Hector. He should never have approached them in the first place. I imagine some of them have no experience of men, and a charming, wealthy older man comes along with his flattery and gifts, and I can see how they'd fall for it."

"What changed your mind?" I say, taking Ffion's hands in mine in a gesture of support.

"I caught him with my maid, Susan. He was trying to... he was... if I hadn't arrived when I did, I can't bear to think what might have happened."

"Good Lord," says Carys. "What a pig! When did this happen?"

"Last week. I'm ashamed it took such an awful event to open my eyes. I should have realised sooner. Now I see how important these Girls' Clubs are. We may not be directly instructing the girls on the ways of the world, but it gives them a space to talk to one another and share any worries they may have. They can learn from each other's experience. How could I not have realised what was going on under my roof?" Ffion splays her hands out in front of her, shaking her head.

"You've had so much going on under that very same roof lately," says Carys, "and besides, Hector has been away at war. You've not noticed anything because until he returned home on leave, there has been nothing to see."

"Did you speak to Susan about it afterwards?"

"Yes, and Mrs Edwards told me it's happened before. Thankfully, she put a stop to it the first time."

"If you didn't know, it can't possibly be your fault. It's not as if you knew and have been turning a blind eye. Some women might well have ignored what was going on, but you intervened before it was too late by the sounds of things."

"What am I going to do, though? I know it's awful to say, but the war has been good to me. I've found a purpose in my life, and it has got Hector from under my roof. When war ends, he'll return, and things will go back to the way they have always been."

"Says who? Ffion, all of us have changed. Goodness, the world has changed. Even when the war ends, nothing will be the same again. And women are on the brink of being granted the vote. We have rights, we have a voice. Let's throw ourselves into this Girls' Club the way we have with everything else the WI has put along our path. For now, let's worry about today, and leave the future for tomorrow."

Chapter Sixty

Angharad

October, 1917

Tonight would be far easier with Carys or Ffion by my side, but Carys can't spare an evening away from the farm and Ffion is tied up at home given it's Matron's day off. The nights are already drawing in and dusk is settling over Llanfairpwll as I walk into the village. I'm grateful for the cover of darkness, for it is a risk coming here tonight.

Never have I felt anything quite like it. This must be what it's like to be a criminal, looking over your shoulder, ducking around corners and jumping at shadows. The shortest walk from my cottage to the school would involve walking directly past Bryn's house.

Only the Colonel could have put me in a position like this. He has a unique ability to coerce with kindness and is impossible to refuse when he makes a request. It should be blindingly obvious I'm the least qualified member of the WI to assist with a Girls' Club, but the Colonel had other ideas. Against my better judgment, I promised I would be here, and how can I break a promise to a man in his position? But if I see Anne, or Bryn, who has forbidden me to go, I will have no choice but to return to the bothy with my tail between my legs.

Even if I make it to the meeting unseen, it will only take a cursory inquiry from Anne to establish my presence. And what will be the consequence? Bryn has the power to destroy me at a time of his choosing.

Never have I so blatantly gone against his wishes that I keep myself out of sight and mind.

When I arrive at the school building, I see Mrs Roberts, the appointed caretaker, has already arrived. Orange light spills from the tall windows onto the street beyond, and as I walk into the building, a fire in the hearth is taking the edge off the chilled air.

"Good evening, Miss Williams," says Mrs Roberts as she arranges a selection of tables and chairs.

"Good evening, Mrs Roberts. Do you need any help?"

"No, it's all seen to, thank you."

"Do you have any idea what sort of numbers we can expect tonight?"

"It's hard to say. Given it's the first meeting, either we'll attract a good amount of girls curious to find out what it's all about, or they'll stay at home hoping others will try it out and report back. We'll just have to wait and see."

A group of WI members arrive and the room fills with excited chatter. Several of them have brought along their daughters, who form a huddle of their own in a corner, talking and laughing at a volume that suggests the sharing of secrets.

Before long, girls outnumber women and cups of tea are being dished out left, right and centre. The door opens and a red-headed girl arrives. From the looks of her, she is on the younger side of the age range, and I can't believe she's any older than fourteen. She steps into the room, then promptly positions herself against a wall. I recognise her movements. She is trying to disappear. A few other girls have noticed her arrival and do nothing to conceal their mirth at the girl's appearance, pointing, laughing and throwing looks across the room that leave no doubt this late arrival is not welcome.

It strikes me that since I arrived, I have been doing much the same as this girl, hiding in the kitchen to the side of the main room, trying to avoid as many interactions as I can. But the sight of this young lady causes me to step out from my hiding place. Her eyes flicker in alarm as I cross the room, and I try to see myself through her eyes. In her position, I'd probably be terrified too.

"Good evening," I say, when I reach her.

"Good evening," she mutters, keeping her eyes trained on the floor.

The girl can't be over five feet tall, and it occurs to me that towering over her will do nothing to put her fears to rest. I take two chairs and position them against the wall. "Would you like to sit down?"

She nods and takes a seat. Her feet barely reach the floor and one of her legs is jiggling up and down as though it has a mind of its own.

"Would you like a cup of tea?"

She nods again. Her fingers are pink from the cold and the thread-bare shirt and cardigan she's wearing can't have given much protection against the weather. I fetch us two cups of tea, and as she takes one, her sleeves roll up and I spot the bruises marring her skin. She catches me looking and quickly pulls the fabric back in place, her cheeks heating with either embarrassment or shame.

"I'm Miss Angharad Williams," I say once I've taken a seat and curled myself up as small as I'm able. "What's your name?"

"Jane."

"Plain Jane," comes a whisper from a group of girls a few feet away. I glare at them and they scuttle off across the room.

"A pleasure to meet you, Jane. Have you come far?"

"No."

Silence stretches between us as we sip our tea. I study Jane over the top of my cup. She is almost as wide as she is tall, her sturdy legs exposed by the tatty stockings which keep falling down around her ankles. Her shoes are held together with string and her red hair is greasy and matted. Jane's face is round and childlike, but there is something captivating about her hazel eyes and I can well imagine her turning into quite a beauty as she grows.

"Is your mother a member of the Women's Institute?" I ask, scrabbling for topics of conversation.

"Mami's dead."

"Oh, I am very sorry. My mami died a while back, too."

Jane looks up at me with a frown. "You don't have a mami?"

"No, Jane, I don't. Or a dadi, for that matter."

"I have a dadi," says Jane, her eyes returning to the ground. "But he's away at war with my brother Rhys."

"Who do you live with then, if your dadi and brother are away?"

"My granny and grandpa."

"I see. And they encouraged you to come here tonight?"

"Said it was a good chance to get me out of the house."

"I see. And do you go to school?"

Jane nods, but her eyes fill with tears.

"Do you enjoy going to school, Jane?"

This time she shakes her head, casting a quick glance at one group of girls across the room.

"How old are you?"

"Fourteen."

"Ah, so you won't have long to go?"

"Two months."

"Those two months will fly by, Jane, believe me. I didn't enjoy school either, but these days it feels like it was the blink of an eye." My own cheeks flush at my lie. When I think back to my school days, I remember every taunt and every beating like it was yesterday, but there's no need for Jane to know this. I want to question where her bruises came from, school or home, but it isn't my place. Before I decide, the meeting is opened and Mrs Sargent sets out the rules and aims of the club. The girls around me smile and fidget in excitement, but at the mention of the one-shilling subscription, I feel Jane stiffen beside me. When I look at her, her face has fallen.

As Mrs Sargent lists some activities on offer and invites the girls to make their suggestions, I lean closer to Jane and whisper to her, "don't worry about the one-shilling subscription. Us WI members have the option to sponsor a girl's place in the club if we wish." I cross my fingers behind my back, disliking how easily lies are spilling from my lips, but knowing instinctively the girl beside me will never accept charity. "I would like to sponsor you, Jane, if that is alright with you?"

"Really?"

"Really, but only if you'd like me to."

"I would, thank you, Miss Williams."

"You're very welcome, Jane."

As the discussion in the room continues, I am glad I'm able to help the girl I very much recognise from my own youth, but at the same time I worry. It seems there's a big enough target on Jane's back already, without her being associated with the likes of me.

When the discussion ends and the girls are invited to choose from a selection of games or crafts, I invite Jane to walk with me and together we cross the room.

"Hello," I say, as we reach another girl who has been sitting on her own since she arrived. "I thought we should come and introduce ourselves. I'm Miss Angharad Williams from the Women's Institute, and this is my friend, Jane. Would you like some company?"

The girl in front of us is a good foot taller than Jane, and built like a beanpole, but they share the same scared eyes and nervous smile.

"I would, if that's alright," says the girl. "My name's Mary, and I've come from Penmynydd, so I don't know many other girls here."

"A pleasure to meet you, Mary," I say, shaking her hand. "Now, I hope you girls don't mind, but I promised to help serve the tea and I'm needed back in the kitchen. Will you be alright if I leave you for a while?"

Mary, the more confident of the two, agrees, and Jane simply nods but gives me a small smile. I return it, then cross the room to the kitchen. Before I return to my duties, I take a moment to watch the two girls. Just as I'd hoped, they soon fall into conversation, and I see Jane smile properly for the first time since she arrived. With a smile on my face, I turn my back on them, confident that just as I have at the WI, Jane might just have found herself a friend.

Chapter Sixty-One

Angharad

October, 1917

As has become our routine, I wait for Anne outside her front gate. It is raining, and my coat is growing heavy and cold, but there is no offer of a hot cup of tea, or the chance to wait in the warm. The brim of my hat has soaked up water and droops over my eyes, so that when Anne appears beside me, I jump out of my skin.

"Guilty conscience?" she asks. "Only you seem a little jumpy this afternoon."

"No guilty conscience," I lie.

We walk to Graig in silence, and it is an effort to shorten my steps so I don't leave Anne behind, much as I'd like to. It is only as we reach the gates to the driveway that Anne places a hand on my arm and speaks.

"A little bird told me you attended the first Girls' Club meeting." Her tone is light-hearted, and I wonder if it might be alright after all.

"Who told you that?"

"Mrs Sargent, I saw her in the post office, and she was singing your praises, saying what a great help you'd been."

"That's kind of her."

"The thing is, Angharad, I felt sorry for the woman."

"Why?"

"Because you've fooled her just as you've fooled the rest of them."

My heart sinks. I should have known I wouldn't get away with such a deceit. I stare at the ground, waiting for Anne to inflict her next blow.

"You know," she says, her tone still light, "I'm beginning to wonder if it isn't time these friends of yours found out about Eddy."

Eddy. The name slices through me like a knife, the pain in my heart as brutal as if I'd been cut with a real blade.

"If these people truly have such a high opinion of you, you should have nothing to fear."

Before I can answer, Anne is striding ahead of me towards the summerhouse. My heart pounds and I feel lightheaded. My mouth is dry as a bone but I've nothing to drink. My stomach lurches and I run across the road and dart behind a bush, retching. I don't know what to do. Should I go to the meeting and get the moment over with? Or return to my bothy and hide away with Betty, as I've always done. Before I can decide, someone calls my name.

"Angharad, I thought it was you. Are you alright? Where's Anne?"

"I'm fine, thank you, Ffion," I say, turning to give my mouth a discreet wipe. "Anne went on ahead."

Ffion frowns. "That's not like her. What's happened?"

"Nothing, nothing. She was keen to get to the meeting, that's all."

"Alright," says Ffion, looking like she doesn't believe a word I'm saying. "How was the first Girls' Club? Did many girls attend?"

"Yes, it went very well, thank you. We'd better get up to the summerhouse, as the meeting will be about to start."

"We've a lady named Mrs. Clowes talking to us this afternoon about herb collecting. She's a government lecturer."

"The government employs women to lecture on herb collecting?" I ask in disbelief.

"I'm sure that is only a small part of her remit." Ffion laughs. "Come on, if she's employed by the government, I expect she is a rather talented speaker, and we might just learn something."

Mrs Clowes' talk is indeed interesting, not least when she describes the work Madge Watt's WI at Wivelsfield does cultivating and selling herbs, but throughout the talk I feel sick. I am sitting beside Anne, whose lips are formed into a permanent smirk. I dare not look at her, for she is enjoying the moment. When I entered the summerhouse, there were no stares or harsh words, so I can safely assume she hasn't revealed my secret yet. Perhaps she is waiting for the end of the evening. Part of me wishes she'd just get it over with.

Professor Robinson stands up next and reads a paper on Food Values and Diet, which the women around me seem to find very interesting, but which goes completely over my head. All I can think about is Eddy. How many months has it been since thoughts of Eddy preoccupied my mind? I have been so busy lately, the time we spent together feels like a distant dream, but Anne's threat has brought my memories back into sharp focus.

As the professor reassures us that enough nutrition can be gained from meals that won't draw so heavily on the nation's food supply, I find myself dreaming of another meal, before we had to worry about the Germans trying to starve us into submission.

Eddy had been out hunting. Having grown up in the home of the local minister, I'd never had use for a gun, and our food was bought from the local market, not shot or trapped by our own hand. But Eddy was always more adventurous than me and appeared one day carrying the carcass of a deer, fur, hooves and head still intact. My horrified reaction had made Eddy scream with laughter, and I'd been given a lesson on preparing and cooking the best cuts of meat. We had eaten Eddy's prize catch by candlelight, accompanied by boiled potatoes, carrots from my allotment, and several bottles of beer. Afterwards, we sang and danced, ignoring the mess of dirty dishes and plates, our attention focussed solely on each other. It was one of the happiest nights of my life.

When my eyes fill with tears, it doesn't seem inappropriate, for the professor has been replaced by Mrs Cotton, who is expressing sympathy for Mrs Jones' and Miss Williams' recent bereavements. More sons and brothers of the village lost to the war. It should bring comfort that my grief is shared with others, but selfishly, I don't believe anybody has ever experienced anything close to the loss I feel over Eddy. There could never have been a greater love than which we shared, it just couldn't be possible.

"Please note," says Mrs Cotton, once a moment of silence has been observed, "that we are no longer in affiliation with the Agricultural Organization Society, but under the Board of Agriculture and Fisheries; the propaganda work of the Institute's being undertaken by the Women's Branch of the Food Production Department, of which Lady Denman is Assistant Director."

The words of Mrs Cotton swirl around me. I'm sure they are important, but I'm struggling to care. Anne taps me on the knee, and I nearly jump out of my skin.

"I think," she says, "that given the recent bereavement our friends have suffered, it would be inappropriate for me to share your secret with anyone today. But rest assured, Angharad, the moment will come soon, so best be prepared." She stands and walks off to fetch a cup of tea and browse the stall of homemade goods that members have donated in aid of the Red Cross. I stay pinned to my seat, Anne's power over me stealing my breath like a hangman's noose.

Chapter Sixty-Two

Angharad

November, 1917

I'm dozing by the fire when the knock comes on my door. Betty barks, her tail wagging as she runs to the front door and begins scrabbling against it.

"Not Bryn or Anne then," I say, on seeing her excitement. My hand flies to my mouth when I open the door to find Charlie and Mr Stephens on the other side. "What? How?"

"I asked Mr Stephens to help me get here," says Charlie. "There was no chance I'd get the chair across the fields myself." He turns to Mr Stephens and the two men shake hands. "Thanks ever so much for your help, Geraint." Charlie talks slowly, his speech exaggerated so Mr Stephens can understand. Mr Stephens gives him a nod to show he's understood, then heads back across the fields towards the farmhouse.

"What on earth are you doing here?" I ask.

"Nice way to greet a fellow. Aren't you going to invite me in?"

Unable to think of a suitable response, I step outside and push the wheelchair across the threshold. It is a relief to grip hold of the handlebars as my hands are trembling at this unexpected intrusion into my privacy. I try not to guess Charlie's reaction to seeing my home, but as is his way, there is no beating around the bush.

"Bloody hell, Angharad. Is this really where you live?"

I position his chair in front of the fire and place the kettle above the flames. "I'm quite comfortable here."

"Sorry, I didn't mean to sound rude. You've made this place very cosy, but when you talked about a cottage, I was expecting more than an old shepherd's hut stuck out in the middle of a field."

"It's a bothy, not a hut, and I don't see why I'd need any more space. After all, it's only me living here." Betty whines and jumps up onto Charlie's lap. "And Betty, of course," I say, tickling her under her chin.

"But I don't understand why you don't live in the farmhouse? There's plenty of room over there."

"My brother didn't think it would be appropriate for me to be living there with Mr Stephens. He thought people would gossip."

"About you and old Geraint?" Charlie roars with laughter and my cheeks burn. Clearly he doesn't think I'd be good enough for even an elderly widowed farmer. "No one in their right mind would think a pretty woman like you would run off with an old codger like him. I'm fond of old Geraint, but give me a break." He laughs again, and it's a relief when the kettle boils and I can distract myself with a practical task.

"I'm assuming you'd like a cup of tea," I say, "but you still haven't told me why you're here."

"Me and Geraint are worried about you."

"Worried about me? Whatever for?"

"Because you've not been yourself lately. When I first moved here, you were always chatting about your Women's Institute and all the different things you were getting up to. But lately, you've barely spoken a word at mealtimes and always have a sad look in your eye. We were wondering if it has anything to do with that family of yours."

"Of course not. Why would you think such a thing?" I hand Charlie his cup of tea, but can't look him in the eye.

"Don't get all coy with me, Angharad. We're friends, aren't we?"

"Yes, we are."

"Friends talk to each other. I'm a good listener, especially after all the time I spent with chaps in the trenches. Use me as your sounding board and consider it payment for all you've done to help me."

"There's nothing wrong with me."

Instead of speaking, Charlie stares at me, refusing to look away until I can bear it no longer.

"I don't have the easiest relationship with my brother and sis-ter-in-law."

"So I'd gathered. But if that's the case, why have you been spending so much time with them lately?"

"They like to keep an eye on me, make sure I'm on the straight and narrow."

Charlie bellows with laughter again, then stops when he realises I'm being serious. "The straight and narrow, hey? And why would they think you'd stray from it? It's not to do with me, I hope?"

With a sigh, I sit back in my chair and take a sip of my tea. "There are things I've done in the past that my brother disapproves of. If those things were ever to become public knowledge, I wouldn't be able to show my face in the village again and would most likely be forced to leave the area. I've no other family, nowhere else to go. If keeping Bryn and Anne happy means I can get on with my life, it's a small price to pay."

"Right," says Charlie, the muscles in his face twitching as he mulls over my words. "And I don't suppose you'll tell me what these dark secrets of yours are?"

"You suppose right."

"Fair enough. But you say you're getting on with your life, and I'm sorry, Angharad, but I don't believe it. You don't mention your friends anymore. And when was the last time you saw Mrs Montgomery?"

"Last month at the WI meeting."

"When was the last time you saw her without your sister-in-law at your elbow?"

"I'm not sure."

"You can't keep going like this, Angharad. Would it really be so bad if people found out whatever it is you're supposed to have done?"

"It isn't a risk I can take, Charlie. I'm a spinster in my thirties. I get by thanks to the arrangement I have with Mr Stephens, but if I were forced to leave the village, there is nowhere I can go. I'm too old and ugly to find a husband and would probably end up in a workhouse somewhere."

"Surely it can't be as bad as that? And it's not true, anyway."

"Which part?"

"About being too ugly to find a husband."

To my surprise, Charlie is blushing. "There's no need to be kind."

"I'm not being kind. Just because I've lost my legs, it doesn't mean there's anything wrong with my eyes. You're a fine-looking woman, Angharad. Any man would see the same as I do."

"Perhaps not the short ones," I say, and Charlie roars with laughter.

"You may have a point there. Not many men like a woman taller than them, but there are plenty of taller chaps out there. It's not like you're six foot."

"You'd be surprised how close to six foot I am."

"So what? Look at me, any woman I find myself with is going to be taller than me, aren't they?"

"You're comparing apples and pears."

"Oh really? So you're allowed to feel sorry for yourself and look at all the worst-case scenarios, but I'm not?"

"I suppose when you put it like that. You're a good man, Charlie. I hope you know how much I appreciate your friendship."

Charlie's cheeks redden again. "I hope you know I'm not the sort of chap who'd think less of you because of something you've done in your past. Blimey, given what I've seen over in France, you could have killed someone, and I'd barely bat an eyelid."

"But not everyone is as kind or open-minded as you are."

"Maybe not. I'd better get back to the farm, but please remember I'm here should you ever need to talk to someone. And don't worry about cooking tonight, me and Geraint are taking care of it."

"You?"

"There's no need to look so surprised. Us men aren't totally incapable."

"But how on earth do you know how to cook a meal?"

"My mami was poorly for a while a few years ago and me and my brothers had to step up as Dadi was as good as useless. I've a few tricks up my sleeve, I'll have you know. And you should see what I can do with a tin of bully beef. I heard the odd rumour of a chap in the trenches eating a rat, but I never stooped that low."

"I hope you're joking."

"I can't say it never happened, but mostly we used rats as a sport. Killing them with a bayonet was a good way to pass the time."

I shudder at the thought, and Charlie laughs again. "Come on, wheel me back over to the farmhouse, and we'll have supper on the table for you at six sharp. It's about time someone looked after you for a change."

Chapter Sixty-Three

Carys

January, 1918

I drop the basket I'm carrying and run across the yard to the sound of the scream. My fingers fumble with the front door's latch, then it bursts open, banging against the wall. The screams grow louder, coming from the kitchen. At the door, I stop running and pause, terrified of what might greet me.

The sound of smashing crockery filters through the door and I push on the wood, the hinges creaking as I hold my breath. Mami is standing in the middle of the room, her hair wild, her face streaked with tears. She picks up a dish and hurls it at the slate floor, china splintering into hundreds of tiny pieces.

"Mami, please, Mami, stop." I grab Mami's hands and she wrestles against me, trying to scratch my face or pull my hair. I whip my palm across her cheek, and she stumbles back, dazed.

"You hit me." Her voice sounds strange, as though it doesn't belong to her body. "Carys, you hit me."

I step forward and wrap my arms around her, leading her to a chair. "I'm sorry, Mami, but you were scaring me." With a gentle push, I get her seated, and only then do I notice the envelope on the table. My heart sinks as tears sting my eyes. I need to read whatever is inside that envelope, but I can't bear to pick it up.

Mami lets out a stream of sobs, each more violent than the last. Her body is no longer her own, as she shakes and shivers on the seat. I pull up a chair in front of her and sit down so close our knees are touching. With her fists clasped in my hands, I force her to look at me. "Take deep breaths, Mami. You need to calm down."

Her body shudders and she tries to pull in enough breath to speak. "P... P... The.... Letter..." A savage scream erupts from her mouth. It is a terrifying sound, like the foxes I hear at night.

Florian bursts into the room and I don't think I've ever been so glad to see anyone. "What's going on?" he asks, staring from me to Mami, then to the letter on the table.

"Can you read it?" I ask.

He nods and pulls a typed letter from the envelope.

"Peter?" I ask.

"I'm so sorry, Carys."

My own eyes remain stubbornly dry. There is too much emotion in the room already without me adding to it. Peter is dead. He is gone, and never coming back.

"Let me make you both some tea," says Florian.

"I broke the teapot," says Mami, her toe nudging the splinters of china around her feet.

"Not to worry," says Florian, "I'm sure I can manage. Carys, why don't you take your mother up to her bedroom? She's had a terrible shock and probably needs to lie down. I'll bring the tea up when it's ready."

"Thank you."

All Mami's rage has left her, and she slumps into my arms like a limp doll as I lift her to standing. Somehow, I get her up the stairs and into her bedroom. She flops onto the bed and curls up in a tight ball, her arms wrapped around her knees.

By the time Florian appears at the door carrying a tray of tea, Mami has cried herself to sleep and I shoo him away with my hand. We creep back downstairs and don't speak again until safely in the kitchen with the door closed. He sets down the tray on the table, steps towards me and wraps his arms around me, holding me close.

Safe in Florian's arms, I let the news of Peter sink in. Still no tears come, my sadness for Mami's loss, and for a future Peter will never get to see sitting in my heart like a stone. Florian strokes my hair and I wish I could stay in this position forever. When I step away, he keeps hold of my arms, looking deep into my eyes.

"Are you alright, Carys?" He is frowning, his stare so intense I want to look away.

"Yes, I am alright."

"You haven't cried."

"No," I say wearily, sitting down at the kitchen table. "I suppose this is news I've been expecting ever since Peter joined up."

"You don't always have to be the strong one."

"What do you mean?"

"I mean, you have had to carry your mother and this farm ever since your father died. There was no time for you to grieve, to lie in bed crying like your mother has."

"Mami isn't right in the head, Florian. I don't know what's wrong with her, but it's more than normal grief. She's a different woman from the one I used to know. Goodness knows how this latest piece of news will affect her. We'll have to keep a close eye on her, make sure she doesn't do anything stupid."

"Fine, so long as you know I am here for you. You do not need to carry this burden alone."

"Thank you," I say, taking Florian's warm hand in mine. "I need to write to my brother William in Canada. It will take a while for any letter to reach him."

"Do you need to do that today? You've had a terrible shock. Surely it can wait until tomorrow."

"There's no time to delay, Florian. We've been keeping the farm going, ready for Peter to take over once he came home, but Peter's death has changed everything. You and the girls will return to Belgium after the war and there is no way I can keep the farm going on my own. Either Will comes back to take his rightful place on the farm as head of the family, or we will have to give the farm up."

"Lose the farm? But that would be terrible."

"Would it? We've been working our fingers to the bone these past years and for what? We can barely scrape enough money to get by despite the hours we work. You hardly get to spend any time with your girls. I attend one WI meeting a month, but that's it for any sort of life."

"We have each other."

I turn away from Florian, unable to see the look I know will be in his eyes. We don't have each other, not really, or at least we do, but in a way that is temporary. Wales is not Florian's home. He's made no secret of his desire to return to Belgium. There's no denying an attraction lies between us, but even if I had the energy for romance, what would be the point? To get my heart broken again? No, thank you.

Chapter Sixty-Four

Ffion

February, 1918

I'm hoping the others will not yet have heard the news and I will be the first to share it. I grip the newspaper tightly between my fingers and know it is a piece of history I shall treasure forever. Perhaps, in years to come, my great-great-granddaughters will discover the newspaper I saved and find it impossible to imagine how the world once was for women, and how significant this step really is.

Angharad is sitting beside Anne as usual, but for once, I don't avoid them. "Miss Williams, Mrs Williams," I say, "have you heard the news?"

"And what news would that be?" asks Anne, sounding utterly disinterested.

I hand the newspaper to Angharad, who scans the headline, then looks at me, her eyes wide. "Is it really true?"

"It's there, in black and white," I say, unable to keep the grin from my face. We both stare at the headline – *Reform Bill Passed: Women's Vote Won.*

Anne snatches the newspaper from Angharad, scans through the article, then drops the paper onto her lap. "Is this really what you're getting excited about?" she says, scorn dripping from her voice.

Any sense of being subordinate that Mrs Anne Williams once felt in my higher social standing is long gone, and it seems she feels she can speak to me as rudely as anyone.

"This is momentous news."

"I don't see what all the fuss is about. Why should women vote? The bible tells us to obey our husbands. We should trust their judgment in such matters. I find it very vulgar to hear women discussing politics."

Not for the first time, I wonder why on earth Anne Williams wanted to join our Women's Institute. "Then we shall have to agree to disagree," I say, managing to smile.

All around us, members are discussing the news. Most of the reactions are positive, although there are a handful of voices who share similar views to Anne. But overall the mood is celebratory, and even when we find out our scheduled speaker, the Hon. Violet Douglas-Pennant cannot attend the meeting, the cheerful atmosphere remains undimmed.

Miss Lamport fills the gap in proceedings, reading an interesting paper on Digestion and Diet. Then, Miss Griffiths of Plas Lwynonn demonstrates a few simple dishes. The poor woman has been drafted in at such short notice she is woefully unprepared. She is missing half the utensils needed, and at one point tries to mix flour and butter together with a teaspoon. By the time her demonstration is over she is red-faced and sweating, but we give her a hearty round of applause, for none of us would have liked to be put in her position, and her attempted demonstration was rather valiant in the circumstances.

After the meeting, we hold a sale of home produce and bottled fruits sent by Mrs Cotton. The sale raises a good deal of money for our building fund, which is growing nicely.

"I shouldn't think it will be long until we have our own premises," I say to Angharad, as the last bottle of preserved fruit is sold.

"It seems rather an indulgence to me," says Anne, taking a sip of her tea and wrinkling her nose.

"It's no such thing, Mrs Williams. Look at how we are outgrowing this summerhouse. We're squashed in here like fleas on a rat! Mrs Jones has been a marvellous sport hosting us for the past few years, but we want our organisation to expand, and at this rate, we'll have to host meetings on the lawn."

"There are other buildings in the village which could be used."

"But it isn't the same as having one of our own. And think of all the trouble it would be to carry in tables, chairs, refreshments and all that go with them each week. No, it is the view of all at the Institute we need our own space. After all, as the Reform Bill proves, times are changing. Just think of all the good we can do if we have a place of our own. The possibilities are endless."

Anne sniffs and walks off to find someone else to talk to, and I breathe a sigh of relief.

"I'm sorry about my sister-in-law," says Angharad.

"Whilst I don't like being rude about your family, that woman would try the patience of a saint. I know we're meant to welcome new members with open arms, but Mrs Anne Williams really doesn't seem cut out to be a member of the Institute. We're concerned with looking outwards at how we can help our community and finding solutions to problems. All she does is look for the problems. She's not much of a team player, is she?"

"I thought she was when we first met," says Angharad, keeping her voice low so as not to be overheard. "She can be very charming when she needs to be. I imagined us becoming great friends."

"She must have changed a lot over the years then," I say, "for I can't imagine wanting to spend more than two minutes in her company, let alone be her friend. Anyway, on to a more cheerful topic, let's hope there is an election soon so we can use our hard-won vote."

"You can, but I shan't be able to. The rules stipulate women must be over the age of thirty and own or live in property of a certain value. I might be over thirty, but there is no way my rented bothy will count."

"And at under thirty, Carys won't be able to vote either."

"Not quite the equal rights we were hoping for then," says Angharad, but she is smiling, for she recognises a big step forward when she sees one. "Speaking of Carys, have you seen her lately?"

"No, and I don't imagine things are easy for her since her brother's death. Her poor mother was struggling enough as it was, without another bereavement on top. Perhaps we should visit her?"

"Perhaps," says Angharad, but I see the way she casts an anxious glance at Anne.

"I'm ready to leave now," says Anne, walking over to us. "Accompany me home, Angharad."

"Of course, sister."

I watch them leave the summerhouse and determine to get to the bottom of whatever is going on between them. For what is the point of gaining ground in women's rights if women like Angharad can be disenfranchised in other ways by members of their own families?

Chapter Sixty-Five

Carys

"Please, Mami, there must be another way."

"You read the letter, Carys. William will not return from Canada. He has made a life for himself there. Perhaps if you had married Dai as you were supposed to, things would have been different, but as I see it, there is no option but to give up the farm."

Whilst deep down I know that what happened with Dai is not my fault, Mami's words fill me with shame. Despite my best efforts, I have not been able to keep the farm going. It turns out women are not as capable as men after all.

"I've written to my sister on the mainland," says Mami. "She is happy for us to stay with her until we can find jobs and get back on our feet."

"When will we leave?"

"I will start the process of ending our tenancy today, then we can begin working through our belongings. We shan't be able to take much with us, I shouldn't think."

"Alright." It is impossible to take in not only Mami's words, but the change in her. She seems to have found a sense of purpose for the first time since Dadi died. Her eyes are bright and there is an energy to her movements I haven't seen for a long time. With a start, I realise she is relieved. All this time I've been trying to cling on to the farm, trying to make things better for Mami, and what she really needed was to leave her memories behind and begin somewhere new.

"Right," says Mami, clapping her hands together. "I'd best get going."

"And I'd better get out to the barn."

I cross the yard in a daze. The farm has been the only home I've known and the thought of leaving it, of leaving Anglesey, is awful. It's good Mami has enough enthusiasm for the both of us, for I feel nothing but sorrow.

"We've another two lambs," says Florian as I enter the barn. "Are you alright? You look as though you've seen a ghost."

"We received a letter from William today. There's nothing for it, Florian. We're going to have to give up the farm. I'm so sorry."

"You did everything you could," he says, climbing over the low fence to come and take my hands.

"But I've let you and the girls down. Mami's gone to speak to the landlord about ending our tenancy. It's not just us that we'll lose our home, but you and the girls as well."

"Don't worry about us, Carys. We will manage. I have friends who've gone to Liverpool where there is plenty of work. There will be people there from back home to help take care of the girls while I'm working. It will all turn out for the best."

Although Florian's matter-of-fact attitude should make me glad, it is not what I want to hear. I want him to be as devastated about leaving as I am, but from the sound of things, he's been planning his escape route for a while now.

"I'll tell the girls when they return home from school," he says, "and I had better write to my friends this afternoon and see if they can secure work for me."

Anger rushes through me and I pull my hand away from his. "Aren't you even a little sad about leaving? I thought we were friends? I thought you cared about me? If anything, it sounds as though you are relieved to be escaping to England." I turn away so he can't see my tears.

"No, that is not how it is," he says, grabbing hold of my arm and forcing me to turn to him. "I don't mind where I work. Whether farm or factory, it's much the same to me. But I shall miss you, Carys, very much."

"I don't believe you."

Rather than using words to put my mind at rest, Florian pulls me close to him. Before I have time to resist, his mouth is on mine, his hands gripping me. I melt into his embrace, the emotions of the morning fuelling our passion.

We stagger to the back of the barn where bales of hay lie stacked together. As we fall onto the soft mound below, Florian's hands find the buttons of my blouse, and I tug at his shirt, the buttons tearing from their threads.

The world around me stills as I give myself to him. I am aware of nothing except the feel of his skin on mine, the warmth of his breath on my neck. There is no time to consider the wisdom of what we are doing as I step into the unknown. The pain when it comes is buried beneath pleasure, the frustration of months and years admiring him from afar finally sated. I close my eyes and give everything I have to the man I love.

When, with a shudder, it is over, we lie beside each other on a bale of hay, each too stunned to speak. Florian's fingers entwine around mine and we cling on to each other. As his ragged breaths slow, he props himself up on an elbow and looks down at me.

"I am so sorry, Carys."

"Sorry? Whatever for?"

"What we just did is a sin. I should never have taken advantage of you in that way."

I raise a hand and brush my fingers across his lips. "Shh," I say, "don't spoil what just happened between us with regrets."

His eyes are shining and I'm surprised when a tear slips down his cheek. "I wish we had met in a different place and time, when we could be together as man and wife. When there was not a war."

"Life is never that simple, though, is it? You have your country to get back to, your girls to look after. Despite her recent rallying, Mami is too fragile for me to leave her, even if there was a way for you and me to be together. It breaks my heart that you will soon leave me."

"I may have to leave you, Carys, but I will never forget you. You must believe that."

"I do," I say, and it is the truth, for I will never forget him. Perhaps one day I will marry and have a family of my own, but whatever path my life takes, I know that Florian Jansen will remain in my heart, and the thoughts of what might have been will plague me for the rest of my life.

Chapter Sixty-Six

Angharad

April, 1918

"I thought that was a most interesting meeting this afternoon."

"Hmm."

"Did you not think so, sister? The suggestion to write to Llangefni County Council about a water scheme for Llanfairpwll seems especially sensible. We are in the twentieth century. Surely it's about time we had a proper water and sanitation system in the village?"

"You seem unusually opinionated this afternoon," says Anne, bringing me down to earth with a bump. "Is there a reason you are so jolly?"

"I don't think I am especially jolly. I enjoyed the meeting, that's all."

"Perhaps you are becoming a little complacent. Do you not believe I will follow through with my decision to inform the WI about your past?"

"No, I know you are a woman of your word."

"Your brother has requested a meeting with you."

"Now?"

"Of course, you don't expect him to make a special trip out to your hovel, do you?"

We reach Anne's house and this time, instead of saying goodbye, I follow her through the gate. I have no idea why Bryn wants to see me, but it can't be for anything good. Anne opens the door and I follow her inside into the gloomy hallway.

"Your brother will be in the parlour," she says.

I knock on the parlour door and wait to be summoned.

"Come in."

"Good afternoon, brother. Anne said you want to speak with me."

Bryn's chair is pulled up to a writing desk covered in sheets of paper. "Sit," he says, pointing to a hard-backed chair.

"What can I do for you, brother?"

Bryn shifts in his seat until he is looking straight at me. "You can help me, sister, by not making a fool of me and bringing our family's good name into disrepute."

"What? I don't understand. I haven't done anything."

"Here." Bryn thrusts the sheets of paper towards me and I realise they are covered in Anne's neat handwriting. At the side of the paper is a series of dates, and next to the dates is a paragraph of writing. With horror, I realise the dates relate to WI meetings, and the notes refer to me.

"What is this?"

"I asked Anne to keep a note of your behaviour at this Women's Institute you insist on attending. It soon became clear you have been making a fool of yourself and we have tried gentle warnings, to no avail."

"But, brother, this isn't true. I didn't cause a disturbance at the February meeting. I was pleased when Mrs Montgomery showed me the newspaper headline about the Reform Bill, but there was no shrieking or jumping around as Anne describes here. And this," I say, turning back through the pages and reading Anne's description of our tea at Plas Newydd, "I wasn't rude to Lady Anglesey. I would never dream of doing such a thing."

"Are you suggesting my wife is a liar?" asks Bryn.

"No, but I am suggesting her interpretation of events is not correct."

"Or perhaps it is your interpretation which is misguided. You have grown so used to the strength of your movements and loudness of your voice you don't even notice it anymore. You think this behaviour is acceptable?" Bryn grabs back the sheets of paper and waves them in my face. "Not only do I have Anne's reports to go by, I also know you deliberately disobeyed my instruction not to attend the Girls' Club. Not only did you attend, you paid the subscription of one of the participants. The only moral instruction those girls should receive should come from the chapel. The chapel, you hear me!"

"We are not attempting to give anyone any moral instruction. The Girls' Club is a place to socialise and learn new skills."

"So you claim, but I'm afraid I do not believe you. It has cost Anne having to attend those sinful meetings each month, but her sacrifice has been rewarded, as we now know the full extent of your corruption."

"My corruption? Brother, I think you are completely misunderstanding the values of the organisation and my role in it."

"How dare you answer back! Hasn't your loose tongue got you into enough trouble over the years? You destroyed our parents' marriage with your baseless accusations. Life in our home was never the same after you claimed to have seen Mother walking with our neighbour."

"But I did see them, and I didn't say it to get anyone in trouble."

"All my life you have been a thorn in my side." Bryn's voice is rising, his skin turning purple. It's as though decades of resentment have been fermenting inside him and this is his opportunity to let out the poison. "Having you as a sister made me a laughing stock at school, but at least I had a loving home to return to. After you destroyed Father's trust in Mother, home was no longer a refuge. And then... *and then...*" Bryn takes a deep breath and gets to his feet. His hands are shaking, his eyes bulging, spittle gathering on his bottom lip. "And then you have the *audacity* to take up with that English *heathen,* bringing shame and humiliation to our family's good name. Was it not enough that you sent our parents to a miserable early grave? Did you really have to torment the living as well?"

Bryn is towering over me, his fists clenched and raised. For a moment, I think he might hit me. I push my chair away and step towards the door. "What happened with Eddy was nothing to do with you. It wasn't a punishment, it was love. We could have happily lived in the shadows without anyone knowing a thing. It was you who destroyed everything."

"Get out of my house!" roars Bryn, slamming his palm down against the table. "You are barred from attending my chapel and if I hear you have ever set foot into that Women's Institute again, I am prepared to take the consequences that revealing your secret will impose on our family. It is better everyone knows the truth about the kind of woman you really are than have you ingratiating yourself into the lives of this community. As far as I am concerned, you are no family of ours. If our paths ever cross again, you will pay for what you have done."

I run from the house, not stopping until I reach the bothy. Betty greets me with her usual enthusiasm, but as I tumble into a chair, my body racked with sobs, she curls at my feet, whimpering in solidarity. What a fool I was to think things would ever be different. How selfish I have been. "I'm sorry, Betty," I say through my tears, "but I fear I may have ruined everything."

Chapter Sixty-Seven

Carys

May, 1918

I force a smile onto my face for the sake of the girls, who are upset enough at the thought of leaving.

"We don't want to go," says Lina, clinging to my legs. "We want to stay at the farm."

I pull her arms away and crouch down until I am at her level. "I know you do, Lina, but we all have to leave the farm."

"You'll come to Liverpool with us?"

"I'm afraid I can't do that. My mami needs me to keep her company when we live with her sister."

"In Liverpool?"

"No, in a place called Caernarfon."

"Is that place near Liverpool?"

"Not so near, but I'm sure I can come and visit you one day if you'd like that?"

Lina nods and sticks a thumb in her mouth. Florian walks into the sitting room, Emma clinging on to his hand. "The cart is loaded," he says. "It's time to go, girls." He takes a step forward and for a moment gazes into my eyes. I want to hold him, kiss him, ask him not to leave me, but I can't.

The four of us walk out into the yard. I turn back to the farmhouse and see Mami watching us through the kitchen window, a handkerchief pressed against one cheek.

"Girls, run back into the house and say goodbye to Mrs Ambrose," says Florian.

The girls do as they are told and in the precious few seconds we have alone, Florian takes my hand. "I shall write to you, Carys."

I nod, for sadness has tightened my throat, making speech impossible. A sniff and a squaring of my shoulders dispel the threat of tears. There will be plenty of time for tears to be shed, and now is not that time.

"Carys..." Florian's fingers stroke my cheek, but before he can say anything else, the girls are running towards us, their arms outstretched. I lean down and give them each a tight squeeze, then Florian lifts them up onto the cart, jumps up himself and takes hold of the reins. "Goodbye, Miss Ambrose, look out for my letter."

With one last wave, Florian tugs on the reins and the horse moves forward, the cart clattering behind it. I stay pinned to the spot, waving until my arm aches and the horse and cart are a mere pinprick on the horizon. A sudden tiredness threatens to drown me, and I lean against the farmhouse wall for support. I turn and look back at the window, but Mami is no longer there.

My eyes remain dry as I cross the yard to the barn. The surrounding air is eerily quiet, and as I step inside the wooden walls, I'm met with the smell of old hay but not the warm fug that living, breathing animals leave in their wake. The only sign of the sheep once housed here are the occasional bunches of wool that cling to nails on a fence, or dance on the breeze.

I try my best not to think of our precious animals and whether they are being treated well on the neighbouring farm. They gave Mami a fair price for them, which was kind, in the circumstances. In three days' time, the keys to the farmhouse will be handed back to the landlord and someone else will move in and fill the farm with life again.

Another wave of fatigue and nausea hit, and I stumble to the nearest fence, leaning against it, trying to pull in deep breaths.

"Carys?"

I turn and see Mami standing in the barn doorway, her arms folded across her chest. "Are you alright?"

"Yes, Mami, I'm fine. It's sad to be leaving, and waving goodbye to our friends, that's all."

Mami frowns and crosses the straw floor until standing beside me. She raises her hand and places the back of it against my forehead. "You've been out of sorts for a few weeks now. Don't think I've not noticed."

"It's all the packing up and worry about the future, that's all."

"Hmm," says Mami, placing an arm across my shoulders. "Let's get you back to the house and sit you down beside the fire."

The relief at finally seeing something of the old Mami is so strong I almost collapse there and then on the barn floor. As my legs buckle, I grip harder on the fence, then transfer my weight to Mami, who guides me back towards the house.

Once we're inside, she pulls a chair close to the fire and helps me down onto it. "You've been working yourself too hard. I should have done more to help. I'm so sorry, *cariad*, for the past year it's as though I've been living in the middle of a bad dream I couldn't escape from, but I'm feeling more like my old self again, and it's about time I looked after you."

"It's alright, Mami. I'm tired, that's all." Mami nods, but I wonder at the truth of my words. The tiredness I've been experiencing lately has been far more extreme than anything I've encountered before.

"What you need is a nice soak. You stay here and I'll fill the copper."

"You don't need to go to any trouble on my account."

"It'll be the last bath you'll have in this house. Everything will be different when we get to the mainland. Let me do this for you, *cariad*. I know you're a woman now, and you've more than proved your strength since your dadi left us, but let's pretend you're still my little girl. Let me do this one thing for you."

"Thank you, Mami."

"It's the least I can do after all you've done for me. Now, it will take me a while to get the copper filled, so why don't you close your eyes and have a little rest?"

I wake to a room filled with steam, and see the copper is filled almost to the brim with warm water.

"Do you feel better after a little sleep?" asks Mami as I stretch my hands above my head and yawn.

"I think so."

"Good. The copper's ready for you. Strip yourself off and I'll fetch the soap. I thought I could wash your hair like I used to."

I smile and fight back tears of relief that Mami has finally come back to me. She shuffles out of the room in search of a bar of soap and I begin to remove my clothes. In my sleepy state, I don't even notice her come back into the room. It is only when the soap thuds against the stone floor that I look up and see the horror in Mami's eyes. She is staring at me and I try to cover my naked body with my arms.

"What's wrong, Mami?" I step one foot into the copper, but as I do Mami rushes forward, grabs my arm and yanks me away from the water.

She takes each of my arms in her hands and stares at my naked body. "Mami, please stop, you're embarrassing me."

"Who did this to you?" Mami's voice is quiet, but her words come out in a rush.

"Did what, Mami? I don't understand?" I look down at my body, but there are no bruises or marks that could cause Mami such distress.

"Who did this to you?" Mami's voice is filled with panic, her eyes looking me up and down. She takes a step away from me and stumbles, grabbing on to the back of a chair for support. With an arm raised and finger pointing at me, this time she cries her question. "Who did this to you?"

"Did what?" Is this another of her funny turns? Was I wrong to think she was over the worst of what ailed her?

"Some man has put a baby in your belly, that's what."

"No!" I look down at myself in horror. "What are you talking about, Mami? I'm not expecting a child."

"You can't fool me, Carys!"

"I'm not fooling anyone, honestly, Mami. I think I'd know if I was carrying a child, don't you?"

"Look at your breasts!" cries Mami. "They're full and round where once they were almost flat. You silly, silly girl! When did you last bleed?"

I try to think back to the last time I had my monthly, but we've been so busy lately, I've stopped keeping track. "I don't know."

Mami sags and I wonder if she'll collapse to the ground, but instead, she walks to me, takes hold of my arm and guides me across the room to where a large mirror hangs on the wall. She cups my chin and forces it up until I have no choice but to stare at my reflection. With horror, I see what she saw. My small breasts are fuller and rounder than they've ever been. The stomach that has always been almost concave is now smooth and protrudes a little, just below my belly button. How could I not have noticed these changes to my body?

"Is this Dai's doing?"

"No."

"Then who, Carys?"

"I won't say."

"You won't say? Do you have any idea the trouble we're in? Good Lord, there is no way I can take you to my sister in this state. Imagine the shame we'd bring on her household! Oh, child, whatever are we to do? My sister will turn us away the second she finds out about your condition!"

"Mami, please, I'm sure we can think of something. Perhaps there's another explanation for the changes to my body."

"Have you been with a man?"

"What?"

"You heard me. Have you been with a man?"

My cheeks flame red in answer and Mami finally collapses into a chair, throwing her head in her hands. As she sobs, I slowly pull on my clothes, knowing what I must do.

"I love you, Mami," I tell her. When I try to put my arm around her, she pushes me away. I lean over and kiss the top of her head. "I'm so sorry, Mami. I hope one day you'll find it in your heart to forgive me."

I let myself out of the room and climb the stairs. In my bedroom, I put all the clothes I own into a small bag, then return to the kitchen, where I add half a loaf of bread and a flask of water to my meagre belongings. With Mami's sobs filling the air, I leave the farmhouse. I can no longer go to my aunt's, but she can. This is my mistake, and she shouldn't have to pay for it. "Goodbye, Mami. Take care," I whisper.

I allow myself one last glance at the farmhouse before I turn and walk away.

Chapter Sixty-Eight

Ffion

May, 1918

The knock on the door irritates me. It is rare that Matron and I find five minutes to sit down for a much-needed meeting and I had expressly asked that we shouldn't be disturbed. Matron seems just as annoyed as I am if her curt "enter!" is anything to go by.

Susan pokes her red face around the door.

"What is it, Susan? Matron and I are trying to have a meeting here. If there is a problem with the soldiers, please refer it to the nursing staff."

"It's not about a patient, madam. There is someone here to see you. A Miss Ambrose."

"I see. Can you explain to her I am in a meeting but will come and find her when we are finished?"

"The thing is, madam, the lady in question is rather distressed."

"Right." I push my chair back and turn to Matron. "I'm very sorry, but it looks as if we shall have to postpone this meeting until next week. Do excuse me."

I'm up and out of the room before Matron can comment, rushing along the corridor with Susan by my side.

"I really am sorry for disturbing you, madam, but we weren't sure what to do with the young lady."

"We?"

"Me and Mrs Edwards. I took Miss Ambrose through to the kitchen so she wouldn't upset any of the patients."

"That was a good idea, Susan. Well done."

We hurry down the stairs, and when we walk into the kitchen, Mrs Edwards is making Carys laugh through her tears. As soon as she sees me, Carys blows her nose on a handkerchief and stands up unsteadily.

"I'm so sorry to barge in like this," she says, "but I didn't know where else to go."

"That's alright, Carys. Susan, I'm going to take Miss Ambrose through to my husband's study. Could you bring a pot of tea through to us?"

"Of course, madam."

"Thank you. And thank you, both of you, for looking after Miss Ambrose while I was otherwise engaged."

"I'll make sure there's some cake on the tray," says Mrs Edwards, and I answer her with a smile.

As a room, I hate Hector's study. It is a dark, depressing place with an ugly great desk in the middle, and the only attempt at homeliness is a drinks cabinet against one wall. The air holds a lingering smell of cigar smoke, despite Hector having been away for months. Given the choice, I prefer to hold meetings in the library, but the chances are Matron is still in there, and at least in the study we are unlikely to be disturbed.

I lower myself into a leather armchair, which squeaks as it takes my weight. "Sit down," I say to Carys, and although she takes the seat opposite mine, she perches on the edge, wringing a handkerchief between her hands. "What's happened, Carys?"

"Oh, Ffion, I've been such a fool."

As Carys bursts into noisy tears, I lean forward and pat her on the arm. "Come on now, it can't be that bad."

"I'll never see Mami again. The farm is gone, Florian and the girls have left, and now I'm alone with nowhere to go. I don't know what to do, Ffion. I can't go to the workhouse, I just can't."

"The workhouse? Whatever are you talking about? I thought you were going to stay with your aunt in Caernarfon?"

"I was, but then something happened and unless Mami went alone, we'd both have ended up on the streets. I've brought such shame on the family. There was no way Mami could have faced her sister with me in tow."

"What exactly have you done, Carys?"

Carys's tears intensify and I try to push away my frustration. I'm already on edge, knowing Hector will arrive home this afternoon, and there is a houseful of wounded soldiers needing my attention. It would be very helpful if Carys could reach the nub of the matter sooner rather than later.

"I've... I'm..." Here a deep flush travels in a wave from her neck to her cheeks and she keeps her eyes fixed on the carpet below. "I think I'm expecting a child."

I lean back in my chair and the leather creaks once more as I let out a long breath. "A child? Are you sure? How long have you known?"

"I didn't know, not until Mami saw me getting into the bath and noticed how my body had changed. I thought my recent tiredness was caused by nothing more than all the work I've been doing on the farm and the worry of preparing to leave."

"Oh, Carys. Mr Jansen is the father, I take it?"

Her head snaps up and she looks at me with wide eyes. "How did you know?"

I can't help but laugh. "It was obvious how you felt about each other. I'm right, then?"

Carys nods, then her shoulders heave up and down in another sob, "Yes, but he's gone, he's gone to Liverpool and I'm never going to see him again."

I cross to Carys's chair, dropping to my knees and taking her in my arms. "You poor, poor thing. It's alright, everything will be alright."

"Can... c... can I stay with you tonight?"

Her request makes me shiver. On any other day, she would be welcomed with open arms, but Hector is on his way home, and I can't risk it. I just can't.

Carys must feel my body stiffen, for she pulls away from our embrace. "You don't want me here. It's alright, I understand. I'm a fallen woman, and you're from high society. Of course, you wouldn't want someone like me turning up on your doorstep."

"No," I say, jumping to my feet. "No, that's not it at all. I would never judge you in that way."

"Then what's wrong?"

I flop back into my armchair and tilt my head back with a sigh. "Hector is home tonight on leave."

"And he'd disapprove of me being here? We wouldn't have to tell him the reason I'm here, would we?"

"It's not that. I'd have no trouble lying to my husband after all he's put me through. The fact is, I don't think you'd be safe staying under our roof. You're an attractive young woman, Carys. And you know what my husband can be like around young women."

"Surely he'd not try anything like that with one of your friends?"

"I wouldn't put it past him. You've been through enough without having to contend with Hector. It isn't worth the risk."

"I'd best be on my way then," says Carys, standing.

"Wait. I can't have you under my roof, but I can give you some supplies. Let me pack you a basket of food and find you some blankets. If you find a suitable outbuilding to sleep in you're welcome to use it, but avoid the stables, as that is one of Hector's regular haunts, and it's best I don't know where you are, in case you're spotted and he questions me about it."

"I'll find somewhere to stay that isn't on your land," says Carys, "there are plenty of outbuildings around Llanfairpwll where I can hole up until I've decided what to do. But some blankets and food would be very welcome."

"Come through to the kitchen and let's see what Mrs Edwards can rustle up."

Mrs Edwards scurries around her kitchen, filling a basket with provisions. She doesn't ask why Carys needs them, but is an intelligent woman and knows something is wrong. I appreciate not only her help but her tact and discretion. Susan appears with an armful of blankets, which we roll up and squash inside a canvas bag.

"Will you be able to carry all that?" I ask Carys when everything is ready.

"Yes, it will be fine," she says, hoisting the bag on her shoulder and hooking the basket over her arm. "Thank you all for your help."

"Good luck," I say, as I show her out of the front door. "Hector is home for five days, but then you must come back, and we'll see what we can do to help you properly."

Carys nods and walks off across the lawn. I watch her, little more than a child herself, with the weight of the world on her shoulders. It's all very well offering my help, but the truth is I have no idea how to help her. She really is in quite the predicament.

Chapter Sixty-Nine

Carys

June, 1918

I stagger up to Angharad's door on trembling legs. Days with minimal food have left me weak and dazed. This is the only place I can turn, and if Angharad can't help me, I don't know what I'll do. When I returned to Ffion's home, her husband was still there, on an extended period of leave due to a stray bullet to the shoulder that had done no lasting damage but had put him out of action for the foreseeable. From the look on Ffion's face, it was clear my being there scared her, so other than some hurriedly smuggled supplies, I left her home with no more certainty than when I arrived. Now here I am, about to beg a friend for help once again.

It only takes three knocks before Angharad opens the door to her bothy. She looks almost as bad as I do, too thin for her broad frame, with pale skin and dark circles beneath her eyes. There is none of the friendliness which once existed between us. She pushes past me and looks around at the open farmland.

"Did anyone see you come here?"

"No, and if they did, why would it matter? Are you ashamed of me?"

"Ashamed of you?" She looks confused, frowning, as her eyes dart every which way.

"I'm sorry to come here unannounced, but there is nowhere else I could go."

"Come in," she says, grabbing my arm, pulling me inside and banging the door shut. Angharad paces the floor of the bothy, stopping at regular intervals to peer out of the small windows. "You're sure no one followed you?"

"Angharad, what's going on? You seem frightened?"

She stops pacing and looks at me properly for the first time. Without answering my question, she narrows her eyes. "There's something different about you. What is it?"

As much as I hate myself for it, I can't stop the tears from falling. I collapse into a chair and throw my head in my hands. "I've made a mess of everything. Dadi's dead, Peter's dead, Mami's gone, Florian's gone. I've lost everything, Angharad."

When my tears subside and I look up, Angharad is kneeling beside me, holding out a handkerchief. She seems to have forgotten her fear and brushes a strand of hair from my eyes. "It sounds as if we've a lot to catch up on. I'll make the tea."

With a cup of hot tea in my hands, I begin my sorry story. "Mami has left and gone to her sister's on the mainland."

"And she left you behind? To run the farm on your own?"

"There is no more farm, Angharad. With Dadi and Peter dead, and my brother William in Canada, we couldn't keep it going any longer. Me and Florian tried to keep our heads above water as long as we could, but it was too much for the pair of us."

"Florian?" asks Angharad with a frown.

"Mr Jansen, our Belgian refugee."

"Oh yes, what a lovely fellow."

Tears burst from my eyes once more. "He's gone, Angharad, and I'll never see him again."

"Mr Jansen?"

"I love him." It comes out as a wail, and I try to get control of myself. "I love him and now he's gone."

"Carys," says Angharad, setting her cup down on the table and taking my hands. "Has Mr Jansen taken advantage of you?"

"No! He loves me too."

"I'm sorry, I don't understand. You and Mr Jansen are courting?"

"We were, but when we had to give up the farm, he had to leave to find work on the mainland. I understand, of course I do. He has to think of his girls. He said he'll write once he finds somewhere to settle and I can join him, but now I've messed everything up."

"And how have you done that, Carys?"

"I'm... I'm... I'm..."

"You're what?"

"I'm carrying his child. I'm going to have a baby. But I don't know where Florian is, or if he'll keep his promise to write. Mami was so upset, I left so she was free to travel to her sister's alone. I don't know what to do, Angharad. I've nowhere to go, no money, no food. I've brought shame on my family and no one in Llanfairpwll will want anything to do with me now. Can you help me?"

"Well, I suppose I have a little money saved. And I can get you some supplies from the farmhouse to tide you over for a while."

"Thank you. Can I stay here with you?" All my hopes are crushed when I look at her. She is aghast at the suggestion, and I wonder if I've got her all wrong. But now isn't the time for pride or disappointment. "Just for a night or two, just until I can find somewhere else to go. I won't be any trouble, I promise."

"It's out of the question," says Angharad, panic in her voice. "If he finds you here... No, I'll fetch you some food, but then you must leave."

"If who finds me here? Mr Stephens? I thought you said he never comes to your bothy? I can stay out of the way."

"Not Mr Stephens," snaps Angharad, but doesn't say more. She pulls a tin down from a shelf and tips coins into my palm. "I'll fetch your food now, but then you must leave."

Anger and shame fill me and I stand so quickly my chair falls to the floor. "No, don't bother. I can see now that I misjudged you. I'll leave now, and I won't trouble you again."

Angharad's face falls, and she looks as if she's about to say something, then clamps her mouth shut. I place the pile of coins down on the table.

"Take them, please."

Now is not the time for pride, and despite my cheeks burning with shame, I pocket the money and let myself out of the bothy. Without looking back, I march across the fields, using the last of my energy. As soon as I'm out of sight, I collapse to the ground, pummelling the damp grass with my fists, and cursing my stupidity. A terrible thought occurs to me. Even if Florian writes to me, I shan't be at the farm to receive his letter. The new tenants move in tomorrow, and once word of my disgrace gets around, they won't be going out of their way to do me any favours. My letter, if it comes, will probably be burned, along with any hopes I have ever had for the future.

Chapter Seventy

Ffion

June, 1918

Despite the summerhouse at Graig now feeling like a second home, I don't enjoy today's meeting as much as I normally do. Mrs Anne Williams' absence is very welcome, and I get the feeling I am not the only member pleased with this recent turn of events. But although I have plenty of friends now at the WI, it is Carys and Angharad I want sitting beside me, and it has now been months since either of them attended a meeting.

I try hard to focus on the discussion around me. Raising money for the British Refugee Fund is a noble cause, and the sale of articles sent by Lady Neave is a wonderful idea, but I just can't seem to muster any enthusiasm for the event.

The only time my interest is piqued is when Mrs Watt stands up and explains her presence in North Wales. It turns out she is here to form a summer school for the instruction of organizers of Women's Institutes, which will be held at Bangor University. It is wonderful to see Mrs Watt again, but her presence dredges up memories which make me simultaneously proud and sad. As she talks about the generosity of the university, in my mind I am travelling with Angharad in the Wolsey, about to attend the meeting which will spark a movement and change our lives. Those days felt so optimistic, and for so long, I felt we were all flourishing within the movement we had helped create. There are now Women's Institutes all over the British Isles, and I want to be able to celebrate that fact with my friends, but they are no longer here.

When Miss Goodwin stands up to give a talk on home remedies, my mind gives up any pretence of engagement and drifts off entirely. I am in Carys's barn feeding a lamb. I am watching Angharad as she puts a broken Charlie back together with her matter-of-fact chatter and optimism. I am waiting at a small rural chapel for Carys, as she arrives to bury her father. I am walking along the shore of the Menai Strait, admitting the worst secrets from my marriage to two women I know will not judge me. I am listening to talk after talk, serving tea after tea, making plans and trying to serve our community as my friends stand by my side.

As soon as the meeting draws to a close, I say my goodbyes, the chatter from the summerhouse fading as I walk across the garden. The thought of returning home makes my heart sink even further. Since Hector's return I have been able to protect Susan, but there have been other girls from the village, if the messed-up hay in the stables and lingering scent of perfume is anything to go by. I now hate my husband so much, I can barely look at him, and try to spend as little time with him as is humanely possible while living under the same roof.

Instead of turning left and heading home, I walk in the opposite direction, towards the woodland which surrounds the impressive Marquis of Anglesey's column. I haven't made it far along the path when a rustling of leaves stops me in my tracks.

"Hello? Is somebody there?"

A hunched figure draped in a dirty brown blanket emerges from the undergrowth and I take a step back. The makeshift hood slips down to reveal the figure's head and my hand flies to my mouth.

"Ffion?" the voice is croaky, unsure.

"Carys?"

Carys steps forward, clutching the blanket tight around herself. Her hair is limp and dirty, stuck down in clumps to her scalp. Her pale skin is now several shades darker, and her nails are black with grime.

"Have you been sleeping out here?"

Carys shrugs, takes another step forward, then collapses to the ground.

"Oh my goodness." I rush to her and help her up. The smell of foul breath reaches me and I turn my head away, but not before I've seen how chapped her lips are, and how sunken her cheeks. "Come on," I say, "let's get you somewhere warm."

Fear of bumping into women leaving the meeting means I take a long way around the outskirts of the village, which is hard going with Carys leaning on me so much I may as well be carrying her. I know I can't risk taking her back to the house, not with Hector prowling around, so I make for the only other place I can think of.

Mrs Edwards answers the door after two knocks, and I wonder if she spends her day off watching what the neighbours are up to, for she must have seen us coming.

"What in heaven's name?" she says, staring wide-eyed from me to Carys and back again.

"I found her in the woods. I don't think she's had a wash or anything to eat for quite some time."

"I'll get some water heating for a bath. You take her through to the parlour. The fire's going in there, so that should warm her up. I'll make us some tea and find her something to eat."

"Thank you, thank you so much."

Mrs Edwards bats away the praise and goes bustling off into her kitchen. I help Carys into the parlour and ease her into an armchair. She's so thin she looks as if she might snap in half.

"You should have come back to see me. I had no idea things had got so bad."

"I went to Angharad." Her voice is a whisper and I have to lean closer to hear her.

"You went to Angharad, yet still ended up sleeping in the woods?"

"She... she didn't want me there."

Fury rages through me. What reason could Angharad have for not helping a friend?

"Here you are," says Mrs Edwards, walking in carrying a tray loaded up with a teapot and cups, several slices of bread and butter and a piece of fruit cake. "If you've not eaten for a while, you'd better take it slow. Have a few bites, then wash it down with some tea."

"Thank you."

"It won't be long until I've got a bath ready for you. I'll call you when it's ready." As Carys grabs a piece of bread and takes a large bite, Mrs Edwards whispers to me, "I'll give you some time alone, Mrs Montgomery, so you can get to the bottom of what's going on."

I reach out, take her hand, and squeeze it. She flushes, then disappears back into the kitchen.

Carys manages one slice of bread and a piece of fruitcake, and colour is returning to her cheeks. "Don't be cross with Angharad," she says, even her voice sounding stronger. "She seemed scared. It was like she wanted to help me, but couldn't."

"Don't you worry about that now," I say. "The important thing is to get you fed, watered and washed, then we can think about what to do next. If you're alright for a moment, I'll see if Mrs Edwards needs any help."

Carys nods and picks up another slice of bread.

"You're wondering if she can stay here?" asks Mrs Edwards as I walk into the kitchen.

"I know it's a lot to ask. I'd invite her to my home, only..."

"You don't need to explain, Mrs Montgomery," says Mrs Edwards, patting my arm and giving me a knowing look. "Besides, you've got enough house guests, what with all those soldiers. Your friend can stay with me for tonight, but I'm expecting my sister tomorrow."

"Thank you. One night will be plenty. I'll have thought of a plan by the morning." I speak with confidence, but in truth, I have no idea what we'll do. But one thing I know is we need to have a talk with a certain Miss Angharad Williams.

Chapter Seventy-One

Carys

July 1918

Thanks to Mrs Edwards' sister falling ill and being unable to visit, I've been able to stay in the comfort of her home for over a week. But now it is time to move on. Ffion has been popping in daily to check on me, patiently waiting for me to regain some of my strength. When I look in Mrs Edwards' mirror, it is a relief to recognise the face staring back at me. Goodness knows where I'll go next, and my future is as uncertain as ever, but the respite Mrs Edwards has provided should give me the strength to carry on a little longer.

I am alone in the house when the knock comes on the door. Mrs Edwards is at work, and for a moment I panic, expecting to find some nosy neighbour taking advantage of her absence. Instead, I open the door to Ffion. I turn, expecting her to follow me inside, but she stays on the doorstep.

"Are you not coming in?"

"Not today. Carys, it's time to speak to Angharad."

"No, I don't think that's a good idea."

"We can't go on forever ignoring what happened. You're physically strong enough now, and I will be by your side. The way she treated you was very wrong, and we need to confront her about it."

"I'm sure she had her reasons for turning me away."

"If that is the case, we deserve to hear them. Come on."

Ffion leaves no time for me to argue and begins striding off along the street. I grab my coat and pull the door closed behind me, running to catch her up. The day is humid and sweat pools beneath my arms and runs down my back, soaking into my cotton blouse. The weather seems to be brewing for a storm, and I hope the same can't be said for our meeting with Angharad.

When we reach the farm, we try Angharad's bothy first, but there is no answer.

"She's probably still milking," I say. "It's still early."

"Let's try the milking parlour then," says Ffion, marching off across the field. She is a woman on a mission, determined to do what she came for. She only slows when we enter the yard.

"Ffion, we don't have to do this."

"We do, Carys."

"Promise me you'll be kind. Angharad seemed scared when I came to see her. I was too upset to realise at the time, but looking back, I think her actions were born from fear rather than judgement."

"Of course I'll be kind," says Ffion. "All I want is to get this matter cleared up in the most amicable way possible."

We find Angharad in the milking parlour with Charlie. She is perched on a low stool and, in a separate stall, Charlie works from his chair. Ffion clears her throat and walks to where Angharad is working.

"Good morning, Miss Williams."

I flinch at the formality of Ffion's words.

"G... good... morning," says Angharad, looking between us with wild eyes. "I'm working."

"Yes," says Ffion, "I can see that."

"I can finish up here," calls Charlie, "if you want to speak with your friends."

"No!" Angharad shouts the word, then looks down at her feet. "Sorry, I didn't mean to shout."

"Well, I'm just about finished here," says Charlie, giving the cow he has been milking a friendly pat. "Why don't I show you ladies over to the farmhouse?"

"That's alright, we'll wait at Angharad's bothy."

Angharad looks up sharply and stares at Ffion. "My bothy?"

"Yes, we intend to speak with you and are prepared to wait as long as it takes."

"Miss Ambrose," says Charlie, breaking the threatening stalemate, "could you help me shift this cow back out into the field? I can manage, but it's always easier with an extra pair of hands."

"Of course," I say, relieved to leave Ffion's side for a moment.

When me and Charlie are a distance away from the milking parlour, he turns to me and says, "I'm glad you've come. I've been so worried about her and I don't know what to do about it."

"You've been worried about Angharad?"

"Yes. She's barely eating these days, and judging from the bags under her eyes, I don't think she's sleeping much either. I've tried asking what's wrong, but she just snaps at me, which is unlike her. Maybe you and Mrs Montgomery will have more luck."

Ffion and I don't have long to wait before Angharad joins us in her bothy. I'm expecting her to be cross at us intruding on her space, but all she seems is tired, wearily filling the kettle and placing it above the fire before slipping into an armchair and letting out a big sigh.

"So," begins Ffion, "you've probably guessed we're here because of the way you treated Carys. You turned her away in her hour of need,

Angharad, and we want to know why. Is it because of your religious beliefs?"

To my surprise, Angharad gives a little laugh.

"I don't think there's anything amusing about the situation we find ourselves in, do you, Carys?"

I feel my cheeks heat as I shake my head. "No."

"Come on," says Ffion as the water in the kettle begins to bubble and pop. "Tell us what is going on, Angharad."

She sits silently for a moment. The kettle whistles and, amid a cloud of steam, she spoons tea into a pot and fills it with water. Her back is turned, but I can see her hands shaking as she sets cups and saucers out on the table. Then she returns to her chair, and without looking at us, begins speaking. Her voice is quieter than I've ever heard it, and we have to strain to hear her.

"I can see you'll not leave this be," she says, "so I may as well tell you everything. I've always been too scared to be honest for fear it would ruin our friendship, but it seems I've done that already, so I've nothing left to lose."

I try to say nothing is ruined, but she holds out a hand to quiet me.

"This is all about my brother and sister-in-law. But to understand, I'll need to go a long way back to when I was still living at home. You may as well take a seat as you could be here for a while."

Chapter Seventy-Two

Angharad

July, 1918

"I was always a disappointment to my parents, I knew that from a young child. I was too big, too clumsy, too loud. Every time my mother looked at me, I could see the disappointment in her eyes. If Bryn had been older than me, things might have been different. From the moment I started school, I was taunted about my size. It was hard, but I learned to ignore the other children and hide myself away as best I could. But Bryn took after my mother and was small for his age. When he started school, being my brother, he was tarred with the same brush. But instead of being called a giant or a troll, because he was short and skinny, the other children called him Jack Sprat.

"Before he started school, Bryn had always been a cheerful little fellow, and we had been good friends. I enjoyed being his big sister and looking after him, but as soon as he started school, everything changed. I never blamed him for resenting me. In his position, I would probably have felt the same. Because of me, he could never make friends, and it left him bitter. At least home was a sanctuary until I ruined that, too."

"I don't think being taunted at school is justification for…" I put a hand on Ffion's arm to stop her speaking, then bend down to pet Betty, who is watching us with knowing eyes from her position on the rug.

"Our house was always rather austere. Father had strict rules and expectations, but in a way that made things easier. We knew what to expect, and there was comfort in that. Then one day I saw my mother out walking with a neighbour, a male neighbour. Father always warned me to think before I spoke, and I should have listened to that advice. Instead, that evening over supper, I announced I had seen Mother out walking with Mr Evans. I was a naïve child, and didn't mean anything by it. All I wanted was to have something to contribute to the supper-time conversation. I only realised my mistake once the beatings started."

"Your father beat you?"

"Not me, my mother, and Bryn on occasions. I sometimes wondered if he considered it worse punishment for me to have to stand by and watch."

"Was your mother having an inappropriate relationship with the neighbour?"

Angharad shakes her head. "I don't think so. Even now, I think they were just on friendly terms. But my father was a jealous man and had a tendency to think the worst of people. He decided there and then my mother had betrayed him and needed to make her pay for her sins. The beatings continued until my father died."

"So there was no respite for your brother at home or at school?" asks Ffion.

"Precisely. My father was a well-respected member of the community. No one would have believed us if we'd told someone what was going on under our roof, and Mother would never have spoken up. She hated me for what I said, even though I meant nothing by it."

"If your father was a violent man, something would have triggered his anger eventually," says Ffion, "and there's nothing to say he hadn't already hurt your mother. He may just have been more discreet about it."

"It's possible," says Angharad, "but I still think my words were the catalyst. Anyway, we continued living our miserable lives for years, until one day, a minister from the mainland visited Father's chapel and brought his young daughter along with him. Both Bryn and I adored Anne right from the start. Now I realise when she spoke to us, she was only being polite, but at the time I'd never experienced friendship, and truly believed Anne liked me."

"How old were you?" I ask.

"Sixteen. Old enough to know better. I'd left school by then, of course, and spent my days doing chores around the house and helping run the Sunday school. Anne was fifteen, so right in the middle of me and Bryn. I could tell he'd taken a shine to her, but knew better than to tease him about it. He'd shown signs of developing the same temper as my father, so I tried to stay out of his way.

"Several more years passed, and Anne and her father visited the chapel every few months. I could tell something was going on between her and Bryn, but still clung on to the notion we were friends. Then, when I was twenty-two, my parents died in fairly quick succession. By then, Bryn had decided to join the ministry. He asked Anne to marry him, and they decided to continue the work of my father and remain at the chapel in Llanfairpwll.

"Even at twenty-two, I knew the chances were I would remain a spinster and expected to live with Bryn and Anne as their housekeeper, or perhaps as a nanny should any children come along. But Bryn had other ideas. It was he who arranged for me to come and live out here and work for Mr Stephens. He told me that whilst Father had put up with me, he didn't intend to. He called me an embarrassment, and worse, and said he wanted me out of sight and out of mind.

"So, I moved out here. Anne would visit me once or twice a week and claimed to be cross about Bryn's decision to banish me, although now I think it was probably her idea."

"But none of this explains the hold they still have over you," says Ffion, her brow furrowed.

"No," says Angharad, her shoulders sagging as though she is suddenly quilted by a deep sadness. "No, it doesn't. And now we arrive at the hardest part of my sorry tale. It's time I told you about Eddy."

Chapter Seventy-Three

Angharad

July, 1918

For so many years, my secrets have weighed me down like a sack of bricks upon my back, and now I have started telling my story, I find I can't stop. Carys and Ffion are sitting motionless, their cups of tea untouched in front of them. I throw another log onto the fire and lean back in my chair.

"I knew my mother had English relatives, but we'd never met them. What I didn't know was one branch had worked their way up in the world and somewhere along the line had reached the level of status and wealth that allowed them to send their children to boarding school and live in a mansion in the Shropshire Hills.

"The first I heard of this family was when Bryn arrived here one day with a letter. He was so angry, his hand trembled as he gave it to me to read. It seemed while we may have forgotten about these English relatives, they had not forgotten about us. The letter explained that a certain Miss Winterbow had gotten herself in trouble and needed somewhere to stay for a few months until the scandal passed."

"The girl was expecting a child?" asks Carys, a hand rubbing gently against her own stomach.

"No. If only it were that simple. The letter didn't explain the nature of the scandal, but informed Bryn that Miss Winterbow would arrive in Anglesey the following week. You can imagine his reaction. He had reached the same conclusion as you, Carys, and was incandescent at the thought of having a scarlet woman under his roof. His words, not mine," I add, on seeing Carys's face fall. "So, Bryn told me that under no circumstances was the woman darkening his door, and instead, she would live with me."

"Living here, in this bothy?" asks Ffion, incredulous. "But there's barely enough room for one person, let alone two."

I shrug. "That didn't seem to matter to Bryn. All he wanted was this young relative as far from his home and chapel as could be, while still honouring his familial duty. To be honest, I wonder if these English relatives even knew Mother had died. Bryn had already gained permission from Mr Stephens that Miss Winterbow could stay with me, so I had no say in the matter. A week later, my world was turned upside down with the arrival of Eddy."

At the mention of Eddy's name, Betty whines, cocks her head and jumps up into my lap.

"Eddy?" asks Ffion with a frown.

"Miss Edwina Winterbow. And not the young girl I was expecting, but a woman of nineteen who had just been expelled from the finishing school she had been attending in the Cotswolds."

I can't help but smile at the memory of Eddy turning up on my doorstep. I'd been a bag of nerves and her reaction to the bothy was nothing like I'd expected. She'd walked in with a huge smile on her face, and had run her hand across every surface, before flinging herself down on the bed, laughing hysterically and exclaiming, "if only Papa could see me now!"

"If she wasn't expecting a child, why had she been sent to you?" asks Ffion.

The smile drops from my face. "She had made allegations against her grandfather."

"What allegations?" asks Ffion, her voice a croak. I wonder if she is picturing her own husband.

"She claimed, and I believed her, that her grandfather had been abusing her in the worst possible way for years. When she finally found the courage to speak up, she was threatened with the asylum, then sent away to finishing school. But what had happened to her had damaged her more than anyone realised, and being called a liar was the final straw. Her behaviour had become increasingly erratic and ended with her setting fire to the school office and being expelled."

"That's dreadful," says Carys, who has turned pale.

"Yes. When she returned home, her father was all for sending her straight to the asylum, but it was her mother who suggested she come to Wales instead. Her mother was a second cousin of mine, apparently. Eddy always thought her mother believed her allegations, but was too scared to speak up. Sending her daughter off to Wales was a way for her mother to absolve some of her guilt."

"What was Eddy like when she was here?" asks Ffion. "Did you ever feel your own safety was at risk?"

"No," I answer honestly. "I always felt Eddy was more of a danger to herself than anyone else. She suffered from extreme changes of mood. One minute she'd be dancing me around the bothy singing at the top of her voice, then the next she'd be curled up in a ball by the fire sobbing her heart out. There was no middle ground with Eddy, but when she was good, she was very good. She's the reason I was able to help you get to Bangor," I explain to Ffion.

"Ah," she says, sharing a smile and a nod of understanding.

"How long was she living here?" asks Carys.

"About six months. In that time, we grew close. Other than Anne, Eddy was my only friend. Living in such a confined space, it could only have gone one of two ways; love or hate. Thankfully, it was the former, and I grew to love her. She was everything I wasn't – beautiful, exciting, adventurous, brave. She brought out a side of me I'd never seen before, and despite what happened, I will always be grateful for that."

"What happened to Eddy, Angharad?" Ffion's voice is soft, as if she knows what happened before I've even told her.

"Coming here was Eddy's last chance. She knew if she was ever sent back, her father would waste no time shipping her off to an asylum. Sometimes she would wake at night screaming from a nightmare where she was carted off never to be seen again." I pause to take a breath, and scrunch my handkerchief in my palm, knowing I'll likely need it soon. "I should have known by then not to trust Anne, but Eddy had instilled in me a love of life that blinded me to the real world. I took Anne's smile to be genuine, her interest nothing more than the concern of a friend. She liked to ask probing questions about my relationship with Eddy, and although I kept some things private, I probably told her more than I should have.

"Anne always came to see me on a Wednesday and a Saturday, but one day she turned up unannounced on a Friday evening. She... she..." My cheeks flush, my breaths come too quickly and I grip the arm of my chair, wondering if I can go on.

"It's alright," says Carys. "We won't judge you, Angharad. Look at me, I'm hardly in a position to, am I?"

I take a deep breath. "Anne came round unexpectedly and... and... she caught Eddy kissing me." I risk a glance at my friends. They are shocked, as I thought they would be, but neither has stood up and walked out yet, so I may as well continue. "Anne went mad, shouting and screaming at us, telling us we were all the worst names she could think of. I saw a different side to her that day and realised what a fool I had been to trust her. Of course, she went straight to Bryn with what she had seen."

I scrunch my eyes up tight and hold a handkerchief to my eyes, even though they remain stubbornly dry. Betty shifts her position in my lap, nuzzling into my side, and to my surprise, a warm hand covers mine. I look up to see Carys's smile of encouragement. I can do this. I can finish my story.

"Bryn sent Eddy home. We didn't even have a chance to say goodbye. In my heart I knew what would happen, even if I didn't want to believe it."

"What happened to Eddy, Angharad?"

"I don't know for certain, but I can guess. I suspect as soon as she arrived home, her father informed her she would be sent to the asylum. Eddy wouldn't have lasted a day in there. She was too full of life for a place like that. So, she took matters into her own hands. It was the gardener who found her the morning after she'd returned home. If she left a note, no one ever told me about it."

"She took her own life?" asks Ffion, and I know she is thinking about the time I almost crashed the car.

"Yes, my darling Eddy took her own life, and mine with it. I had been naïve to think Eddy and I could continue living as we were. Someone was bound to find out eventually, but I thought we'd have longer than we did. When Bryn and Anne came to tell me the news of Eddy's death, they seemed pleased. I couldn't understand it. Ever since, they've held my secret over my head like an executioner at the guillotine. You know what will happen if they share my secret. I will have to leave Llanfairpwll and there is nowhere else I can go. I've been at their mercy for so long now, I can't even remember what it is like to be free."

My friends stare at me, and I try to read the emotions on their faces.

"Goodness," says Ffion eventually. "That is quite the tale, Angharad. This tea has gone cold. Let's make another pot."

As Ffion bustles around with the kettle, it feels as if I'm in the dock waiting for my sentence to be passed down. Will they forgive me? Or have I just ruined everything again?

Chapter Seventy-Four

Angharad

July, 1918

"So you prefer women to men?" asks Carys with a frown.

"No, generally I have always found men far easier to understand and get along with than women. Until I met you, of course."

"You know what I mean, Angharad."

Never one to beat around the bush, Ffion sets it out in layman's terms. "Carys is asking if you prefer to be in romantic relationships with women rather than men."

"Well, I have only ever had one romantic relationship, and that was with a woman, but actually, the answer to your question is no."

"You prefer men?"

I throw my hands up into the air, unsure quite how to answer.

"It's alright," says Carys, placing a hand on my arm. "Take your time."

That she should touch me after what she has just learned is more than I could ever have dreamed of. I'd expected total and immediate rejection. But here are my friends, wanting to understand me.

"For me," I say, trying to explain things properly, "it's not about whether someone is a man or a woman. I have only truly loved once, and yes, Edwina was female, but I can't say I'm particularly attracted to the female form. It was the person inside the body I fell in love with."

"So Eddy could just as easily have been a man?"

"In theory, yes, I suppose so. But it is unlikely I would ever have had the chance to get to know a man as well as I knew Eddy, and men are rather put off by my size. That being said, Eddy could have come wrapped in any package and it would have made no difference to me. She was my soul mate. My best friend. The physical side to our relationship was negligible in the grand scheme of things. We were each other's supporter, each other's protector. Only I couldn't protect her in the end." As much as I'd like to control my emotions, I can't. I collapse in on myself, the grief as sharp as it was the day I first learned of Eddy's death.

Ffion and Carys crouch beside me, wrapping their arms around me. They say nothing, holding me as my body heaves with violent sobs. Only when my tears subside does Ffion speak.

"You know, Angharad, what happened to Eddy wasn't your fault."

"It was, if I hadn't been so careless, if I hadn't opened my big mouth to Anne, if she hadn't found us like she did..."

"Eddy was damaged by what had happened to her and it made her ill, Angharad," says Carys. "Just like those poor souls returning from the war are ill. Just like Madge Watt's husband was ill."

"Carys is right. You'll hate me for saying this, but I don't think you can even blame Bryn and Anne for what happened."

My head whips up and I glare at Ffion. "Can't blame them? They sent her away! They ruined my life, and they have been holding my secret like a dagger over my head ever since!"

"That is all true, and everything you described is a despicable way to behave, but they didn't sign Eddy's death warrant. It was her illness and all she'd experienced that did that, Angharad. Goodness, if we'd been having this conversation two years ago, I would have given you a very different response, but you've both seen the men who come to the convalescent home. Some of them are so damaged by the things they have seen, have experienced, that no one could hold them accountable for their own actions."

"But I need someone to blame!"

"Do you?" says Carys. "I tried that when we lost the farm. I know it's not the same, but I was so angry, so hurt. I blamed Dadi for dying, my brothers for leaving us, Mami for not being strong enough to keep going, but all blame does is eat away at you from the inside. You are the only one who suffers from holding so much anger in your heart."

"It hurts so much," I say, the physical pain of reliving my loss causing me to double over.

"And part of you will always hurt. But from how you've described Eddy to us, that isn't what she would have wanted."

"How do I get better? How do I continue to live? It's too much to carry."

"You're strong, Angharad, and I don't just mean physically." Carys stands up and looks down at me, her hands on her hips. "For years you've lived under the threat of your brother, but not once have you crumbled. Somehow, despite him, you've built a life for yourself, found friendship and purpose. I don't think you actually realise how much admiration we all have for you."

"Carys is right," says Ffion. "We all look up to you. And if we can recognise your worth, it's about time you learn to value yourself."

"I thought you'd both hate me when you found out the truth."

"Hate you?" Carys laughs and throws her hands up in the air. "I'm an unmarried woman expecting a child, who's brought disgrace on her entire family."

"And for years, I turned a blind eye to my husband's mistreatment of other women. Neither Carys nor I are in any position to sit in judgment over you."

"Thank you. Thank you both."

Ffion and Carys each take an arm and pull me up off my chair. "Now we've finally got all that out of the way," says Ffion, "we need to make a plan."

"Yes," says Carys, sharing a look with Ffion. "You can't go on like this, Angharad. It's about time we broke your brother's hold over you once and for all."

Chapter Seventy-Five

Angharad

July, 1918

"D o you hate me?" I ask, trying to gauge Charlie's reaction. He's stunned and looks rather upset.

"It's a lot for a chap to get his head around. I've never come across a woman who prefers women to men."

"I think most women prefer women to men," I say, trying to lighten the mood.

"Not in the way you're describing."

"I'm sorry."

"What for?"

"You seem so disappointed in me."

"I'm disappointed, yes, but with the situation, not with you."

"I don't understand."

"I suppose... I suppose I always wondered..."

"Wondered what?"

"Whether one day you might see me as more than your friend. It was stupid, of course. What woman in her right mind would want a man like me?"

Charlie's revelation stuns me into silence. I stare at him, and a warm glow sweeps through my body.

"Say something, please. I've just made a complete fool out of myself and you're staring at me like I've got two heads."

"Sorry, you've shocked me, that's all."

"Forget I said anything. I should have kept my big mouth shut."

"No, it's not that." I try to express my thoughts. It never occurred to me I could have more than one love in my life. One felt too much to ask, any more felt plain greedy. And besides, who would want a woman who looks like I do? I let my eyes rest on Charlie and feel a rush of affection towards him. "I had never been attracted to a woman before I met Eddy, and I haven't been since."

"Then why did it happen?"

"I don't know. It was like magic. From the first day Eddy arrived, we just clicked. It never occurred to me there would be anything other than friendship between us, and it was Eddy who pushed things in a more romantic direction."

"So where does that leave us, then?"

"It leaves us as the good friends we are, with the possibility that one day, once all this has died down, if we keep an open mind and both feel the same way, then maybe that friendship might grow into something else."

Charlie grins at me. "That will do me for now."

Mr Stephens walks in and raises an eyebrow as he looks between our red faces.

"Mr Stephens, I wonder if we could have a word?"

Mr Stephens watches my lips moving, nods, washes his hands at the sink, then sits down at the kitchen table.

"Do you remember my friend who stayed with me a few years ago, Miss Winterborne?"

Mr Stephens scribbles on his piece of paper. *Yes, lovely girl. I was sorry about what happened to her.*

"So was I, Mr Stephens. Well, it seems my brother and sister-in-law feel our friendship was inappropriate."

Mr Stephens frowns.

"They think we were involved in some sort of romantic relationship."

Mr Stephens tips his head back and laughs. Charlie catches my eye and raises an eyebrow, and heat floods my face.

Don't worry, writes Mr Stephens, *if your brother suggests that to me, I'll set him straight.*

"Thank you. There's something else I'd like to discuss with you. It is rather delicate. You remember my friend, Miss Ambrose?"

Mr Stephens nods.

"Well, I'm afraid she's got herself into a bit of trouble. You see, she is expecting a child."

Mr Stephens frowns and writes one word on his paper. *Father?*

"The father doesn't yet know about the baby, but I am going to do my best to find him. The thing is, Miss Ambrose has nowhere to turn. Her family have had to give up their farm after her father died and her brother was killed in the war. Her mother has moved to the mainland, but Carys, Miss Ambrose, has nowhere to turn."

Mr Stephens scribbles on his paper. *Not under my roof.*

My heart sinks, but I try the only option left to me. "No, of course not. But what about under mine? She could stay with me in the bothy until I'm able to track down the father of her child. You wouldn't need to see her, and no one would need to know she is there."

I wait with bated breath for Mr Stephens to write his answer. He holds his pencil between his fingers, twirls it around, holds it to the paper, removes it, and lowers it again. Instead, he answers with a shrug and a curt nod, gets up from his chair and stomps out of the farmhouse.

"Was that a yes or a no?" I ask Charlie.

"I think it was a yes, but he can't be seen to be condoning such a thing. I might be putting words into his mouth, but knowing Geraint, he'll turn a blind eye if Miss Williams stays with you. But, I must say, I'm shocked to hear she's expecting."

"So was she," I say, and we both laugh. "I'm going to do my best to make things right for her."

"I'm sure you will," says Charlie, wheeling his chair closer and taking my hand. "You're a woman in a million, Angharad Williams, and we're all lucky to have you as our friend."

Chapter Seventy-Six

Angharad

August, 1918

"It's so strange to think this time last year I was in the middle of harvesting hay. Things seemed difficult then. Now, looking back, it feels like some golden age."

"It will be alright," I say, giving Carys a reassuring pat on the back. I haven't told her yet that I visited her farm, but no letter had arrived for her. Florian might wait until he's settled before writing to her. I may be worrying about nothing. "You know, I've been told I'm not welcome at chapel. I'm not sure we'll be allowed in."

Carys smiles at me. She seems so well compared to how Ffion found her only weeks earlier. "Maybe not, but you'll have to face your brother one day, and today's as good as any. I'm so grateful for all you've done for me, Angharad."

"It's nothing. The extra help on the allotment has been wonderful."

"I know, but I've invaded your privacy, and I know that can't be easy."

"What are friends for?" I say as we walk through the chapel gate. My heart sinks at the sight of Anne standing outside. What is she doing there?

Anne places an arm across the doorway. "You are not welcome here."

"Pardon?"

"You heard me. You are no longer welcome in this chapel."

"Mrs Williams, I'm sure this must be some sort of misunderstanding."

"Don't you dare utter my name, you little…"

"Anne, please."

"And as for you," she says, a shower of saliva landing against my skin. "I should have known you'd be involved in any scandal. From what I've heard, you're housing this Jezebel."

I glance at Carys, who has turned very pale. How does Anne know about the baby? "Sister, I'm sure this can all be resolved with a calm discussion."

"We will not taint ourselves by talking with the likes of you. You should have been more careful, Angharad. Goodness knows you've had enough warning. The Women's Institute is on their summer break, but the second their meetings resume, I shall go to the committee and inform them of everything I know."

For a moment, I cower as has always been my nature, but then a new feeling takes hold. "Do you know, Anne, I couldn't care a jot if you speak to the committee. Miss Ambrose and Mrs Montgomery already know everything there is to know about my past and the knowledge has done nothing to dent our friendship. Perhaps the other women of the WI shan't be as understanding, but I'm willing to take that chance. In fact, please tell them all you know. I'm fed up with carrying around secrets and shame."

"And what about your employer, eh? What will you do when Mr Stephens finds out? He's a God-fearing man. There's no way he'll allow you to live on his land when he finds out what you are."

"Actually, I've already told him, and he accepts me as I am. He also knows about the situation Miss Ambrose finds herself in, and whilst he may not approve, he is a man who takes Christian teachings seriously, and has taken Jesus's advice to love thy neighbour."

Anne stares at me open-mouthed. She begins to splutter out words, then clamps her mouth shut.

"Right, Miss Ambrose, why don't we walk to Menai Bridge, and see if we can find a chapel that will welcome us?"

"Do you know, Miss Williams, that sounds like a splendid idea."

Before Anne can spill any more of her poison, we turn and leave the chapel behind us.

"Are we really going to walk all the way to Menai Bridge?"

"No, we can find a new chapel to attend another week."

"It feels strange not to be attending chapel."

"I know. But at least I've had a chance to get used to it these past few months."

"You were very brave, standing up to Anne like that."

"I should have done it years ago."

"Shall we walk down to the shore? It's a beautiful day."

"Why not?"

Carys links her arm in mine, and we make our way down the lane which leads to the banks of the Menai Strait. When we reach St Mary's churchyard, the sound of an organ reaches us and mixes with the bird-song beyond the church walls.

We enter the churchyard, then Carys stops walking and closes her eyes. "Do you think God will ever forgive the sin I have committed, Angharad?"

I take a moment to find an answer. "Do you know, Carys, I'm really not sure I believe much in God these days."

"What?" Carys stares at me in horror as the surrounding air fills with voices from the church singing 'Guide Me, O Thou Great Redeemer'. "You don't believe in God? But you're a minister's daughter!"

"Perhaps that is why." I laugh to lighten the mood, but the frown doesn't leave Carys's face. We continue to walk through the graveyard, and I stop beside two very familiar gravestones. "My parents," I explain, bending down and placing a hand on the cold stone.

"You know, Angharad, what happened to Eddy, all that has happened to you? None of it is God's fault. Any blame falls firmly at the feet of man."

"Perhaps, but even if that were true, how can you reconcile the suffering caused by the war with a supposedly loving God?"

"It wasn't God who started the war, was it?"

"No, but why has He done nothing to intervene? Why did He do nothing to help Eddy? Goodness knows I've prayed enough over the years, and not one of those prayers has been answered."

"I'm no theologian, Angharad. I can't say any of my prayers have been answered either, but I believe God gave us the gift of free will, and it is up to us how we use it, for good or evil. Besides, look around us. There is so much beauty here. How could that have been created by chance?"

We walk through a rusty gate and follow a narrow path down to the shore. The ribbon of water sparkles beneath a bright summer sun and the distant mountains are soft in the hazy light. Deep inside me, I feel the flutter of a faith I thought long vanished.

"I worry about finding a new chapel," says Carys. "After all, if I'm barred from attending your brother's in Llanfairpwll, who's to say another minister in another village or town won't feel the same?"

"Then perhaps we give up on chapel for the time being. Perhaps we hold a meeting of our own, in the farmhouse each Sunday. It has been years since Mr Stephens has made head nor tail of a chapel service, but between us we could speak slowly, write things down."

"You'd do that for us, despite your own shaky beliefs?"

"Maybe it's time I gave this God of yours another chance. Maybe it's not that my prayers weren't answered, but that I was asking for the wrong thing. After all, look at all I have in my life. I never dreamed of asking God for friendship. It seemed impossible, and yet here you are."

"Perhaps that is what's meant by God's plan. It might not be the path we wished to take, but the right one nonetheless."

We sit down on a grassy bank and gaze at the surrounding beauty. I take Carys's hand in mine. "Your baby will be a gift from God, however it was conceived."

Carys frees her hand and rubs it against her stomach. "I hope you're right, Angharad. I really do."

Chapter Seventy-Seven

Ffion

September, 1918

"Mrs Montgomery, Miss Williams, do come in."

"Thank you," I say, giving Angharad's fingers a quick squeeze as we cross the threshold of Graig. We walk into the drawing room and find the four women we are here to see already settled in chairs with cups and saucers beside them. Once the preliminary greetings are disposed of, Angharad and I sit beside each other on the settee. I can feel her legs shaking beside me, and plant a smile on my face that I hope gives a show of confidence.

"So," says Mrs Jones, "we were most intrigued by your request to meet."

"And we are most grateful for you accepting, and for hosting this meeting in your home."

"What I don't understand," says Mrs Jones, "is what was so important it couldn't be discussed at one of our regular committee meetings?"

I take a deep breath. It's now or never. "The matters we wish to discuss are of a personal nature, and we wanted to bring them to you first. One of these matters involves a certain Mrs Anne Williams, and although she hasn't attended a meeting for a few months now, there is no saying she won't appear when we least expect her."

At the mention of Anne, the other women shift in their seats and some of them frown. So, it is not only me who has found her an obstructive, negative presence on the committee. Angharad's foot is tapping rapidly on the carpet below, and I decide it will be best to deal with her situation first. She is clearly in no state to plead her case herself, so I launch straight into the heart of the matter.

"You will be aware, I am sure, of Angharad's relationship with Mrs Anne Williams." The ladies around me nod and I smile at them. "They are sisters-in-law, but I'm sure all of us can appreciate not all family relationships run as smoothly as we would like." At this, there are titters of laughter and knowing looks. "Unfortunately, this is the case for Miss and Mrs Williams. Relations between the two of them soured some years ago, and whilst I believe family disputes should largely remain private, in this case, as their dispute directly affects the running of the Institute, I felt it important to bring the matter to you."

"Affects the Institute?" asks Mrs Jones. "But how?"

"Mrs Anne Williams has been threatening to make public an episode from Angharad's past, unless she ceases all contact with the Llanfairp-wll Women's Institute."

There are gasps from the assembled ladies.

"Miss Williams and I feel enough is enough, so we are here to get things out in the open, so to speak." I look across at Angharad, who has her hands folded in her lap and her eyes on the floor. "The information Mrs Williams has been holding over her sister-in-law is a relationship formed between Miss Williams and a distant cousin some years ago. The young lady in question was sent to Anglesey after suffering terribly at the hands of a male relative."

One woman chokes on her tea, and another raises a hand to her mouth.

"Miss Williams opened her home to this young lady, Miss Edwina Winterbow. Given all Miss Winterbow had been through, and I shall spare you the details, she needed a great deal of comfort. Miss Williams and Miss Winterbow grew extremely close and formed a strong bond. Unfortunately, Mrs and Reverend Williams disapproved of the closeness Angharad and Edwina shared and took to calling in unannounced. On one of these occasions, Mrs Williams walked in while Angharad was comforting Edwina and assumed the worst."

The ladies around me are frowning in confusion.

"Mrs Williams felt the relationship between Angharad and Edwina was unnatural, inappropriate. She and her husband arranged for Edwina to be sent back to England, where, I regret to inform you, she took her own life." I've been trying my best to present as sanitised a version as I can muster of the story, but there's no point beating around the bush where Eddy's death is concerned. "You can imagine how this upset Miss Williams terribly. But worse still, for several years now, Mrs and Mr Williams have been threatening to tell villagers about the relationship between Angharad and Edwina, unless Angharad conforms to their wishes and keeps herself to herself."

"Blackmail?" asks Mrs Jones, her eyes wide.

"I suppose you could put it in those terms, yes."

"But I don't understand the problem? I had two aunts who lived together as companions all their lives. There was nothing seedy about it and they were perfectly happy."

"Quite. Such living arrangements can be rather common. But it is my belief Mrs Anne Williams intended to make this relationship sound sordid."

"And this is why you've stopped attending meetings, is it?" asks Mrs Jones, directing the question to Angharad.

"Yes," says Angharad, lifting her eyes for the first time.

"Well, I really can't see any problem here," says Mrs Jones. "I am very sorry for the loss of your dear friend, Miss Williams. And I am sorry you felt unable to come to us with this information sooner. Regardless of anything Mrs Williams may tell us, you can rest assured your position in this institute is secure. You are a valued member of our organisation, and don't forget the principles we are founded on, those of inclusion of different backgrounds and political beliefs. As an institute, our survival is reliant upon being open to women regardless of their background."

"I'm pleased you mentioned the principle of tolerance the Women's Institute is based upon," I say, grateful to have at least cleared up one matter, "for that brings me on to the second matter we wish to discuss."

Angharad and I keep our composure until we are safely away from Graig and out of sight of any other women leaving the home. I turn to her and squeal with delight, then grab her in a tight hug. When she pulls away, she is laughing. "I can't believe they were so accepting of my situation."

"You realise this means you are free now, Angharad? With the Women's Institute on your side, you're practically invincible. And what about Carys's situation? Wasn't that a turn up for the books?"

"I know. I feel terrible I'd been expecting the worst."

"It helped when you said you'll try to get in touch with Mr Jansen. It made the whole thing sound far more palatable. And I think the war has changed people's views about these things. The amount of women becoming pregnant by soldiers who are only passing through is of great concern. At least in this case, we might reunite the parents and prevent too great a scandal."

"Only if I can find Florian, and even then, there's no saying he'll step up and do the right thing."

"You saw the way he looked at Carys, we both did. And the few times I met him, I felt he was a good man. I'm sure he'll come through for us."

"Then I'd better get on with finding him, hadn't I?"

Chapter Seventy-Eight

Ffion

October, 1918

The summerhouse is eerily quiet. At least half our number is absent due to either being struck down with the illness themselves or caring for family members who have been. I probably should have stayed at home, as influenza is rife among the soldiers I'm housing, but after a very long few days, I needed to escape.

"Goodness," says Angharad, coming to stand beside me, "it's quiet in here today."

"It's the influenza," I say. "It's everywhere in the village. Please tell me Carys hasn't fallen ill?"

"No, but we thought it was best she stays at home, just in case. Are you alright? You're looking a little peaky."

"I'm fine, just tired from all the extra care our patients have needed."

"The flu has reached the convalescent home?"

"It certainly has, more's the pity. Mrs Edwards is struck down, so Susan and I have been trying to manage the cooking between us. We've tried to isolate the patients who have it, but it's tricky."

"Is your husband at home?"

"He was, but when the first few soldiers fell ill, he decided to stay with his mother on the mainland."

"Not London?"

"No, he thinks the influenza will be worse there. I heard from the children. Both Mary and Rebecca have had it but recovered quickly enough not to need sending home. The boys have escaped it so far, but I'm assuming it's only a matter of time. Our speaker for today, Mr Price F. White, is struck down and unable to attend."

"What was he due to speak on?"

"The Fuel Question. Miss Lamport has stepped up to take his place, though I'm not sure how much she knows about the subject. Given our low numbers, it might have been better to forget about any talk and simply enjoy a cup of tea and the chance to rest our legs." I fan myself with my hand, the room suddenly feeling rather stuffy.

"Are you sure you're alright, Ffion? You don't look terribly well."

"Truly, I'm fine. Let's find somewhere to sit down."

In the end, Miss Lamport does a sterling job of tackling the Fuel Question, and thankfully keeps her talk brief. I seem to have something stuck in my throat and it is an effort not to cough and disrupt the ongoing discussion. Angharad must notice, for she gets up and returns with a glass of water for me. I take a long drink, but my throat feels as dry as before.

The suggestion is made to postpone the next meeting, given the current epidemic, and all agree this is a sensible idea. Mrs Cotton and Mrs Jones speak briefly and the meeting draws to its conclusion with the opportunity to browse the produce stall, although there isn't much to see with so many of our usual contributors absent.

"Shall we get a cup of tea?"

"Yes, let's." But when I try to stand, my legs suddenly feel wobbly, and I flop back down again. I am very cold, but then a surge of heat rushes through me and I am forced to remove my cardigan. I try to look up at Angharad, but my eyes ache.

"We need to get you home," says Angharad. "I think you've caught the flu."

"Oh no, I'm fine," I say, as the room around me spins. The women nearby back away, eyeing me with mistrust.

"Is everything alright here?" Mrs Cotton asks Angharad.

"No, I think Mrs Montgomery is unwell. Given your recent poor health, it's probably best you leave this to me."

The women scatter to the edges of the room as Angharad eases me to my feet and supports my weight. It is terribly embarrassing to have caused such a scene, and I pray to God I am simply tired, and have not brought the infection into the group.

"I know this isn't very dignified," says Angharad, when we get outside, "but we're not going to get very far like this. It will be easier if I carry you."

"Carry me?" My voice sounds far away, and my throat is so dry it is difficult to speak. "There is no need to carry me, Ang...." My legs lose feeling, and I collapse to the ground. From the summerhouse I hear exclamations of distress, but they sound so far away as though part of a dream. I'm aware of strong arms scooping me up, and I bury my head against Angharad's chest as she holds me tight to her. "Lucky you're so strong." Did I just speak, or did I imagine it?

I must have fallen asleep, for the next thing I know, I am being carried through the house, and Angharad is talking to someone.

"She has come down with influenza, Matron. Can you show me to her room? We need to get her into bed."

"Yes, it's up here."

I bump against Angharad as she carries me up the stairs. I want to giggle at being carried through my home but can't get the muscles in my face to move. It is so cold here, so very cold. Angharad lays me down on the bed and must tuck me in, for I feel the coolness of cotton sheets and the warmth of woollen blankets covering my body. Just as I slip towards sleep, I hear Matron speak.

"Miss Williams, I've just come from the village. It sounds as if your brother and sister-in-law are very unwell. If you want to go to them, I will make sure Mrs Montgomery is well taken care of."

Before I hear Angharad's reply, sleep overtakes me, and I fall into oblivion.

Chapter Seventy-Nine

Angharad

October, 1918

The decision is an easy one to make. Whatever Bryn and Anne have done to me, they are family, and I shan't abandon them in their hour of need. When I reach the bothy, instead of going inside, I bang on the door. Carys answers, but it takes me a moment to catch my breath and explain what is going on.

"I can't come in. I've just been with Ffion who was taken ill at the meeting. The last thing I want is to pass the illness on to you. I've also heard that Bryn and Anne are extremely unwell with it. I'm going over to their house now."

"After all they've done to you? Surely not. I can understand helping Ffion, but not them. Come inside. I'm sure you won't have picked up any germs at the meeting."

"I can't risk it, Carys. It's not only you to think about, but the child you are carrying. And I must go to Bryn and Anne. Whether or not I like it, they are my family. I need to be there for them."

"You'll be putting yourself in harm's way."

I shrug. "And what if I am? I've no husband, no children who will mourn me if I succumb to the illness."

"Don't talk like that, Angharad. It isn't right. There are plenty who would be devastated were something to happen to you, and I'd be top of that list."

"That's very kind, Carys, and I promise I won't take any unnecessary risks. Could you please pack a bag with a few of my clothes? I shall probably have to stay at Bryn's house, and I can't see any of Anne's clothes fitting me, can you?"

Betty runs out from between Carys's legs and jumps up, licking my hand.

"Why don't you take her with you?" calls Carys as she packs up my clothes.

"Anne hates dogs."

"I don't think Anne's in a position to complain by the sounds of things, and I don't like the idea of you being in that house with them. At least with Betty there, you'll have an ally. If they become too nasty, she can bite them for you."

"Carys!"

Carys's laughter floats through the door and I pick Betty up and scratch under her ears. "Of course I was joking," says Carys, handing me a carpet bag, "but not about the company. Goodness knows how long you'll end up staying there. It would put my mind at rest to know Betty is with you."

"Alright then. Looks as if you're coming with me," I say, kissing the top of Betty's head before setting her down on the ground.

"I'll drop round food for you later. I doubt they'll have anything in the house if they're as poorly as you say they are."

"Thank you. That would be very helpful, but I want you to put the food on the doorstep, then walk away. You mustn't catch this illness, Carys."

"I'll be careful, I promise."

"Good. Wish me luck."

"Good luck!" calls Carys as I turn and head toward the village.

When I reach Bryn's house, all the curtains are drawn, and no light seeps through. I knock on the door, but when no one comes to answer, I try the handle and let myself in. Betty runs in ahead, then stands in the middle of the hallway, whining. "It's alright, *cariad*. You stay down here, and I'll see what's going on."

The sound of coughing reaches me from upstairs. My heart pounds as I climb towards the bedrooms. The first door I try opens with a creak. It takes my eyes a moment to adjust to the darkness, but when they do, I see Bryn and Anne lying in their marital bed. The smell in the room is terrible, and I rush to the window and open it, taking in a deep gulp of fresh air. I open the curtains a crack, and the light that trickles in shows just what I am dealing with.

Anne has her back to me, facing the wall. Her clothes are soiled and her body trembles. She is muttering, as though in the middle of a nightmare, and her arm flails out above her, as if she is trying to bat someone away. At least she is moving, unlike Bryn, who is lying so still beside her for a moment. I wonder if he is dead. His skin is waxy, his lips a strange blue colour. When I touch his shirt, I find it soaked with sweat. The bedclothes beneath them are putrid and once I have checked on the girls, changing the sheets will be the first thing I see to.

I am almost too afraid of what I'll find to try the next door. But what is the point of being here if I am not prepared to help? With a gentle nudge, the door creaks open. A set of bunk beds sit on either side of the room.

"Aunt Angharad?" says a quiet voice.

"Yes," I say, walking to the far side of the room. My youngest niece, Efa, is sitting up in her bed, trying to use her colouring pencils in the dark.

"Everyone is unwell except for me."

"Thank goodness you are alright at least. Shall I open the curtains a little so you can see your drawing better?"

"Yes, please."

I cross to the window and pull back the curtains enough to let a shard of light into the room. The air here is stuffy and smells musty, but nothing like in Bryn's room, so I only open the window a crack. With more light to see by, I check each bed. Bethan, my eldest niece, is in a deep sleep, but when I touch her forehead, it is warm but not hot and it seems she no longer has a fever and might be over the worst. In the opposite beds I find Mari, whose body is still hot and damp to the touch but who is mercifully fast asleep, and Sara, whose sheets are tangled around her slim body, but who, like Bethan, appears not to have a fever.

"Efa," I whisper as I stand beside her bed. "As you and I are the only people here who are not unwell, shall we become nurses for a few days?"

"I don't know how to be a nurse, and Mother has said I shouldn't speak to you."

Anger and sadness bubble up inside me, but I push the feelings aside. "Perhaps not, but your mother is very sick and needs our help. I'm sure she won't mind you talking to me for a few days, just until she is feeling better."

"Alright, but I still don't know how to be a nurse."

"Neither do I, but I know how to care for animals, and I don't suppose humans are all that different. Why don't you be my assistant? Together, we'll help your family get better."

"Alright." Efa holds her arms out and I realise she wants me to lift her down. I place my hands beneath her arms and once on the floor, she takes my hand. "You know," she says, "I've always wanted to speak to you."

"Well, now you have the chance. But we'd better get straight to work and get your family well again. Come on, there's lots to do."

Chapter Eighty

Carys

October, 1918

In the absence of Angharad, the farmhouse looks unloved. Pots and pans sit waiting to be washed beside the sink and the curtains in the parlour have not been opened.

"I'm sorry about the mess," says Charlie. "I can't reach the sink and I'm still too unsteady on my new legs to stand for any length of time."

"Mr Stephens could reach."

"Don't be too hard on him, Carys. Without Angharad here, we're flat out trying to keep things going."

"Then let me help."

"Not in your condition."

"Charlie, I'm pregnant, not ill."

"Still, I wouldn't want you near the hind legs of a cow."

"Then at least let me help here in the house. We need to keep a steady stream of meals going to the Williams house, and there isn't enough room in the bothy for me to cook proper meals."

Charlie runs his hands through his thick brown hair. "What was she thinking, Carys? Going off like that to help her brother, I just don't understand it. Sometimes I think she's too kind for her own good."

I watch Charlie as he sighs and shakes his head. It is obvious he cares for Angharad, and I wonder how deep those feelings go. If I knew him better, I'd be tempted to ask.

"I'll take some cawl over to her this afternoon. If I make a big enough batch, there'll be plenty for you and Mr Stephens as well. At least we've no shortage of veg, thanks to Angharad's allotment."

"No shortage of milk, either. We're far luckier than some."

"Aren't we just," I say, shivering, as I wonder what would have become of me had Angharad not taken me in.

"Can I come with you when you take the food?"

"Are you sure? Don't you have things to be getting on with here?"

"I do, but I'm worried about her. Goodness knows how those relatives of hers are treating her."

"She's stronger than you think."

"You didn't see the effect their threats had on her. It was like she shrivelled up, shrank in size. I was really worried about her for a while there."

"You're a good friend to Angharad, Charlie. I know she values your friendship a great deal."

"She does?"

I can't help but smile at the hope and joy in his eyes. "Yes, she does. Now, you get out to the barn and get on with your work, and I'll make a start clearing up in here. Oh, and you'd best warn Mr Stephens I'm in his home. I don't want him being too shocked if he walks in and finds me here."

"Don't worry about Geraint," says Charlie. "If he was that disapproving, he'd not have let you stay in the bothy. He's got a good heart, and a sensible head on his shoulders. He's not one to judge."

"That's just as well. Now, off you go. I'll call you when there's some food on the table."

"Thank you, Carys."

"Of course."

As I potter around the kitchen, I notice how my stomach keeps getting in the way. It's becoming harder and harder to bend down, and when I fetch water from the well, I have to do a most unladylike squat in order to pull up the pail. When I wipe down the table, my stomach bumps against the wood and I can't reach as far as I'd like. It's the same when I wash the dishes, but I can't resent the round ball beneath my apron. Despite my being terrified for the future, the child I am carrying belongs half to me and half to Florian, and that makes it precious. I have no idea how I'll provide for the pair of us, and force my thoughts onto the practical matters of today, rather than my fears for the future.

From the basket I filled earlier, I pull potatoes, carrots, swede and leeks and begin chopping them finely before taking a bowl from the shelf and scraping the vegetables into it. Next, I go into the pantry and take a joint of lamb from its paper wrapping. A wave of nostalgia hits me and for a moment I am back on our farm, but I shake the memory off, knowing it will only bring sadness.

Once the meat has been chopped into cubes and rolled in flour, I grab a pan from its hook below the shelf, add a knob of butter and wait until I can hear it fizzing on the range, before adding the lamb. It fizzes and pops, and the air fills with the sweet smell of butter-coated meat, making my stomach rumble.

Once all the ingredients are added and bubbling away in the pan, I turn my attention to other jobs Angharad has not been able to do. I sweep the flagstone floor, then go upstairs and remove sheets from the bed, returning downstairs with an armful of cotton ready to be scrubbed when we return from the village.

"Dinner is ready," I call out into the yard when the cawl has thickened up and the meat flakes off my fork.

Charlie and Mr Stephens enter the farmhouse together, Mr Stephens giving me a brief nod, before sitting at the table and tucking into his food. Neither Charlie nor I linger over our meal either, knowing we are needed elsewhere. The thought of entering the village is making my heart beat faster than I'd like. Since my pregnancy became obvious, I have avoided the gaze of others, despite Ffion and Angharad's assurances that I would still be welcome at the WI. Perhaps I'm a coward, but I can't bear the thought of other women sizing up my bump and whispering about the situation I've got myself into.

"Let's go," says Charlie, staggering to the sink on his new legs. I wonder if he'll drop the bowl he is carrying, but he makes it to the sink without incident and turns to us with a grin. "First time I've done that," he says, "but I think I'll use the chair to get into the village."

We set off along the road and I wonder what passers-by will make of us, Charlie in his wheelchair and me waddling along with my belly poking out of my coat. At least the bump provides a useful shelf for me to balance the pot of cawl on as we walk and wheel our way closer to the village.

I needn't have worried about folk's opinions of me, for the streets are deathly quiet, as though it is too dangerous to step out into the chill autumn air for fear of catching drops of sickness on the passing breeze. A few curtains twitch as we walk past a row of stone cottages.

"People are scared," says Charlie. "All this time we've been worried about the Germans, and now there's this threat much closer to home. Have you heard of any fatalities?"

"Yes, unfortunately I have. Older folk and the very young seem to be worse off, although others are not immune. The Edwards of Llangefni lost a son aged only twenty-six to influenza."

"I read in Mr Stephens' newspaper that three cups of Oxo a day keep influenza at bay."

"Do you believe it?"

"No, but if others do, this influenza pandemic will be good for business. I've heard the same about Bovril. Apparently, the makers are struggling to keep up with demand."

"At least someone is feeling the benefit, I suppose. Do you think we should try it, the Oxo I mean? I'm sure I saw some in Mrs Stephens' pantry."

Charlie shrugs. "I suppose it can't hurt."

"You know the school and Sunday school have been closed for the time being?"

"Really? Goodness me, Carys, what is going on with the world?"

"I know. I worry about the country my child will be born into. With war and so much sickness around, it feels like a foolish time to be having a baby."

"Well, there's little you can do about it now," says Charlie, nodding at my bump.

"I suppose not. Here we are." I walk up to the Williamses' front door and knock, before placing the pan of cawl down on the table.

A young girl answers the door with a frown and I take a step back. "Who are you?" she asks.

"My name is Miss Ambrose and I'm a friend of Miss Angharad Williams. Is she here?"

"Aunt Angharad," shouts the girl, "there's someone to see you."

Footsteps sound on the stairs, then Angharad appears, looking tired but otherwise well. "Carys, how lovely to see you. Oh, Charlie is here too. How wonderful."

"We bought you a pan of cawl," I say, pointing down to the front step.

"That's very kind of you."

"Can we eat it now?" asks the little girl.

"This is my niece, Efa," says Angharad, ruffling the girl's hair. "She's been a marvellous helper to me the past few days."

"We're playing nurses," says the girl.

"Not just playing," says Angharad. "Look how much better your sisters have got since you started looking after them."

The girl beams with pride, then her face falls. "But not Mother and Father."

"No, not yet, but I'm sure they'll be better soon. Efa, it looks as though Miss Ambrose has brought some bread and milk as well as the cawl. Why don't you take those through to the kitchen, and I'll follow you with the pan in a moment."

The girl picks up a basket containing milk and bread and disappears back into the house.

"How are Bryn and Anne?" I ask once I'm sure the girl is out of earshot.

"Not good. Not good at all. I'm very worried about them. Anne seems to be a little better today, but if anything, Bryn is worse. They're so ill, I'm not sure they're even aware it's me who's been caring for them."

"And how are you? Have you shown any sign of catching the sickness?"

"Not yet, and I'm praying it stays that way." A cry comes from somewhere above our heads, and worry covers Angharad's face. "I'd better go, but thank you so much for the food."

"Take care of yourself," calls Charlie, and from the earnest expression on his face, I can tell he means it.

We walk away from the Williamses' home in silence, and I suspect, like me, Charlie is offering silent prayers that Angharad will remain well and will come back to us soon.

Chapter Eighty-One

Angharad

October, 1918

The cry had come from Anne, who I find leaning over my brother's still body, trying to shake some life back into him. When I run into the room, she looks up, her eyes flashing with anger.

"What are you doing here? You're not welcome in this house."

I could stop to tell her that the clean sheets she's lying on are thanks to me, not to mention the clean nightdress she wears. I could tell her that over the past three days, while she has slept, I have nursed her three eldest daughters back to health. Instead, I say, "what's the matter with Bryn?"

"I don't know," cries Anne, forgetting to be angry with me for a moment. "He was making a strange wheezing sound like he couldn't breathe. It woke me up and then he seemed to stop breathing altogether. You need to do something. You need to do something. Now!"

I rush to the bed and take Bryn in my arms, lifting him until he is sitting in the hope it may clear his chest and make breathing easier. He flops around like a rag doll and it is only my arms that are stopping him from falling back to the bed. I hold my cheek to his mouth and feel a feather-like tickle of breath.

"He's still breathing, but he is very unwell." I prop an extra pillow behind his neck and head and turn my attention to my sister-in-law.

"You're looking better. Let me feel your forehead." Before she can protest, I place a hand against her head and my shoulders sag with relief to find it no longer sticky with sweat.

"I'm looking better?" she asks. "How long have you been here?"

Efa strides into the room, the apron I found for her skimming the floor. "Aunt Angharad has been here for three days and you have been asleep that whole time. We have changed your sheets and your clothes and helped you drink some water. My sisters are all feeling much better because we have been excellent nurses." Her confidence suddenly disappears, and she looks at Anne from beneath her lashes. "I know you told me not to talk to Aunt Angharad, but she was the only one well enough to talk to."

Anne has the good grace to blush. At least I hope it's embarrassment rather than fever causing her cheeks to redden.

"As your daughter says, I have been here for three days. I heard you and my brother were unwell and came to help."

"Betty is here too."

"Betty?" says Anne, lying back against her pillows, as though speaking has used the last of her energy.

"Aunt Angharad's dog. She's friendly."

"I know you don't like her being in your house, but I've made sure she stays downstairs."

"Where have you been sleeping?" asks Anne, her voice slightly slurred as though she is about to drift off herself.

"In a chair downstairs."

I wait for her to make some snide comment about me invading her home, but as her eyes flutter shut, she whispers, "thank you."

For the next two hours, I stay by Anne and Bryn's bedside, praying there will be some change in his condition. As Anne sleeps peacefully, my brother is in the grip of fever, his body pouring out sweat one minute, and shivering the next. I'm about to get up and go in search of fresh towels, when his shivering reaches new heights, his body shaking uncontrollably. The movement wakes Anne, who turns to her husband and lets out a scream as pink-tinged foam appears on his lips.

I jump to my feet and rush to Bryn. The movement causes his blankets and sheets to slip and, with horror, I realise his feet are black. "Bryn," I say, kneeling beside him and pressing a hand to his forehead. "Bryn, it's me, Angharad. I know we've had our differences, but I'm here to help you."

"What's happening to his face?" screams Anne, as the area around his cheekbones turns a blueish-black colour.

"Bryn is very poorly," I say.

"I can see that," snaps Anne, some of her old vigour returning. "Do something, Angharad. Save him!"

But at that moment I don't know what to do. I am paralysed with fear as my brother struggles for breath.

"Do something!" screams Anne.

"Help me turn him," I say.

"Why?" The word comes out as a wail.

"Propping him up didn't seem to help, and neither does lying flat on his back. It's all I can think to do, unless you've a better idea?"

Anne shakes her head, and together we turn Bryn onto his side. For a moment, his breathing seems to ease, but then the awful sound starts up again, as if he is drowning, right here in his bed with not a drop of water in sight. The air in the room is fetid and hot. The smell of sweat and something rotten sticks in my nostrils and trickles of perspiration run down my back. Bryn makes a wheezing sound I know will haunt my dreams, and then the room falls silent.

"Bryn?" says Anne, shaking her husband's shoulders. "Bryn, wake up." Despite her weakness, she pulls herself onto her knees, her body folding over his as tears consume her.

I climb onto the bed behind her. "Anne," I say, trying to pull her away. She slaps me out of the way and continues shaking Bryn's shoulders. "Anne, leave him be. He is at peace. He is with the Lord."

"I don't want him to be with the Lord!" she cries. "I want him here, with me!" Any energy she has deserts her and she collapses into my waiting arms. I pull her close, holding her ravaged body and stroking her hair as the sobs come thick and fast. "I want him here, Angharad. I want him here with me."

"I know you do, I know. Hush now, hush, I'm here."

I can't say how long we stay like that, but it must be a while, for the light changes in the room, softening the whitewashed walls and dark-stained furniture until it almost feels we are living in a dream.

"Do you feel strong enough to move?" I ask Anne, when her tears finally subside.

"I don't want to leave him," she says, her voice hoarse.

"I know," I say, rubbing her back, "but Bryn will still be here and you can come back and see him. But he needs to be alone now, Anne. I need to clean his body and see to certain things, as goodness knows how long it will take a doctor to arrive."

"Why are you doing all this?" she asks. "You hated him. You hate me."

"I didn't hate him," I say, shocked to realise this is true. "He was my brother, and I loved him."

"But we made your life miserable."

"That is very true, but we are family, Anne, no matter what."

There is a knock at the door, and I release Anne from my arms. "Hello?"

"Aunt Angharad, it's me. Is everything alright?"

Efa must have known something was wrong, to have stayed away from this room for so long. "I'll be out in a moment, Efa. You wait there."

"Alright."

"How will I tell the children?" asks Anne, her eyes filled with tears.

"Would you like me to do it?"

She nods, then raises her hand to her mouth. "I haven't even asked about the children. Are they well?"

"They weren't, but they're all on the mend now."

"Thank the Lord," she says. She glances across to Bryn, then closes her eyes tight. "Take me away from here, Angharad."

"Alright. Let's get you settled downstairs in the parlour. I'll make a bed up for you in there and you can get some rest. You have been very unwell, Anne, and it will take some time for you to regain your strength."

"Will... will... you stay with us?"

"I'll stay as long as it takes to get you all well."

"And... and... Bryn..."

"I'll make all the arrangements. Don't worry." I scoop Anne up into my arms and carry her out of the room. Efa is waiting on the landing, her thumb stuck in her mouth. "I'm going to make your mother a bed in the parlour beside the fire. Can you bring some blankets and cushions down for me? Then I'd like you to go back to your bedroom so I can come and talk to you and your sisters about what is happening."

With a nod, Efa goes to the cupboard and begins pulling out everything we need. I carry Anne down the stairs and settle her in a chair while Efa and I work together to form a makeshift bed in front of the fire.

"Thank you," I tell the girl. "Now go up to your bedroom and wait for me. I shan't be long."

Anne is already drifting back towards sleep. As gently as I can, I ease her out of the chair and into the bed on the floor. I don't imagine it is all that comfortable, but it is better than sharing a bed with her husband's corpse. Her eyes are closed, and I assume she is asleep until I begin to creep out of the room.

"Angharad?"

"Yes?"

"I think we misjudged you. I think Bryn and I got things terribly, terribly wrong."

"Hush," I say, "there's no need to worry about that now." But I'm not sure she hears me, as her breathing has deepened and her face is smooth and free from the grief of moments before. I close the parlour door behind me, place a hand on the bannister, and prepare myself to break the terrible news of Bryn's death to his children.

Chapter Eighty-Two

Ffion

October, 1918

I'm sitting up in bed with a newspaper spread across my lap when they walk in. "Oh, how lovely to see you!"

"We heard you were well enough to receive visitors," says Carys, perching on the edge of my bed.

"Mrs Edwards sent us up with this," says Angharad, laying a tray of tea and biscuits down on the bedside table before sitting herself in a chair. She looks exhausted, and I worry she may be ill herself.

"How are you feeling?" asks Carys.

"Much better, although I'm still as weak as a baby. I'm one of the lucky ones. Do you know we lost two of our men in the epidemic?"

"That's dreadful," says Angharad, her eyes filling with tears. While she's always been sensitive, her reaction to the news surprises me.

"Are you well yourself, Angharad? You don't look in all that great shape."

Angharad manages a small smile. "I'm not ill, just tired. I've been caring for Bryn, Anne and their daughters, who all succumbed to influenza."

"Good Lord, how awful for you. Are they all recovered?"

Angharad pulls a handkerchief from her pocket and blows her nose. "Anne and the girls are on the mend, but Bryn... well... he wasn't strong enough to fight it."

"He's dead?" At the same moment, I feel both glad and guilty for the relief that overcomes me.

"I know it should feel a relief after all he's done to me, but all I feel is sadness."

"That's understandable," says Carys, taking Angharad's hand. "He was your brother, after all."

"How is Anne coping?" I ask, trying to imagine the dour woman with anything other than the pinched lips and scowl.

"Badly. Her mother arrived today and is talking about taking Anne and the girls back to the mainland to live with her. It has surprised me just how upset Anne has been. I'd never thought her capable of feeling such love, but it seems she loved my brother deeply. It's probably wrong to say, but the experience has made her seem more human, somehow."

"It's not wrong, it makes perfect sense. And if a reconciliation can come from this, all the better."

"Yes," says Angharad, although she doesn't sound convinced. "Anyway, how are you? Is there anything interesting in that newspaper of yours?"

"As a matter of fact, there is. Did you hear that only two weeks ago, Germany asked the Allies for an armistice?"

"Yes, we read about it in Mr Stephens' newspaper."

"Good. Today it's being reported the Allies have taken control of all of German-occupied France and part of Belgium." At the mention of Mr Jansen's home country, Carys visibly tenses, and I curse my insensitivity. "I don't think it's too optimistic to say this war will be over soon."

"That is good news," says Carys, clapping her hands together. "Such a relief."

"Yes. And between the recent news and all the time I've had to think whilst lying in this blasted bed, I've made a few decisions."

"Such as?"

"I've decided to close the convalescent home for starters. We've been taking in fewer men recently, and now we are down to five soldiers, all of whom can be accommodated in the military hospital in Bangor."

"It's a wonderful thing you've done here," says Angharad, "and I expect it will also be wonderful to have your home back."

"It will, it really will, especially with the children coming home at Christmas. My eldest son should be with us this year, and I want the house to feel like a home for them."

"Of course you do," says Carys. "And good on you for putting yourself and your family first for once."

"Speaking of putting myself first, I may have done something rather rash."

Angharad and Carys both stare at me, eyebrows raised. "You? Do something rash?" asks Angharad in mock surprise.

I pull myself higher against my pillows and fold my arms across my chest. "I've written to Hector, informing him that this coming Christmas will be the last he spends in this house."

"You've what? Surely you're not talking about divorce?" asks Carys, open-mouthed.

"Oh, goodness no, that would harm me more than him and I'd never be able to collect enough evidence about him. No, divorce is not an option, but separation is. He already spends most of his time in London, and the only thing he comes here for is the fishing, hunting and young women, all of which he can find elsewhere."

"What if he doesn't agree?"

"I've told him if he doesn't agree to my demands, I'll go to the police about the attack on Susan, and if they don't believe me, I'll try the newspapers. In truth, I don't think either a policeman or journalist would for a second take any action on my allegations and would laugh me out of the door, but my husband is a vain man, and any threat to his reputation should be enough to make him see sense."

"Good for you," says Angharad, patting my hand.

"Well, with women getting the vote and all we've done with the WI and setting up the convalescent home, I wondered why I stand back and accept Hector's behaviour when I'm so capable and firm in all other areas of my life." I throw my hands in the air. Tiredness comes in a wave and I slump back against my pillows.

"We'll leave you to rest," says Carys, heaving herself off the bed.

"That baby is growing fast," I say, as her coat slips to reveal the bump beneath it.

"Yes, too fast," says Carys. "I still don't know what I'll do when it arrives. But let's not think about that now. You need to rest, and we need to get back to the farm."

"It was good seeing you both," I say, trying to hide a yawn behind my hand, "and you have my deepest condolences, Angharad. Tell me when the funeral is taking place, and I'll do my best to be there."

"You concentrate on getting yourself well," says Angharad.

No sooner have my friends left the room than my eyes close and I fall into a deep sleep.

Chapter Eighty-Three

Ffion

November, 1918

T he sound of tyres on gravel causes me to rush to the window. The last of our patients was transferred to the military hospital in Bangor only two days ago, and the last thing I need is a visitor before Mrs Edwards, Susan and I have returned the house to its former grandeur.

My heart sinks as Hector climbs out of his motor car. I've had no response to my letter and have been dreading this moment. He strides up to the front door and pushes it open. I hear the rustle of his coat being removed and the click of the hat stand as it wobbles against the tiles below. The drawing-room door opens and Hector strides into the room, arms stretched wide.

"Darling, good to see you've got rid of all those wretched lame ducks you had staying here." He pulls me into his arms, then kisses me on the cheek the way one might kiss an elderly aunt. Then again, I am old, by Hector's standards.

"Did you get my letter?" I ask, stepping away.

"No, what letter? Never mind any talk of letters. I've just heard the most remarkable news. The war is over! The Armistice has been signed and hostilities should end..." he checks his wristwatch, "right about now."

"Oh," I say, thrown from my train of thought by this truly marvellous news. "How wonderful."

"We should celebrate. I'll go down to the cellar and get us a bottle of champagne."

Hector is halfway to the door before I manage to organise my thoughts. "Wait."

He spins round, sighing in frustration. "What is it?"

"Did you get my letter?"

"No, I have no idea what you are talking about, darling."

"Sit down," I say, "just for a moment."

"Fine," he huffs, "but I really can't see what could be more important than the war ending." He perches on the edge of a chair, his leg twitching as though ready to spring up at any moment and start celebrating.

"The letter I sent was about us."

"Us?"

"You and I. Our marriage."

"A love letter?" Hector chuckles. "Don't you think you're a bit long in the tooth to be sending that sort of correspondence?"

"It wasn't a love letter," I say, his laughter igniting the anger I've been carrying for years. "I was requesting a separation."

"What on earth are you talking about, woman?"

"I want a separation from you. I don't want you living under this roof. Not after everything you've done."

The smile drops from Hector's lips, and his eyes are hard, the muscles in his face taut. "And what is it I'm supposed to have done? In case you hadn't noticed, for the past few years, all I've been doing is fighting for my country."

I resist the urge to tell him that sitting behind a desk issuing orders could hardly be described as fighting. "I know what I saw with Susan."

"Who's Susan?"

"Our maid."

He seems genuinely confused, his brow furrowed as he searches back through his memory. Goodness me, how many more have there been since Susan?

"I walked in on you attacking her."

"Attacking?" Realisation dawns, and he laughs. "You call that attacking? I call it making love, a perfectly natural act between a man and a woman."

"Except that at the time Susan was not a woman, she was little more than a girl. She was younger than your eldest daughter, for crying out loud!"

"Is this jealousy rearing its ugly head, darling? I suppose at your age it is inevitable."

"This is not jealousy, quite the opposite. I can't believe it has taken me so long to come to my senses! How can I put my all into an organisation designed to support women while living with a man such as you? Everything we do is about building women up, educating, enlightening, and yet here you are, tearing away young girls' dignity and rights whenever the mood takes you."

"I have never received any complaints."

I can't believe he is actually smirking. The nerve of the man. "I no longer want to live under the same roof as a man such as you."

"I hope you're not suggesting divorce? It would bankrupt us, not to mention the scandal. Women don't come out of divorce well, as I'm sure you are aware."

"I'm not asking for a divorce, I'm asking for a separation. You seem happy enough to spend much of your time in London as it is."

"And what if I want to come back here?""Then I shall be forced to go to the police and newspapers about exactly the type of man you are."

"Police? Newspapers?" Hector tips back his head and laughs loudly. "If I am to leave this house, it shall not be as a banishment, but because I can no longer stand the sight of you. You were pretty enough when we married, but the years have not been kind, darling. Why do you think I have to look elsewhere for a little romance? You're an embarrassment, Ffion. An embarrassment and a bore."

"Then you shouldn't mind spending more time apart, should you?"

"I've had enough of this," he says, standing. "I'm getting myself that bottle of champagne and a single glass. I can't bear the sight of you."

Hector marches out of the room and I take a series of deep breaths, determined not to let his words have the desired effect on me. Instead, I make my way to the stables, saddle Bluebell and head toward the Stephens farm.

As I canter along the deserted lanes, the air around me fills with the sound of bells chiming from every church and chapel in the vicinity. The sound, combined with the cutting cold of the air rushing past my face, is exhilarating, and despite my recent conversation, I whoop with delight, my chest filling with laughter.

By the time I arrive in the farmyard, my cheeks are red from the cold and aching from smiling. Carys and Angharad run from the house, Charlie and Mr Stephens following behind.

"Are we right in thinking the bells bring good news?" asks Carys, her eyes wide with hope.

"They do indeed. The war is over. We are free."

As we embrace, I see Charlie lean against Mr Stephens' arm, tears of relief sparkling in their eyes.

"This calls for a toast," says Charlie. "Give me five minutes to dig out the brandy, then meet us in the parlour."

"Isn't this the most wonderful news?" says Carys, beaming. "How did you hear?"

"Hector told me."

"Hector? He's at the house?"

"He didn't receive my letter, or so he claims."

"Goodness, so he has no idea about your plans?"

"Oh yes, I told him."

"You told him?" Angharad looks at me with something like admiration. "How did he respond?"

"With as much arrogance as I've come to expect. He didn't agree to my suggestion of a separation, but he didn't disagree either. It wouldn't surprise me if he spends more of his time in London and his visits to Anglesey become fewer and far between. And if I have to share a house with him, at least it is large enough for us to avoid each other most of the time."

"You're a brave woman, Ffion Montgomery," says Carys.

"We all are," I say, linking arms with my friends. "And that alone deserves a toast. Come on, let's celebrate."

Chapter Eighty-Four

Angharad

"Why, Miss Williams, what on earth is the matter?"

"Is Mrs Montgomery home?"

"She is, yes."

"Then do you think you could fetch her for me, Susan?" I ask, trying to maintain my patience whilst conveying a sense of urgency.

Susan scuttles off and after a couple of minutes of foot-tapping and pacing up and down the length of the front step, Ffion appears.

"Carys is having her baby," I say, leaving no time for pleasantries. "I have no idea what to do, but thought you might, given you've children of your own."

"I always had a midwife with me. I'm not sure how much help I can be."

"You'll be better than me. Please, Ffion, please come with me."

"How did you get here?"

"I ran."

"Right, well, I'd suggest speed is of the essence. Come on," she says, pushing past me to where the Wolseley sits on the drive.

"Won't your husband mind?"

"Goodness knows. He went off in a huff back to London, but not before he spent a vast amount of our money on a brand new Morris

Oxford." She opens the boot, grabs the hand crank, passes it to me, then climbs into the passenger seat.

"You realise I haven't driven a motorcar for quite some time," I say, turning the crank until the car roars into life. When I climb into the driver's seat, Ffion is grinning at me.

"This brings back fond memories," she says.

"It certainly does." Despite my worry for Carys, I can't help but smile as I ease the car along the drive. So much has changed since I first drove Ffion to Bangor. The engine hums in a deep bass as I pull out onto the lane and increase my speed.

"Does driving bring back memories of Eddy?" shouts Ffion above the engine noise.

I turn to her and smile. "Yes, but those memories no longer hurt as they once did. And I've new memories to add to my collection. Whenever I see a motor car these days, I think of you."

Ffion smiles and leans back against the leather seat, looking satisfied. We don't speak again until Mr Stephens' farm comes into view.

"How long has Carys been in labour?"

"I set off to find you as soon as the pain started."

"In that case, we could be in for a long night. First babies take their time arriving in the world. Have you had any luck getting in contact with Mr Jansen?"

"I told you he wrote to Carys at the old farm at last?"

"Yes, have you told her about it yet?"

"No, I didn't want to get her hopes up. Besides, it was only a brief postcard wishing her well. The important part was the return address he'd included. I sent my letter off to him two weeks ago, but have heard nothing since, which doesn't bode well."

"No, but he always struck me as a good sort. Let's hope he replies soon."

I pull the car into the yard and switch off the engine. "It will ruin your lovely car if I try to drive it over to the bothy. We're best off walking from here."

"Angharad!"

I turn around to see Charlie standing in the farmhouse doorway. "I'm sorry, I don't have time to stop. Carys is having her baby."

"I know. She's here. I went over to the bothy to speak to you and found her doubled over in pain. I thought it was best to bring her here as there's more space. Don't worry, Geraint knows, and has headed off to the pub to get out of the way."

Ffion and I run over to the farmhouse and Charlie leads us through to the small room beside the parlour he uses as his bedroom.

"I've got some water on to boil, and I found some towels in the cupboard."

"Thank you. We'd better check on her."

"Just shout your instructions through and I'll do all I can to help."

"Thank you."

We find Carys kneeling on Charlie's bed, her palms pressed against the wall, her hair damp with sweat. She grunts and lowers her chin to her chest, her muscles tensing. Beside the bed is a puddle of water and I step over it to reach her.

"It's alright," I say, rubbing her back. "We're here now. We came in Ffion's car, so if I need to fetch the doctor it will be a darn sight quicker than if I were on foot."

"I think…" says Carys, stopping to pant, "it might be too late for a doctor."

Ffion walks to the end of the bed and gently lifts Carys's nightdress. "Good Lord," she says, dropping the fabric and staggering back. "The head's already out. Carys, you're doing very well, but I think you should be lying on your back."

"Not... argh..." She bears down again and I stand helpless at her bedside, completely at a loss as to how I can help.

Ffion is doing a much better job at taking everything in her stride. She lifts Carys's nightdress again and shakes her head. "Angharad, tell Charlie to prepare a basin of warm water and we're going to need plenty of towels. I was wrong when I said we'd be here all night. One more push and this little mite is going to be out in the world."

"Charlie? Charlie, we need that water now." As I run to the door, I hear Ffion whispering gentle encouragement to Carys, her hands poised ready to catch the child when it arrives.

"Everything alright in there?" Charlie asks when I meet him in the kitchen.

"I feel so useless, but Ffion is doing so well. Her years running the convalescent home seem to have paid off."

"I don't remember there being much call for midwifery while I was there," he says with a grin, placing a set of towels on my shoulder and a basin of warm water into my arms. "Good luck with it all. Let me know when it's safe to come in."

I nod and make my careful way back to the bedroom. I may not have many skills, but not spilling any water would be a good start. Just as I reach the door, a cry stops me in my tracks. It is not the cry of a birthing mother, but a higher-pitched, angry sound. I nudge the door open with my shoulder and place the water on the table so heavily that some sloshes over the rim of the bowl. There on the bed, purple and covered in a sticky substance, is a tiny bald creature, waving its arms and legs in the air and screaming at the top of its lungs. Ffion grabs the towels I have forgotten are on my shoulder, and begins rubbing the small creature. A smile spreads across her face and tears fill her eyes. Carys flops down on the bed, her eyes filled with wonder.

"Don't get too comfortable," says Ffion, "there's a way to go yet till you're done, but would you like to meet your son?"

Carys opens her arms and Ffion deposits the tiny bundle within them. I reach a hand to my face and realise my skin is damp with tears.

**

It turns out babies are a conundrum. On the one hand, they are tiny beyond belief, their delicate fingers and toes daintier than those of any doll I ever owned. On the other hand, it's impossible to understand how something so large could have fitted in the stomach of someone as small as Carys.

"You can hold him, Angharad. He won't bite."

I look down at my dinner-plate-sized hands, a wash of shame reddening my cheeks. "Oh no, I couldn't do that. Look," I say, holding my hands out to Carys. "I'd hurt the baby. I'd crush him."

Despite her exhaustion and all she's just been through, Carys laughs. "Hurt him? What a lot of nonsense you sometimes speak, Angharad. Here."

Before I can stop her, she leans forward with a wince and places the wriggling little dot in my hands. My body shakes, my heart hammering with fear that, worse than crushing the baby, I'll drop him.

"Those hands are safe as can be. See," says Carys, "he's stopped grizzling. Try holding him close to you."

With as much care as I take over the hens' eggs, I lift the baby closer to me. He meets the cotton of my dress and snuffles and nuzzles into me. Tears flood my eyes and trail down my cheeks.

"It's alright," says Carys. "You're doing so well with him. You're a natural."

A natural? Not a disaster? Not a danger? I allow myself to be brave and loosen my grip, allowing a thumb to caress the fuzz on top of the baby's head. He snuffles again, then stills, his tiny eyelids fluttering. He is the most beautiful thing I have ever seen and as I cradle him, I make a silent promise. His arrival in the world may not be under the best circumstances, and his family situation is a complicated one, but I will do whatever it takes to make his and his mother's lives as happy as they can be.

"Everything will be alright, little one," I whisper, placing a light kiss on the top of the baby's head. "Everything will be alright."

Chapter Eighty-Five

Angharad

December, 1918

When I see him walking across the field, I'm so relieved I could cry. With a quick glance to check Carys is still sleeping, I click open the door as quietly as I can and let myself outside. As I cross the field, I wave and increase my pace.

"You received my letter," I say as I reach Florian.

"Yes, and I'm sorry it's taken me so long to get to you. I had to arrange for the girls to stay with a neighbour for a night or two."

"You're settled in Liverpool?"

"As settled as it's possible to be when you're a refugee. I've found work in a factory and the girls are alright, but they miss our life on the farm. How is Carys? Your letter sounded urgent. Has she taken ill?"

"Before we see Carys, I need to explain what's been happening here these past few months. Let's sit down for a moment."

We perch on a fallen tree trunk and Florian frowns. "Angharad, whatever has happened, please just tell me. I can only spare a day before I need to get back to the girls. Everything is uncertain right now. With the war ending, we shall soon need to return home. There is much to do, much to think about."

Florian's face is so earnest that for a moment I waver over whether I should have summoned him here, but then I remember my friend and her beautiful little boy. "Florian," I say, "Carys has a child, a son."

"What?" Florian runs a hand through his hair, staring at me with wide eyes. "When did this happen?"

"She found out she was expecting a child not long after you left Llanfairpwll. Each week I've been pestering the new tenants of the farm to see if you'd written. I can't tell you what a relief it was when you finally did."

"Yes," says Florian, shaking his head in confusion, "but what does this child have to do with me?"

"It wasn't an immaculate conception."

Florian's brow furrows, then his eyes widen in understanding, a flush creeping up his neck. "The child, it is mine?"

"Yes," I say. "You have a son, Florian. Would you like to meet him?"

Florian jumps to his feet, his eyes trained on the bothy. "Carys is in there? With the baby?"

"She is, but I haven't told her I wrote to you. Would you mind waiting outside so I can tell her you're here? It could be quite a shock."

"Of course, yes. It will give me a chance to take in this news."

We cross the field towards the bothy, but as we come nearer, I stop and turn to him. "You need to understand that this has all been very difficult for Carys. Her mother went to the mainland, leaving Carys here alone, and for a while she had nowhere to turn. I'm ashamed to admit this, but Carys came to me for help, and I turned her away. So did Ffion, for different reasons, although she did her best to help. I thought it was best you know how hard this has been for her."

Florian nods. "I can imagine, and I feel terrible for the part I have played in this. How have the villagers responded to the news?"

"Some better than others. At least the Women's Institute chose not to sit in judgement, although Carys hasn't attended a meeting for some months, for fear it would make other members uncomfortable. We've done our best to look after her, but this has been a lonely experience for her. While you take in the momentous news I have shared, perhaps you could consider what will happen next. You know how hard life will be should Carys remain an unmarried mother and her child a bastard."

Florian nods again. I pat his arm, leave him standing outside the bothy and step inside. Carys and the baby are both stirring.

"Goodness," says Carys. "How long have I been asleep?"

"About an hour."

"I must get up. I can't believe I've been so lazy."

"Carys, you were up every two hours in the night with this little monster," I say, leaning over the baby's basket and stroking a finger across his cheek. "But, yes, it is better you get up, as you have a visitor."

"A visitor? Is it Ffion?"

"No," I say. Carys pulls herself up to sitting, and the mattress sags as I sit on the end of the bed. "Now, I don't want you to be cross, but I've been making regular trips to your old farm hoping Florian might have written."

Carys's face falls. "I gave up hope of hearing from him a long time ago."

"I know. But I didn't. Several weeks ago, when I visited the farm, they handed me a postcard. It was from Florian and was addressed to you. I know I should have given it to you there and then, but I didn't want to get your hopes up. Instead, I wrote to him."

"And did he reply?"

"No, not exactly."

"I thought as much."

"No, Carys, that's not what I meant. He didn't reply in writing but replied in person."

"What do you mean, Angharad? You're speaking in riddles."

"He's here, Carys," I say, unable to keep the smile from my face.

"Here?" She jumps out of bed and begins smoothing down her hair and adjusting her skirt. "Florian is my visitor?"

"Yes, he is. Shall I show him in?"

Carys pulls the baby from his basket and clutches him to her as if for protection. I walk to the door and call to Florian. When he steps inside the bothy, it is as though time stills. He and Carys stare at each other, neither speaking. Without a word, I slip from the room. As I pass the window, I see Florian rush to Carys, smothering her and the baby in kisses. Carys passes the baby to Florian, and he takes him. "I named him Ieuan," I hear her say. "It means gift from God."

As I turn to walk to the farmhouse and leave them in peace, I marvel at the bravery of my friend. Few in her position would consider the child a gift from God, but Carys is one of a kind, and if Florian has any sense, he'll hold on to her tight and not let go again.

Chapter Eighty-Six

Angharad

December, 1918

We've agreed to meet by the statue of Nelson on the shore below the church. I'm glad, for it means I can arrive early and gather my thoughts on this historic day with only seabirds and distant mountains for company. Betty barks at a gull swooping just low enough to taunt her and I laugh. "Of course I'm not truly alone, am I?" I bend down and stroke Betty's coarse fur.

Anne wasted no time taking her daughters away to the mainland after Bryn's death, and despite the slight thawing in our relationship, I know I shall probably never see them again. Perhaps when she's old enough, Efa may write, but it's more likely she'll settle quickly into her new life and forget all about me.

In the distance, I see Ffion picking her way along the rock-strewn shoreline towards me. The sound of young girls' chatter reaches me on the breeze, and I know Carys must be nearby too. Charlie has stayed back at the farm, but will meet us at the chapel later.

"You can be a foolish woman sometimes, Angharad Williams." Eddy's voice is so clear in my mind she might as well be standing next to me. "Stop living in the past and look at all you have. Ffion, Carys, Charlie, Mr Stephens, all your friends at the WI, Betty. I could go on, but I think I've made my point. And speaking of Charlie, I wouldn't mind if something happened between you one day. You don't need to save yourself for the ghost of a woman who loved you once."

"I still need you." My voice is shaking. I need to regain control before my friends reach me. What will they think if they find me shedding tears of sorrow on such a momentous and happy day?

"*Cariad*," says Eddy, and I know it's only in my mind, but I can almost feel the warmth of her breath against the back of my neck. "You don't need me anymore, you haven't for a long time. Hold me in your heart just as I hold you in mine, but don't let what happened between us define you. It's time to look forward, not back. Go on, *cariad*, go to your friends."

Ffion is within shouting distance, and she waves her arms in the air and lets out a whoop of joy. Her cheeks are pink from the cold, her eyes shining and her mouth spread in a smile. As she calls to me, breath pours from her mouth in a cloud. "Is Carys here yet?"

"No, but I think I heard the girls, so she can't be far away."

Ffion reaches me and pulls me into a brief, firm hug. "Today is a day of change. How are you feeling?"

"Free."

Ffion studies my face for a moment, then nods in understanding. She leans over and places a cold kiss on my cheek, then blows on her hands to warm them. "Oh, thank goodness, here they come."

I turn to see Carys, Lina, and Emma breaking into a run as they step onto the narrow beach. When they reach us, they are out of breath and giggling. "Lina wanted a race, but I think I'm getting too old for such things."

"Where's Ieuan?" asks Ffion.

"Florian has taken him up to the farm to see Charlie."

"Daddy said today is just for girls," says Emma, who has grown at least an inch since I last saw her.

A look passes between Ffion, Carys and me as we acknowledge the significance of today. "Shall we go?" asks Ffion.

"No time like the present," I say, fixing a lead around Betty's neck.

"Are you sure you don't mind coming with me?" asks Ffion. "It seems awful that you are not allowed to join me inside."

"One day we shall," says Carys, linking one arm in mine and one in Ffion's. "Today is just the start, you'll see."

We walk into the churchyard to a sea of faces we recognise. At the WI, the non-political nature of our meetings is firmly upheld, but today, our fellow members are out in force to have their say.

"Miss Williams, Miss Ambrose, Mrs Montgomery!" Colonel Stapleton-Cotton waves and we cross the churchyard to greet him. "Isn't the turnout tremendous?" he says, waving his arms at the crowd of husbands and wives waiting for the church to open its doors.

"It is indeed," says Ffion with the smile that hasn't left her face all morning.

"Is Mr Montgomery not joining you today?"

"No, unfortunately, he has been detained in London."

"That is a shame," says the Colonel, as Carys and I exchange a knowing look. In the end, just as Ffion predicted, Hector had taken himself off to London, not quite with his tail between his legs, but with the understanding he would not be welcome in Llanfairpwll should he decide to return.

"A shame you ladies can't participate in today's events. You should have brought the wedding forward a few hours, Miss Ambrose."

Carys smiles. "And overshadow all this?" She waves her hand at the waiting crowd. "I don't think so. There'll be plenty of chances in the future for me to wield a pencil and put my cross in a box."

"Indeed, there shall."

With a creak of ancient hinges, the church doors open and the crowd shuffles forward, excited chatter filling the air.

"Go on," I tell Ffion. "We'll be waiting for you here once you've made history."

She laughs and I expect the Colonel to follow the crowd in his chair, but he hangs back. "You deserve to be in there today," he says, his smile dropping, his tone serious. "Never underestimate the voice you have, Miss Williams, or the contribution you have made these past years to village life. The part our institution has played in getting us through this war may not be glamorous enough to make the papers, but we have achieved more than I ever believed possible, and you've played no small part in that."

"Thank you, Colonel. I appreciate your kind words."

"Not kind, Miss Williams. Honest." He salutes me, nods to his wife Jane, who takes charge of his bath chair, and together they make their way towards the church to cast their vote.

Fifteen minutes later, a flushed Ffion is walking towards us.

"Tell us everything," says Carys.

"Was it frightening?" asks Lina.

"No," laughs Ffion, bending down to look Lina in the eye. "But it was very official."

"What does official mean?"

"It means important. The man inside had to check my papers to make sure I was who I said I was, then I waited until my name was called, and I was handed a piece of paper called a ballot paper. I was shown into a private booth, where I made my choice of candidate."

"Who did you choose?" asks Emma.

"That is private," says Carys.

"Yes," says Ffion. "Only I and the clerk who checked my ballot paper know who I voted for."

"How did it feel?" I ask.

Ffion stands and looks me square in the eye. "It felt as if history was being made. It was as though this day will be looked back upon in years to come as a turning point for women." Her eyes fill with tears, then she laughs and gives a little shrug. "It also felt a bit like being back at school, and as simple as drawing a cross in a box. Mundane and extraordinary all at once."

"Can we go now?" asks Lina, tugging on Carys's hand.

"Oh, yes," I say. "In all the excitement I'd almost forgotten we have a wedding to get to."

Lina lets out a dramatic sigh and I wink at Carys.

"Come on," says Ffion. "Let's walk back to my house. Have you girls ever been inside a motor car?"

They shake their heads, a look of awe filling their faces.

"A motor car?" asks Carys with a frown.

"You didn't think we were going to make you walk to your own wedding, did you?"

"But with your husband... away... and your chauffeur not back yet, who will drive us?"

Ffion tips her head back and roars with laughter. "Oh, Carys, just you wait and see. You're not going to believe your eyes."

Chapter Eighty-Seven

Angharad

December, 1918

All passengers bar Ffion sit in a stunned silence as I replace the crank in the footwell and grip on to the steering wheel. We're out on the open road before anyone speaks.

"Angharad," says Carys. "Where on earth did you learn to drive?"

Ffion turns in the passenger seat and says, "Eddy taught her."

"Oh," says Carys, her eyebrows raised.

"Who is Eddy?" asks Emma.

Neither Carys nor Ffion speak, and I realise they are waiting for me to fill the silence. "Eddy was a very good friend of mine."

"Does he live in Anglesey?"

"No, Eddy died some years ago."

"Like our mother."

"Yes, like your mother."

"Did you love Eddy?" asks Lina.

I look in the rear-view mirror. This is no flippant question. Her head is tilted to one side, and her brows are drawn together. A serious question deserves a serious answer. "Yes," I say. "I loved Eddy very much."

Lina leans forward in her seat and her small hand rubs my shoulder in a gesture that causes a lump to form in my throat. "Don't worry," she says. "My daddy loved my mummy very much, and he was terribly sad when she died. But now he loves Carys, so everything is alright again. I'm sure you will find someone to love again one day, Angharad."

"Out of the mouths of babes," mutters Ffion.

I think of Charlie, and the possibilities of our burgeoning friendship. There's no saying what will happen there, but if the past few years have taught me anything, it's to expect the unexpected and keep an open mind and heart to opportunities as they present themselves.

"We're nearly there," I say, needing to get my emotions under control.

"You're a very good driver," says Emma. "I thought being in a motor car would be scary, but I feel safe with you."

"I'm glad to hear it."

We pull up to the small chapel where Carys's family has worshipped for generations, and I switch off the engine. Charlie is waiting for us outside, looking dapper in his suit. He is standing on his new legs and leaning on the walking stick, which keeps him steady.

Carys climbs out of the car, her mouth open. "Who did all this?" she asks, pointing to the winter foliage and berries which adorn the chapel entrance.

Ffion blushes slightly. "Angharad and I came here last night to give the building a festive feel. We know that there may be sad memories associated with this place..." Her pause allows us all time to remember the last time we gathered here, when Carys buried her much-loved father. "We thought the decorations give a feeling of hope and Christmas cheer."

"They certainly do," says Carys, her eyes glistening with tears.

"There's one more surprise," says Ffion, walking around the car and opening the boot. She pulls out the bouquet she has prepared and Carys is unable to keep the tears at bay.

With trembling hands, Carys takes the bouquet from Ffion. A base of fern leaves gives way to sprigs of mistletoe and dried baby's breath. It is beautiful, delicate, homely, and made with love.

Ffion's cheeks turn pink. "I hope you like it. The mistletoe symbolises love and protection, and the baby's breath signifies new beginnings."

"I love it," says Carys, pulling Ffion towards her.

Ffion disentangles herself from Carys's arms and returns to the boot of the car, where she pulls out two smaller bouquets. "Of course, your two bridesmaids each need a bouquet, too." She hands the girls their flowers and their faces light up. "And," she says, taking a bag and balancing it on the bonnet of the car, "I know you didn't want any fuss and are happy wearing your Sunday best, which looks lovely, by the way. But I thought you should have something a little special on your wedding day. Here." Ffion pulls out an intricate lace shawl. I help Carys out of her woollen overcoat, and Ffion drapes the shawl across her shoulders.

"You look beautiful," says Emma.

"Like a princess," says Lina.

"I don't deserve all of this," says Carys.

"You deserve all of this and more," says Ffion. "Come on, we need to get you married."

Charlie greets us at the door and explains Ieuan is with Mr Stephens.

"Goodness, we should probably help old Mr Stephens, don't you think, Angharad?"

"Geraint's completely taken with the little mite," says Charlie. "If anything, I think you'll have a job prising Ieuan away from him." He turns to Carys. "All set?"

"Ready as I'll ever be."

Charlie, Ffion, and I make our way into the small chapel. The congregation is made up of us, Mr Stephens, the minister, and a nervous-looking Florian who is waiting for his bride at the front.

"I organised one more surprise," whispers Ffion as we take our seats. "Remember Miss Thomas, who played for us all those years ago when we launched the first British Women's Institute?"

I follow Ffion's gaze to a young girl positioned at the side of the chapel behind a large harp. Her delicate fingers pluck the strings, and as she does, weak winter sunlight breaks free from the clouds to stream through the chapel's windows.

Ffion sniffs, and I don't need to look to know tears are running down her cheeks. As Carys walks up the aisle with Emma and Lina following behind, it isn't just Ffion shedding a tear, there isn't a dry eye to be seen. Even Mr Stephens' cheeks shine with dampness as Ieuan coos and gurgles in his arms.

Carys reaches the front of the aisle and Florian takes her hands in his. At that moment, they only have eyes for each other. My mind drifts to the strict moral rules my father instilled in me. To him, the union taking place in front of me would have been classed as sinful. Goodness, to much of society, the union would appear sinful. But as Ieuan gurgles and Carys and Florian's eyes shine with love, all I can see is the purity of their bond. After the darkness of war and all the loss we have all endured, as they make their vows, to me the marriage signals hope for the future. It restores my faith in the goodness of everyday folk, and the light that can shine in even the darkest moments.

After the ceremony I offer to drive the newlyweds and their three children to Bangor station, but Florian has organised a carriage to take them on the short journey, and I can see it is a matter of pride that he provides for his family.

"We'll miss you," I say, pulling Carys into an embrace.

"Liverpool isn't so far away. Perhaps you can come and visit us?"

"I'd like that very much."

Ffion joins us and we stand in a small circle, holding on tight to each other's hands. "You're going to miss the WI Christmas party," she says, her voice catching.

"I'm sure there's a branch in Liverpool, and if not, I'll have to start one."

Although our eyes shine with tears, we are all smiling. As hard as it is to say goodbye, we all know this is the best outcome any of us could have wished for.

"I don't know what I would have done without the pair of you by my side these past few years."

"Likewise," I say.

"It's what friends do," says Ffion. "We hold each other through sadness and celebrate life's successes. We carry each other when we are weak, and dance together in moments of joy."

"What will I do without you?" asks Carys, her face falling.

"You're a survivor, Carys. And you've a loving husband and three beautiful children by your side. You've nothing to fear."

"And besides," says Ffion. "You've sat through three years of WI lectures and demonstrations. If that hasn't prepared you for life, I don't know what would!"

We all laugh, our hands drop to our sides, and Florian walks over and puts an arm around his wife.

"I can't thank you both enough for all you have done for us."

"It's nothing," I say, "just take good care of our friend."

"I will," he says, and I don't doubt it.

We hug Lina and Emma goodbye, then the newly formed family of five climb into the carriage and we stand and wave until they disappear over the horizon.

"Well," says Ffion with a sigh, "that's the end of an era."

"Yes, but we can write, and there's plenty to keep us busy here."

"Such as?"

"Well, for starters, we've a WI Christmas party to organise."

We climb into Ffion's car and begin the journey home. I know we are as sad as each other to say goodbye to our dear friend, but if the past few years have taught us anything, it's that we have the resilience to carry on whatever life throws at us. As the chapel becomes a tiny dot in the rear-view mirror, we discuss tea, cake, dancing, and what the focus of our WI might be as we race towards not only a New Year but a new beginning for the world.

Chapter Eighty-Eight

Angharad

December, 1918

As I stand outside the school building, a flutter of nerves reminds me just how far I've come. Orange light and the sound of joyful chatter spills through the windows. Once my legs would have turned to jelly at the thought of so many people in one room, and I'm shocked as it occurs to me the flutter in my stomach is excitement rather than nerves.

"Sounds busy," says Charlie.

"Between ninety and one hundred people accepted the invitation," I say. "It's why we've had to hold it at the school."

Charlie reaches up and takes my hand. I squeeze it and smile down at him. "I thought I might try dancing tonight," he says, knocking his knuckles against a wooden leg.

"Are you sure you're ready for that?"

"I will be if you dance with me."

My cheeks warm and I drop his hand, walking behind his chair so he doesn't see my embarrassment. "Why don't we leave the wheelchair in the cloakroom? I doubt there'll be much room for it in the hall."

"Good thinking."

"Angharad, Charlie!" Ffion runs over to us, almost stumbling on her high heels. She is wearing a beaded silk and chiffon cream and rose-pink dress and looks more glamorous than any time I've seen her.

"Blimey," says Charlie, his eyes widening at the sight of Ffion. "You scrub up well, Mrs Montgomery."

"Thank you, Charlie."

A pang of jealousy takes me by surprise as my old insecurities rear their ugly head. It is a timely reminder never to get too complacent and remember I am and shall always be a work in progress.

We enter the school, and the local man roped into manning the door invites us to leave our coats and Charlie's wheelchair in the cloakroom. I unbutton my coat slowly, desperate to delay the moment my outfit is revealed. If only Ffion hadn't persuaded me to accompany her on her shopping trip to Bangor. Women like me don't need satin dresses. What on earth was I thinking, letting Ffion talk me into this? I look ridiculous! To have spent so much of my savings on one dress? I must have been out of my mind!

As I ease my arms out of my woollen coat, I want the ground to swallow me up. Eyes trained to the ground, I hand over my coat, my cheeks burning as the satin grazes my hips and flutters around my ankles.

"Bloody hell, Angharad," says Charlie. When I finally meet his eye, my cheeks redden even further. "I thought Ffion looked a picture, but you, well, you look marvellous. Really marvellous."

"Let's get into the hall," I say, desperate to get away from Charlie's wide-eyed stare.

"I knew that dress was worth every penny," Ffion whispers in my ear.

Despite having spent the afternoon decorating the schoolroom, it still takes my breath away when I walk in. The candles pour golden light onto the holly, ivy and mistletoe displays. Paper decorations hang from the ceilings and the tables are illuminated by thick candles in broad glass jars.

"It looks magical," says Charlie, maintaining his balance with the help of me and his walking stick.

"Look," says Ffion, "there's the Colonel and Mr and Mrs Jones. Oh, goodness, and there's Mrs Watt. What a wonderful surprise!"

We make our way to their table, and it is no surprise to find Madge Watt holding court.

"Merry Christmas," says Ffion, my heart racing as she introduces Charlie as *Angharad's good friend*.

"I hear you're working up at the Stephens farm," says the Colonel as Charlie takes his seat. I smile, knowing they will be locked into conversation for quite some time.

I sit next to Ffion, and opposite Mrs Watt.

"I've just been telling these good women how your Women's Institute is an inspiration across our great nations," says Mrs Watt. "You ladies of Llanfairpwll made history when you took a leap of faith all those years ago. Of course, I had great faith in you, even then, but you've surpassed all my expectations. The work you did for the food supply, the knowledge you've shared, the money you've raised. Heck, you've even employed a nurse and are, I hear, in the process of doing something about the area's ridiculous lack of water supply. I am very proud of my association with you all."

For a moment I wonder if Mrs Watt has been on the sherry, but then I realise we are all drunk. Drunk on hope and freedom, drunk on the relief of surviving all we have had to endure and how we have come through it stronger and more determined than ever.

As Mrs Watt and the other ladies at our table discuss plans for the future, I catch Ffion's gaze and we share a smile.

"Are you setting any resolutions for 1919?" she asks me.

"I hadn't really thought about it."

"Well, you'd better get your skates on," she says, "there are only five hours until we enter the New Year."

"I think," I say, looking around the room, "setting any New Year's resolutions would be rather pointless."

"Oh? And why is that, then?"

"Because the WI will throw plenty of new challenges my way regardless of any I set for myself."

"That's true enough," says Ffion, laughing.

"How about you? Is there anything you'd like from 1919?"

Ffion's face flickers with emotion. She closes her eyes and lets out a long breath before opening them again. "I'd like to spend more time with my children. Is that a selfish wish?"

"No," I say, patting her hand. "It's not selfish at all."

"I want to raise my sons to respect women and ensure they don't take the same path through life as their father. And I'd like my daughters to go through life with their eyes wide open."

"I think that's a very noble ambition. But you realise you are already achieving that aim."

"What do you mean?"

"Children are very astute. They will have been watching you these past few years, Ffion. They will have seen a strong woman who has stood up to a weak yet angry man, a woman who puts others before herself and uses the privilege she was born into for the betterment of those around her. Look at all you did with the convalescent home, all you contribute to the WI."

"Thank you, that's very kind of you to say."

I shrug. "It's the truth. Shall I get us a drink? I feel we should make a toast to whatever the next year will hold for us."

"What a wonderful idea."

"I'll be back soon."

I stand and begin weaving around the tables, and I am stopped so many times and drawn into conversation, I wonder if I shall ever make it to the drinks table. My mind strays back to three years ago. If I'd had the confidence to enter a room such as this, it would have been to sit in a corner and try to shrink from public view. How much has changed in three short years!

Just before I reach the table where drinks are being served, my eye is drawn to the far corner of the room. There, in my mind's eye stands Eddy, a smile spread across her beautiful face. She is holding a drink in her hand and watching me with a look of pride. She catches my eye, lifts her hand to her mouth, plants a kiss on her fingers, and blows it across the room. She raises the same hand in a gesture of goodbye, lifts her glass in a toast, gives me one last smile, then walks out of the room.

With shaking hands, I take two glasses from the table and turn back to look at all my friends and acquaintances gathered under one roof. A part of me will always miss Eddy and all we shared, but my future is spread before me. Whatever the next year and those that come after hold, I am no longer alone. I will navigate the future with an armour I never thought I'd possess – friendship. And now, on the eve of 1919, I can't think of a better toast than that. "To friendship," I whisper. I raise my glass, lift it to my lips, then with a smile step forward to join the party.

***

Thank you for reading The Ladies of Llanfairpwll. If you enjoyed the book I'd be very grateful if you could leave a review, and if you'd like to stay in touch, and recieve a bonus chapter about when Angharad met Eddy, you can join the monthly 'LK Wilde Readers' Club' newsletter at www.lkwilde.com

Separating Fact from Fiction

An Author's Note

The 'Real' Ladies of Llanfairpwll
Members of the first WI in Britain- started in 1915 in Llanfair PG,
Anglesey, North Wales. Image courtesy of the Anglesey Federation of
Women's Institutes, published with permission.

Whilst many of the events in this novel are based on fact, I wanted
to make it clear where I allowed myself some artistic licence and why.

Ffion, Carys and Angharad are all fictional, as are their personal stories. Side characters such as Colonel Stapleton-Cotton, Mrs Watt and Mrs Jones are real, but all thoughts and conversations they express are fictional. My aim with these characters, whether fictional or otherwise, was to bring to life the facts surrounding the formation of the first WI, whilst also exploring issues women at the time faced.

At the start of the novel, Ffion attends a meeting at Bangor University at the invitation of Colonel Stapleton-Cotton. There is no evidence of a lady such as Ffion being invited, however Jane Stapleton-Cotton attended the meeting, so there was at least one woman present. Given the significance of this meeting to the formation of the WI, I wanted readers to experience it through a character's eyes, which is why Ffion turns up there!

The second thing I'd like to address is Bryn's opposition to the fledgling WI. There is no evidence to suggest the inaugural WI in Llanfairpwll suffered any such resistance, however there are documented cases of this occurring in other places where women tried to set up their institutes, and I was keen to reflect this broader resistance in the novel.

We don't know where Mrs Madge Watt stayed while in Llanfairpwll, so I decided it would be rather fun to have her stay with Ffion. It is also unlikely she attended the Christmas party in 1918, but I allowed myself artistic licence here, as we know she kept in regular contact with the Llanfairpwll WI and attended many meetings and events over the years.

I have found conflicting evidence about whether Plas Llanfair, the home I gave to Ffion, was indeed used as a temporary convalescent home for wounded servicemen. A report into *First World War Military Sites: Infrastructure and Support* by Gwynedd Archaeological Trust suggests it was, 'despite no evidence for this being found in newspapers'. However, in *War, Peace and the Women's Institute* by Barbara Lawson-Reay, the author writes that the real resident of Plas Llanfair, Mrs Bella Clegg, was commandant of Bodlondeb Red Cross Military Hospital, Bangor. For anyone wishing to know more about the real 'Ladies of Llanfairpwll', the aforementioned book has a wonderful 'Who was Who' chapter listing members of the Llanfairpwll WI along with their biographies. The section on Mrs Bella Clegg is absolutely fascinating and the description of her tireless work for her community inspiring.

I have tried to keep dates of meetings, and the subjects of talks and demonstrations accurate, although given I only had access to the titles of these talks, conversations among members and speeches by visiting guests are all imagined.

Not only are records of these early WI meeting minutes available to view at the Bangor University Archives (which I had the pleasure of visiting), they are also documented in a wonderful book *A Grain of Mustard Seed* written in the 1950s by Llanfairpwll WI member Constance Davies.

The history of the WI is fascinating, and a subject I very much enjoyed exploring during writing this novel. I have only scratched the surface of all the WI has achieved over the years, so if you would like to know more, the following books proved especially informative and engaging: *A Force to be Reckoned With* by Jane Robinson, *War, Peace, and the Women's Institute* by Barbara Lawson-Reay, *The Story of the Women's Institute Movement* by J.W. Robertson Scott (published in the 1920s).

If you ever get the chance to visit Llanfairpwll, the WI museum housed in the toll house (WI hall) is wonderful and well worth taking the time to visit (contact the Anglesey Federation to arrange a visit).

More information on the Women's Institute can be found at www
.thewi.org.uk.

Acknowledgements

Thank you to Audrey Jones from the Anglesey Federation of Women's Institutes for meeting me. Audrey was so generous with her time, and her passion for the WI was inspiring. She explained the organization and its history, answered my many questions, showed me around the museum, and brought humanity to the people and events I'd read about in books. Any errors in depicting the history of the WI are down to me.

To find out more about the history of the WI, their current work, or to find a local group visit- www.thewi.org.uk.

Huge thanks to my editors, Jo Egleton and Tom Fosten, for their un-wavering desire to make this novel the best it could be. Their feedback was constructive, insightful and at times made me laugh out loud (Tom, I shall never describe a reverend as 'veneered' again, or keep sending a man with a wooden leg striding around the Anglesey countryside)! I'm so very grateful for their help in pushing the novel, and me to be the best we could be. Thank you to Jen and Pete, who read an early draft of the book and, as well as making helpful suggestions, gave me the encouragement I needed to continue working on it.

Thank you to Julia Gibbs, proofreader extraordinaire, without whom this book would mistake-laden and very annoying to read. Your hard work adds the final polish a manuscript needs and I'm very grateful you possess the skills I lack!

Thank you to Jarmila Takač, for taking the vaguest brief I've ever given her and creating such a beautiful cover.

Thank you to Sue and Pete, the wonderful Airbnb hosts I stayed with during my Anglesey research trip. They went above and beyond with their hospitality and invited me into their home, and their information on growing veg brought Angharad's allotment to life in my mind.

Thank you to the staff at the University of Bangor Archives for the warm welcome I received when accessing their wonderful records.

Enormous thanks go to my boys, Joe and Tom. There has been a lot of negative press lately about teenage boys, but I'm fortunate not to recognise the stereotypes so often thrown around. Whilst engrossed in pushing this novel towards publication, the boys have cooked me meals, helped with housework and admin tasks, and dolled out hugs freely. Without theirs and my husband's support, there would be no book. They are my champions and inspiration, and this book is, like all my books, for them.

And finally, thank you for reading this book. The support I've received from readers over the years has surpassed all my expectations and spurs me on to tell more stories. Thank you all.

Book Club Questions

1. Angharad struggles with her past and the fear of it being exposed. How does this shape her interactions with others and her journey throughout the novel?

2. Do you think Angharad's response to Bryn's threats was justified? Would you have reacted differently?

3. If Angharad hadn't met Eddy, or suffered such a significant loss, do you think she would have still become involved in the new Women's Institute?

4. The Women's Institute represents progress and empowerment for the women of Llanfairpwll. How does its establishment challenge the traditional roles of women in the village? Do you see any parallels with modern movements?

5. How does the novel's setting, both in time and place, enhance the story? What unique challenges do the characters face because of the war and rural life?

6. Do you think Bryn's actions were purely out of malice, or could there be more to his motivations? Did your feelings towards him change throughout the novel?

7. How does Angharad's friendship with the women of the Institute change her? What role does female friendship play in the novel?

8. The Women's Institute pushes against societal expectations. Which of these challenges stood out most to you? Are there any societal taboos today that feel equally difficult to overcome?

9. How does the novel showcase Welsh culture? Do you think it could have been explored more?

10. The women face resistance when trying to assert themselves. Did their struggles resonate with any issues women still face today?

11. How do secrets shape relationships in the novel? Did the story's resolution provide enough closure for Angharad's struggles?

Also By LK Wilde

People say you get one life, but I've lived three.

I was born Ellen Hardy in 1900, dragged up in Queen Caroline's Yard, Norwich. There was nothing royal about our yard, and Mum was no queen.

At six years old Mum sold me. I became Nellie Westrop, roaming the country in a showman's wagon, learning the art of the fair.

And I've been the infamous Queenie of Norwich, moving up in the
world by any means, legal or not.

I've been heart broken, abandoned, bought and sold, but I've never, ever
given up. After all, it's not where you start that's important, but where
you end up.

**Based on a true story, *Queenie of Norwich* is the compelling tale
of one remarkable girl's journey to womanhood. Spanning the
first half of the 20th century, Queenie's story is one of heartbreak
and triumph, love and loss and the power of family. It is a story
of redemption, and how, with grit and determination, anything
is possible.**

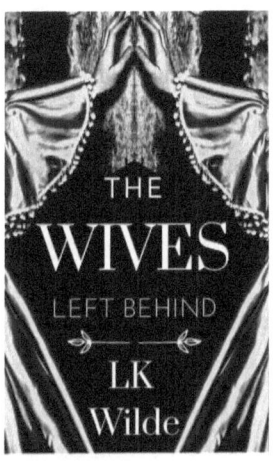

**1840, Cornwall. The victim, the accused, and the wives left be-
hind. Welcome to the trial of the century...**

Based on a true story.

When merchant Nevell Norway is murdered, suspicion soon falls on
the Lightfoot brothers. The trial of the century begins, and two
women's lives change forever.

Sarah Norway must fight for the future of her children. Battling against her inner demons, can Sarah unlock the strength she needs to move on without Nevell?

Maria Lightfoot's future looks bleak, but she's a fighter. Determined to rebuild her life, an unexpected friendship offers a glimmer of hope...

With their lives in turmoil, can Maria and Sarah overcome the fate of their husbands? Or will they forever remain the wives left behind?

Book 1 in the Cornish feel-good *The House of Many Lives* series

Kate is stuck in a rut, She works a dead end job, lives in a grotty bedsit and still pines for the man who broke her heart.

When Kate inherits a house in a small Cornish town, she jumps at the chance of a fresh start. A surprise letter from her grandmother persuades Kate to open her home and her heart to strangers.

But with friends harbouring secrets, demanding house guests, and her past catching up with her- can Kate really move on? And will her broken heart finally find a home?

Island life is hard... leaving is harder.

1913, Northumberland.

Clara Robson adores the rhythms and barren beauty of island life. As her feelings for best friend Jimmy grow, she hopes to one day recreate the happy marriage her parents share. But tragedy is about to strike the Robson household, leaving Clara's plans in tatters...□

Jimmy Watson is desperate to escape the island and the father he despises. The only thing standing in his way is his burgeoning love for Clara. But when his father leaves him for dead in the middle of the north sea, Jimmy's hand is forced and he joins a Scots herring crew headed south.□

Clara is sent to the mainland to live with her wealthy, estranged grandparents. Homesick for both her island and Jimmy, a chance encounter with a group of herring girls offers her an escape from her gilded cage.

1913 is a record-breaking year, but as Clara and Jimmy chase shoals of silver darlings to Lowestoft, their paths are dogged by war, injury, and misunderstandings.

Set adrift from all they know, will they find each other again? And will they ever find their way home?

About the Author

Author and musician LK (Laura) Wilde was born in Norwich, but spent her teenage years living on a Northumbrian island. She left the island to study Music, and after a few years of wandering settled in Cornwall, where she raises her two crazy, delightful boys.

To keep in touch with Laura and receive a 'bonus bundle' of material including an additional chapter about when Angharad met Eddy, join her monthly Readers' Club newsletter at-

www.lkwilde.com

Or find her on social media- @lkwildeauthor

Finally, if you enjoyed this book, please consider leaving a review or rating on Amazon. Reviews are so important to indie authors as they're the best way to help more people discover the book!